HART STREET LANE

RETURN TO DUBLIN STREET
BOOK THREE

SAMANTHA YOUNG

Hart Street Lane

By Samantha Young

Copyright © 2025 Samantha Young

Cover Design by Hang Le
Couple Cover Photography by Wander Aguiar
Edited by Jennifer Sommersby Young
Proofread by Julie Deaton

PROLOGUE
MAIA

It was past seven, and I was already late to get home for no-doubt the healthiest takeout my fiancé Will could find. My assistant Eli had left an hour ago with the rest of our team, including our boss, Christina. I was ready to be done for the day. Therefore, the sight of Becky Carruthers sashaying my way in her six-inch heels filled me with agitation.

Just five seconds. If she'd been five seconds later, I'd have already gotten on the lift and escaped.

She gestured with an impatient, demanding flick of her wrist, and I stupidly looked straight at her, losing my chance at plausible deniability.

"I'm surprised I caught you. You're usually well gone by now." Becky halted in front of me and thrust her tablet into my face.

Since her observation was deliberately incorrect, I forced the irritation out of my tone. "Problem?"

I loved my job as the senior fashion buyer at Pennington's, one of the oldest department store chains in the country. Since Pennington's Edinburgh was the flagship store, we were the cogs and wheels of the entire company, making all inventory and marketing decisions for our website and the four Pennington's stores across the UK. The offices were on the two floors above the large bookstore next to Pennington's, and we had direct access to the department store from there.

It was fun and exciting to stay on top of trends and travel for the Big Four. I flew out to Paris, New York, London, and Milan for fashion month at the end of September, early October, to see fashion collections and trends before they made it to the retailer level. I made selections and predictions based on our customer data, and we were then sent samples that I got to muse and mull over with my fashion buyer assistant Liza and my boss Christina, who was head of buying. Eli was my personal assistant, but they were interested in working their way up, so I encouraged them to offer opinions too. Our profit margin suggested my team had an excellent eye. There had been several seasons where an item had gone viral from Pennington's, kicking off a national trend. I even enjoyed negotiating with suppliers, managing our budget, and collaborating with marketing on promotions.

That is ... I *used* to enjoy collaborating with marketing.

Becky was hired as marketing manager eighteen months ago, and she was driven to the point of driving me insane. If it were up to Becky, we'd all work sixteen-hour shifts and have no life at all. That was fine. Kind of. However, her passive-aggressive suggestions that I didn't work hard enough and that I was relying on my wealthy fiancé for financial stability were not fine. Becky was full of snide comments I had to pretend I didn't hear for the sake of professionalism. Not to mention that since Becky's arrival, Liza had become somewhat frosty and aloof with me. Sometimes downright rude, and since I was her boss, I should call her out for it. But the situation had made me paranoid. Especially considering our relationship was fine until Becky entered the picture.

"Head office just gave their go-ahead to an idea Nadia on my team came up with." Her lips pinched, and I knew she was pissed that Nadia had come up with an idea she hadn't.

I glanced over the email. It was confirmation that the marketing department had been given the green light and a considerable budget to proceed with their new marketing campaign. Apparently, to boost the company's social media presence and bring them into this decade, Nadia had suggested running a campaign following an engaged couple through their wedding journey. Pennington's would supply everything for the hen night, stag do, ceremony, and reception, homeware for their new home together, and a luxury five-star honeymoon. The couple wouldn't have to pay for a thing, but they'd have their lives splashed across Pennington's socials for months as the campaign unfolded.

It was actually kind of genius.

"Well done to Nadia."

Becky grimaced, and I shifted uncomfortably at her jealous annoyance.

"Just let me know what you need. Happy to source whatever. I bought several gowns from Vienne's upcoming bridal collection for the store, and there are stunning options for the campaign. Anyway, we'll talk tomorrow. I'm late for Will."

Becky's gaze flickered to the elaborate diamond engagement ring Will had slipped onto my finger at around the same time Becky joined our Edinburgh store. "What a luxury it must be not to have to worry about working your-self into the ground because you have a fiancé with an amazing job." She tilted her head as she repeated a comment I'd heard from her almost every week since she started working here.

I gave her a tight smile. "We still have our own flats. No one else pays for my life."

She blinked, clearly surprised I'd responded. "Oh. That's a little defensive. I didn't mean to hit a nerve. Anyway." She stepped closer, and I visualized drawing a crazy mustache on her face so I wouldn't call her a passive-aggressive cow. "I think you and Will are the perfect couple for the campaign. I already ran it by Hilary, and she agrees."

Hilary Erstwhile was head of marketing and publicity. While she was Becky's direct boss, she was also kind of my boss because she was CEO Iain Erstwhile's sister.

"Wait. What?"

Becky shrugged. "I asked around. You and Will haven't finalized your wedding plans yet, and let's face it—this is for social media. People don't want to follow the story of ugly or old people." She smirked nastily. "You and Will *are* inarguably a beautiful young couple."

That had to be one of the nicest things she'd ever said to me.

On the back of a truly vapid and horrible sentiment.

"You're successful and attractive, and you'd look good in the photos."

"I also work for Pennington's, so it seems like a conflict of interest."

"Not at all. It reinforces the idea that Pennington's is a family company who looks after their own. People love that."

"I'm not up for having my life splashed across social media. But thanks."

Becky scowled. "They probably won't pick you, but as marketing manager, I have to put forward an idea for a couple. Hilary has signed off on this. Are you really going to leave me high and dry, Maia? We're supposed to be a team."

The wee rotten ... I clenched my teeth to hold back my annoyance. "As a team, it would have been more considerate of you to ask me before you suggested it to Hilary."

She rapidly blinked her dark brown eyes, feigning innocence as she reached out to squeeze my arm in fake reassurance. "Oh. Well, of course. You're right. Next time, I definitely will."

"You'll find someone else. Have a good night." I turned away, choking back the multitude of obscenities I wished I could hurl at her, and pressed the button for the lift. When I stepped on and turned as the doors closed, Becky didn't hide her vindictive glare. Why would she? There was no one around for her to pretend to be nice in front of.

———

When Will and I met at a rugby game, we'd both been amazed to discover we lived minutes from each other. My two-bed flat was buried behind Hart Street, on Hart Street Lane, and his much larger flat was on Albany Street. I was only a ten-minute walk north from Pennington's on Princes Street. Will's place was on my way. Often, I'd either stop by his for dinner or stay overnight instead of heading home. It was never the other way around. He said my flat was too small, but really, I think Will just preferred his place. I didn't care enough to squabble about it.

Once we were married, we were going to find a home together anyway, so the point was moot.

Though I would miss my flat on Hart Street Lane. An attractive apartment in Edinburgh's historical New Town was a long way from the forgotten Glasgow tenement I'd grown up in.

"Sorry I'm late!" I called as I let myself into Will's place.

The apartment was typical of the Georgian architecture in this area of Edinburgh. High ceilings, ornate cornicing, floor-to-ceiling windows with working wooden shutters. Will's flat had been renovated so that part of the wall separating the kitchen and living room had been removed to allow a semi open plan feel.

Other than the biscuit-colored paint on the walls and the original hardwood floors, the space was masculine. Dark cabinets and black marble countertops in the ultra-modern kitchen. Black leather sofas and glass-top tables. There were no drapes or cushions or rugs. And anytime I'd tried to introduce a wee bit of soft femininity, Will shot me down. He'd promised when we had our own place we'd work together to compromise on the interior design.

I strode into the living area to find Will sitting with his hands grasped together between his knees, his head bowed.

I halted as he lifted his chin to look at me.

Between the strange atmosphere in the room and the pleading sadness in his gorgeous blue eyes, my stomach turned over.

"We need to talk."

There was a sense of what was coming as I dropped my key on the sideboard and walked slowly across the room. The smell of Thai takeout drew my attention to the kitchen where the food had been plated, most likely cold now.

I sank down onto the sofa opposite my fiancé and twisted the engagement ring nervously on my finger. "I know I'm late again." But it wasn't like I was the only one who was ever late home from work. Of the two of us, Will was the one who constantly changed our plans because of his job. Will owned his own company, a thriving business. He worked in exposure management and traveled around the country, and sometimes abroad, identifying and assessing risks to organizations, i.e., cyber threats, terrorism, natural catastrophes.

Last year the company's gross profit was five million pounds. And it was growing. I was proud of him. Though I could do without him telling everyone how much his company made last year. In fact, everywhere we went lately, all Will did was talk numbers and income. He'd always been ambitious since I'd known him, and I loved that about him, but this past year his drive for financial gain had become somewhat of an obsession.

It was also the reason we'd made no plans toward our wedding. We hadn't even had an engagement party yet, and we'd been engaged for eighteen months. I had close friends and family who hadn't met him!

"That's not what this is about." Will took a shuddering breath, his eyes washing over my face. "Christ, you make this hard when you walk in here looking like that."

Make what hard? I felt nauseated.

Will had been distant for weeks.

I'd ignored it because I'd hoped it was just work that was keeping him busy.

"Looking like what?"

"So beautiful I sometimes can't believe you're real."

When we first met, his compliments had filled the empty place inside me that constantly battled a sense of unworthiness. But over the last three years, my feelings about his focus on my outward appearance had grown complex. Sometimes I no longer knew how his compliments made me feel. Maybe because I was obsessed with my appearance to the point of anxiousness, and his preoccupation with it only worsened my hyperfocus on my exterior presentation. And not for the reasons people might think.

"What's going on?"

Will nodded nervously. "You … uh … you know Birgitta?"

Instantly, I stiffened.

Birgitta was Will's ex-girlfriend from university, a Swedish international student at Edinburgh. They broke up because she returned home after graduation. Then, a year ago, Birgitta moved back to Edinburgh for a job, and she and Will struck up a friendship. It made me uncomfortable because it was clear the Swede was not over Will, and she treated me with icy politeness.

"Nothing has happened," Will hurried to assure me. "I wouldn't do that to you."

I wanted to be relieved but felt increasing panic instead. "Okay …"

"But … there are … there are strong feelings still."

A hollow hurt expanded across my chest. "From you or her?"

Will grimaced guiltily. "From us both. I tried to deny it, but … she and I have been meeting for lunch every week and talking for ages on the phone … and I realized I still have feelings for her."

I could barely hear past the blood rushing in my ears as I tried to remain calm. "You've been carrying on an emotional affair with her."

He dared to flinch. "If you want to label it as such. Though it was never my intention."

"I'm labeling it as such because that's what it fucking is." Tears burned my eyes as I stood to move away from him.

"Don't swear, it's crass."

I whirled on him in outrage. "Fuck. You."

He sighed heavily and then nodded. "Sorry."

I began to pace as visions of the safe future that had been laid out before me wavered at this news. Will wasn't perfect. But I hadn't been looking for an idealistic romance. Maybe as a teenager in the flush of first love with Charlie, my high school boyfriend, I'd thought it possible. But that fell apart, and this person I'd loved was suddenly gone, and it reminded me too of ... I just ... I decided I didn't want to go through life experiencing that over and over again. I'd wanted someone steady. Someone who had control over every aspect of his life so he'd never bring chaos into mine. I'd had enough chaos to last a lifetime.

Will made me feel secure. Sometimes we'd be in the middle of a mundane task and he'd pull me into his strong arms, and a peace and calm unlike anything I'd ever known would wash over me. I felt loved and safe. And I thought ... I thought I'd get to feel that way for the rest of my life.

This ... this wasn't what I'd ever expected from him.

"What do you want me to say?" My lips trembled as I held back tears, defensively crossing my arms over my chest. If I looked at his handsome face, I'd cry, so I stared out his large windows at the rooftops of the Georgian buildings across the street. The clouds above them hung heavy and gray. A typical spring evening in Edinburgh.

Yet not typical.

A typical evening meant curling up beside Will on his

uncomfortable sofa with a plate of healthy Thai food I didn't particularly enjoy, watching a documentary until I could safely excuse myself to read the latest bestselling thriller novel. Then Will would come to bed, and we'd have sex. Sometimes I'd come; sometimes I'd fake it. Will always came. It hadn't mattered to me because I didn't care about the sex. I adored the intimacy. The expression on his face as he moved inside me, like I was everything in that moment. The way he whispered he loved me before I fell asleep in his arms. That was the part I held on to.

"I need time." Will stood to face me. "Marriage is a huge deal, Maia. And I do love you. But ... I'm still in love with Birgitta too. So ... I'm asking you to give me some time with her ... to figure out if she's who I want."

My jaw dropped.

"You're asking me to step aside so you can fuck your ex for an indeterminable amount of time to decide whether you want me or you want her?"

His eyes flashed with anger. "You know that's not what I mean."

Was this actually happening? "You want me to wait patiently for you to decide if you love me the most?"

"If you love me and want a future with me, I don't think it's unreasonable."

Oh my ... I gaped at this man who I was realizing was either a freaking narcissist or the most entitled wanker who'd ever lived.

The saddest part was that he didn't even realize he was plummeting me back to the worst thing that had ever happened to me.

My mother finally choosing her addiction over me.

I hadn't been enough for her. Not enough to fight it.

Will didn't know about my mum's addiction, though.

Suddenly, looking at him was like looking at Mum. And I felt the very opposite of safe as the tears spilled over without my control.

"Maia—" His face crumpled, his eyes brightening with tears as he reached for me. "Please don't cry."

"Don't touch me!" I stumbled away from him, wiping furiously at the salt water dripping down my cheeks.

"Maia, please. Just think about what I'm asking. *Please*."

How could this be?

How had everything changed in a matter of minutes?

The terrified wee girl in me wanted to plead with him to take it back, to pick me. *Pick me!* I wanted to scream.

The words sent me spiraling back in time to a day I'd like to forget. It knocked my breath out of my chest.

I'd begged someone who was supposed to love me once before. And when she laughed in my face, I'd promised myself, *never again*. Instead, I'd finally battled my sense of self-worth long enough to be brave enough to go find my dad. It was the best decision I ever made.

So, I shoved down my fears and panic and held tight to my pride. "Do you honestly think I'm going to wait around for you to decide that I'm worthy of your love?"

Will shook his head. "That's not what I'm asking."

"Aye, it is." I reached down to grab my bag from the couch. Then I slipped off the engagement ring and placed it on the kitchen peninsula. I'd never really liked the ring anyway. It was too big and in your face. "Have a nice life with Birgitta."

I turned to go, and Will grabbed my biceps, spinning me back to him. His guilty expression was now harsh with desperation. "No. Stay and talk to me about this."

I calmly but firmly yanked my arm out of his hold. "There's nothing left to talk about. The minute you asked me to wait for you to decide if you loved me best was the minute you lost me."

"Damn your pride, Maia." Will searched my face, a frantic panic in his eyes that didn't make sense. If he loved me ... why?

I took him in. His dark blond hair was always styled to perfection. The hard physique beneath his crisp shirt and expensive suit trousers. While I swam three times a week, Will hit the gym every morning before work. He ate clean. Didn't drink. Didn't smoke. He had a boyishly handsome face. The most beautiful blue eyes framed by thick dark lashes. Three years of memories tightened like a vise around my chest. Three years of kisses and hugs and sweet words whispered in my ear. Him introducing me to people with this glowing look of pride.

But beneath his supposed love for me, he'd been holding on to Birgitta all this time. And he wanted me to wait around until he'd decided which one of us he loved the most. I wondered whether Birgitta had agreed to such uncertainty.

Well, I wasn't Birgitta.

I had more fucking pride than that. "You're not some prize to be won, Will. I used to think so. Until this moment. But you don't get to have your cake and eat it too. If you loved me, you wouldn't even think about asking this of me." I shook my head in disgust. At him. At me. At three years wasted. "You don't love me. You just like the way I look on your arm."

"Damn you for saying that," he bit out.

"Damn me? What else am I supposed to think? 'You make this hard walking in looking like that.' Clearly, this" —I gestured to my face and body—"was the only thing about me you actually loved."

"Maybe because that's all you give me. You for damn sure never give me you. You never talk about your mother, about your past or about anything real. It's all about appearances. Your career is all about appearances too, for Christ's sake. Why do you think I even started turning to Birgitta in the first place? She has depth. *She's* more than a pretty face. She doesn't spend hours in the bathroom looking at herself in the mirror or deciding what dress will look best on a tiny percentage of the female population. Birgitta does clinical research that helps people. She's smart and driven and more than her face. Did you ever think your vanity is the reason I even considered Birgitta again?"

His words crushed me. Were so physically debilitating, I stumbled back from him.

Will's eyes widened, instant remorse etching into his features. "Maia ... fuck. I didn't ... I'm sorry."

Fresh tears fell, and I hated him for those too. I tried to get my breath back as I wiped at them.

"Maia, I'm so sorry." He reached for me again.

I slapped his hand away. "Don't fucking touch me." I glared at him, disbelieving I had been ready to marry this arsehole. He didn't know a thing about me. "You have no idea why I am the way I am, but if you think I give a shit about my appearance because of vanity, you know *nothing* about me. You don't know what it's like to have grown up the way I did. To have someone else's shame crawl on your skin. To have people look at you like you're trash, and not for anything you did." I brushed impatiently at my quickly falling tears. My chest hurt so fucking badly, I was surprised I could force out the words. "The hair, the makeup, the clothes ... it's just armor. It makes me feel safe."

Will gaped at me. "Why have you never told me that? If I'd known that—"

"It doesn't matter now." I scrubbed my cheeks, knowing I was taking all my makeup with it and, for once, not giving a shit.

"It does. I want to know." He looked like he was going to move toward me again, so I physically retreated.

"No." I shook my head, dread a dark pit in my stomach. "You don't get to have it."

"Maia—"

"I could never marry you now. Only a narcissist would ask his fiancée to wait around while he fucked another woman so he could decide whether said fiancée was worthy of him."

He flinched again, taking a step back.

"Goodbye, Will."

"Maia—"

"I'll arrange to get my things later."

"Maia, please."

I had only so much strength left, and I wanted to walk out with my head held high and my eyes clear. I strode across the room, my stiletto heels stabbing his precious hardwood floors, and I slammed out of the flat so hard, I heard his period windows vibrate.

I hurried through the streets of New Town, not meeting anyone's eyes, desperate to get back to my flat before the avalanche of emotions collapsed over me.

As soon as my flat door closed behind me, I let the pain that had built up in my chest out in harsh, sobbing cries. And when the pain became too much to bear on my own, I fumbled for my phone and thumbed through my contacts, the names blurry through my tears.

After a few rings, she picked up. "My? How are you, sweetheart?"

"Grace," I sobbed my stepmother's name.

"My, what's happened?"

I couldn't speak.

"Are you home?"

"Y-yes," I forced out.

"I'm on my way."

CHAPTER ONE
BAIRD

The early-morning traffic was light across the city center. It meant I got to the gym on Queen Street in minutes on my black Honda Rebel 500. When I was looking for a motorbike three months ago, all the reviews said the Honda was best for commuting. The gaffer hated it, but it was easier to park than my BMW M2, the sports car I bought because it was comfortable for a man my size—I'd wanted something with some speed to it. The gaffer fucking hated that too.

It was so early, a chilled fog hung over the top of the Georgian buildings as I swung my leg off my bike and yanked my helmet free, which I only wore because it was illegal not to.

A sexy blond approached the gym entrance as I took the protective headgear off, and she flashed me a come-hither smile. Inside, I felt nothing. Maybe a bit naked as I ran my hand through my new hairdo. On the outside, my grin was wide. "Morning, gorgeous."

"Good morning." She gave me another hot smile before she entered the building.

Anticipation filled me as I followed her inside.

But not for her.

There was only one reason I got out of bed two hours before I needed to.

Hurrying through my routine, I shoved my clothes into a locker and raced as quickly as a man could in swim shorts on wet tile flooring. The whole place reeked of chlorine and that only upped the anticipation.

As I stepped out into the pool area, my eyes scanned its length. It wasn't a leisure pool, so it was only twenty meters and not very deep. This was for laps and exercise only.

There were only two people in it at this hour—a guy who kept glancing across the pool to the dark-haired female who had no idea she was being watched. I scowled at the fucker before turning back to the woman.

Her dark head bobbed in and out of the water, and my pulse picked up as she cut through it with the precision of someone who had been swimming for years.

I ran another hand through my hair, still not used to it, and walked to the pool's edge to slip into the water.

The sound brought Maia MacLeod's gorgeous face up as she drew to a halt mid-stroke.

Air seemed to fill my whole fucking chest as our eyes met.

This was what it felt like every time.

We swam together three times a week. We hung out whenever she could get away from that prick of a fiancé.

It had been almost two years since we'd met. And she still knocked me for six.

I pushed through the water toward her as she floated in the middle of the pool. Her eyes narrowed as she studied me, then widened when I drew to a stop in front of her.

"You cut your hair!" Her exclamation bounced around the tiled room. She winced. "Sorry. But you cut your hair."

I'd never given a fuck about what anyone thought about my appearance. So, I'd cut off my hair on a whim last night, wanting a change, not thinking anything of it. Then I started to worry what Maia would think. One of the few compliments she'd ever paid me was that I had "gorgeous hair."

It had been so long I had to wear it up all the time.

I'd had the barber lop most of it off, keeping it long enough that it still fell into my face. Belatedly, I realized I'd have to wear a headband now to keep it off my face at work.

I gave Maia a cocky grin I didn't particularly feel. "Fucking awesome, eh? Feels light as a feather." I shook my head like a dog at her, and she let out a peal of laughter I felt in my dick.

She placed a hand on my shoulder for stability as she reached up to draw her fingers through my hair. I held back my shudder, leaning into her without thought. My hand found her waist under the water, and my blood heated as I studied her while she wasn't looking into my eyes.

Under the bright lights of the pool area, Maia's irises were a striking violet. I'd never seen an eye color like hers. They stood out against her dark lashes, tan skin, and dark hair.

The first time I saw her, we were in a club. She was kind of like a cousin to my best mate Callan's fiancée, and they'd bumped into each other that night. The lights flashed across Maia as she'd talked animatedly.

And it was like the dance floor fell away from beneath my feet.

I knew then that I'd met the one.

Don't tell me how.

It was all gut instinct.

I'd lived my life on gut instinct, and it hadn't steered me wrong.

Maia MacLeod was THE ONE.

Unfortunately, she was engaged to this financial prick arsehole wanker I'd like to suffocate with my goalie net.

Still, I trusted my gut. I pursued a friendship with Maia to see if my gut was right. And almost two years later, through hell to boot, here we were.

And I was in love with Maia MacLeod.

If I had to watch her marry that Will guy, it would break me more than the brain injury I'd suffered last season ever could.

"Well?" I gave her waist a squeeze, for once glad Maia wore a full bathing suit to swim in so I wouldn't feel her soft, bare skin against my palm.

Her eyes met mine, and she smiled. "I like it. You look really handsome."

My heart turned over in my chest. I grinned. "I think you mean I look sexy as fuck."

Maia rolled her eyes and pushed away from me. "Are you here to swim or to preen?"

I spread my arms wide, deliberately showing off my cut physique. "I can do both!"

Maia's gaze roamed over me for a second, and I tried not to let my cockiness show too much. Her fiancé worked out. But he was at least six inches shorter than me, so I made him look like a toothpick in comparison.

However, I also knew there wasn't a vain bone in Maia MacLeod's body. Some folk might think so because she was mind-blowingly stunning and she always looked good. But she'd shown me photos of her when she was a young teen with her big hair and nerdy glasses. I thought she was cute as fuck, but Maia said she got bullied a lot. I'd like to punch the wee bastards who messed with her head back then because they'd skewed Maia's self-perception. Yet, I also knew they were the reason Maia didn't put much stock in people's appearance. If she liked you, it was because you were worth liking.

Maia liked me for me, just like I liked her for her.

But that didn't mean I couldn't remind her I was built like a brick shithouse and had stamina for days.

A tinge of red on the olive of her cheekbones was visible even from a distance. Maia quickly looked away and resumed her swim.

I smirked but decided not to torture her. "First one to ten laps buys breakfast!" I shouted before racing toward the opposite end of the pool.

"Hey! That's a three-meter head start!" I heard Maia yell back.

When I reached the end of the pool, I waited for her to catch up. "I can't help it if my big-dick energy propels me through the water."

Maia burst into laughter, and I leaned into her unconsciously. Her sweet smile was *life*. "Believe me, you do not have big-dick energy."

Affronted, I clasped my chest in feigned outrage. "How dare you?"

She shoved me playfully. "Big-dick energy is when you're quietly confident. You're as quiet as football fans on game day."

"Fine. I have loud big-dick energy," I said *loudly*.

"Trying to have a quiet swim here, mate!" the other bloke in the pool yelled over at us.

He was just pissed because I was with Maia. "Apologies,

mate. I have loud big-dick energy," I whisper-shouted at him.

Maia made a choking sound, and she gave the guy her back as she shook with laughter.

My cheeks hurt from grinning. Finally, I drew her into my chest with a less than platonic one-armed hug. "Ready to race again?"

Her expression turned contemplative. "I don't know. I don't think you ca—loser buys breakfast for a week!" She suddenly dove into the water ahead of me, her arms swiping through the pool like blades as she front-crawled her way to victory.

By lap five, merely because I had almost a foot on her, I would have overtaken her.

But there was no bloody way I was letting her pay for breakfast.

———

Breakfast consisted of coffee and smoothies. Maia had somehow managed to do a full face of makeup and fix her hair by the time our orders arrived. She came out of the women's locker room to find me chatting with the blond from earlier.

The blond had made the approach, but it was only polite to flirt with her for her bravery. I respected a woman who went after what she wanted.

We exchanged numbers as Maia appeared.

Maia gave the blond an awkward smile that made me feel like shit. I hated when she caught me flirting with other women, but at the same time, she was engaged to someone else.

The blond gave Maia a smug smirk that instantly made me delete her number from my phone as she walked away.

An arrogant man might think this encounter was the reason Maia was quiet.

But one, Maia had made it clear we were just friends. And two, something had been off with her for a few weeks now. I'd tried multiple times to find out what was going on, but she always turned the conversation back to me. The only time her eyes lit up was when I made her laugh. I was worried about her.

I pushed again for the hundredth time. "You know, you can talk to me," I told her as we finished up.

I was known as the life of the party. The fun guy. A good laugh. But there was more to me than that. I cared about my friends and family. Would do anything for them, including having the tough conversations. Thankfully, my sport had begun to realize the importance of mental health and there was less stigma around talking about our feelings now. So, I was there for those who needed to unload whatever shit was on their chest. I didn't waste that energy on people who didn't matter, so most people never witnessed that side of me.

"Same, you know." Maia considered me as she tucked a strand of hair behind her ear. She wore small diamond hoops today. She also wasn't wearing her engagement ring, though she always took it off to swim. The absence of it felt like a weight lifted off my shoulders. "You usually leave for training by now. Why are you dragging breakfast out?"

Because the new owner was a dick and in turn, the gaffer was riding my fucking arse all the time.

I shrugged.

"Baird ... what happened?"

"You haven't seen the papers this morning, then?"

Maia frowned. "You know I don't read that crap. Is ... is there a story in it about you?"

"I went to a house party at the weekend. I got a little fucked up and someone took photos."

She yanked her phone out of her purse, and I almost regretted telling her as she googled me. I knew the photos she'd find. Me, clearly shit-faced, on some stranger's couch with two half-naked girls sprawled across me.

Maia's shoulders tensed as she stared at the photo. "Did you take anything?"

Something like shame heated my cheeks. I'd never had anything harder than weed.

Until this weekend. "I ...tried some coke."

She sucked in a breath.

It wasn't something I was intending to do again. I just wanted to let loose a bit. Unfortunately, this was the fifth story about my partying that had made it into the papers in the last six months.

"Whose party was it?"

"Dunno. Just some people I met when I was out."

Her head snapped up, her eyes flashing angrily. "Random strangers who could have done anything to you ... and they did. You took coke. And they sold photos of you, Baird. You're lucky there were no photos of you taking the coke."

Irritation and guilt were not a good combo for me. "I don't need this judgmental shit from you, My. I'm about to get fucking reamed enough as it is when I go into training."

"As well you should. I have never felt our age gap more than I do right now."

"You're four years older than me, My. That's it. I was probably *fucking* before you were." It wasn't like me to be crass toward her in that way. I winced, regretting the words.

Before I could apologize, Maia pushed her chair back and stood. She pressed her hands to the table to lean toward me so she could hiss quietly, "My mum used to end up at random people's houses to get *fucked up*."

Surprise cut through me. "My—"

"My mum was an addict," she confessed. "Heroin."

"Maia—"

"Partied hard. It started out like this. A little experimentation here and there." She waved a hand at me and straightened, sorrow flicking across her beautiful face. "It quickly snowballs. And I don't need that shit in my life again."

Before I could say a word, she stormed out.

Panicked, I pushed away from the table and was out of my seat so hard the chair toppled. I didn't take time to right it. Instead, I raced after My.

I caught up with her as she stepped outside the building.

"Maia." I rounded in front of her on the pavement.

She glared up at me, but there were tears in her eyes. The sight of them killed me.

"Never again." I took her gently by the shoulders, hoping she could read my sincerity. "I will never touch the stuff ever again. I can't. I'd lose my spot on the team. It was a mistake. I promise you I will never do it again."

"Don't do it for me. Do it for yourself, Baird. Do it for your sister and your mum who love you and count on you."

I released her like she burned to the touch. Because *Maia* didn't love me and count on me yet. But ... there were tears in her eyes, and that meant something.

"I'll do it for me. But I am doing it for you too. You ...

your friendship means more to me than a few minutes of partying. I didn't ... I didn't know about your mum."

Maia grimaced and looked away. "I don't tell a lot of people."

"You can tell me anything."

She nodded, but it was weak. "I have to get to work."

"I'll see you soon."

She didn't quite meet my eyes as she waved and walked away. "Next time," she said over her shoulder.

Dread filled me because I knew that I'd inadvertently broken some kind of trust with her.

I ran a hand through my wet hair, my fingers sliding over the right side of my head with an awareness I couldn't shake. My last scan showed the skull fracture I'd suffered last season had healed.

But it was there, like a fucking phantom crack.

Maia disappeared around the corner out of sight.

"Fuck." I kicked my motorbike, taking sadistic pleasure in the pain that ricocheted up my shin. I glanced back down the street where she'd just been. "Fuck, fuck, fuck."

CHAPTER TWO

BAIRD

"Oi, oi! What's the tea, boys?" I announced as I strutted into the locker room of Caledonia United Football Club a half hour later like I hadn't a care in the world.

Caley United FC was currently Edinburgh's top team in the Professional League and number two overall. Glasgow's teams had been dominating the top of the league table for decades, and finally after making our way up, we'd knocked Kingston United into third place last year. This year, we were aiming to take the number one spot from Dalmarnock Thistle. There wasn't much of the season left, but we were on course to do it. It was a lot of pressure.

And I had external shit going on too. My teammate and best pal, Callan Keen, and I had a small real estate portfolio, but we were planning our future, knowing football was a short-lived career. We'd put together a business proposal to turn Blantyre Castle, an estate on the coast just outside Edinburgh, into a hotel and spa. That castle was owned by Braden Carmichael, who was Beth's, Callan's fiancée's, dad. Instead of buying it off him, we got into business with him.

Callan, because of the association, had decided to be a bit more hands-off with the project than planned. Which meant I was coordinating the management of the renovation with Braden and his team.

Was there any wonder, on top of the season, I needed to blow off steam whenever I got the chance?

"You cut hair!" Kaito Tanaka, our Japanese central defender, stopped in the middle of the room to gape at me. "Your sex power is gone."

I gave a bark of laughter as I self-consciously ran my hand through my hair. "Nothing on earth could take my sex power, Kaito, mate. Trust me."

"Baird." Callan stood up from the bench at his locker area. He was the team's captain and the league's best midfielder. "You're late. Gaffer wants to speak to you."

"No nice hairdo?" I spun around, arms wide. "I always compliment you on any physical changes you make to your appearance."

"Is that before or after you mercilessly mock him?" John queried from opposite Callan.

Callan spoke before I could. "Fuck your hair. You're late."

I shrugged. "I'll pay the fine." The gaffer fined us fifteen quid for every minute we were late.

John Tessier, my other best mate and the team's Canadian center forward, stood up from tying on his football boots. His brow was furrowed. I knew that worried expression. He and Callan had been giving me that look for over a year. "It's not about being late."

"It's about your tabloid exploits." Eric Baumann, our Swiss left wing, shrugged on a T-shirt. He scowled at me. "No one cares about your hair. You're making us look like a bunch of unprofessional pricks."

My anger and fear that simmered just beneath the surface started to boil. But I grinned with my usual carefree cockiness. "I thought I was the only one in the photos. Did I miss something?" I winked at him because I knew my blasé attitude would piss him off more. Didn't take much. Eric was a temperamental turd.

Baumann was suddenly in front of me, blocking my path. He was a good few inches shorter, but that didn't stop him from stabbing a pointed finger too close to my nose. "Every single one of us represents this team when we're on the outside."

"I'd suggest you get that appendage out of my face before I use it to plug your arsehole."

I heard choked laughter around me as Baumann's cheeks turned purple with anger.

"Listen—"

"Enough!" the familiar voice of the gaffer rang around the locker room.

Dread cut through everything else as I turned to look at Brian O'Kelly.

Brian had been Caledonia United FC's manager for four years now. Most clubs went through managers faster than an entire football team going through a year's worth of toilet paper. Yet Brian was still here because three years running, Caley United had gone from middling it along in the Pro League to coming in second.

His assistant manager Sven followed him everywhere. A quiet but strategic man who I think some of the players failed to realize was Brian's trump card. Sven didn't have the demeanor to manage a group of testosterone-fueled athletes from all walks of life and all different cultures who needed a helluva lot of coaching to gel as a team. But Brian did. And Sven was the strategist. Together they were the perfect football manager.

Right now, they wore twin expressions of disapproval directed at me.

Disapproval from authority figures fucked with my head.

Call it being raised by a single mum I'd do anything for.

"Looking good, Gaffer." I saluted him, instantly knowing it was the wrong move.

Kept making those lately.

The image of Maia walking away this morning caused a wee ache behind my sternum.

The gaffer pointed a thick finger at me. "You. In my office. Right. Fucking. Now."

Everyone shut up, and I felt all the lads' stares.

My cheeks burned, though I kept my swagger as I walked through them. Callan patted my shoulder as I passed. "It's all good," I assured him.

"Is it?"

I ignored that as I had ignored any attempt he and John had made to figure out what the hell was going on with me since I'd fractured my skull during a game two winters ago. We were playing Dundonald United. Their striker, Juan Perez, had jumped to intercept a pass with his head. I'd lunged to the edge of the penalty box to defend the net at the same time. Perez headered me instead of the ball. It knocked me out instantly and I'd suffered a hairline fracture to my skull.

The injury had put me out of the sport until this season.

It had also scared the absolute shit out of everyone who loved me. Because in the past, an injury like that had been fatal.

So, I partied a wee bit harder than I used to. I lived life to the fullest.

However, I still turned up to games, and I'd made more saves this season than any other goalie in the league. I showed up whenever Braden called and knew exactly what was happening with our project at Blantyre.

What was the big damn deal if I needed a goddamn escape now and then, a thrill away from the day-to-day pressures?

Life was short. I knew that better than anyone.

As soon as Sven shut the gaffer's office door behind us, the gaffer spoke with a calmness I hadn't expected. Unfortunately, his words were harsh. "Burbank wants you gone."

Fred Burbank was the club's new owner. Unbeknownst to all of us, the deal was underway last season. We found out with the rest of the world at the beginning of last summer that Caledonia United had been sold.

To Fred Burbank. An American-born, self-made billionaire who bought Caley because owning a UK football team looked fun.

That was a direct quote.

We all thought it meant he'd bugger off and let the gaffer run the show. It didn't. Burbank was more involved than our previous owner. And apparently image was important to him.

"Because of the papers this morning?"

The gaffer narrowed his eyes. "Because it's the fifth goddamn time you've been in the papers this season!"

My pulse raced, but I didn't let it show. "I have a contract," I reminded him.

"You do. Do you also know what is in that contract?"

I shrugged.

"Don't you shrug at me, boy."

Chastened, I nodded. "Sorry, sir. I don't know."

"A misconduct clause." He crossed his arms over his chest. "It states that if you engage in behavior that brings negative attention or causes the club to be perceived negatively by the press, the contract is null and void."

Craig Bennet at the tabloid newspaper in question had it in for me. If he could find a story on me, he fucking would. "It's not my fault a shit stain of the journo world wants to spin my partying into something bad. I'm still out there on the field making the most saves."

"I know that. But what you do off the field matters. I know you lads need to decompress, but this is taking the partying to a new level. Now you've been late to nearly every training session for three weeks. That's not on. Burbank is done."

"I have a contract." My palms suddenly felt clammy.

"See"—he pointed at me—"that look of panic is the only thing saving you right now. Because for a second there, I wasn't sure you cared. Does it even compute that the goalkeeper with the most saves in the league didn't get picked to play for Scotland in the European championship this year?"

I attempted to hide my wince. Because of course that fucking stung. Callan got picked to represent us at the Euros for the second year running, and I was pleased for him. But it was just another thing the scum journos were yapping about and how the snub was most likely due to my "erratic" behavior off the pitch. "Of course it computes."

"Right. Well. I convinced Burbank to give you one more chance to clean up your act. If this latest article constitutes misconduct, it constitutes an antisocial behavior fine."

Wonderful.

I gave a lift of my chin to say I understood, but I was pissed off.

"And you're going to have to work to turn your act around. No more parties unless you're with Keen or Tessier. One more party with a bunch of fucking strangers who'll sell shots to the tabloids, and you're done. Moreover, I want you to act responsibly—volunteer at Keen's fiancée's food-bank. Go make some kids' day at a primary school. Every spare minute you've got, I'm going to fill it with positive press opportunities, and you are going to do every single fucking one of them. You might not be playing on a pitch this summer, but you will be playing for the cameras. Understood?"

I ran a hand through my hair and exhaled heavily. "You know I have another business. It takes up a fair amount of my time, and I was relying on the summer to make a lot of headway." While we still trained as usual from the end of May to August, we had no games scheduled until the new season started.

"I don't give a damn about your other business. That's your concern. You signed a contract and took a lot of money from this club, and it's all there in black and white, McMillan. We own your arse for the next year. And if you want us to own your arse again the following year, you better get your shit together. Because you are a fantastic goalie, but there are some talented goalkeepers on the rise, and Burbank's got his eye on them. Understood?"

Burbank was a turd-smeared cock. "Understood."

"Fine. Go put a bloody headband on that hair."

Nodding, I turned to leave.

"McMillan."

I glanced back at the gaffer. His expression was about as

soft as he knew how to make it. "Maybe it's time to see the team's therapist again."

I tensed. After my accident, the team had insisted I see a counselor. She had to give me the all-clear to play too. "She said I'm fine."

"That was last year. Your behavior has changed since then."

"Is it mandatory?"

Whatever he heard in my tone made the gaffer huff, "Nope. For now."

Without a word, I strode out of his office. Every single one of my team members looked at me expectantly, like they'd known I was walking to my possible doom. I grinned, spreading my arms wide. "Since you clearly all find me so pretty you can't look elsewhere, you'll be pleased to know you'll be looking at my sexy mug for the foreseeable future."

A few good-natured "fuck offs" were sent my way, but I saw the genuine relief on their expressions.

On Callan's and John's too.

But I also saw their worry.

Since I couldn't deal with it, I winked at them and marched over to my locker to get changed for training.

CHAPTER THREE
MAIA

My gut seemed to be in a constant state of churning. For a month. It had been a month since my breakup with Will and the churning wasn't just grief. It was from lying and evading.

The truth was I was ashamed by our breakup.

Those old insecurities and fears about people's perception of me felt like bedbugs crawling all over my skin.

Being rejected by a fiancé who paid out thousands of dollars for an engagement ring surely revealed the truth about my worthiness. Years I'd fought to shed the shame I'd felt because of my mother. The shame piled on me by schoolmates who didn't care I was already living in hell and decided to make every day worse by reminding me who my mum was and who I was by association. Then there was the shame I felt about leaving her behind after years of parenting *her*. Layers and layers of shame.

I wished I could wrap myself in my dad and Grace's love and pride and let everything else be washed away. Yet I couldn't. When Becky was the first person at work to notice I wasn't wearing my engagement ring, I lied and said it was being cleaned. Then Beth noticed, and I fobbed her off with the same lie.

For a month.

The only people who knew the truth were Grace and Dad, and I'd sworn them to secrecy until I was ready to explain the situation. Because I didn't fully understand. I felt at once heartbroken and relieved, and I didn't know how to make sense of the relief just yet. But there was this feeling of one weight being lifted from my shoulders, only to be replaced by the evasion of truth.

I was now single.

Will and I had broken up.

The future loomed uncertain and not very safe at all.

I was so unbalanced and lost in the chaotic dichotomy of my emotions.

Perhaps that's why I lost my shit at Baird this morning. After our swim, I'd hurried back to my flat to change into my work clothes. I was shaken by my anger at Baird's behavior. I hadn't realized until that moment how attached I'd gotten to him. For weeks I'd been plagued by guilt for not telling him about my breakup because he was one of the few people in my life who seemed to notice the change in my demeanor. It had been on the tip of my tongue to tell him when he'd revealed the whole tabloid fiasco.

Baird McMillan was one of the most frustrating men I'd ever met.

He presented this carefree, jack-the-lad persona to the world, and he *was* endearing, funny, and charismatic. I loved that about him. He'd kind of pushed his way into my life with his gregarious affection. I couldn't deny him. It was like telling a golden retriever you didn't want to be friends. Will hadn't been all that excited about my burgeoning friendship with Scotland's hottest Professional League goalkeeper.

Yet Baird had hidden depths that only those close to him ever got to see. He was deeply loyal and would do anything for his friends. He was protective of women, probably because he was raised by a single mum and his big sister. And he was currently spiraling after his head injury. I could see it happening and I didn't know how to stop it, and he didn't want to talk about it.

Experimenting with hard drugs was crossing the line, though, and I'd taken it personally when I shouldn't have. But I also … as much as it would hurt to walk away from a friendship that had quickly become important to me … I couldn't have that specific kind of chaos in my life.

I couldn't go back there.

Ever.

Not even for Baird.

With that in mind, my melancholy was multiplied by a hundred that morning as I walked into Pennington's. I took the lift to the top of the Edwardian building, my heels clacking on the marble-tiled flooring. Smiling at colleagues and murmuring good mornings, I was hoping to get to my office and bury my head in our winter budget. We were always two seasons ahead, so our summer and autumn products were already well underway in terms of ordering, shipping, and merchandising.

"Maia." Christina Gault, head buyer and my boss, stuck her head out of her office door. "A word."

Her tone was clipped, but Christina always spoke that way, so I didn't think much of it as I followed her into her office. She leaned her pencil-skirt-clad bottom against the edge of her desk and crossed her arms over her chest.

"Why didn't you tell me you'd agreed to put your name forward for Pennington's social media campaign?"

I furrowed my brow in confusion. "What are you talking about?"

My boss gave me an impatient look. "The social media campaign to follow an engaged couple through their journey to marriage."

My stomach dropped as the conversation I'd had with Becky the night I'd broken up with Will came back to me. I'd forgotten all about it. "What are ... what? I didn't agree to anything. I said no."

Christina dropped her arms from her chest. "Becky insists you agreed."

That little ... "I didn't. I promise I didn't."

My boss muttered a curse under her breath. "Well, this is a pickle, isn't it."

Oh no ... no, no, no. "Please tell me she didn't put me forward and Pennington's selected me and Will."

"They selected you and Will."

"Christina, I can't do that campaign." Blood rushed in my ears, my cheeks burning with anger and panic. "I specifically told Becky no."

"Why would she think you said yes?"

"Because it's what *she* wanted to hear. She needed to suggest someone, and she set her mind on me. Christina, this crosses a line professionally. I didn't give my permission for her to do this."

Letting out a long, frustrated exhale, Christina rounded her desk to sit in her chair. She studied me for a few seconds until I had to bite back an irritated *"Well, say something!"*

"The wheels are already in motion. Legal drew up a contract for you and Will to sign."

"Then they'll need to shred that contract."

"I don't think you understand what I'm saying. Becky took this to Hilary, who took it straight to Iain. They want one of their own in this campaign. 'Look how we treat our employees.' 'Come spend your money at a department store who cares.' All that kind of nonsense. And let's be honest here, Maia, you've got the face and body of a cover girl. You'll look divine in a wedding dress and a bikini for your honeymoon."

"I have to do bikini photos for social media?"

"Yes."

"No."

Her lips pinched. "Yes. Hilary and Iain are in raptures over this idea. I ... I think you're talented and I'll fight for you. But I can't tell you that I have it in my power to protect your job if this goes south."

I gaped at her. "Are you saying if I say no, they'll fire me? I didn't say yes in the first place. That can't be legal."

"It's your word against Becky's. They'll think you got cold feet and messed them around."

"B-b-but," I spluttered. *I'm not engaged anymore*, I wanted to scream.

Oh my God.

"You're right. Legally, they can't fire you for this. But they'll find a way to get rid of you. Pennington's want only team players in their company. They value loyalty. And I doubt very much they'll give you a reference when you try to move on."

I was going to be sick. Everything I'd worked for ... "And they'd see this as disloyalty? Me saying no?"

"Yes."

"But I didn't agree to this," I repeated lamely. I could tell her Will definitely wouldn't agree to it but then I'd be outright lying to her about the state of my relationship by suggesting we were still together.

Christina stood up abruptly. "It is unfair. I absolutely agree. But look at it from a positive place, Maia. Your entire wedding and honeymoon are now bought and paid for. And since you select our bridal collections, you know you're going to love your dress. I'd say this is a win. Just don't let it interfere with your work. Tomorrow afternoon, we have a meeting with Hilary. I'm sure legal will be sending the contract over for you and Will to sign too, and I'd suggest getting independent counsel to look over that and not our in-house. Okay, off to work."

I left her office in a panicked daze.

Eli, my assistant, greeted me from their desk just outside my office. "Morning, boss. Ooh ... why do you look like someone just peed in your Birken bag?"

"Um ..." I stopped beside their desk, trying to shake off my mounting anxiety so I could bury my head in work. "Did Liza send over the data from our customer feedback surveys yet?"

Eli shook their head.

The report was overdue. With a sigh, I left my purse on Eli's desk and marched down the hall to the shared office spaces. Liza's desk was in the open-plan office area with all the marketing department, finance, and HR staff.

I didn't particularly want to face Becky right now, but I'd emailed Liza several times for the customer feedback document this week. Before Becky's arrival, Liza and I had gotten along great. She was a wonderful assistant buyer and eager to work her way up. However, ever since she and Becky got buddy-buddy, our working relationship had deteriorated. I hated confrontation, so I was trying my best to avoid out-and-out reprimanding her.

Thankfully, Becky was nowhere in sight, but Liza was standing by the coffee machine, flirting with David from accounts.

"Liza."

She turned slowly, not quite meeting my eyes. "Maia."

"I need the customer survey report ASAP."

"Yeah, I'll get to that this afternoon."

"It's not done?"

She stiffened. "We've had other things to prioritize. The trend forecast, for starters."

"I want the customer survey report by noon."

When she didn't move, I bit back my irritation. "Now, Liza. Please and thank you."

She shot David a petulant look and then moved past, avoiding my gaze. "Whatever," I heard her mutter under her breath.

It was loud enough for David to hear because he gave me a *What the hell?* look.

And all I could think was: *Fuck my life.*

Seriously. Fuck. My. Life.

CHAPTER FOUR
MAIA

I didn't know how I made it through work that day. Autopilot switched into gear, and I tackled tasks while my mind cooried up in the corner in panic mode. How the hell was I supposed to get out of this idiotic campaign without losing everything? I'd chosen not to tell Hilary the truth about Will just yet because I had to believe there was a way to get out of it without humiliating myself in the process. One positive was that it did, for the first time in a month, distract me from the hurt in my heart.

Liza, thankfully, emailed the report I wanted, but I could feel the frost even in her three-sentence email.

Becky approached during my lunch hour to congratulate me. I could tell by the smug gleam in her eyes that she knew I was miserable. The urge to unleash the past month of emotions on her was real, but ever the professional, I nodded along to whatever she said, dissociating so I wouldn't claw off her face.

By the time I'd walked up through the wide, perfectly symmetrical Georgian streets of New Town and then downward onto Hart Street, my pulse raced as my mind whirred with possible solutions. Hart Street was two rows of Georgian terraced homes and black wrought iron gated facades. There were a couple of new architectural additions to the street. Near the top of the road, there was a lane between the buildings called Hart Street Lane. Unlike the Gothic, creepy alleyways up on Old Town, this narrow lane was a well-lit, flower box–laden pathway into the back of the homes.

It had a tree-surrounded courtyard and in the middle of the clearing what had once been an old schoolhouse was now four flats. There was a main entrance, with two flats on the ground floor. My flat was on the top floor across the landing from my neighbor Geri Mills. Geri was a seventy-eight-year-old artist and self-proclaimed spinster. She said *spinster* had always been a filthy word, but she took pride in the fact that she'd lived a happy, sex-filled life without being "bogged down by the terrible business of marriage and cohabitation."

"That's what spinsterhood really is, my dear. Happiness," she'd told me a few months after I moved into my flat. "A beautiful girl like you ought to have lots of sex, but never tie yourself down to one person."

Suffice it to say, Geri did not congratulate me when Will and I got engaged.

She probably would once I told her the engagement was off.

The thought made my stomach drop as I glanced at her door before unlocking mine.

It was a two-bedroom flat, it had high ceilings and a bay window that mostly looked out at tree branches, making me feel like I was anywhere but in the middle of the city. It was a little dark because we were surrounded by foliage and buildings, but it was cocooned away from all the hustle and bustle.

As I pressed a hand to the hallway wall for balance to loosen my ankle-strapped high heels, my attention snagged on my photograph wall. For years, I grew up in a home with no family portraits.

With no family, really.

When I moved in with Dad and Grace, I'd become almost obsessive about cataloguing life and displaying my happy memories. Will called my wall of photographs "clutter."

It wasn't clutter to me. It was the visual representation of a life I was grateful for because it hadn't always been this way.

My handsome dad and beautiful Grace. My wee brother Lachlan who grew up so fast across those pictures on the wall. A baby in my arms when I was seventeen. A teenager last Christmas, his arms crossed over his chest as I squeezed him into my side for a cuddle for the camera. My face was lit up with laughter because he was so annoyed by the affection.

I didn't see enough of him. Lachlan, or Lockie as we called him, would be a man before I knew it.

I was thirty years old and having to start my romantic life all over again. There was no way I could face my career being wiped out too.

My misty eyes moved over the wall as I stretched my sore feet into the hardwood floors. There was a photo of my extended family, all the amazing, kind people who'd welcomed Dad, Grace, and my dad's sister Shannon into their lives. It was from my sixteenth birthday party at the Italian restaurant D'Alessandro's. The restaurant was owned by my uncle Marco's family.

Marco wasn't really my uncle, but he was close friends with Dad and Aunt Shannon through his wife Hannah, a member of the Carmichael clan. Her best friend was Cole, and Cole was married to Aunt Shannon. Cole's sister, Aunt Jo, was best friends with Joss Carmichael, my pseudo-cousin Beth's mum. And there were a lot more of us than that.

We were a large, complicated, tangled bunch who loved one another so much.

I'd gone from being alone to having a huge family within the space of a few months. It had been over-whelming in the best way.

Now there were photos of them all over my wall.

Pics of my best friend from high school, Leigh, hung there too. From fifteen years old to now. She lived and worked in Glasgow, but we tried to see each other as often as we could. Other than Beth and my cousins, my social group was scattered all over the world. I'd met most of my current friends when I went to uni in London. My closest friends were my two roommates, Penny and Davina. Penny now lived in Texas and Davina was in Dubai.

The truth was ... since I'd met Will, my social world had become his. When we were together, we hung out with his friends. Hence why none of my cousins or Leigh had met Will—in the three years we'd been together.

That said everything. Why hadn't I realized that wasn't normal?

Hurt flared across my chest.

My gaze landed on a photo of Will and me. Grace had taken it. He was kissing my cheek, and my face was scrunched up in laughter. We looked happy.

Tears dripped down my cheeks and I wiped them away wondering how I could have been so wrong about that. It was a shock to realize I no longer trusted myself—no longer trusted my feelings. I took the picture off the wall and then reached for the other three photos of us together. With a sick, churning stomach, I shoved them into my side table drawer to deal with later. Then I kissed my fingertips and pressed them to a photo of Dad, Grace, and Lockie as I passed it to venture into the kitchen.

It was moments like these I wished I was a daily wine drinker. Like Will, I wasn't big on alcohol. If I was out with the girls, I'd have a few cocktails, but that was it.

Stopping in the kitchen, I realized I'd intended to make a snack, yet I wasn't hungry. Turning around, I wandered out of the kitchen, through the sitting room, and back out into the hall. My bedroom was on the same side as the living room and had a lovely, leafy view. The second bedroom was so small I'd turned it into a wardrobe. It was fair to say I loved clothes. I loved how they transformed a person. So, I had rails of clothes, far more than one person needed, and boxes and boxes upon shoes. Thankfully, this extra space allowed my bedroom to remain mostly clutter-free. Shutting the blinds, I changed out of my tight-fitted pencil dress into joggers and a cropped tee.

I'd barely pulled the tee on when my doorbell rang, setting off the app on my phone. I hurried into the hall to pull my phone out of my purse. Ignoring the notifications that I had missed calls and a bunch of unanswered texts from Will that had piled up over the past month, I tapped on the doorbell app.

There wasn't a security door into the building, so I'd installed the camera doorbell. The camera app flared to life and my heart skipped a beat at the sight of Baird.

If Will really wanted to talk to me, he could come to my

flat. Like Baird. Who didn't like how we'd left things and had shown up mere hours later.

A pleasant ache scored across my chest as I opened the door to him.

His gorgeous, dark eyes held mine for a second, and I felt more than a sizzle of the physical attraction I'd gotten very good at ignoring. Baird McMillan was probably the most beautiful man I'd ever met.

However, lots of women thought so, and he was the biggest flirt on the planet.

Baird was a good-natured lothario. He'd never intentionally hurt a woman. I think he'd chew off his own arm first. But this was a man who could flirt with a lamppost. He'd never be satisfied with the same woman for the rest of his life. He was heartbreak waiting to happen for anyone who fell in love with him, so he'd never be a romantic possibility for me.

That didn't mean I couldn't enjoy looking at him.

This morning he'd not only surprised me with the tabloid story but with his haircut.

I'd loved his long hair. Yet he was sexier than ever with it shorter. It was wet right now and hanging across his temples in waves. He had to brush it out of his eyes, his big, tattooed hand impatiently swiping at it.

My dad had tattoos. Nearly all my uncles had tattoos, including Uncle Cole. Baird could give Cole—one of the best tattoo artists in the country—a run for his money. Baird had a full sleeve of artwork all the way to the fingers on his right hand. This past year, the tattoo collection had grown. Now he had tattoos across his chest and up onto his neck. They were Celtic tribal in style, and Cole had expertly shaded the designs so the ink wasn't overly prominent.

If you'd asked me whether I'd be attracted to a guy with a neck tattoo, I would have said no.

And I would have been wrong.

Last year, I'd told Will I was finally ready to get a tattoo, and he'd talked me out of it. He said tattoos were trashy and I'd regret it. Looking back, Will could really be a bit of a dick.

"You're still mad at me." Baird's broad shoulders slumped.

I realized I was scowling at the memory of my ex-fiancé and smoothed my features.

My chest squeezed at Baird's forlorn expression. The man was six foot five, built of pure muscle, and he could squash most people between his giant paws. Yet he made me feel protective of him.

"Nope." I stepped back, gesturing for him to come in.

Baird had only been at my place once before. Thankfully, I'd tidied up last night and there were no underwear drying on my radiators.

His expression lightened with relief as he strode in, giving me a flash of that cocky grin. Baird didn't talk much about his dad because he'd taken off when he was a baby, hence why he'd taken his mother's surname instead. But he did tell me his dad was Scottish Italian, and I gathered that's where he'd inherited the olive skin that made his teeth gleam white.

The smell of bergamot and lemons accompanied him, and I felt another flush of inappropriate attraction. Especially when my gaze devoured his broad back and tapered waist as he strolled down my hallway.

He was like a Marvel superhero brought to life.

"Tea? Coffee? Water?" I asked, trailing him, pulling a

wee bit self-consciously at my crumpled cropped pajama tee.

"Chamomile." Baird followed me into the compact kitchen. He seemed to fill the entire space as I made us both tea.

"What brings you here?" I asked, even though I suspected I knew. He made it difficult to stay annoyed with him.

"To apologize."

I glanced over my shoulder, and his gaze jerked up from my lower back to my face. It was not unusual to catch Baird staring at my arse or legs or chest. We were friends, but he was a man who loved women, and I did have all the female bits he adored, so I didn't take it personally. "You don't need to."

"I do." He took the mug I offered. "Maia, you're my friend, and I don't want to lose your friendship."

I gently tapped my mug against his. "Well, cheers to that. Come sit."

Once we'd settled in my living room, him making my sofa look tiny and me in my armchair facing him, I asked, "What's going on with you?"

Baird pushed his hair off his face before taking a sip of the tea. I waited. He gave me a small, sexy grin at my serious, determined expression. "I'm fine, babe."

Babe.

The one and only time he'd met Will, he called me *babe* so many times I thought Will's head would explode. When Will went to the loo, I'd had to ask Baird not to do it in front of my partner. He'd grinned like an idiot who'd won a pissing contest. I'd playfully tried to shove him into the bar counter. *Tried* being the operative word. It was like trying to shove a hundred-year-old oak tree. That only made Baird laugh harder. But he'd stopped calling me babe in front of Will.

"I don't believe you. If you don't want to talk about it, fine. But just be honest."

"I am fine." He leaned forward. "I've got a lot on my plate. The season, the castle reno ... and I just need to decompress a bit. I might have gone about it the wrong way."

"Are you talking about the partying or the dangerous hobbies?" I referred to the past few months of extracurricular activities that included him snowboarding on one of the most difficult trails in Switzerland, tandem skydiving in Fife, and motor racing against his friend, Daire Montrose, a Scottish *Formula 1* driver. I repeat: He thought it was a good idea to race against a Formula 1 driver!

Baird grinned unrepentantly. "You say dangerous, I say fun. And I'm going to take you skydiving one of these days. I see the way your face lights up whenever I mention it."

I wrinkled my nose because he wasn't wrong. There was a part of me that longed to shrug off this safe little cocoon I'd built for myself. When I mentioned to Will it might be fun to skydive, he'd scoffed and told me I'd hate it. I thought he was simply protecting me from myself.

Yet, if I thought about it, I used to take calculated risks before I met Will. Going off to London for university was the biggest one. Had I stopped living a bit after I met Will? Had I allowed him to stifle me?

Hmm.

"Hey. You okay?" Baird leaned forward, brow furrowed with concern.

"Don't change the subject," I evaded. "You know you've gone off the rails since ..."

"'Going off the rails' is a bit dramatic. I'm enjoying life.

But the partying stuff ... It won't happen again. It can't. The new club owner has me by the balls."

"What do you mean?"

"Not only can I not put another foot wrong but he wants me out in public doing positive PR. Volunteer work, that kind of thing."

I tried not to chuckle. "Well, that sounds awful. What an evil thing to make you do. Helping people."

Baird made a face at my sarcasm. "Ha, funny. C'mon. It's not about the helping part. It's the PR part. I mean, I hate that fake bullshit. I know it's a reflex for people to film absolutely everything, but filming your 'good deed' to post on social media gives me the fucking boak."

"Right?" I agreed. "Every time someone shares one of those reels where they film themselves doing something nice for a stranger or a friend, and people are all like 'You're the loveliest, you're the kindest,' I'm like, really? You're buying into this? It's self-aggrandizing, narcissistic BS. You do a good deed because it's the right thing to do. It's not something that's premeditated. You don't film yourself doing it to post on socials to have a million strangers pat you on the back."

Baird chuckled. "Tell me how you really feel, babe."

"I just did."

"Well, exactly. I'm going to be that wanker posting my good deeds online."

"It's different. You have to do what you need to, to stay on the team."

"Aye, well, I'd already decided after this morning not to be a prat." His eyes darkened. "And I willnae try a hard drug again. I mean it, My. I felt like shit after it, anyway. It's no' for me." His accent thickened with his emotion.

Relief moved through me. "Good. I'm glad to hear it."

"Do you ...uh ... do you ... can you tell me about your mum?"

The thought of explaining my background nauseated me. It was like being stripped naked in front of people so they could judge all my defects. I rubbed at my eyes, giving my pulse a minute to slow.

"Let me just take out my contacts and then I'll tell you." I placed my mug on the coffee table, stood, and strolled into the bathroom.

"I forgot you wear them," he called after me.

"I don't forget. They're a pain in the butt, and there are many times I've been tempted to spend my well-earned savings on laser surgery."

I heard his approaching footsteps as I pulled my contact lens solution out of the bathroom cabinet.

"You should just do it."

He filled my peripheral. I turned my head to find him leaning against the doorframe, arms crossed over his chest, his biceps straining the sleeves of his T-shirt.

"I can't spend my savings on eye surgery."

"Why not?"

"Because I'm saving for a deposit on a house. In this city, that might take me a million years. Not all of us are professional footballers, you know."

"I rent." He shrugged.

He did. He rented the coolest flat I'd ever seen down in Dean Village. His bedroom looked like it was floating above the kitchen in a glass cube. No joke. "But you can afford to buy."

"Get the laser surgery, My. Life is short."

I muttered under my breath about responsibilities and such as I tipped my head to capture the contact off my eyeball.

"I don't know how you touch your eye like that."

I frowned as my vision blurred in front of me. "You get used to it." I fumbled for my glasses and shoved them on. Vision clear, I put everything away and then walked over to him. "All done."

Baird's eyes swept over my face. There was a roughness to his voice as he said, "You're right. Don't get laser surgery."

"Why?"

"The glasses are sexy. You look like a hot librarian."

"Flirt." I gently shoved past him and reached for a hair tie off my sideboard. With a swish of my long hair, I tied it up into a messy bun as I returned to the sitting room and flopped back on my armchair.

The good thing about never wanting to pursue a romantic relationship with the most beautiful man I'd ever met was that I didn't give a shit about my appearance.

My breath hitched at the realization. Because honestly, the only people I'd ever been comfortable not being "well-presented" in front of were Dad, Grace, and Lockie.

Baird was the least judgmental person I'd ever met, though. He made me feel like I could be fully myself with him.

"You all right?" he asked as he sat down again, his long legs sprawling toward mine.

"Uh ... fine."

"You sure?" His gaze dropped to my hand for some reason. "You're not wearing your engagement ring. I thought it was because of swimming ... but ... you've been off these past few weeks."

Just like that, the truth blurted out of me. "We broke up."

Baird's face slackened. "For real?"

"He asked me to step aside while he tried to figure out if he wanted me or his ex-girlfriend."

"Are you fucking joking?" Baird exploded from his seat. "I am going to fucking rip off his nutsack!"

I launched out of my armchair, grabbing Baird to halt him from his angry departure. "Stop! Stop. Will's not worth another tabloid exploit."

"*You* are!"

While that was lovely, I tugged harder. "Baird, please."

Just like that he stopped, whirled, and yanked me into a bear-hugging crush. "Fuck, My, he's a prick. He never deserved you, babe. Never."

I accepted his embrace, pressing my cheek to his warm, hard chest. Tears burned my eyes because why didn't Will believe I deserved better? *He* was the one who had spent three years in my bed. The warm, safe envelopment of Baird's masculinity only reminded me that cuddles like this were no longer a certainty in my future. My favorite thing about Will had been his hugs.

A sob caught in my throat.

"Fuck, I'm going to kill him." Baird's voice was gruff with emotion as his embrace tightened. "Nutsack. Off."

A giggle broke through my tears, and I leaned back to look up into his beautiful dark eyes. It amazed me that he could make me laugh when I was at rock bottom. "Stop threatening to take off his nutsack. Trust me, he needs all the help he can get in that department." Catty, but I was allowed to be.

Baird's eyebrows shot up. "Oi, oi. Spill the tea."

I smirked at his playfulness. "Nope."

"If he not only chose another woman over you but failed to bring you pleasure, I feel like it's almost a legal requirement for me to remove his nutsack."

"We are not talking about that. Especially since that's the least of my problems."

Instantly, Baird became serious. "What's happening?"

I sat down and proceeded to tell him about the situation at work. "And now I could lose everything I've worked for because I don't have a fiancé to present to them," I finished on a shaky exhale.

"Well, isn't Becky a conniving wee rat." Baird shook his head. "I'm sorry. That's shit ... I don't know what to ..." His expression suddenly slackened and then immediately intensified. "I think I'm having a plan. Aye. There is definitely a plan forming." Baird stood, pacing my small living room. "Two birds. One stone. It could work. It could totally fucking work."

I peered up at him in confusion. "What are you rambling on about?"

He suddenly whirled on me. "I'll be your fiancé for the campaign."

CHAPTER FIVE
BAIRD

Maia gaped at me from her armchair, those phenomenal violet eyes wide behind her black-framed glasses. She looked adorably shocked and confused.

All the while my heart raced like a motherfucker as I waited for her response.

So okay, what I'd suggested sounded crazy.

But in my mind, it was the perfect plan.

"I'm sorry, can you repeat that?" She shook her head, blinking rapidly. "I thought I heard you say you'll be my fiancé for the campaign."

"I did." I grinned. "It's an amazing plan."

"I—"

"Think about it." I lowered to my haunches in front of her so she could see my sincerity. "I need to clean up my public image. What better way than to show I'm settling down with my Mrs.? You need a fiancé. And not to sound like a wanker, but I think Pennington's would be pretty fucking happy to switch out a finance guy with a professional football player for their campaign. End result—you get to keep your job."

Maia smacked her hands down on my shoulders to shake me. "Baird, we would be getting married. Not just engaged. Like, *married*. In front of the entire country, I might add. Globally, if this goes viral."

Nerves fluttered in my stomach. The good kind. "Aye. I know. We'll just get divorced after a year or so." Or not. By then, I hoped I'd convinced Maia I was the one. That was the third part of this exceptional plan, but I couldn't share that with her.

I was a mess of emotions for this woman. The feel and sound of her crying in my arms was like a nightmare. Will ending things broke my heart for her, but the selfish arsehole in me was elated. Totally fucking elated.

This was my in.

But Maia needed time. Only a self-involved prick would outright pursue her after she'd broken up with her fiancé. Pretending to be her fiancé allowed me to stealth seduce her.

Somewhat manipulative?

Aye, probably.

However, I knew I could make Maia happier than anyone else could if she gave me the chance. I'd lay the world at her feet.

This was the best plan I'd ever had in my life.

"No." Maia dropped her hands from my shoulders. "That's insane. I'm not asking you to fake a marriage with me. I think it's illegal."

I laughed as I stood up because she was so goddamn cute. "It's only illegal if you're doing it so someone can get a visa."

"Well … it doesn't mean it's right. It would be totally selfish of me. Baird … our lives will be splashed across social media, and because of who you are, the tabloids will follow this story. Do you realize this could mean you can't have sexual relationships with other women unless you completely trusted they wouldn't sell the story to the newspapers?"

Affronted that her first thought was that my libido couldn't take celibacy, I scowled. "Do you think I'm some sex-crazed animal or something?"

Her expression slackened with surprise. "Of course not. I just … you're … you flirt with everything that moves, Baird. You're only twenty-six years old. Pretty sure months without sex will have an adverse effect on you."

"I can do it. I'm offended you think otherwise."

"You know I don't mean to offend you." Maia stood to face me, squeezing my arm in reassurance. "I just don't think you've thought this plan through."

"Look, if you don't want the added scrutiny of the media, I get it." I did, but I was fully disappointed she didn't see merit in the idea.

"It's not really that … it's just … I've alluded to it before, but I was always under a microscope at school. Before I moved in with Dad. For all the wrong reasons." She tugged nervously at the cropped top that kept revealing flashes of smooth olive skin. "It might be a bit of a trigger for me if that were to happen again."

Concern had me reaching for her waist, needing to touch her. I gave it a squeeze. "Does that have anything to do with your mum?"

Maia gave me a sad smile. "I wonder how many people realize how perceptive you are for your age."

I narrowed my eyes. "Stop banging on about our tiny age gap."

"I'm thirty. In woman years, that's like a ten-year age gap, not four."

"Bullshit." I tugged her with me to the couch, so she had no choice but to sit cuddled up next to me. "Talk to me. Because I am not giving up on this plan until you can convince me you really hate it."

Maia pulled her knees up onto the couch and stretched her arm out along the back of it. I liked that she was already so comfortable with my proximity. It gave me hope for the future. And the success of the most amazing plan a man in unrequited love had ever dreamed up.

Yet, I did not love the expression on Maia's face. The tightness around her mouth and eyes as she looked into mine and quickly glanced away.

Like she was ashamed.

Fuck.

"Babe, you can tell me anything. I am a judgment-free zone."

She picked at the fabric of her sofa, her throat working as if against emotion that choked her.

Wanting to alleviate the tension, I offered, "I know a guy, and I'm not naming names, who let a lassie stick a Barbie doll up his arse, and his butthole vacuumed the doll right up there. Sucked it right in and they couldn't get it out. He had to go to the hospital."

Just like that, Maia's eyes lit with shock and laughter. Her lips trembled. "You do not."

"I fucking do. And until now, I'm the only one other than the doctors and his lassie who knows about it because"—I gestured to myself—"judgment. Free. Zone."

Maia suddenly cackled, and I grinned as she bowed toward me with the force of her amusement.

"Do you know what's even better?"

She shook her head, wiping tears of laughter from her eyes.

"It was Interior Designer Barbie."

Maia howled and I joined her, rubbing a hand over her knee, grateful I'd lifted her mood. "I don't think that's quite the interior she had in mind for designing."

"Stop!" Maia wheezed, shoving me.

"I don't think she wanted to be quite as involved in the demo either. Especially anal demolition. What a stinkin' mess."

She pushed me even harder as she laughed and squealed, "I-I'm g-going to pee myself! Stop!"

"All right, all right. I'll stop. But do you get my point?"

She nodded, removing her glasses to wipe at her eyes. Her long lashes spiked with the wet and made her irises look even more violet. Once she caught her breath, she smiled at me. Such a sweet, sexy smile. "Is that a true story?"

"Absolutely. I've got way worse than that, but I don't want to traumatize you. My friends know I don't judge and that they can tell me anything, so I get all the juicy stories."

Maia considered me, a soft expression on her face. "Okay. Well ... this isn't quite 'Barbie up the butt' level of story."

I waited patiently.

She exhaled but then began. "I grew up not knowing who my dad was. Mum finally gave me a name after years of me begging to know. By that point, she was addicted to smack. We lived in this terrible block of flats where people are just forgotten because it was the only place we could afford. I was scared every day. Not only because of where we lived but because I'd taken on the role of parent and I was terrified of my mum overdosing. Also Mum always had some guy around who liked getting strung out with her. As I got older, that got more dangerous for me."

The thought of anyone trying to hurt her like that ... "My, I'm sorry."

"People at school knew my mum was a heroin addict. And kids are not kind. I was bullied constantly. Other parents didn't want their kids around me. I felt ashamed every single day of my life. I had to turn up at school in too-small clothes and I would steal soap just so I could get washed because Mum had spent her benefits on drugs."

My stomach knotted and I slid my hand over her knee again, soothing, comforting her.

"When I was fifteen, one of her boyfriends tried ... he tried to ..." She looked down, picking at her nail nervously. "Well, you know."

"Fuck," I hissed out angrily, trying to contain the emotion.

"I got away. But when I told Mum, she slapped me. Told me I was lying. It broke something in me because I always made excuses for her because I loved her. I always had compassion for her, even though her addiction was ruining us. But when she hit me and didn't take my back, something died between us. I told her she had a choice. It was me or heroin." Maia's lips trembled, and I saw all the agony in her eyes as she met mine. "She didn't choose me."

If I didn't already know I was in love with Maia MacLeod, I would have known right then. Because my chest goddamn *ached* for her.

"She didn't deserve you," I whispered.

"I know." She nodded, reaching for my hand on her

knee. "I know. But even knowing something doesn't mean you can rationalize it quite that easily. Anyway, I took off. I went in search of my dad, and I found him here in Edinburgh. It was hard for him finding out he had a kid and had missed all this time with me, but he didn't turn me away. He fought for me. He and my stepmum Grace tried to make up for the first fifteen years of my life.

"The most important thing for me was having people around who loved me and wanted the best for me. But I also noticed something that was a byproduct of that. I was now wearing decent clothes and had a good family at my back. People didn't know about Mum. And they treated me so differently from before. I watched how they treated the kids at school who clearly didn't have much. Not just like they had less than, but like they *were* less than. They treated them like I had been treated in my previous life. Like I was nothing. Uneducated. Trash."

"Then they were cunts."

Maia blinked at my crudeness but then smirked. "Aye, they were. But as much as people don't want to believe it, the way you present yourself to the world matters. I began to hyperfocus on my presentation in the hopes no one would ever guess where I came from and who gave birth to me. I'm ashamed of her, and I'm ashamed of myself for being ashamed of her. I'm ashamed of myself for leaving her behind because I did love her."

"Of course you loved her. But you're allowed to be ashamed of a woman who put you at risk and didn't fight for you. And you are not your mother."

"Rationally, I know that. But I carry a lot of guilt." I shrugged sadly. "Anyway, there's something else you should probably know before agreeing to this."

"All right ...?"

"We don't talk about it a lot because of how sensitive a subject it is, but my dad has a record. He went to prison before I came into his life."

Shock thrummed through me. Logan MacLeod was a bit of an intimidating dude, but he also was an upstanding guy who managed a couple of Braden Carmichael's businesses for him. I tried to keep my expression neutral. "Why did he go to prison?"

"My aunt Shannon had a boyfriend who was abusing her. One day she tried to leave, and he beat her to a bloody pulp and almost raped her."

Fucking hell. I pictured My's tiny wee aunt and felt a murderous urge to kill some guy I didn't know. And I understood why Logan MacLeod went to prison. "Your dad hurt him," I guessed.

"He put him in a coma." Maia shrugged. "Maybe I should feel otherwise, but I don't blame my dad for doing what he did, even if the law does."

"I don't blame him either, My."

"I didn't think you would." She smiled gratefully. "But my parents have pasts that other people would judge if they ever made it into the public sphere."

"They won't. We'll make sure of it."

"My point is, I've worked hard to get to where I am. The idea of splashing myself across social media and tabloids to be put under scrutiny ... I don't know if I'm built to deal with it."

Damn it. How could I argue with that?

"But then ..." She nibbled at her lips. "I don't want to lose my job. And the campaign would only be for three months."

Hope began to bloom. "It might be fun, My."

She considered me. "Would it really help you out too?"

"Absolutely. It might even get me out of phony volunteer shite. Plus"—I wiggled my eyebrows in exaggeration—"can you imagine the look on Becky the Rat's face when you tell her you're now engaged to a professional footballer?"

Maia let out a gleeful snort of amusement, and my heart turned over.

"Is that a yes, My? Are we doing this thing?"

CHAPTER SIX
BAIRD

Driving through the streets of Falkirk felt strange now. It was my hometown, and yet I hadn't lived there since I was eighteen. I'd played for the local team's under 18s and got talent-scouted by Caledonia United. Since my big sister Ainsley had already made the move to Edinburgh, I liked the idea of being close so she had family in the city. Even if it meant leaving my mum and grandparents behind.

For a while, they made the effort to come into the city to see us, but my gran had a bad fall last winter and wasn't able to travel as much.

Ainsley and I were driving home for Friday night dinner with them. I couldn't do the weekend because I had a game, and I needed to tell them about my plans with Maia.

I still couldn't believe she'd agreed to marry me.

"It's weird," Ainsley murmured as I drove along a street we used to ride our bikes on. The hill below it led down to a huge park near the primary and high schools we'd attended. The houses here were a mix of council and owned, pre-war and midcentury. I didn't remember the parking being so bad, but now I had to slow right down to get my vehicle through the parked cars.

"What's weird?" I asked as I indicated to turn up the hill and onto the street my grandparents' house was on.

Our mum had moved us in with Gran and Granddad after our dad bolted. We didn't remember him. All we knew was his name (Andrew Mancini) and that he was Scottish Italian. Mum didn't like talking about him, and I refused to be curious about the arsehole who fucking abandoned us. Ainsley was a wee bit more interested than me, but I told her to leave me out of it if she ever decided to go searching.

As far as I was concerned, Granddad was the only father figure I'd ever needed.

"What's weird?" I repeated as I pulled up to the house. My grandfather had been smart and years ago had the curb dropped so he could turn the front garden into a driveway. It was tight maneuvering, but I managed to reverse the BMW in.

"Everything is so familiar, but it feels like we lived here in another life."

I switched off the engine. "Aye. That's a good way to describe it."

"I wish we could talk them into moving closer to us."

"I know. I suppose it wouldn't be fair. They've lived here their whole lives."

My sister sighed. "Aye, I suppose."

It was tight getting out because we were parked right up against Mum's car but I managed. It was easier for my tiny big sister.

Ainsley eyed me as we walked up the steps to the front door. "Are you going to tell me why you're acting shifty?"

"Shifty? When the fuck have I ever been shifty?" I asked this just as Mum opened the door.

Mum was blond and blue-eyed. Unfortunately, both me and Ainsley got our coloring from our dad. Both dark-haired and brown-eyed. Thankfully, I'd gotten my height from my mum's side of the family who were Scandinavian. Ainsley got her height from Granddad's side. It annoyed her to no end that she was a foot shorter than me while Mum and Gran were five foot nine.

"Less of the swearing," Mum said, pulling me into a hug. I gave her a tight squeeze. I'd missed the hell out of her.

"How are you, Mum?" I asked as I released her.

"Wondering why your sister is calling you shifty." She hugged Ainsley and murmured in her hair, "What's he up to now?"

"Nothing." I grunted and walked inside, kicking off my trainers because Gran had never allowed us into the house without taking off our shoes first.

It was an end-of-terrace 1930s home. A small central hallway branched off into the downstairs loo, kitchen, and living room. The stairs were next to the front door and led up to three bedrooms. Upstairs had been tight living quarters and as I got older, Mum ended up sharing with Ainsley. There was no doubt in my mind Ainsley took off for Edinburgh Uni to study art history just so she could get some space.

Now I studied those stairs, worrying about Gran having to climb up and down them.

Mum caught my expression. "I know." She squeezed my shoulder. "I've tried talking to them about making a move."

"I could source a nice bungalow somewhere nearby if it's the location that's an issue."

Ainsley kicked off her shoes. "Maybe we can talk to them today."

"We're not deaf, you know," Granddad called from the living room. "We can hear you plotting our lives out there."

I grinned, a feeling of home hitting me right in the chest at the sound of his voice. Striding into the living room, I found Gran in her armchair at the large bay window and Granddad in his by the fire. He got up to greet me, and I tried not to notice how much stiffer and slower he was. I couldn't imagine life without these two, and I didn't like to think of them as elderly. But they were.

"Granddad." I hugged him, patting him gently on the back.

"Nice to see you, son." He gave me a solid pat and a crooked grin. "You finally cut that bloody hair. Looks good. Though you could still take it a bit shorter."

I chuckled because he'd been good-naturedly taking the piss out of my hair for years. Ainsley had greeted Gran first, so we swapped. I leaned down to kiss Gran's cheek, noting how soft but thin it felt against my lips.

As I pulled back, I studied how deeply lined her face had grown in the last year. How puffy and dark the circles under her eyes were. She'd aged since the fall. "Beautiful as ever, Granny."

"Och, away with you." She gestured impatiently to the couch. "Sit down, sit down. Catch me up on your news. Tell me about the haircut."

And as I settled onto the couch, I realized Ainsley was right. Being back in Falkirk with my grandparents felt like reliving memories of a past life. It made me sad. And I decided I might try to talk them into moving to Edinburgh to be closer to us.

"So, are you going to tell me what's on your mind?" Mum asked, closing the kitchen door behind her.

Ainsley and I were doing the dishes after dinner because they didn't have a dishwasher.

"You noticed the shiftiness too, did you?" Ainsley teased.

"Aye, I did." Mum took a seat at the small breakfast nook. "Mum and Dad are watching their soap, so we have some privacy. Talk to me, Baird. I know when something is bothering you."

The thought of explaining my plan filled me with nerves. "Aye, I do have something to tell you." I turned from the sink, crossing my arms over my chest. "Ains, can you sit for a minute too?"

"Now I'm worried. You sound very serious." She dropped the dish towel and sat on the chair opposite Mum, bringing her knees up to her chest.

"It's nothing bad." I tried to alleviate the worry wrinkling my sister's brow. "At least I don't think so."

Mum pinched her lips together but gestured for me to continue.

I quickly but quietly relayed my and Maia's plan.

Ainsley and Mum exchanged incredulous looks throughout and stared at each other once I'd finished talking, as if silently communicating.

Finally, Ainsley turned to me. "I think it's a bad idea to fake-marry a woman you have feelings for."

Both Mum and Ains knew I was head over heels for Maia because, along with Callan and John, they were my confidantes. I hadn't told Callan the extent of my feelings because Beth was Maia's cousin and I didn't want him to have a secret from Beth. John knew, though.

"Or a genius idea. Gives me time to win her over." I grinned. "And I have every confidence I can do it."

"She'd be a fool not to fall for you, son," Mum opined loyally.

"Maybe," Ains huffed. "But she's also just gotten out of a very serious relationship. I doubt Maia wants to jump into anything serious with Baird."

Irritated, I scowled at my sister. "Why are you pissing in my Cheerios?"

"Baird," Mum muttered, wrinkling her nose in disgust.

My sister pinned me with her bold stare. "Because I love you and I don't want you to get your heart broken. Plus, you do realize the tabloids will be all over this."

"That's the point. Cleaning up my image. Baird McMillan, family man."

"Family man?" Mum squeaked. "Is there something else I should know?"

I winked at her. "Not yet, anyway."

Ainsley made a sound like she was going to be sick.

"Okay, I want grandbabies, but twenty-six is too young."

"Maia is thirty. We can't leave it too much longer." I was only half joking.

"She's older than your sister?"

"Four years is nothing."

"I don't know. Maia's a pretty mature thirty-year-old." Ainsley studied me, mischief dancing in her eyes. "Maybe you're not grown up enough for her."

I pushed off the counter, gesturing to myself. "I am mature. I am fucking Bitto Storico."

"Language." That was Mum.

"Sorry. I am bloody Bitto Storico."

"I give up," Mum murmured.

Ainsley screwed up her face. "What is Bitto Storico?"

Mum already had her phone out googling it, and she let out a bark of laughter and held the screen up for Ains.

Ainsley read it out loud. "It's the world's most mature cheese." She shook her head while Mum giggled to herself. "One—how do you know these things? And two, cheese? You choose cheese for your analogy? Really?"

"Why not? It's delicious. As am I."

"Okay, okay." Mum stopped laughing and gave me her authoritative face. "If you can't have a serious discussion about a serious thing you're about to undertake, do we really think you should be doing it?"

"Och, you know I'm being serious. I'll prove how serious I'm being." I licked my suddenly dry lips. "You said I could have Aunt Sigrid's ring when the time came." I referred to my aunt Sigrid from our Norwegian side of the family. They stayed in touch with us via Gran, and we'd even visited their home just outside Oslo when we were kids. And they'd come to visit us. Aunt Sigrid was one of Gran's four siblings. She had no children of her own and she'd died a year after her husband. She'd split her small estate between her nieces and nephews. Mum was her favorite, and she'd left her engagement ring to her. Mum had then promised me that I could give it to the lassie I chose to spend the rest of my life with.

I didn't know much about jewelry, but I knew that ring was cool as fuck and way better suited to Maia than the monstrosity Will the Prick had given her.

"She has violet eyes," I metaphorically pulled the ace out of my sleeve. "It's meant to be."

"Oh my God." Ainsley gaped at me. "So she does."

"Really?" Mum pressed her fingers to her lips, eyes wide.

Because Aunt Sigrid's engagement ring was a sapphire almost the exact color as Maia's eyes.

The kitchen fell silent for a few seconds. Then Mum grimaced. "I think I'm more worried than ever. I don't want you to get hurt."

I shrugged, unable to do my cocky "nothing ever bothers me" act with my mum and Ains. "I think she's worth the risk."

Mum shot up from the chair and I'd barely got over the surprise of the sudden movement before I was pulled into her embrace. "I hope it all works out the way you want, son." She leaned back to clasp my face in her palms. "I'll go get the ring. And I'll want to meet Maia. Very, very soon."

I nodded, a lump forming in my throat at the bright tears glistening in my mum's eyes.

It hit me that if I didn't convince Maia to give me a real chance, I'd be breaking more than my own heart.

Mum quietly left the kitchen to get the ring.

I turned to Ainsley.

"I'll break her face if she hurts you," she announced, tilting her chin up, dark eyes flashing with protectiveness.

I contemplated my big sister. "Appreciate that, Ains. But I'd appreciate it even more if you'd give Maia a chance."

"I don't know Maia well enough to not like her. Do I think she's a bit aloof? Yes. You clearly see another side to her, so I'm inclined to like her because of how much you like her. But that doesn't mean I won't break that gorgeous face of hers if she hurts you."

"One, Maia isn't aloof. Far from it and you'll find that out. Two, you know I won't let you near her gorgeous fucking face, even if she hurts me."

My sister's expression softened. "She better deserve you, B."

"I hope we deserve each other." I shrugged. "She's … Maia … she's the one, Ains."

Ainsley couldn't wipe the concern off her face as she nodded slowly. And again, I hoped like fuck I would prove myself right.

CHAPTER SEVEN
BAIRD

The last time I'd been this nervous before a game was my first match after recovering from my injury.

I suppose that variety of nervousness had never gone away, but I'd found a way to compartmentalize those feelings.

This was different. These nerves had nothing to do with the game and everything to do with the fact that Maia was coming to see me play for the first time. It was a qualifying home game against Kingston United and would determine if we made it into the final against Dalmarnock. It was a big game.

And yet I was still more nervous about Maia. I'd gotten her VIP access so she could come meet the gaffer and we'd tell him we're engaged.

First, I had to give Callan and John the skewed version of the truth we'd decided to give everyone other than our parents. The locker room was not the place to do it, so I had them follow me into one of the empty offices.

"What's going on?" Callan crossed his arms over his

chest, frowning. I knew his concern came from love, but man, I was getting sick of seeing that expression on his face.

Just blurt it out. Rip it off like a Band-Aid. "Maia split with her bloke a while back. I took my chance, proposed, and she said yes."

It was mostly the truth.

Unfortunately, I couldn't tell them the whole truth because it would mean asking Callan to keep a secret from Beth, and I didn't think that was fair.

"Is this a joke?" Callan's arms dropped to his sides.

"Nah. Never been more serious." I pulled the ring box out of my back pocket. "Asked my mum for Aunt Sigrid's ring." The lads knew all about it and had taken the piss out of me for years because I hadn't shown any signs of ever getting serious enough with a lassie to use it.

"You've never been in a serious relationship," John said, taking the thought out of my head. "How the hell do you go from screwing around to engaged?"

"Aye? Can you not just date for a bit? Why the need to jump right in?" Callan demanded.

I snorted. "Mate, you proposed to Beth six months after you met. I've known Maia for over a year."

"Technically, Beth and I have known each other since we were sixteen. We were dating for six months before I proposed. Unless Maia's all right with you showing up in tabloid photos with half-naked women, I'm thinking there's a plot hole here."

Bloody Callan. Too smart for my own good. "Fine. She broke up with Will a while back, but I only just got up the courage this past week to propose. She said aye. That tells you everything. That's all that matters. I'm not going to stand here and explain myself. It's happening. That's final."

Callan stared at me like I'd grown three heads. "You're serious? Have you been in love with her this whole time?"

I side-eyed John, and Callan followed my gaze. John gave him a tight-lipped nod and then sighed. "Sorry, buddy. But I promised Baird I wouldn't tell you. He didn't want you to have to keep a secret from Beth."

"I'm in love with Maia," I confessed.

Callan closed his mouth. I waited.

And waited.

Then my best mate nodded slowly as he processed all this new information. "Okay. Well, I ... I'm happy for you, man. But I think getting engaged right away is a mistake."

"Callan—"

"Nah. I'm worried about you. You're doing a complete one eighty from sleeping with everything that moves to proposing to a lassie. Your behavior is ... erratic."

"So was yours when you were falling in love with Beth and didn't want to man up and admit it," I snapped back.

"Okay, okay. None of that." John stepped between us calmly. "You guys need to chill."

"He needs his head sorted." Callan pointed angrily at me.

"Aye. I do." I nodded, my words taking the wind out of his sails. "But did it ever occur to you that Maia might be the one who can help me do that?"

My best mate's shoulders slumped.

Then, "Well ... fuck."

I curbed a smug response.

His eyes narrowed. "I'm cautiously offering my congratulations."

My amusement fled. "You can stick your judgmental cautious congratulations up your arse."

"For fuck's sake, Baird. People who care about you are allowed to be concerned for you."

"Well, I'm sick of it. I'm a grown man. I can handle myself. This is what I want. This is who I want, and that's that."

Callan peered at me for a few seconds. A few more and I was out the door. Thankfully, his expression relaxed, and he rounded the table to embrace me, giving me a manly thud on the back. "Congrats. I'm always here for you."

"I know, bud. Sorry for being a prick and making you worry. I'm all good."

John was next to embrace me. "Thank the ever-loving gods she loves you back. I was worried you were going to pine your life away."

Callan huffed. "How the hell did I miss this?"

"Because his pining looks a lot like how he flirts with everyone."

"Fuck off," I replied good-naturedly, even as guilt and unease rode my shoulders. It was one thing evading the details with half-truths but another entirely to perpetuate a lie.

And the fact was that Maia wasn't in love with me.

Not yet, anyway.

———

Minutes before we left the locker room for the field, Maia texted to let me know she'd arrived. Her presence was like a shot of adrenaline. I went out there with my game face on.

Kingston United might have kicked our arses if I hadn't had Maia in the back of my mind.

She fired me up.

Our opposition was determined to take us down, and

our defense was apparently asleep on the job. There were about twenty goal attempts from Kingston. A few of them went so wide I barely had to bother. The others, I saved like the machine I was. Nothing was getting past me today.

They awarded me Player of the Match.

Caledonia United were into the final.

"*Oan yersel*!"

The lads smacked me on the back, trying to climb me like a tree, as we strolled into the locker room after the press line. Even having to face tabloid arsehole Craig Bennet as he asked me whether my performance was an attempt to stop the owner killing my contract didn't bother me. "Nah, mate. I'm just phenomenal at a job I love." I grinned at him like I didn't want to punch his scummy wee face and moved on to the next interviewer.

We were all glad to get back to the locker room, though. The gaffer patted my shoulder in a fatherly gesture. "Brilliant, McMillan. Brilliant, lad. More of that in the final, eh, and we might just win this thing."

I was not averse to a little positive attention, and I was fucking made up that we were in the Cup final, but I also really wanted to see Maia and give her the ring. The nerves wouldn't abate until I did that and there was no going back on our plan.

Unsurprisingly, I was the first bloke out of the showers and locker room. I said hello to some of the lads' partners waiting in the family room. Maia stood by herself, looking around, shifting her weight from one leg to the other like she was uncomfortable. I frowned, wondering if anyone had approached to welcome her. It was a damn shame Beth hadn't been at the game to keep her company.

Maia's face lit up when she noticed me, and my heart turned over in my chest.

She was so stunning I didn't think there would ever come a day when she didn't knock the breath right out of me.

"You owned it, Baird!" Eric's lass, Katrin, yelled happily from within the circle of her cluster of WAGs (wives and girlfriends).

I gave her a chin lift because I was annoyed Maia was standing on her own. When someone was on their own and you had people around you, it was up to you to make that person feel welcome. Sometimes this crowd was cliquey, and it bugged the shit out of me.

As soon as I reached Maia, I swept her into my arms and she let out a squeak of surprise as I lifted her off her feet.

She laughed softly and embraced me before I lowered her. Maia grinned, those violet eyes shining brightly. "I'm definitely going to call you Bear from now on."

I wrinkled my brow on an affectionate smile. "Bear?"

"Aye. I swear when you were defending the goal at one point, you looked like a hard-bodied grizzly bear towering over the other players. Then the first thing you do when you see me is bear-hug me."

I chuckled at the imagery. "I like the addition of hard-bodied."

She rolled her eyes. "Well, you're not exactly soft like a bear."

"No, I am definitely not soft."

She glanced shyly away. I'd never seen My react shyly to anything I'd said. It was absolutely, incredibly adorable. "Anyway ... you were amazing. Congrats on getting into the final. It's phenomenal."

"I was showing off for you," I replied honestly.

Maia shook her head with a laugh like she thought I was teasing.

"Come with me." I grabbed her hand and led her past everyone, not giving them the time of day. I had a mission to complete.

"Where are we going? Am I allowed down here?" Maia hissed uncertainly, tugging on my hand as I led her through doors and down corridors.

"You are if you're with me." The office where I'd broken the news to Callan and John was free, so I pushed in and shut the door behind us.

That's when the nerves kicked in again.

Maia glanced around the clinical space, tucking a strand of silky dark hair behind her ear. Christ, even her ears were cute and perfect. She wore classy little diamond studs that winked in the light. I hoped the diamonds weren't from Will or we'd have to replace them pronto.

"And we're in here why?" My asked, arching an eyebrow.

Here goes nothing.

I tugged the ring box out of my pocket. "If we're going to do this, you need to dress the part." I opened the box.

Maia's jaw dropped. "Where?" she wheezed out. "How? What?"

I snorted. "Give me your hand."

Maia gaped. "Huh?"

Shoulders shaking with amusement, I reached for her manicured left hand and slipped the ring onto her ring finger. It fit. Perfectly.

Meant to be.

An unexpected flush of arousal shot through me seeing the ring on her. My dick started to harden.

Fuck.

Kaito's naked arse. Baumann's naked arse. That time the

team tried to make me eat sheep balls. The gaffer's naked arse. Ugh. Aye, that did it.

I cleared my throat. "It was my aunt Sigrid's engagement ring, so it's vintage. Mum said it's a *violet* sapphire. I thought ... it's kind of perfect for you. Cannae believe it fits."

Maia looked up from the ring. "It's stunning, Baird. I can't ... I can't wear this. It's too special."

"We need a ring, and I happened to have this one. I know you'll take care of it."

"I will." She clasped it to her chest, eyes a wee bit bright, like she was fighting back emotion.

I reached for her other hand. "Hey, I didn't mean to upset you."

"It's not ... you didn't. I just ..." Maia lifted the ring into the light. "When Will ... when we ended our engagement, I was genuinely heartbroken. But lately, there are things that make me question our relationship. Like the engagement ring he gave me."

Our eyes locked, and I trembled against the need to kiss her, soothe her, make her realize I would hand her the world.

"This is a ring I'm supposed to wear for the rest of my life. It should be exactly the right ring for me. Yet Will chose this huge diamond that was showy and obnoxious. I felt awkward when people would comment on it. But this ... this *is* perfect for me. How do you know that and he didn't?"

Because I know you. I love you. *Not who* I *want you to be.* I held back the desperate words. "Because I pay attention, My. Maybe you're starting to realize Will the Prick *didn't* pay attention."

Her answering laugh sounded like a half sob. "Aye, I think you're right."

I tugged her into a cuddle. "Are you okay?"

Maia hugged me tightly. "Aye. I will be. Thanks for trusting me with your aunt's ring."

I want to trust you with it for the rest of my damn life.

Clearing my throat again, I released her before I did something like kiss her until neither of us could breathe. "Now for the fun part. We go tell the gaffer we're engaged."

She nibbled on her lush lower lip. "I feel bad telling your manager before I tell my parents."

Shit. "We ... we can wait. If you want."

"No. Let's do it. I'll tell my parents tonight."

At her disturbed expression, I was almost afraid to ask. "You don't think it'll go well?"

She grimaced. "Not because it's you. But because I'm 'engaged' again after only a month of breaking off my last engagement."

"One, don't air-quote *engaged*, or you'll give this whole thing away."

Maia snort-laughed but nodded.

"And second, you're telling them the truth. That this is ... fake." I hated that word. "So, I'm sure they'll be fine."

"Hmm. I'm glad one of us thinks so."

CHAPTER EIGHT
MAIA

I couldn't stop staring at Baird's ring.

Not just because it was a family heirloom he'd entrusted me with but because it was the most perfect engagement ring in the world. I'd never seen a sapphire that matched the color of my eyes before. My eyes were a gift from my dad. A gift I treasured because they were such an unusual color. Aunt Shannon, dad's wee sister, had the same violet eyes too.

I didn't even know this color of sapphire existed. The sapphire looked around two carat and was a rectangular cushion cut, set in platinum, and flanked by three round-cut diamonds, two hugging the sapphire and one at the base in a triangular cascade into the band. Six round-cut diamonds in total. It was beautiful but understated. Baird told me his aunt's husband had bought it from a jeweler in Austria in the 1960s. I loved it had history, but I was also taken aback that Baird had bestowed a piece of jewelry upon *me* that was clearly important to his family instead of keeping the engagement ring for the woman he would eventually marry after we divorced.

One day, I was going to be a divorcée. I wasn't sure either of us had processed how big that was and how it might impact us down the road.

There were lots of things we hadn't considered when we impulsively decided to do this. For instance, I certainly hadn't predicted how attached I'd get to this freaking engagement ring after only a day of wearing it.

Forcing my gaze from my ring finger as the lift taking me up to the Pennington office floor drew to a stop, I strolled across the marble floor, making a beeline for my office so I didn't have to speak to anyone yet. Well, anyone other than Eli.

I had hoped to come into the office after a good sleep, feeling well-rested and ready to face my entire team with the news, but it had taken me forever to drown out the voices of my family last night.

Having decided it was best I face my dad and Grace alone, I'd left Baird after he'd introduced me to his manager, who was shocked to say the least. Brian seemed resigned to the news, though I got the feeling he wearily accepted this as another crazy thing Baird was doing this year. He ended our conversation saying he hoped this meant Baird was finally going to settle down and get on with the game and that his performance today gave him hope that might be true.

Brian's behavior toward Baird irritated me because my friend had been through so much, and his actions of late were clearly him acting out against the fear he'd experienced after his injury. He wouldn't talk to me about it, but I thought for sure the men around him at the club would have a better handle on it. Apparently not. It seemed it might be down to me to push Baird and get him to open up and talk about the lasting effects from the head injury.

Callan and John were lovely, though Callan did remind me I needed to call my cousin Beth to tell her the news.

However, I had my parents to deal with first.

After evading the truth with Callan, John, and Baird's gaffer, and feeling icky after it, I was so glad I didn't have to lie to my parents about the engagement.

At least I was at first.

Until my dad shot up from his couch and demanded, "Are you insane?"

My stepmum, Grace, an elegant Englishwoman, spoke with a softness that belied the steel in her spine. "Logan, I don't think that language is helpful."

"Insane?" He glowered at Grace. "You don't think this scheme is insane?"

She glowered right back. "I wouldn't use such a hostile word, no."

My dad's handsome face softened minutely. He turned to me. "Okay, what I meant to say is ... I'm worried about you."

I looked at Grace. She nodded and gave me a concerned but reassuring smile.

"Didn't you hear what I said about my job? What my boss said?"

"Aye. And it's illegal. They can't fire you."

"Not outright. But they'll find a way to do it legally. I've seen it before. They're big on loyalty and team player stuff at Pennington's. I've worked too hard to lose my position now."

Dad slumped into his seat. "So, you're going to lie to the entire world and get married to a man you don't love?"

"It'll help Baird's image too," I responded weakly.

"I think this is a very big, fraudulent plan, and maybe I

wouldn't be so worried if it weren't for the fact that Will broke your heart five weeks ago," Grace offered quietly.

Dad nodded. "What Grace said."

Despite my hammering pulse, I firmly pronounced, "I'm doing this. It's a blip of time in the grand scheme of things. It's not illegal because we're not doing it for a visa or something like that."

"I think you'll find falsely making a statement in your marriage vows is considered perjury in this country and therefore is illegal," Grace relayed.

My heart stopped. "Grace!"

"What? I'm just letting you know what you're really gearing up to do."

Damn it. I did *not* know that.

Was it going to stop me, though?

Nope.

"Well, I didn't want to lie to you guys when I'll have to lie to everyone else. I told you the truth. But … you can't tell Lockie." Guilt consumed me. "He's too young. He might tell the wrong person and then I really will get into trouble."

Dad's jaw clenched before he unclenched it and snapped, "You're going to lie to your wee brother? What if he gets attached to Baird? You know he's a Caley fan and already worships the ground that bloke walks on."

"It's just for a little while. Stop acting like I'm committing a big crime that's going to emotionally scar everyone." I stood up, trembling. "Except for that one time I went to a club with Layla the sociopath when I was sixteen, I have always done the right thing. The expected thing. I decide for once in my life to take a risk and do something a wee bit mad that will help my career, and you're acting like I've robbed a goddamn bank!"

Dad and Grace stared at me stunned.

I was stunned.

The first year with them had been the most tumultuous. I was a teenager, devastated about my mum and terrified Dad would fail me; therefore, I'd acted out quite a bit. Until it occurred to me if I kept acting out, I would really push Dad and Grace away.

Instead, I became obsessed with people-pleasing. In a way, I also think it was a form of absolution with other people because deep down, part of me believed I was in the wrong for leaving my mum behind.

I'd people-pleased with Will too. We hadn't compromised on anything. I'd just given in so I wouldn't upset him or rock the boat.

Baird, it seemed, made me feel a wee bit reckless.

The fear of upsetting my parents was like a sickness in my gut. I stood there, frozen, waiting for them to react.

Grace sighed heavily. "You're right, sweetheart. I mean, I still don't agree with the plan, but it is your life and it's not like you're hurting anyone."

"Lying isn't hurting? Lying isn't selfish?" Dad glared at his wife.

Remorse worsened my nausea. I didn't want Grace and Dad to fight.

"The only people it might hurt are Maia and Baird, and that's their risk to take," Grace replied with a bite in her calm tone. "As for selfish ... I think Maia's earned the right to be a little selfish. Don't you?"

Did I mention I adored my stepmother?

Dad swallowed hard, his words thick as he responded a few seconds later, "Aye. I suppose in that you're right."

Suffice it to say I'd left my parents' house uncertain and filled with guilt at the friction I'd caused. I couldn't sleep.

Hence the need for three coffees before I even left my flat this morning.

The last thing I needed was to see an email from Will when I logged into my work computer.

I'd opened it before I even realized who had sent it.

Maia,

I can't believe you blocked me. We need to talk. Please. Call me.

Will

I immediately blocked his email address.

My phone screen suddenly lit up and a text message popped up from Baird.

Be there at 12.

Butterflies fluttered to life in my belly as I replied.

Thanks. See you soon.

He sent me the blowing-kiss emoji, and I rolled my eyes, grinning. He was adorable.

My hope was that his presence would bolster me today while we awkwardly explained to my boss and my boss's boss about the change in situation. I'd already contacted Christina last night to tell her I needed an emergency meeting with her and Hilary about the campaign. She'd bluntly responded this morning that we'd meet at noon, and I'd quickly relayed that information to Baird. Thankfully, his morning training session ended just in time for him to join me here.

———

Baird called up five minutes before the meeting, and I ran downstairs to the delivery entrance to let him in. Eli took Baird's call, so they were full of questions and eyebrow waggles, but I had to tell my bosses first before I explained anything to Eli and Liza.

Baird looked incredibly handsome in his black dress shirt and dress trousers. The shirt sleeves were rolled up to his elbows, revealing his strong forearms and tattoos. And it was open at the collar, so he didn't look too formal. Yet the transformation was amazing. He looked ... older. Sexier.

Heat flushed through me. "You look hot."

Baird chuckled at my confused tone as he stepped into the building, his body brushing against mine. "I'm offended by how surprised you sound."

"No ... I just ... I mean ... you look different."

"Thought I'd dress the part. Look responsible and all that." His gaze moved down my body as I shut the door and locked it. "Is this what you wear to work?"

I glanced down at my cropped white button-down shirt and wide-leg black suit pants. The shirt had long, stiff bell sleeves and showed a good expanse of my bare stomach. Ten years ago, my boss would have told me to go home and change. Now, crop tops were in, and as a fashion buyer, I liked to wear the products I bought for the store.

"What's wrong with it?" I wrinkled my nose in mock irritation as I strode past him.

"It's sexy as fuck. I like it." He walked into the small lift, and it bounced with his weight as he squeezed in. His citrusy aftershave filled my senses, and my cheeks flushed again. Hiding my reaction to his nearness, I stabbed at the button that would take us upward where I could get some distance from him.

Baird reached for my left hand and lifted the ring up in the light. "Fuck, it suits you."

There was such gruff emotion in his voice, my heart stuttered for a minute. Because the emotion matched the strange expression on his face.

"Bear?" I whispered, confused suddenly. And not quite sure why.

He blinked like he was coming out of a trance and then gave me his usual playboy grin and wink. "Let's show it off to Becky and watch her turn purple."

Relieved, I laughed and tried to tug my hand back.

Baird entwined our fingers together instead. "Need to walk out there looking the part," he reminded me.

In other words, there was no putting distance between us.

We walked into the upper offices of Pennington's hand in hand, with Baird practically brushing his side up against mine. He smelled so bloody good. My body tingled in a very specific way, and I cursed inwardly. It had only been five weeks since Will and I broke up, but apparently, I was feeling the dry spell.

"This place is cool," Baird muttered, glancing around.

The offices were cool because of the Edwardian architecture. High ceilings, marble floors, intricate cornicing, and interesting pillars. Not all but some of the offices still had the original wood paneling on the outer walls with mottled privacy glass above.

"They're waiting for us in Hilary's office." I led him to the other side of the upper floor just before the open-plan offices. Hilary's door was ajar, and an irritated flush moved through me to find Becky already seated beside Christina.

Hilary leaned her suit-clad bum on the edge of her vintage captain's pedestal desk. Everyone straightened, eyes widening at the sight of the big, handsome guy clutching tightly to my hand.

Or rather who *I* was clutching tightly to.

Baird's hand pulsed around mine as he offered me silent comfort and reassurance.

"Well ... what's this?" Hilary stood from the desk to face us.

"Hilary, Christina ... Becky," I forced myself to be civil and acknowledge her (unwanted) presence. I licked my very dry lips. "I ... I broke up with Will a while ago—"

"Because Maia and I fell in love," Baird cut in, and I knew it was because the trembling in my voice was so apparent. "Not the best situation, but without going into the details, Maia left Will for me." He held up my hand, flashing the engagement ring. "I'm Baird McMillan, Maia's actual fiancé."

My smile trembled. "Just thought you should know."

My friend cleared his throat as if trying to shove down his laughter at my silly add-on.

"Wait ... Baird ..." Christina's eyes widened with delight. "As in your friend, Baird, the Caledonia United goalkeeper?"

"As in her *fiancé*, the Caledonia United goalkeeper," Baird corrected.

"Oh my god, this is brilliant." Christina stood up and came over to embrace me. "Congratulations, darling. This campaign is going to be amazing. I mean, obviously congrats on falling in love and getting engaged—" She spun to face Hilary. "But this campaign is going to be amazing."

Her reaction was better that I could have hoped for!

We waited tensely for Hilary to decide to disagree or agree.

"I'll call legal right away to change the contracts. Iain is a huge football fan. He's going to love it." Hilary eyed Baird in a very female way that had me unconsciously pushing into his side. "You're beautiful. You're going to look so much better in a tux than Will." She cut me a look. "No offense."

"I'm getting married in a kilt," was Baird's gruff response.

"We planned for a tux, no?" Christina shared a look with Hilary.

Then I dared to speak up, "We do have a collaboration with MacGregors for our Edinburgh store. We offer it in our bridal collection." I referred to an exceptional Edinburgh kiltmaker who had a small collection in our store.

"That's right." Christina considered Baird, her eyes devouring every inch of him. "Actually, I do think he'd look better in a kilt."

"Kilt it is. I don't care, as long as we get this contract signed." Hilary peered at Baird. "There's nothing in your contract with Caledonia United that would forbid this collaboration, is there?"

Baird squeezed my hand and admitted, "You *will* need permission from the club."

What? I tugged on his hand, but Baird held it fast as he continued, "I spoke to my gaffer this morning and relayed the situation to him. He thinks it might be good for my image, so I don't think you'll have a problem. He's expecting you to contact him."

Hilary nodded briskly. "Fine, fine. I'm sure Iain can make all of that happen with one phone call."

Christina side-eyed Becky. "Becky thought Maia was here to tell us she wasn't doing the campaign. Aren't you glad you were wrong?"

I could only imagine my colleague had been preening at the prospect of me pissing off the Erstwhiles.

Sure enough, Becky looked like she'd sucked on a lemon. "Of course," she forced out and gave me a false smile. "Congratulations, Maia. How fortuitous for you that you upgraded your fiancé just in time for the campaign."

Baird stiffened at my side.

Hilary's expression sharpened and Becky seemed to realize her passive-aggressive comment was spoken in company and not whispered in my ear. She beamed. "It's such great news for the campaign. I can't wait to get started."

———

I thought I'd feel a sense of relief as I walked out of my boss's boss's office with Baird still holding tight to my hand.

Instead, I was shaking with dread at the massive lie we'd just told.

This was surely bad for my karma.

Baird led me back to the lift. "I need to get over to Blantyre. I've got a meeting with Braden. Otherwise, I'd stay for lunch."

"No, you go do what you need to do," I replied a little numbly.

Baird stopped and turned to clasp my face in his large palms. His thumbs stroked my cheeks as his warm dark eyes held mine. I shivered at the intensity of his expression. "It's all going to be okay," he promised on a whisper. "I won't let anything happen to you. We'll get through this, and it'll all be good. You're my best friend, My. I'm going to take care of you."

Perhaps it was the tumultuous chaos of so many emotions in such a short period, but my eyes stung with unshed tears.

Before they could spill over, Baird bent his head and gently, so very gently, brushed his mouth over mine. My lips tingled like I'd touched electricity. I felt that soft caress in all my erogenous zones.

A tiny brush of his lips.

And I felt it everywhere.

I gaped up at him in shock.

"Becky's watching," he murmured. Then his lips pressed a little harder to mine before he released me. Baird stroked my cheek one last time. "Call me if you need me."

I nodded, speechless.

As Baird disappeared onto the lift and out of sight, I felt uneasy for a whole different reason.

It never occurred to me that when our fake relationship imploded, it would be a danger to more than just my career.

CHAPTER NINE
MAIA

As usual, I was in the pool before Baird had arrived at the gym. I was in the middle of a length when I heard a splash and someone cutting quickly through the water toward me. I sped up to get to the shallow end and turned just as Baird reached me. He stood, pushing his wet hair off his face, his biceps bulging. In my periphery, I saw water droplets trickling down his tan, sculpted, inked chest.

Like always, I kept my focus fixed firmly on his face and off his magnificent body. Before I'd done it out of consideration for Will because I knew I'd be upset if Will was ogling another woman (if only I'd known he was ogling another woman in every way a man could). Now I restrained myself for my own peace of mind.

Baird gave me his killer smile. "That's it done."

A wee bit mesmerized by his mouth (his lips had proved distracting ever since he'd kissed me two weeks ago), it took me a minute to process his words.

"What's done?"

"The contract."

Surprise shot through me. "How do you know?"

"Did you not check your emails this morning? That's everything tied up between the club and Pennington's. I tell you, I don't know what Iain Erstwhile promised, but I've never seen a contract move that fast."

"Wow, it's done." *Oh my goodness, we are really doing this?* "That means the campaign will start at the end of the month." Just two weeks from now.

"Aye." Baird seemed so unbothered. "Don't tell me you're getting cold feet now?"

"You saw the plans, right?" The marketing team at Pennington's had already drawn up a schedule for us even before the contracts were signed. As long as the schedule didn't interfere with Baird's training or matches, we were penciled in to do photoshoots and video shoots for the social media campaign. Everything from an engagement announcement to bridal wear to our wedding gift list to the actual wedding (oh my goodness, we were going to get married in front of the public!), to our honeymoon.

It was starting to become a reality.

My dad was right. What we were doing was kind of insane.

My chest felt tight.

"Maia." Baird reached for me. "Are you okay?"

"We're getting married."

He embraced me, pressing my cheek to his hard chest. The feel of his strong, wet body cut through my panic. I'd never been more aware of him, and I didn't know why it had to happen now of all times. "I promised you everything would be okay, and I meant it."

"None of that funny business in here!" a belligerent male voice echoed through the pool area.

Baird turned in the water and I stood on tiptoes to see over his shoulders. An elderly gentleman was easing himself into the pool, glaring daggers at us.

"I'm hugging my fiancée. Only a pervert *perverts* a hug," Baird snapped back in annoyance.

That was the thing about my now fiancé. He was as laidback as a sunbathing walrus until someone upset a woman he cared about.

The man stuck his finger up at us before pushing off into a swim.

"What a turd," Baird muttered, turning back to me. "You all right?"

I gently eased out of his delicious arms. "Just a momentary panic. If you hadn't noticed, I'm quite a private person. I think I've posted five photos on socials in the last two years." Baird, much to Hilary's delight, already had a substantial social media following.

Many of his followers were women. Who were probably going to lose their minds when we announced our engagement.

The thought dredged up my main concern on Baird's part in this plan: his playboy ways and just how difficult he was going to find it to abstain for three and a half months. Pennington's wanted us to pick a venue from their selection for an August wedding. They would have to pull some major strings to host this wedding so quickly. But at least it would be over with by then. Once we completed the honeymoon shoot, of course.

"We can still make this go away," Baird offered quietly. "If it's too much."

And lose my job?

Irritate his club who were already at their wit's end with him?

"No. We're too far in it now. Let's swim. Swimming helps." I pushed off before Baird could stop me.

The pool had always been the one place I could drown out the negative thoughts that often consumed my headspace when I was younger. Will didn't know that was why I swam every week. I realized that I'd kept a lot of myself from my ex. Maybe because deep down, I'd known he wasn't the right man for me? That thought hurt, so I pushed harder in the water until it faded.

For once, Baird didn't try to joke or playfully pull me out of my worries. He let me swim, like he really understood that's exactly what I needed.

There Baird McMillan went again, surprising the heck out of me in the best way.

———

Unfortunately, this ... this was not a surprise.

Standing awkwardly at the edge of the cafeteria watching Baird flirt with the redhead who was sitting in what should be my seat, I felt a flush of agitation. He leaned in and whispered something in her ear that made her guffaw. She slapped his hand and squealed, "You're so bad!"

Ugh. Could this scene be any more cliché?

A sick feeling churned in my belly.

Baird's flirting had never bothered me before. It was almost a weekly occurrence for me to exit the locker room and find someone practically draped over him.

But here we were on the cusp of the biggest lie either of us would ever undertake, and he couldn't stop himself from flirting with another woman on day effing one!

Sometimes, just when I thought Baird was more mature

than everyone assumed, he'd do shit like this and remind me of our age gap. The level of my annoyance shocked me as it propelled me forward toward the table to slap some sense into him.

The arsehole had the audacity to look up at my approach and grin, totally oblivious to his wrongdoing. I did not smile back.

His expression fell.

I looked at the redhead. She scowled at me as if to say, "And you are?"

Therefore, I answered her out loud. I lifted my ring finger, letting the sapphire wink in the light. "I'm the fiancée."

Her expression turned ashen as she turned to glower at Baird. "You're an arsehole." Then she stood and shook her head. "I'm so sorry. But you should know he's an arsehole and good luck with that." The redhead grabbed her backpack and hurried away, cheeks blazing.

To my shock, Baird was on the cusp of erupting into laughter. "What. Was. That?"

Was he kidding me?

I dumped my bag and took the seat the redhead had vacated. That stupid smile disappeared at whatever he recognized in my expression. "You promised me that I was safe with you," I hissed at him. "This is a big bloody lie we're about to tell the whole world. And you promised I was safe. I used to only be semi-joking about it being a physical impossibility for you to not flirt with everything that moves ... but now I am seriously worried that you're going to mess this up. We're both on dangerous ground with this lie. We cannot screw it up and get caught with other people."

Baird scowled. "My, I was only flirting with her. That doesn't equate to sex, to cheating."

I tried to ignore the flash of hurt or what the hell it meant. I didn't want to think about it too deeply. "That's not how other people see it. If Will flirted with other women in front of me, it would have not only pissed me off, it would've hurt my feelings. Very badly. People in serious relationships, unless otherwise agreed upon, don't do that to each other." I slumped in the chair and gazed across the mostly empty cafeteria. Dread settled in my gut. "I knew this would be your Achilles heel, and still I agreed to it."

"What the fuck does that mean?" he demanded.

My brows nearly hit my hairline at his tone. "You know what it means. You don't have a monogamous bone in your body. *My* whole body is full of them! In the real world, you and I would never be in a relationship for that very reason. And the idea of constantly having to remind you that you're supposed to be pretending to be the antithesis of commitment-phobic exhausts me."

Baird gaped, stunned. His reaction confused me because I didn't think I'd said anything we both didn't already know. Then he practically whispered, "Is that what you think? Is that what you've thought of me this whole time we've been friends?"

"Eh, have you ever tried being monogamous? I don't think so. Do you flirt with anything that offers you a smile? I do think so."

"Don't be condescending, Maia." Baird suddenly pushed up from the table, his expression blank in a way I'd never seen. "I have to get to training."

It took me so long to compute what was happening, he was halfway across the cafeteria when I thought to shout, "Bear!"

"We'll talk later," he said over his shoulder.

Then he was gone.

My cheeks burned as the two girls at the next table stared at me. I turned away and muttered to myself, "How the hell am I the bad guy?"

CHAPTER TEN

BAIRD

The last time I was in this foul a mood was not long after my injury. In fact, I think this mood was fouler than that. Baumann and I nearly got into it in training when he started taking the piss out of me about my quick engagement to Maia. He kept saying shit about how many women I'd slept with and asking what was so special about Maia. When he used the word *pussy* in relation to her, I lost my mind. Callan and John had to hold me back. Thankfully, the gaffer had been near and heard, and Baumann got a fine for being a prick.

The truth was I was only this enraged with him because I was angry at myself.

And confused.

This whole time Maia had thought me incapable of being a one-woman man.

I'd never even crossed her mind as a viable candidate to be her man.

I'm fucking down bad at the gym and she's not only oblivious, she's impervious!

Ainsley was right.

I'd gone into this whole scheme like a cocky bastard, absolutely sure I now had a clear path to making Maia fall for me. There was even a part of me that hoped My already had feelings for me, ones she'd kept locked up tight because of Will.

But nah.

This whole time she'd written me off.

"Got any plans for the weekend?" Freddie, our youngest and newest player, fell into step beside me as we all trudged, soaked with sweat, across the field toward the locker room. Freddie had replaced Botan, a Japanese player who'd left to return to Kyoto this season. The coaches had run us ragged this morning in preparation for this weekend's final.

"Not really," I muttered. I wasn't in the mood for small talk. But the team was pissed about the loss of Botan, and Freddie had been taking the brunt of that. Baumann and some of the other lads were giving him a hard time. I forced myself to be polite. "You?"

"Jumping on a train to see my girlfriend." Freddie grinned like a man in love. Bloody hell. Poor lad.

"She live far?"

"Ae?" he asked like he hadn't heard the question.

"Does she live far away?" I repeated.

"Ae."

I cut him a sharp look to see if he was being deliberately annoying. "Eh?" I copied him.

Freddie frowned. "I said Ae."

"I know you said *eh*. Can you no' hear me? I asked where does she live?" For fuck's sake. Why was everyone being deliberately exasperating today?

Freddie was equally exasperated. "She lives in fucking Ae. A. E. The village."

Muffled laughter sounded behind me, and I glanced over my shoulder to find Callan and John practically falling over themselves in hysterics. At my expense. "Like I was supposed to know there's a village that sounds like a Scot asking a fucking question!"

At that, they all burst out laughing and I stormed ahead.

It wasn't like me.

Usually, I'd be peeing my pants at the situation.

Maia was messing with my sense of humor, and that pissed me off too.

Surprisingly, the lads let me be. We all showered, everybody giving me space. But once I was tying on my trainers, Callan stopped in front of me. He had all his gear on, ready to go. "Fancy grabbing a bite with me and John?"

I nodded because I was being a pissant and I didn't want to be.

Not long later, we'd settled in at a New Town pub near my place. As soon as we'd ordered food, Callan said, "What's wrong? First, you nearly tear Baumann apart for being his usual prickish self and then you didn't find the Ae thing funny. That's just no' you." I could see his lips twitching like he wanted to laugh at it again.

John was outright grinning about it.

It cut through my black mood. "It was funny."

"Really funny." Callan cleared his throat. "Anyway, what's going on?"

I considered how to phrase what I needed to ask them without giving away the truth of the situation with Maia. "Would ... would Beth be pissed off if you flirted with another woman? Like, I've seen you around other blokes with her and know you get pissed when they flirt with her ... so ...?"

He and John exchanged a knowing look.

Unsurprisingly at this point, it annoyed me. "What was that?"

Callan eyed me. "Is Maia pissed off because you're flirting with other women?"

Kind of. Just not for the reason my mate would assume. Or for the reason I wished. When she first approached, flashing her engagement ring at Sophie, the sassy redhead, I thought she was jealous. I was elated!

I was wrong.

"Aye."

"Beth would probably be more confused and hurt than pissed off," Callan replied. "To be fair, if she flirted back with any of the arseholes who pant after her, it would fuck me off."

"Which we all know is man code for hurt." John shrugged.

Me and Callan nodded in agreement.

"Why is that, though?" I asked, genuinely wanting to understand. "To me, it's harmless flirting. A bit of good-natured banter. It doesn't mean anything."

"That's not necessarily true," Callan explained. "If you're both in agreement that flirting with other people is harmless and allowed, then flirt away. But flirting for many people is a signal that you're sexually available. Say I didn't see it that way, but Beth did, and it bothered her, I would quit doing that shit in a heartbeat. Folks say you should never change yourself for someone, but there are small changes you can make that are worth it if it protects the people you love. Now I've vowed to protect Beth. Even from me. Most of the time, I do it. I'm not perfect and sometimes I unintentionally hurt her in small ways and vice versa. However, flirting with other people when I know it hurts her is an intention to cause her harm. So why the fuck would I do that?"

Shit.

Maia had said if Will had done that, it would have hurt her feelings.

"If you've made a commitment to Maia, you flirting with other women is telling her that you're saying to strangers you're sexually available when you're not. How the hell is she supposed to feel about that?"

I scrubbed a hand over my face as the last year of my behavior played out in my head. One-night stand after one-night stand. Flirting constantly, and many, many times in front of Maia. I know I was a free agent and she was with Will, so I wasn't surprised she never took my flirting with her seriously. "She's ... she's worried I'm not capable of monogamy in the long run."

John winced. "Is ... did she break it off?"

"No, no. But we had a barney this morning because I flirted with some lass at the gym. You know I appreciate the balls it takes for a woman to make that approach. Me flirting back is just respecting the move."

"And disrespecting Maia in return," Callan said flatly.

It was like he'd punched me. "Do ... you think she felt disrespected?" Because for a moment, I thought I saw more than concern on her face. I thought I'd seen disappointment and pain. But maybe that was me imagining something that didn't exist between us.

"Abso-fucking-lutely. Christ, Baird, what will it cost you to turn the other way when a lass flirts with you? Fuck all. It'll cost you fuck all. But not turning away ... it's probably going to cost you Maia."

Callan's blunt assessment knocked me on my arse.

Maia was right.

Her words had wounded me this morning, but she was right.

How could I expect her to take me seriously if this was how she felt about the flirting? "I screwed up. And I'm not just talking about today. I have been screwing this thing up the whole time I've known her. She's been building a case against me—" I cut my words off before I revealed too much. "I have to show her I'm in this. Or I'll lose her." Correction: I'd never win her.

"No flirting." John wagged his finger comically at me. "Actually, since it's such an inherent part of who you are, you just need to channel all of that into Maia."

"I can do that." I nodded. It would be the greatest pleasure of my life to channel all my sexual energy into Maia MacLeod. By the time I was done, she'd take me seriously.

She had to.

I was Baird McMillan.

Once I set my heart on something, that was me. I was all in.

And I was all in on Maia.

Losing her ... losing her now that I was so close to being with her ... well ... it just wasn't an option.

CHAPTER ELEVEN

MAIA

The day Baird stormed out on me I'd gone back and forth on whether I was in the right or wrong. My friend was usually so easygoing that I'd started to question if I'd been too harsh with him. I was on the cusp of calling him to apologize when I walked up the stairs to my flat and found Baird sitting outside my door, waiting for me.

The first words out of his mouth were, "I'm sorry, Maia. It won't happen again. You are safe with me. I promise."

At that moment, I experienced a falling sensation. Like I was literally dizzy at his pronouncement. When my reply was to ask him to come in, he'd stood up, grinned at me in relief, and drew me into a bear hug.

For some weird reason, I almost burst into tears.

Later that night as I got into bed, I realized part of the reason Baird's apology made me so emotional was because that was twice now we'd argued, and he'd been the first one to show up in person to apologize. To fix it.

All of Will's texts and then his email about wanting to talk … not once did he walk his arse to my front door.

I was realizing more and more as the weeks went on that what I'd had with Will had been superficial. That messed with my head just as much as he'd messed with my heart. Because what did that say about me? That I'd been ready to marry a man I was hiding my true self from? A man who had made all the decisions about our lives and rarely ever compromised to give me what I wanted from it—and I'd allowed him to do that. Why hadn't I pushed back? Why did I always have to people-please?

Though ... I didn't feel the need to do that with Baird. He was the first person in years I'd had any kind of conflict with.

Huh.

Thankfully, I didn't have much free time to dwell on all that. The last few weeks had been a whirlwind of preparation for the beginning of the social media campaign. The production team had already filmed us doing a short introduction that they'd post after the campaign and engagement announcement.

On Saturday, I'd traveled with my pseudo-cousin Beth to Glasgow for the Cup final. Her parents, Braden and Joss (who were like my aunt and uncle), were there too to support Callan, along with Beth's siblings, sixteen-year-old Elle and twenty-two-year-old Luke. Our other "cousin" Lily joined us with her boyfriend Sebastian, who was a huge Caley United fan.

"I know we've to keep your engagement on the down low for now," Lily had said as soon as she saw me, "but congrats." As she hugged me, she warned, "You should also know January is plotting your very slow and painful death."

I laughed as we drew apart. "Why?"

Lily's adorable dimples creased her cheeks. "Because she's had a massive crush on Baird since they met."

My smile had fallen. "Are you serious?"

"Aye, but she'll get over it."

"I don't know." Sebastian draped his arm around his girlfriend, drawling in a posh Etonian accent. "*I'm* not quite over it."

"Hey, I thought your man-crush was on my fiancé, not Maia's?" Beth teased. She'd already congratulated me in the car on the drive over. She'd also proceeded to pepper me with a million questions I did not want to answer in front of her family.

My aunt Joss had finally said dryly, "Perhaps Maia wants to keep her private relationship with her fiancé *private*?"

"Right." Beth had nodded like she understood, then mouthed at me, "We'll talk later."

I couldn't say I was looking forward to having to lie to her.

Once Sebastian had assured Beth that Callan was his number one and Lily had assured me January wasn't seriously plotting my untimely death, we'd settled in to watch the match.

Unfortunately, our boys didn't win.

They played valiantly, and it was some game. I'd always been more of a rugby fan than football, mostly because Grace's best friend was a rugby player and she'd gotten me into the sport.

But having people I cared about on the pitch really made me invested. My voice was hoarse from screaming and shouting right alongside Beth and Sebastian.

After the game, Baird, Callan, and John were gutted.

So close and yet so far.

I hadn't known how to be with Baird in front of everyone. Therefore, I decided to shove aside the lie between us and embrace the truth. He was my friend. And I hurt for him. I'd hugged him hard, and Baird had held on to me like I was a lifeline.

Afterward, he didn't want to join us for dinner. I left with him because it would look weird if I didn't. However, when we reached the city center, he'd given me a sad smile and said he needed to be alone for a bit, and I found myself dropped off on Hart Street. Watching him drive off, knowing he was hurting, plagued me all night. I'd texted him to check in over the weekend, but he wasn't very chatty. That only made me worry more.

I didn't know what to expect when he showed up for the video shoot this morning. It was day one of our schedule. Today we were shooting our parts in the campaign and engagement announcement film Pennington's wanted to release at the end of the week. Christina gave me the day off work, which meant I had to make up the hours over the next few days. I felt awful that Baird had to muster up enthusiasm to do this just days after his Professional League championship dream was crushed.

My jittery nerves were already at peak level. Of course, the production team didn't know we were acting the part of newly engaged lovers, which added to my nervousness.

The production had been in South Lanarkshire since the wee hours of the morning. They had spent the past few weeks gaining permits and permissions so they could arrange our announcement using their homeware products on a huge field where Baird and I were to fly over in a hot air balloon. Since I didn't have a car, Baird was going to drive us to the site, but he'd texted me late last night to tell me he wasn't in the city, so he'd just meet me there.

I knew he was suffering from the loss, but I was anxious about where he was and what he was doing. My chest burned every time I considered who he might be doing it with. Never mind the fact that he knew I was in a bit of a state about our plan and I'd wanted his support.

I told myself I was being selfish, that I hadn't just lost a national championship and been subjected to the relentless abuse of so-called fans and the tabloid media.

Yet there was a part of me that feared Baird was ultimately one of those guys who was really good at apologizing but who never really changed.

A trailer had been set up for us, filled with the outfits I'd helped select from our line-up. Becky had wanted me in something showy and expensive from the store, but I'd convinced Hilary and Christina that because the announcement was a big, over-the-top production, we should find ways to advertise items that were more affordable. We already had access to data that told us there were people who didn't even step inside Pennington's because they thought the products were out of their budget. Yet we had a vast range in our stores, and I wanted to appeal to the market we were currently missing out on.

I won that argument. And the evil eye from Becky.

Once my hair and makeup were done, I dressed in a fairly inexpensive pale green, calf-length cami dress that didn't flash a lot of skin but molded to my body. It was sexy without being too sexy for a retailer ad campaign. As I slipped on the brown leather flat sandals we'd chosen, Gail, the production assistant assigned to me, popped her head in to let me know Baird had arrived ten minutes ago. They were rushing him through hair and makeup.

Relief and irritation flooded me, and I felt a little dizzy.

After downing my third glass of water, I excused myself to use the portable restroom. We were supposed to have warm, clear skies all day and I was already feeling it. It was a surprisingly balmy morning for the first week in June. When I came out of the restroom, assistants were fussing over Baird. Fixing his hair, brushing lint off his shirt.

I'd also chosen items for him to select from and was weirdly happy to see he'd picked my favorite shirt among the lot. It was an army-green cotton short-sleeve button-down, with turn-back cuffs and a Cuban collar. On Baird, the sleeves were a little tight around his biceps, but he looked exactly how I imagined he would. Cool as hell but classy. He'd paired it with dark denim jeans with turnups and kept his biker boots on.

The look worked for him.

He was hotter than hot.

As if he felt my attention, he turned his head ever so slightly to meet it. His eyes roamed down my body and back up again. My breath caught at the heat in his gaze.

I reminded myself not to take his perusal too seriously. Especially as I didn't know where the hell he'd been last night.

Knowing we had a bunch of cameras to face while we pretended to be in love, I didn't approach Baird with the intention of arguing. However, every step I took toward him, I grew more and more irritated.

"Hey, babe. You look amazing." He drew away from the assistants to place a hand on my waist. He bent his head to brush his lips over mine.

It startled me for two point five seconds before I realized we were supposed to be an engaged couple. My lips tingled and I tried not to tense.

"You ready for this?" Baird asked.

I glanced around to make sure there wasn't anyone in immediate earshot and then I turned to him and asked quietly, "Where were you?"

His hand fell away from my waist at my tone. "I know I'm a bit late. Traffic was busier than I thought it would be."

"I know traffic was busier. I know this because the taxi cost me over a hundred quid to get here."

Baird winced. "Shit. Sorry."

"I don't need to rely on you to take me anywhere, but next time, give me more notice so I can arrange better transport."

"Maia—"

"Were you out carousing last night?" I studied him, looking for signs of a hangover.

Baird's eyebrows pinched together. "No. I wasn't."

I waited for him to tell me where he was.

At his silence, I shook my head. "This is a disaster. This is going to fall apart. I'm going to lose my job."

Suddenly, he took hold of my right biceps and tugged me toward the trailers.

"What are you doing?" I hissed. "People are watching."

"Fuck them." He threw open the trailer door, and I hurried in after him, my cheeks blazing with embarrassment. Baird released me to stride through the trailer, checking to make sure it was empty, and then he turned to me. "I had the worst fucking weekend of my career. We thought we had it. And we lost. You have no idea what that feels like. And it would be nice if you could think beyond yourself for just one bloody second."

I swallowed hard at his uncharacteristic reprimand. "I ... I am really sorry about the championship, Baird. You know I am. And you know I feel that for you. But this"—I gestured around us—"is terrifying. And the first day we start it, you're nowhere to be seen and you're off getting fucked somewhere on who knows what with who knows who. You promised. You promised you wouldn't and that you could do this for three months. Just three months, Baird, and then you can go back to your empty parties and as many women as you want."

Suddenly, the air in the trailer grew thick as I watched Baird's eyes darken with the kind of anger I'd never seen from him. At least not directed toward me.

"Well?" I jutted my chin in defiance of his outrage.

He kept his distance and sucked in a breath before releasing it. "Do you want to know where I was last night? I was with Callan, collecting John from Newcastle. Because before the game, the owner told John he's not renewing his contract. One of my best mates is off the team. The gaffer was pissed as hell because he knew that would mess with our heads going into the game, and it did. So not only are we losing John to Canada, but we also lost the championship, and we're going forward with an incompetent fucking owner who didn't have the common sense to wait until he delivered that soul-destroying news.

"John fucked off to Newcastle to get absolutely smashed, got into a bit of bother, and Callan and I hauled our arses down there to get him. I didn't get home until four o'clock this morning, and I was late getting here because I was trying to get a bit of sleep before launching into this circus with you."

I closed my eyes as regret and shame filled me, followed by sadness for Baird and John. "Bear ..."

I opened my eyes as Baird finally closed the distance between us. He bent his head toward me and I flinched at the reproach in his expression. "I wish you'd stop deciding who I am for me. I wish you'd start trusting me. I'm not your mum, Maia."

My body physically jerked at his words.

His reproach softened to regret. Then he shook his head and muttered a harsh *fuck* under his breath before he marched out of the trailer.

CHAPTER TWELVE
MAIA

My stomach was sick as we approached the hot air balloon, and it wasn't nerves about the flight. Before this morning, I'd been looking forward to it. I'd never been up in a hot air balloon before. Will and I had the opportunity when we were in Barcelona last year, but Will said he was pretty sure I'd hate the experience, so we didn't bother.

Yet another unsubstantiated comment I'd swept under the rug.

I glanced up from beneath my lashes at Baird who hadn't looked at me since I'd followed him out of the trailer. Between the murmurs and worried glances, I knew the team could sense we were at odds with each other.

What I was just beginning to realize was how much I detested being at odds with Baird.

It was confusing to find myself arguing with him when I never argued with Will about anything, and yet I felt wretched at the very thought of Baird hating me.

It took a lot to make Baird dislike anyone. However, I had been judgmental and untrusting and self-involved.

We were mic'd up, so they could hear us clearly during filming. Mine was taped onto my back, causing a pronounced bulge, so our cameraman had been informed to try to avoid filming me from behind. Baird's was more concealed under his shirt.

The low roar of the propane burner drowned out the rushing of blood in my ears as we stopped before the balloon.

"This is Nicholas, your pilot." Gail gestured to an attractive dark-haired man around my age. "Nicholas, these are our lovebirds, Maia and Baird."

Nicholas gave us a chin lift. "Nice to meet you. Use the steps to climb aboard."

He pointed to barely there footholds attached to the basket he was already standing inside.

"Ladies first," Baird said without meeting my eyes.

I put my foot in the first hold, but I was shaking so hard, I slipped.

"Easy." I felt his familiar strong hands on my waist. "I've got you."

That was Baird. Being kind even when he was angry with me.

The problem came in trying to hike my leg over the basket in this dress. I'd stupidly assumed there would be a door on the basket when I'd chosen my outfit. I was about to hike up my dress when I remembered something. I glanced over at the crew, who already had a camera in my face. "Can you not film this part, please?"

The cameraman, Mike, just said, "I have to film everything."

"She said no." Baird glowered at Mike.

Mike shrugged. "I take my orders from my boss."

The air turned menacing as Baird gruffly asked, "Is that

what you think?" Then he covered the camera lens with his big hand. "No look-y without permission-y."

The words were playful; his tone was not.

Mike swallowed nervously as he lowered the camera.

I reluctantly hiked my dress up as far as I could without being indecent and tried to swing my legs over without flashing anyone. But it was proving impossible. I could feel my cheeks burning as I realized this and lowered my leg.

"My."

I looked up to find Baird standing beside me, his expression blank.

"Come down." He gestured for me to come off the footholds.

I did it without thinking.

As soon as my feet hit the ground, I hurried to lower my dress back into place. Then Baird bent and lifted me into his arms like a groom with his bride. I let out a little squeak of surprise as he lifted me up and over into the basket. I grasped onto the sides for purchase as he released me.

He was mad at me, but he saw me struggling and did something to help.

Reeling, I hadn't quite gotten my emotional footing when the basket jolted again as Baird bounded inside with an athletic ease as impressive as him lifting me into it. Nicholas steadied me, his hands on my waist, and warning flashed in Baird's eyes. Nicholas released me like the propane burner wasn't the only thing on fire.

It was louder than I expected inside the basket.

"Here's the script!" The director, Bruno, suddenly appeared outside the basket, holding out a piece of paper to us. "Once you're up there and you see the announcement, Mike will film this introduction piece."

I was shaking so badly, the paper trembled. Baird

gently took it from me, pressing his side into mine as we looked it over. It was a robotic script where we introduced ourselves, who we were, our ages, and what we did for a living.

Baird shoved it back at Bruno. "We can do it without a script."

"You don't need to because you have a script."

"Let me rephrase—we're not using your crappy script. We're going to sound like ourselves up there or we get out of the basket."

I gaped at Baird.

Lately, he was surprising me at every turn.

Who knew buried beneath his charm and easygoing nature was a stubborn mule with a spine of steel?

It was more than kind of hot.

And he hated me.

Bruno snatched the script back. "Just try not to veer too far away from it."

At that, we stood back to let Mike climb aboard.

"Ready?" Nicholas asked.

After we'd all nodded our agreement, I latched onto a corner of the basket, my stomach flipping over as the grounds team untied the anchors and we floated steadily upward.

Despite the turmoil of emotions roiling inside me, I couldn't help but delight in the sensation of watching the ground fall farther and farther away. It was a slow ascent entirely different from any other experience I'd had flying. The higher we climbed, the clearer the Edinburgh skyline became in the northerly distance.

I was aware of Nicholas talking, but I wasn't processing anything. I was too busy enjoying the serene experience as the air gently blew through my hair.

A tap on my shoulder finally brought me out of my reverie.

Mike looked impatient. "Can you stand with your fiancé so I can film you two enjoying this experience ... together?"

Oh crap.

I looked over at the other side of the balloon where Baird stood, arms crossed over his chest, stance wide, absolutely towering over everyone else in the balloon as he stared with uncharacteristic broodiness out at the world.

That's when I realized I wasn't comfortable moving around the basket when it was in flight. The movement triggered a bout of vertigo.

"Oh God." I clambered for one of the roped corners and sucked in a breath, squeezing my eyes closed.

"My."

I opened my eyes to find Baird in front of me, scouring my face in concern. "You all right?"

I relaxed at his gentle tone. "I'm fine. Until I move, apparently." I shot a look behind him at Mike. "They want us standing together. Enjoying it together."

"Okay. Why don't you turn to look out? I'll stand behind you."

I did that and found my equilibrium again. Until Baird's heat hit my back as he pressed his body to mine. He leaned his hand on the edge of the basket, our fingers touching, while he held on to the rope, just above where I held it.

I attempted to relax, but I was hyperaware of his hard chest pressing into me.

We both knew that we couldn't say anything right now that would give away our ploy or our earlier argument, since everyone could hear everything we said.

Something in the distance on the ground thankfully distracted me from my friend's hot proximity. "Look!" I pointed toward what was starting to become clearer, laid out on a field.

Sure enough, drone cameras circled the area. Below us, spelled out across two fields using a substantial number of plates, vases, and other items from Pennington's homeware department, were the words: "We're Engaged! Maia MacLeod Said Yes to Baird McMillan!"

"That's cool," Baird murmured against my temple, leaning further into me until I could barely breathe. Surrounded by his heat and the delicious scent of his after-shave rendered me speechless for a few seconds.

"Right, let's do this," Mike announced loudly. "This is where you turn to the camera and introduce yourselves. Then, Baird, we'll get one of you kissing the bride-to-be."

At least the moment was being recorded, and I could look back on it to see what actually happened. Because *in* the moment, I was in an utter daze as Baird turned us to the camera, his arm around my waist, holding me tight to his side as if holding me up.

Of course, Baird had dealt with the media for years, so he was able to switch off the tension between us and switch on his affable, affectionate persona. I was aware of him introducing himself and then clasping my hand tight to his chest as I blurted out who I was and how I worked for Pennington's as a fashion buyer.

Then, Baird was kissing me.

Not the lip brush from before.

While it was PC for the camera (no tongue), he kissed me with such conviction, I felt it everywhere. My skin was on fire as he dipped me over his arm to kiss me even harder. My fingers curled into his shirt, my legs trembling, and this time not from vertigo.

This was no sloppy boy-man kiss.

This was the most perfect kiss anyone had ever given me. And the friction of his short beard against my chin was so delicious, I was pretty sure I'd never been more turned on.

Once he released me, he continued to stare at my mouth.

I gaped up at him, wishing he'd kiss me again, but this time with tongue.

"Perfect!" Mike yelled, making me jolt.

I straightened, wobbling with the movement of the balloon, and Baird's hold around my waist tightened. I wondered if he read my confusion for what it was.

My cheeks blazed at the thought.

"We can head back down now," Mike told Nicholas. Then he winked at us. "Nice work, you two. Glad to see you got over whatever lover's tiff that was before we got on here."

I stiffened at the reminder Baird was mad at me.

The renewed tension thrumming through Baird's body told me he'd remembered he was pissed off at me too.

Just like that, my mood plummeted faster than the balloon as it descended toward the ground.

CHAPTER THIRTEEN
BAIRD

The production team had us hang around for ages until they were satisfied with the shoot. Finally, they let us go, and My and I went back to the separate mini trailers to change into our own clothes. I was quick, so I assumed I would be out first, but when I strolled to where I'd parked, I saw Maia with her phone to her ear.

I was still butt hurt, so I was tempted to keep walking, but as always, I found myself drawn to the bloody woman.

Then irritated when I overheard her telling someone she was waiting on an Uber.

"It won't be long, Grace ... aye ... Grace, they're safe ... I know ... but where would I park it?"

Not caring if I was interrupting, I said, "Cancel the Uber. I'll give you a lift."

Maia whirled around, wide-eyed. "Uh ... aye, that's Baird ..." Her gaze washed over my face as if searching for something. "Hang on a minute, Grace." She lifted her phone from her ear and replied hesitantly, "It's fine. It's already on the way."

"Cancel it. I'm giving you a lift." My tone brokered no argument.

I heard the voice on the end of Maia's phone get louder and she pressed the device back to her ear. "Okay, okay. I will. I will ... I promise ... I am ... are you serious?" Maia rolled her eyes and then nodded at me. "Lead the way."

She did not hang up the phone.

And I understood why when she said, "I am literally following him to his car ... oh my goodness, you take over-protective to new levels."

Ever the gentleman, I opened the door for her and waited until she was in before I closed it and rounded the hood to get in the driver's side.

As soon as I was in, Maia sighed. "Baird, we're on speaker. Will you please tell my stepmother that I am in the car with you so I can hang up and cancel my Uber?"

My lips twitched despite the tension between us. "Maia is in my car, Mrs. MacLeod. I'll see her safely home."

"Thank you, Baird. Call me Grace," she replied in a gentle, very posh English accent. "Take care of My for me."

I couldn't help but grin outright. "Precious cargo, Grace."

As I started the engine, Maia took Grace off speaker and said into it, "Happy now? *Grace* ... I'm not telling him that! Goodbye!" She hung up with a huff, her fingers flying over the screen.

I pulled the car onto the road, heading back into the city. "Tell me what?"

"Nothing. It's too embarrassing. She's lucky my dad wasn't in the vicinity. He's super possessive of her."

I frowned. "Like ... in a controlling way?"

"Oh God, no. Like Grace would let him. Nah, he's just ... my dad and Grace are the kind of in love you usually only see in movies. Dad's kind of old school, though. He doesn't want men hitting on her, and he doesn't want Grace thinking other men are attractive."

"That's not old school. No guy wants to see other guys hitting on their girlfriend or wife."

"I wouldn't—" She cut off.

"You wouldn't what?"

I felt her perusal and glanced at her quickly before concentrating on the road.

"Bear ..."

My hands tightened around the steering wheel at the nickname. I glanced at her again and was shocked to see tears there. "Maia ..."

"I'm so sorry," she blurted out. "I was going to say something there that was ... well, I've been unfair to you. I've been assuming I know you when clearly there are lots of things I've yet to learn. But more than that ... I know you're not my mum. It's not just Mum. It's ... it's Will."

My heart kicked up speed. "Will?"

"His betrayal completely caught me off guard. And it's not that I don't trust you ... it's just that ... well, I don't even trust myself. It's messed me up completely. It's taken me back to a place I thought I'd gotten past ... but I haven't. That's not your fault, and I shouldn't be making it your problem. I'm so sorry for jumping to conclusions and assuming the worst. More than that, I am so sorry about John."

Regret for my words in the trailer pummeled me. Of course, Will had fucked her up. "My, what I said about thinking beyond yourself—"

"You were right."

"Nah. It was harsh. You didn't deserve that."

"You didn't deserve my mistrust."

"Let's agree we're both sorry and move on, then."

When I glanced at her, she gave me a warm, sweet smile I felt in my dick. "I can do that. I hate arguing with you," she said.

I wouldn't mind it so much if we could end the argument with me inside her, but ... patience. "Me too," I replied gruffly.

"So, how did you think it went today?"

We chatted a bit about the first shoot of the campaign. Then I dared, "I didn't cross the line with the kiss, did I?"

I swore her breath hitched a bit. "Oh. No. No, the kiss was perfect."

"Perfect, aye?" I flashed her a cocky smile.

Maia huffed, "For the shoot. It was perfect for the shoot."

We talked and joked and teased each other all the way back to her place, and while I was still gutted about John, at least I felt better about me and Maia.

"How is John feeling?" she asked as we entered New Town.

"Lost. His ... his mum died four years ago, and he and his dad ... their relationship fell apart after that. Caley"— my throat grew thick—"Caley became John's family." I drew the car to a stop on Hart Street, right next to the lane that led to her place.

Switching off the engine, I turned to see Maia's eyes were bright with unshed tears. I reached over to pat her knee. "I know. It's shit."

"It's beyond shit," she whispered, blinking rapidly. "Poor John."

"Callan and I asked him to join our company so he could stay here."

"That's a great idea."

"I don't know. Property management isn't his passion."

"But it'll give him a legal reason to stay until he figures out a way to remain in the country doing something he loves."

"I tried to tell him the same thing, but he's just ... wallowing right now."

"By himself?"

"That's what he wants."

Maia leaned into me. "There are times when we leave the people we care about to wallow, and there are times when we don't. Let's go get him."

Surprised by the suggestion, I quirked an eyebrow. "Now?"

"Yes. It's only four o'clock. Let's see if Callan's free and we'll all go out to dinner. Me being there will make it seem less like an ambush."

"Is it an ambush?"

"Kind of. We'll lull him into a false sense of 'We're just here taking your mind off it' and then hit him with the 'Come work for us until you discover what it is you want from life now.'"

My chest fucking ached as I stared into her beautiful face because it wasn't only the perfect arrangement of Maia's features that made her gorgeous. She was gorgeous right down to her very soul. "Okay. Let's do it."

MAIA

"You must be pleased with how the campaign is starting."

I glanced up from the latest national sales reports, my brain still on my last thought about meeting with Christina to discuss ending our relationship with a certain designer. This was the fourth season we were at a loss on sales for the items. I knew the designer was a friend of the Erstwhiles, but the clothing was much too punk rock for our clientele, and we were continually putting what items we had into sales stock, sometimes having to slash eighty percent off the retail value to move it.

The sound of Becky's voice was the last thing I wanted to hear when I was contemplating such a difficult conversation with my boss.

And the catty look in Becky's eyes was the last thing I wanted to *see* when I'd had my fill of cattiness for the day. Usually, Eli was there to block her entry, but they'd already left for the day.

I made a noncommittal sound of agreement. "I'm sorry,

Becky. I really need to get this report finalized before I finish up."

"Finishing early again?"

What a little ... "Technically, I'm already into my overtime. You and I are the only ones left at the office."

"Yes, well, I'll be staying until the work is done."

"My work will be done once you go back to yours."

Her eyes flashed at my rare bite back. It was clearly taken as antagonism because she leaned her arse on my desk and said with saccharine falseness, "You mustn't pay attention to all the comments online. You know how people enjoy tearing others down."

"I'm not paying attention to the comments."

At noon, the first video went live on Pennington's social media. The team had edited it together well. It showed us on the hot air balloon, Baird pressing his chest into my back as we looked out at Edinburgh. Music played over the edited videos as I pointed down at the field where the announcement had been spelled out. The drone camera footage had been knitted in nicely between that, and then a voiceover actor explained to the viewer who we were and how they were following our journey to marriage. The music died down so Baird and I could be heard introducing ourselves ... and then our kiss.

A kiss that looked pretty realistic. In fact, my whole body had flushed hot from top to toe when I watched us. We looked ... *right* together. And that freaked me out.

The video went viral. Hilary was ecstatic. The follower count on Pennington's socials had already seen a huge bump. So had my own followers. And Baird's.

An hour ago, I made the mistake of checking the comments. There were so many girls crying over Baird being off the market. Literally. The comments were filled with the sobbing emoji. Then there were the catty comments about how I'd never hold his attention and eventually he would cheat. There were even volunteers to help him cheat! Lots of people placed bets on how long the marriage would last. Then there were the comments about how disappointed in Baird they were for choosing "a typical WAG." What did that even mean?

In among all that were comments about how our chemistry was fire. People defended me. My DMs exploded with a mix of congratulatory messages from complete strangers and disgusting sexual overtures from people who wanted to hook up with me.

I wondered if Baird was being treated to the same.

"I do know people like to tear others down. I do indeed know that," I said a little too pointedly.

Becky's eyes narrowed and she pushed off my desk. "Well, even if you and Baird don't last, at least your wedding is free."

I hated how much she was going to gloat when Baird and I got divorced. But I refused to give her the satisfaction of knowing she'd annoyed me.

"Silver linings." I gave her a fake-ass smile back and turned to my computer. I stared at it intently until her heels finally clacked out of my office.

Ten minutes later, I finished up and hurried toward the lift to get away before Becky accosted me again. I'd just stepped out of Pennington's when my phone rang. It was Baird.

The relief that washed over me should have been worrying. I'd kind of expected him to text once the video went live, and when he didn't, I'd secretly panicked he was in regret mode about the campaign. Then I wondered if that was being self-involved, considering he was showing John around Blantyre Castle today.

After our shoot on Monday, we convinced John to join us for dinner. Callan met us at the restaurant, and I think my presence helped take their minds off everything. Until Baird gathered the courage to press John a wee bit more about joining the business. He explained it was a way to keep him here until he figured out what he wanted to do. They'd gone back and forth and didn't really come to a decision. I felt terrible for John because what he wanted to do was play football, but his agent couldn't drum up any interest from UK teams or anywhere in the world and had suggested they part ways. John was teamless and now agentless.

Yesterday, Baird texted and told me John had agreed to try working for them and was shadowing Baird at Blantyre today.

I answered the phone, eager to hear Baird's voice. "How did it go?" I asked, trying to be supportive and not self-involved.

"I'll tell you about that later." His deep voice in my ear was an honest-to-goodness balm to my soul. "How are you doing with the video going viral so quickly?"

"We knew there was a possibility that could happen."

"Well, this is it. We're in it now." His tone was teasing, and I took that to mean there was no regret.

I bit my lip. "Did you read the comments?"

"I never read the comments. Did *you* read the comments?"

"Maybe."

"Trolls?"

"Maybe."

"They're just angry, jealous morons hiding behind their phones."

"I know that."

"Aye?"

"Becky was salivating, though."

"Becky needs someone to remove that Barbie doll from her arse," he muttered.

That stopped me in the street as I threw my head back on a dirty cackle of laughter.

Baird's voice was warm with amusement. "Or maybe it's a GI Joe."

I snorted. "Oh, you have no idea how much I needed that."

"I'm glad."

"Do you want to come over? We'll order takeout?" I blurted. I hadn't seen him all week because he had to miss our last swimming session for a work thing.

And I missed him.

"I'll be there in ten." He hung up without another word.

I burst out laughing again, anticipation thrumming through me as I hurried through New Town to my place.

Not wanting to analyze why, I was already mentally searching my closet for something cute but casual to change into and cursing myself for being behind on my laundry because I had this slouchy cropped tee that fell off one shoulder that would've been perfect. But it was in the wash.

Considering alternatives, it took me a second to process the visual at the top of my stairs.

Standing outside my flat was Will.

A very, very angry-looking Will.

The sight of him brought back a flood of conflicting emotions. Mostly hurt. And resentment.

Cautiously, I approached, pulling my keys from my purse. "What are you doing here?" I asked once I reached the landing.

He huffed, "What am I doing here? I've had to resort to hunting you down because you blocked me everywhere else."

Stay calm. Do not give him the satisfaction of seeing emotion from you.

"When someone blocks you, it means they don't want to speak to or see you, Will. It means you should probably not *hunt* them down." I jammed my key into the lock. "Go away."

"Not until we talk. Please. I'll just come back tomorrow. Or I'll camp out here."

I frowned, letting out a huff of heartfelt annoyance. "Fine. Come in. But you get five minutes. That's it."

As soon as I entered my living room, I dropped my purse on my coffee table and whirled around.

Will was not at my back.

"Will?"

He appeared in the doorway, his expression pinched. "You ... you took down the photos of us. From your wall."

Oh.

Guilt pricked me. Followed by irritation that I'd feel guilty for something I totally had the right to do!

"We're not together anymore so, yes, I took them down."

His handsome cheeks turned ruddy. "And are we not together anymore because I asked for space to figure things out or are we not together anymore because you were fucking the Caley United goalkeeper behind my back?"

Rage unlike anything I'd experienced in a long time flushed hotly through me. It made my voice low, my tone seething as I responded, "No. I did not cheat on you. Baird and I were just friends. At least on my side of things. But after you emotionally cheated on me and we broke up, he told me he had feelings for me."

Will's jaw clenched before he hissed back, "We hadn't broken up. You blocked me!"

Was he insane? There went my vow not to engage with him.

"I blocked you because we broke up! We broke up the moment you asked me to wait around while you decided which of your girlfriends you thought deserved you."

Will strode toward me, his expression so uncharacteristically aggressive I tensed but refused to step back. "Therefore, you decide to get engaged weeks later to another man? And to do it publicly. What? To humiliate me?"

Oh my goodness. How had I not realized how self-involved this prick was? "No. Becky put me forward for the campaign without my permission, and if I didn't do it, I'd lose my job. The engagement was never supposed to be this public."

"Oh, that's right. Blame a colleague. Blame everyone but yourself."

All the months I'd complained about Becky he'd never taken my side in it.

Not like Baird.

I realized that while there were a million ugly things I wanted to spew at this man, he wasn't worth it. He wasn't worth the energy.

"Get out, Will. I don't know what your purpose in coming here was, but get out."

Instead, Will crossed his arms over his chest. "I'm not leaving until we talk about this. For once, we're going to argue, Maia, instead of you sweeping it under the rug or you appeasing me."

Well, at least he had a modicum of insight and perception.

"The problem is, Will, I don't care to anymore. I don't want to argue with you. Leave."

"No. I want to argue because I don't think this is done between us."

"Oh, you're leaving," a deep, familiar voice announced before he appeared, striding into my living room.

My whole body relaxed at the sight of Baird and something dark and wrathful flashed in his eyes when he noted my relief.

He stopped at my side, his arm pressing into mine. "You heard her. Get the fuck out."

Will tilted his chin in defiance. "What kind of man swoops in to steal another man's fiancée?"

"The kind who wants her more than you do. Also, she wasn't your fiancée anymore. Now get the fuck out."

"You have no idea what I want. You're an ill-educated athlete who can barely string a sentence together. Do you really think you can give her what she needs?"

"How dare—"

Baird cut off my indignant reaction by squeezing my arm. I glanced up to find him wearing a peculiar expression as he stared Will down. His mouth was curled like he was almost smiling, but his usually warm, dark eyes glinted like hard obsidian.

"You know what your problem is, mate ... you thought so highly of your fucking self that you believed a woman like Maia would actually wait around for you."

Will had the decency to flinch.

"Now you're in the midst of a reality check. Maia

MacLeod is top tier. There is no getting better than My. She's kind, she's smart, she's funny, she gives a shit about people, she's driven without being a ruthless dick about it, and somehow, unbelievably, she's all these things when she doesn't have to be because she's a smoke show, and the world's a superficial dumpster fire that puts more stock in that than what lies beneath. But Maia is all that and more because she's beautiful down to her fucking soul. And you …"

I watched in stunned silence, my heart pounding in my ears as Baird dragged his gaze disdainfully up Will's body until he met his eyes.

"You were punching way above your weight when she said yes to you. You're such an arrogant prick, you didn't think so. You'd convinced yourself it was the other way around. But now you know that as soon as she was free of your bullshit, there were thousands of guys lined up who would give their left nut for a chance at her. And I'm actually smarter than you because I wasted no time. I've wanted her from the moment I met her, and I was biding my time until she realized you didn't deserve her. Here you are, now that you know you were punching above your weight, and you're what? Trying to shame and gaslight her into taking you back?"

My goodness. I could barely catch my breath. Not just from the lovely things Baird had said but because he was right. Will had thought he was doing me a favor being with me. And he *had* come here to shame and gaslight me!

My ex seemed as stunned by Baird's speech as I was.

Baird stepped into Will's personal space with an air of crackling intimidation. "See, you've got a problem there. Not just because Maia's wise to your bullshit now, but because you've got me literally standing in your way. And

I'm not better for Maia than you are because I'm good-looking, fantastic in bed, a successful national sportsman." He smirked cockily. "I could go on ... but the point is, I'm better for Maia because I know I don't deserve her. No one deserves all the tremendousness that is Maia MacLeod. And knowing that, I'm going to work my fucking arse off to make sure *I* never lose her. So, why don't you go back to your college sweetheart who you probably don't deserve either ... because Maia no longer exists for you."

Will swallowed hard but stupidly replied, "Are you threatening me?"

"Nah, mate, if I was threatening you, I'd have stuck the head in you. This is just your first warning."

My body was confusingly hot and languid, and I refused to acknowledge that I might be turned on by Baird's protectiveness. Not a very feminist response.

Will stepped back nervously and then shot me a look of disgust over Baird's shoulder. "It's all words, Maia. He'll be screwing around behind your back before you know it."

"What? You mean like you were?"

"I never cheated on you." Will gave me sad puppy-dog eyes. "I wish you'd given me more time."

My patience snapped. "The fact that you can still say that after everything Baird just laid out tells me that you actually are a narcissist. I didn't want to give you more time. I didn't want to be a choice you had to make between me and someone else. I am worth more than that." Correction: I had to convince *myself* I was worth more than that, and I hated him for making me doubt it. "What aren't you getting about that?"

Will looked away, the muscle in his jaw ticking. "I do. I do get it. I'm ... I'm sorry."

At my silence, he looked back at me. "But this ... this

Neanderthal ... he's going to hurt you too," he warned before marching out of the flat.

I flinched at the sound of my door slamming.

"I hope he didn't just chip my doorjamb."

Baird whirled to gape comically at me.

Then we kind of stood there staring at each other, Baird's expression softening into concern as my heart rate increased. His words swam in my mind and caused an ache in my chest.

Because I wished he'd meant them.

"You're a good actor," I finally said. "For a second there, I almost believed everything you said."

He swallowed hard, his gaze searching. "My—"

The loud ringing of his phone cut him off.

CHAPTER FIFTEEN
BAIRD

My ringing phone was a blessing and a curse. I swore under my breath and yanked it out of my pocket. "It's Ainsley."

"Answer it," Maia said. "I'll get changed."

I nodded, my eyes following Maia out of the room as I put the phone to my ear. "Ains, what's up?"

I'd been on the verge of blurting the truth to Maia about my feelings, to tell her that everything I'd said to her arsehole ex was true.

It was too early. Too soon. We'd only just gotten over our argument at the shoot. I still had a lot of foundation to lay before she was truly ready to hear that I was in love with her.

"Eh, I'm calling about the campaign going live," Ainsley replied. "It went viral. Mum's freaking out a wee bit. I don't think any of us were expecting it to take off in such a big way. Even the media is talking about it."

Aye, I'd talked with my agent on the way to Maia's because interview requests were coming in. I told her to turn them down because My and I had already agreed we only wanted to do the campaign and not make a huge deal about it. We'd laid down that law with Pennington's too, when they'd tried to sneak obligatory yeses to media requests into the contract.

"Aye, I know." Day one and it already had two million views.

"I hate to be a superficial cow, but it's because you're hot. Together, I mean. You two look right together, wee bro."

"I'm at Maia's right now," I said so she'd know I couldn't respond directly.

"Ah, okay. Tell Maia I'm asking for her and that she looked beautiful in the video. And good luck cracking that hard head of hers because if she doesn't realize she's into you after that fucking kiss, you're going to need a nutcracker the size of a Range Rover."

I grinned smugly because after watching the video, I properly got a look at how dazed and flushed Maia was after our kiss. She was into it. "Aye."

"Okay, I know you cannae talk, so I'll let you go. Call me."

"Will do."

We hung up just as Maia wandered back into the living room in a pair of leggings and an oversized T-shirt tied at the waist. Her hair was up in a messy bun and she'd popped her glasses on.

I wondered what it was that made a person the most beautiful human you'd ever seen. Like, I'd met a lot of attractive women, but none of them made my fucking chest ache like this.

"What?" She cocked her head quizzically.

"Nothing, babe. Just making sure you're all right after that scene with the ex."

Maia moved into the kitchen to grab us beers out of the fridge. She handed me one, and I sat down beside her. "You know, I think it was a good thing. I told you on Monday that I started to recognize upsetting things about my relationship with Will. Him coming here just drove it home ... he isn't the one. Marrying him would have been a huge mistake because everything you said to him about how he saw himself in the relationship was true. He thought he was better than me and that I was lucky to have him."

"Imagine calling me an ill-educated Neanderthal when he thinks that."

Maia scowled. "He's wrong."

"I mean, I'm not exactly educated."

"You don't have to have a college degree to be smart or educated, Baird. You've seen more of the world than Will has. You've met people from all walks of life doing what you do. You know how to treat people because you had a mother who taught you well. The only thing Will's mum taught him was how to look down on people. Thankfully, he missed his dad's lessons on how to be a lecherous perv."

I went from enjoying her kind words to readying myself to punch an old man in the face. "Please do not tell me your ex's dad came on to you."

Maia shook her head. "Not, like, overtly. But I'd catch him staring at my breasts all the time. When we talked one on one, he'd stare at my mouth. Once he helped me out of the car and he 'accidentally' groped my arse."

"That's coming on to you, My." I seethed, taking an aggressive swig of beer. Some men were fucking animals. And that was an insult to animals.

"Hey." Maia soothed a hand over my shoulder. "Good news is, I never have to see him again. Better news"—she turned into me—"I'm completely over Will."

My heart jumped. "For real?"

"For real." She smiled. "I just ... our relationship was so surface level. It never would have lasted. He didn't make me feel safe to be myself, but I'm to blame for staying with someone like that too. Now I feel like this massive weight is off my shoulders. Like ... I'm free of something. It feels great."

"I'm glad, babe."

"I'm also starving, so let's order food."

Triumph made me restless, like I needed to burn off the excess. Part one in this plot was to make sure Maia was over the ex. Part two was to make Maia fall in love with me. I was ecstatic part one was completed so much quicker than anticipated.

However, Maia wanted to chill, so I had to contain the restlessness.

Not long later, I'd kicked off my boots and switched to water because I'd ridden my motorcycle over. We were watching a crime show on Netflix and trying to make a dent in our huge order of Chinese food—I'd have to work it off in the gym tomorrow. Like always, it was comfortable and easy hanging out with Maia.

But I wanted to show her that I was the one and that she could really talk to me. That *our* relationship was not surface level.

"Kath, my agent, she called today about media interviews. A big morning show wants to interview us. I shut her down."

Maia paused the TV show, turning to give me her full attention. She was curled up on the end of the sofa, her knees to her chest. Her toenails were painted pink and she wore a gold toe ring on her right foot, second toe. It was sexy as fuck. She drew her arms around her knees, almost protectively. I shifted on the couch to face her.

"Wow. That's a lot. So quickly. Just one video."

"Aye, I know."

"How do you feel about it?"

I decided to be honest. "On the one hand, I'm used to it. I've had clips from games go viral. And this one girl put together a montage of me without my shirt on that went viral."

Maia's lips trembled with laughter. "Of course it did."

I grinned. "I can't help that I'm a sexy beast, awright."

"No, you cannot."

"Anyway," I said, attempting to get serious again, "I've experienced that. But this feels different. I'm not worried for me, but I'm worried for you. I don't want any of this messing with your head."

"I've already decided to come off socials while we're doing this."

"That's probably a good idea." I studied her thoughtfully. "Is there anything else bothering you about it?"

Maia pursed her lips. "I'm terrified we'll get caught in the lie and both suffer the consequences of that. I feel guilty for lying."

"No one can prove this is a lie, Maia. No one is going to find out. And we feel guilty because we're not arseholes." Anyway, hopefully soon, it would not be a lie.

She gave me a grateful smile and then sighed. "I guess the only other thing I'm worried about is it affecting my family. That's it, really. Nothing else."

I wondered if she was lying to herself or if she just didn't want to talk to me.

My therapist's way of getting me to open up was to share something vulnerable about herself. Borrowing a page from her book, I confessed, "I sometimes wonder if my dad is out there, watching videos of me, watching my games. Or if he deliberately avoids them. Or worse, if he doesn't even know it's me."

Her eyes widened and then she unlocked the protective cage of her arms and shimmied along the couch to place a comforting hand on my knee. "Bear. I ... I know it's not quite the same, but I get it."

"It is the same, Maia. We both have a parent who abandoned us."

Maia's eyes brightened with tears. "People ... they keep trying to tell me that my mum didn't choose because her addiction is a disease ... and rationally, I know they're right. But irrationally, it hurts that she didn't fight her addiction for me. That she let me go instead. And I feel like a hypocrite for feeling that way because I didn't fight for her. I left. I chose myself too."

"You're allowed to feel like your mum didn't choose you." I threaded our fingers together and squeezed. "No one can tell you how you feel. You feel like she abandoned you. That's the end of the sentence. There are no 'buts.' And I choose to disagree with you that you left her. You were fifteen, Maia. From what you've told me, you were a child forced to be a parent, and you decided to find the one parent who would look after you instead. I think what you did was brave."

Her hold on my hand tightened. "Thank you. And about your dad. I ... I think deep down, there's a part of me that's scared Mum will see this and she'll show up. As guilty as I feel about leaving her ... I don't want that, Bear."

"Not at all?"

She shook her head. "There's too much damage. The thought of her in my life terrifies me."

Now I held on tighter. "Then she will never be in your life again. I promise you that. As long as I'm around, she will never get near you."

Maia gave me a sad smile and then moved closer, dropping her head to my shoulder, cuddling in. "I'm sorry about your dad, Bear. I'm sorry he's in the back of your mind too."

"Aye, me too. I don't ever want to meet him. Genuinely. And so I worry that he'll make an approach because of this."

"He won't get past me," she whispered, a fierceness in her tone.

I smiled before I pressed a quick kiss to the top of her head. "At least we've got each other."

At that, Maia snuggled in even more, her knees touching mine. I reached for the remote to restart the show, satisfied I'd made a small breakthrough with My tonight.

When she fell asleep, I discovered when Maia was out, she was out. Not once did she wake up as I lifted and carried her into her bedroom. I laid her down on the bed and gently extricated the holder from her hair so the silky dark strands spilled freely across her pillow. Not once while I did this or when I untucked the duvet to cover her up did she wake. Or when I took her glasses off and set them on her bedside table. I put her phone on charge and held the camera up to her face to unlock it just so I could make sure her alarm was set.

Maia didn't even blink.

And she snored quietly.

I stared down at her, wishing like hell I could get in beside her. Wishing like hell it was my right, my place in her life to get in the bed and spoon with her. I fucking loved spooning, but girls tended to take spooning to mean something it wasn't, so I'd stopped doing it.

With Maia, it would mean something.

I wanted to spoon with Maia MacLeod.

Impatience rode me.

"One day," I murmured, before I bent down to press a kiss to her forehead.

As I was leaving the flat, filled with that impatience but also hope for the future, my phone buzzed. I pulled it out of my pocket to see it was a text from Callan.

> Just giving you a heads-up, mate. Sorry people are pricks.

Attached to his text was a link to a video. I turned the volume down as I exited Maia's building and strolled over to my bike.

The video was of a fit brunette, telling the world she'd fucked me a few weeks ago and I was clearly cheating scum. She'd posted the clip from the tabloid newspaper that got me in trouble. She was one of the girls in it. I did not remember sleeping with her.

I didn't remember her, full stop.

Feeling sick, I turned and looked up at Maia's dark flat.

What kind of shitstorm was this about to unleash on us?

On the possibility of us?

CHAPTER SIXTEEN
MAIA

Discombobulated.

I'd always liked that word.

I was discombobulated when I woke up the next morning in my bed, unable to remember how I got here. Quite quickly, I realized I must have fallen asleep on the couch and Baird had not only put me to bed, but he'd made sure my alarm was set. For a few minutes, I just lay there staring at my ceiling, heart racing, because of the squishy feeling in my stomach.

I recognized that squishy feeling.

It was accompanied by other feelings I'd been ignoring for a few weeks now.

"Damn," I murmured, flushing hot all over with realization. "I'm crushing on my best friend."

There.

It was true.

I was developing a big, juicy crush on Baird McMillan, the absolute worst romantic candidate in my life.

Aye, he was sweet and funny and protective and considerate … but he was also a giant man-whore who had no intention of settling down.

Groaning, I covered my face with my hands. Why did I have to complicate this? I was totally crushing on him because of all the nice things he said yesterday, and he was just saying those things to make a point to Will.

Right?

I threw off my duvet with a groan and sat up, reaching for my phone. My stupid pulse leapt at the sight of the text notifications from Baird (among a few from family and friends). Baird had placed my glasses on my side table. Butterflies erupted in my belly at his thoughtfulness.

I made a whining sound. "Come on, really? Baird?" I asked myself out loud.

Not that Baird wasn't crush-worthy of course. But he wasn't for me. I did not do casual anything.

Grumbling, I put on my glasses and tapped my phone screen.

The first text said:

U were out so put u 2 bed.

The second text said:

I'm sorry bout this.

This turned out to be a video a girl had posted claiming that Baird was a cheating snake because he'd had sex with her only a few weeks ago. While it was the giant splash of cold reality I needed to remind myself that Baird was not the one for me, I was upset for him. I didn't want the world thinking that about him. Or that I was the kind of girl who would put up with that.

A third text stated:

My management advised me 2 respond.

Then there was a link to another video.

This time it was Baird on his own socials. The sight of his handsome face stirred another flutter of butterflies, despite everything. I didn't know where he was, but it was a close-up, handheld selfie video.

"Oi, oi, everyone," he said with less enthusiasm than usual. "I don't usually respond to bullshit videos, tabloid crap, and such, but I felt it was necessary. Maia and I have been friends for over a year. We didn't get together until just a few weeks ago after the alleged stupid video that's circulating. Maia knows my past. I know hers. Our engagement might seem quick to everyone, but once we knew we wanted to be together, we didn't see any point in hanging around. We're committed to each other, and videos coming out of the woodwork intended to damage us won't. Those people are showing themselves for the petty humans they are. That's all I'm going to say about that. My love to our friends, family, and supporters. Thanks for being happy for us."

I was at once bemused by how well he lied about the state of play between us and proud of him for being so straightforward and direct. Looking at the comments, most people really appreciated that about him and were being supportive. There were some arsehole remarks. When I saw more than a few questions about why I wasn't in the video with him, defending him, my cheeks burned with irritation.

I found myself typing before I could think: ***All of this, Bear. I love my BFF. Heart emoji.***

Two seconds later, a notification banner dropped to tell me Baird had liked my comment.

Then he responded. ***Love my BFF too.***

I knew he meant it platonically, but it still made me feel all squishy again.

My phone beeped.

It was Baird.

U got my txts then …

My fingers flew over the screen.

We're all good. People are creeps.

We won't let them win.

Thanks for putting me to bed.

The dots popped up on the screen instantly. And then:

Anytime. Ur cute when u snore.

I made a noise of indignation.

I do not snore!

U do. It's cute.

I do NOT.

OK. Whatever u say, babe.

I sent him the middle finger.

He sent back a crying-with-laughter.

Grinning, I got up to prepare for the day and the inevitable commentary from Becky's peanut gallery.

I fought against the overwhelming urge to ask Becky why she was stalking me after she accosted me before I even got to my desk.

"I just wanted to say I'm so sorry about Baird. Men will be men, I suppose, and sometimes they need more than a pretty face. Hilary wants to see you in her office to make sure this awful revelation isn't going to hurt the campaign." Becky had given me big Bambi eyes filled with fake sympathy wrapped up in malice.

Instead of calling her out for her unkind "pretty face" comment, or calling her a stalker, I shrugged with a nonchalance I knew would annoy the absolute heck out of her. "There's no issue. Baird and I are stronger than ever. Jealous people do destructive things. Don't they?" I gave her a pointed look, and her fake sympathy slipped. I brushed past her, feeling like I was starting to win against her bullying.

I spent the next ten minutes reassuring my boss that all was good in the world of Maia and Baird.

However, at lunchtime, I broke my promise to myself that I wouldn't check the comments. I found myself back on Baird's post. Hundreds of people had liked my comment. And there were replies like, "Aw, she calls him Bear!" and "I want a love like yours!"

But there were also comments like, "You're a bad feminist!" and "You should be ashamed of yourself for taking back a cheater!" and "As a woman, you should believe women." Like Baird had committed some crime against a girl he hooked up with consensually at a party.

Seriously, the illogical, emotionally unintelligent crap people posted was exhausting.

It was like Baird knew I'd looked at the comments only for them to upset me because a text from him popped up on my phone.

> We're goin' out 2nite. U, me, Callan, John, and Beth.

I quickly texted back:

> Where?

A few seconds later he replied:

> Niteclub. Blowin' off steam/damage control.

I hadn't been dancing in such a long time, and he was right. We needed to be seen together outside of the campaign.

> Tell me where? When?

> Pick u up at 8 pm.

I replied with a heart emoji and turned my phone on silent to get back into a work headspace. Yet, within minutes, I was striding out of my office and into our wardrobes where we kept all the new products we were still reviewing and all the products we'd already decided on. There was a dress on one of the rails I'd been eyeing for weeks.

It was a thin-strapped minidress with a slim A-line

silhouette and a risqué side split. It contoured to the body and was handsewn with shimmering midnight-blue sequins. On the left side of the abdomen, the midnight blue was broken up with a gold sunburst and on the right side of the hem was a cascade of half-moons.

It was sexy and flirty and classy all at once, which was hard to pull off with a minidress. The one on our rails was my size. Kismet! Grabbing it, I hurried to Christina's office and knocked on the door.

Upon entering, I held up the dress. "Baird and I are going out in public tonight to do damage control."

"Yes, I saw that unfortunate video. How are you?"

"I'm fine," I replied honestly. "Baird didn't cheat on me."

My boss didn't look so certain, but her gaze moved to the dress. "Well, that's stunning."

"Yes, and it's up for preorder so it's not available yet, but I need to look amazing tonight, and I wondered if I could buy this with my discount?"

"No." Christina shook her head but with a small smile. "Take it. A gift from Pennington's as part of the campaign."

I gaped at her. The dress was worth seven hundred pounds. "Are you sure?"

"Of course. I assume we'll see it all over social media tonight. Marketing can make up a post later tagging the designer and the link to the preorder. I'll talk to Hilary."

"Thank you, Christina." I meant it in more ways than one.

She gave me a kind smile but then shooed me out. "Now go work."

I had every intention of going back to work, but first I needed to find the perfect pair of shoes to match my dress.

When I sat back down at my desk fifteen minutes later,

it occurred to me I might not just be dressing up to be seen tonight.

I might have been a grown woman, but I was also a woman with a developing crush on her best friend/fake fiancé, and I wanted him to notice me. Not just flirt casually like he always did but really notice me and think I was the most beautiful woman in the room.

"Oh, Maia." I dropped my head in my hands, my words muffled, "You're in big trouble."

BAIRD

It was official.

Maia MacLeod was trying to kill me.

She stared at me.

While the blood pounded in my ears and flew straight to my dick.

A minute ago, when I'd knocked on her flat door, she'd yelled "Come in!" and I'd marched inside, pissed off to find the door unlocked. "I could have been anyone, My!" I called to her, stopping in the doorway of her living room/kitchen. She wasn't in there.

"I knew it was you from the camera app!" Her voice traveled from the direction of her bedroom.

"I'm just sayin', keep your flat door locked. You ready?"

"Putting on my shoes." She sounded a little out of breath.

And then she was there—my lecture on security for a single woman living alone dying in my throat—standing in front of me in a dress that somehow managed to be classy as fuck and the sexiest piece of clothing I'd ever seen in my life. Maia looked like she was ready to hit the red carpet.

Her dark hair flowed down her back and shoulders, sleek, straight. I wanted to fist all that hair in my hands as I—

"Fuck," I huffed out, scrubbing a hand down my beard.

The dress had a modest neckline, but it sculpted to her breasts, her small waist, her luscious hips, and there was a split in the hem that was definitely going to kill me. Her long, gorgeous tan legs looked even longer in the sky-high, barely there strappy sandals she wore.

"My face is up here." Her words trembled with amusement.

I reluctantly dragged my gaze back to her face. Her makeup was more than usual. Smoky eyes that made the light violet color even more striking.

"Do you even know how beautiful you are?" My voice was rough with the magnitude of my feelings for her.

Maia appeared happily surprised and shocked the hell out of me by asking, "Really?" Like she didn't know.

That pissed me off. It pissed me off that Maia MacLeod had lived thirty years on this planet and was so damaged by her worthless mum and her moronic ex that she didn't know she was a fucking goddess among us mere mortals.

I took a step toward her, forcing myself not to touch her, to push too fast, too soon. "You're always the most beautiful woman in the room, Maia. Always."

Her lips parted on an exhale. "I think you mean that."

"I do mean it. I've always meant it."

She glanced away, a shy, sexy smile curling her lips. "I always just thought ... you know ... you flirt with everyone."

Shit.

It looked like Callan and John were right. That part of my personality really was coming back to bite me in the arse.

"Doesn't mean what I say isn't true." I bridged the

distance between us and held out my hand. "Ready to do this?"

Maia eyed my upturned palm and slowly reached out to take it, my aunt's ring sparkling in the light. I threaded my fingers through hers and squeezed.

She licked her lips, her gaze searching as if she wasn't quite sure what was happening between us. Good. I didn't want her looking at me with benign comfort. I wanted her off-kilter. I wanted her heart racing, her skin hot, and I wanted her questioning everything she thought she knew about what we were and could be.

"You look great too," Maia opined quietly. "You always do."

"I know that, beautiful, but I appreciate the compliment."

She smacked my arm with her free hand. "Cocky bugger."

Laughing, I shrugged and began leading her toward the exit. "You say cocky, I say self-aware."

Her resultant snort-laugh made me feel about ten feet tall.

———

The club we were meeting our friends in was on George Street, so only a few minutes' walk from Maia's. While she managed in her heels with ease on the pavement, the cobbles were a bit of an issue, and I couldn't say I didn't enjoy being able to put my arm around her to keep her steady.

As we strolled toward the pillared entrance of the club, three guys walking toward us practically tripped over themselves ogling Maia. Possessiveness thrummed through me, my hand tightening around hers as I glanced over my shoulder to see they'd turned to watch her walk away. They were whistling under their breath and smacking each other in that "*Check her oot, mate*" silent language when they noted my death stare.

They quickly turned around, and I shook off my uncharacteristic response.

I'd been with attractive lassies before who garnered a lot of attention and it never bothered me. I'd been out with *Maia* while she was getting attention and didn't let it get to me.

Tonight, I felt weirdly uptight about it.

I told myself to get a grip as we walked up to the bouncers instead of waiting in line. "Baird McMillan."

They didn't even check the list. One of them glanced between us. "Saw you two on the news. Congratulations." He stepped aside and gestured for us to go in.

"Thanks, mate." I could hear the whispers starting in line as recognition hit the would-be clubbers.

I searched Maia's face as we walked inside. "You sure you're up for this?"

"Damage control," she replied quietly.

A hostess greeted us like we'd been announced. "Your party is waiting for you."

We followed her through the already busy club and upstairs where the hostess unclipped a roped-off area and led us toward a table. Callan, Beth, and John were already seated alongside my sister. I shook my head as we approached. "Cannae take you lot anywhere, you bougie bastards with your VIP sections."

They laughed and greeted us as Maia and I slid into the booth beside them.

"Maia, that dress is to die for." Beth had to raise her

voice across the table to be heard over the dance music. "Is that from Pennington's?"

Maia nodded. "They let me have it for free. Marketing, they said, in case someone takes a snap of it tonight."

"Well, at least there are perks to being under a microscope," Ainsley offered. She studied Maia. "How are you doing with all the scrutiny?"

"I guess we're about to find out."

Protectiveness had me sliding my arm around her shoulders to pull her into my side. I'd asked her ages ago what perfume she wore because she always smelled amazing. She said it was 21:50 Rêverie. I inhaled it now, denying myself the urge to press a reassuring kiss to her plump lips.

A server appeared at the table to take our drinks order. Once she left, I turned to Callan. "Did you organize the VIP section?"

He shook his head. "Nah. They recognized me when we arrived and led us up here."

"Nice."

The drinks soon arrived, and we fell into easy conversation, talking about our weeks and everyday crap. Things got a bit awkward when Beth asked, eyes glinting with curiosity, "So ... I'm dying to know how this happened." She gestured between us.

Guilt tore through me. Around this table sat my favorite people in the world, and I hated lying to them. Maia tensed.

It was Ainsley, the only one who knew the truth, who came to the rescue. "I think it's better not to talk about that stuff in public. Prying eyes and ears, you know."

Beth grimaced as I offered my sister a grateful smile.

"Oh, of course." Beth nodded. "You're right. I'll get the tea later from Maia." She gave her pseudo-cousin a pointed look. I guessed that perhaps Maia had been avoiding her.

This was the worst part.

Though I couldn't deny that Maia snuggling against me soothed my discomfort.

Not long later, after our third drink, Maia turned to me and said, "I want to dance."

"That's where the camera phones are," I reminded her.

"We came here to be seen, so we might as well enjoy ourselves." She started to slide out of the booth. I had to curb a masculine groan when I found myself face-to-face with her sequins-covered arse. Such a perfect, pert peach of an arse. John chuckled across the table, and I shot him a wry look.

"She's trying to kill me."

My friend flashed a wide grin. "But what a way to go."

I chuckled and followed Maia out of the booth.

"I'm dancing too." Beth waved at John to let her out.

Ainsley nodded. "And me."

Callan snorted. "I guess we all are, then."

"Nah. I'll stay here." John let Beth out, eyeing the table of women across from us. One of them, an in-your-face stunning blond, was eyeing him right back.

"Enjoy!" I winked at him and followed Maia down the stairs. I hurried to keep up with her because even though she traversed them like a pro in her sky-high heels, she'd had three cocktails.

As soon as we hit the floor, I put my hands on her hips. She glanced over her shoulder up at me, her eyes bright enough that I knew she was tipsy but not drunk. Heat shot through me as she started popping her hips from side to side as she guided me in a dance-walk into the middle of the crowded dance floor. Just as I was turning her to face me, a strange woman pushed into my personal space, literally shoving Maia away so she could thrust her fingers into my hair.

"You cut it!" The unfamiliar blond pouted drunkenly as she pressed her body to mine.

I didn't know this woman. She'd *shoved* Maia. There were probably camera phones coming out as we stood there. Wondering how to extricate myself as quickly as possible, I didn't have time to figure it out. She was not so gently thrust aside.

By a seriously pissed-off Maia. "Do you know her?"

I shook my head, worried about where this was going.

Maia turned to the blond who staggered to right herself. "You do not touch strangers without their permission. You do not shove me, and you do not touch him."

"Fuck," the blond whined, stumbling. "Shorry. Jusht a Caley fan is all." She turned away to start dancing again.

I tried not to smile as Maia gaped at me. "Do you have to deal with that all the time?"

In answer, I wrapped my arm around her waist and drew her against me. "It comes with the territory."

Maia rested her palms on my chest, her violet eyes wide with concern. "No, Bear. It shouldn't. People don't get to touch you unless you want them to."

"As sweet as that is, My, I'm six foot five and built like a brick shithouse. I can take care of myself. Promise." I leaned down to say quietly in her ear, "Do I have permission to touch you like I would if we were really together?"

The sound of her breath catching went straight to my dick.

I felt her nod and then heard her whispered *yes*.

Anticipation thrummed through me as I brushed my lips against the side of her neck. Then another and another until her head fell back to let me kiss her throat. Her fingers curled into my T-shirt, and I felt the shiver that rippled through her.

Oh fuck.

Sliding my hands down her waist, I cupped her arse and began to sway my hips to the music. Lifting my head from her throat, Maia met my heated gaze as she met the beat with her own hips. Abruptly, my mind flashed to her riding me, her cheeks flushed, her lips parted on cries of pleasure as our hips met, grinding together, me thrusting up into her.

All the hot blood coursing through my body traveled south.

Her lips parted as my hardness became evident.

"Fuck. Couldn't help it. But I can back off," I forced out gruffly.

Her eyes grew hooded and she shook her head, pressing deeper into me as she slid a hand around my nape. "Damage control," she whispered before she pulled my head toward her.

As our lips met, I squeezed her arse and groaned into the kiss as she whimpered. Her tongue touched mine and I swear I exploded into a raging fire. I let go of her arse to cup the back of her head, to hold her to me so I could kiss her like she was my next breath. Everything about this woman was right. The taste, the feel, the smell. She was my match. The missing fucking piece.

Unbelievably, she kissed me back with the same hunger, the same desperation I felt.

It was wet and sexual and undeniably the best fucking kiss of my life.

I was vaguely aware of wolf-whistling, but it was the hard smack on my back that had me reluctantly releasing

Maia. She panted for breath, her lips swollen, her lipstick smudged, cheeks flushed, eyes bright with arousal.

Bloody hell.

I turned to glare at the intruder and found Callan grinning at me.

"You two are going to get us kicked out."

"Facts." Beth pushed into his side, pretty eyes dancing with laughter. "I'm surprised Maia isn't pregnant from that kiss."

Before I could let that go to my head, Callan's expression transformed to something more serious as he leaned in. "A lot of cameras on you, mate."

Shit. I looked up and found Callan was right. A bunch of clubbers were filming us. I nodded at my friend and protectively pulled Maia closer. Callan and Beth melted away into the crowd on my periphery. I only saw My.

Her fingers moved over my mouth. "Lipstick," she explained as she wiped it off.

"I'm going to need a minute before you step back." My voice was hoarse with need.

"Oh." She bit her lower lip with a shy understanding that was so sexy, I was pretty sure I was never getting out of the club without a hard-on.

"Just try not to ..." I waved a hand, palm out, over her face. "Be you, right now."

Maia let out a bark of laughter. "What am I supposed to be?"

"Not so bloody gorgeous inside and out," I grumbled.

"Hmm." She let go of me but didn't move away. Instead, she stuck her fingers inside her cheeks, pulled her mouth apart, and stuck out her tongue as she cocked her eyes.

It was my turn to laugh in surprise. "What the fuck are you doing?"

She waggled her tongue at me.

"Weirdly, that isn't helping my situation."

Maia dropped her hands but only to lean into me as she cackled with laughter, her tits pressing into me.

I grinned as I stroked her waist. "Not helping either."

She beamed up at me, so beautiful it hurt. "I don't know how to help, then."

Glancing around, I saw Beth and Callan dancing all sexy and into each other. Since the moment Beth came back into Callan's life, she was all he could see. There wasn't anyone else for him. I finally understood the feeling. However, the lucky bastard could prod his cock into his fiancée's arse as much as he wanted while they danced. My gaze swung past them to see Ainsley was all over some redheaded lassie and beside her was John with the blond from upstairs.

I whistled between my fingers and every single one of my companions looked at me.

I gestured to John. He appeared annoyed but came over. "What is it?"

"Switch places with My."

He looked incredulous. "Fuck off. People are filming you, dude. I'm not ending up in the tabloids under the headline SECRET GAY ROMANCE IN SCOTTISH FOOTBALL."

I laughed because it was funny, but John moved to leave so I grabbed his arm, my eyes darting pointedly south. "Seriously, mate. Just stand in front of me until I get things under control. I don't want this situation in the tabloids either. SCOTTISH FOOTBALLER CAN'T CONTROL HIS DICK AROUND HIS FIANCÉE isn't a headline I think Maia will enjoy."

John shook his head in mock disappointment. "What are you? Fourteen?"

Maia was in a flood of giggles at my predicament.

"Everything she does makes me hard." I shrugged unapologetically.

At that, Maia's head whipped toward me, her laughter dying. Her expression slackened. "Seriously?"

Why deny it? "Seriously."

"You're pathetic." John huffed but gently moved Maia aside to step in front of me with his arms crossed over his chest. "The gaffer naked in a sauna with Baumann."

"That's just cruel."

"Your grandmother doing the nasty with your grandfather."

"Hey, keep it respectful. Though, that is working." I gestured for him to continue. "Right, next."

"Your mom and the gaffer."

"That's uncalled for."

"In the sauna with Baumann and a tub of Marmite ..." He continued on in graphic detail until I wanted to be sick. And it worked like a charm. Any sexy feelings I had were obliterated.

"Oh, enough. That was overkill. I think I'm scarred." I narrowed my eyes on my friend. "You are one disturbed Canadian."

John chuckled, not disagreeing.

I shot a look over his shoulder at Maia who was dancing but also eyeing me in that curious, searching way she'd started to do recently. As if she might be beginning to wonder if I'd been into her all along. It was about time she began to believe it. My blood started to heat again. "Fuck. I'm getting a drink."

John smacked me on the shoulder as we turned toward the bar. Then he gripped my neck to pull me toward him so he could whisper, "You haven't fucked her yet."

I jerked back from him.

John shook his head with a sigh. "Secret is safe with me."

"John—"

He waved me off and headed back to his blond.

Shit.

CHAPTER EIGHTEEN
MAIA

As I spun on the dance floor to Queen (the music was a great eclectic mix of new and old hits), my mind spun too.

Baird's erection situation had been hot. Then funny. Now it was confusingly hot again. He was a young guy. Twenty-six. But ... John was right. This was a situation a teenage boy might find themselves in. Somehow it wasn't off-putting. It was ... it was seriously hot that Baird found me so attractive he couldn't get a handle on his hard-on.

However, that also meant that Baird genuinely wanted to have sex with me.

We couldn't have sex.

I mean, we could, and it would maybe defuse the heat between us.

God, that kiss ... My lips still tingled.

No. I shook my head. A one-night stand would ultimately make me feel icky.

I wasn't built for casual sex.

Right?

Or did I just *think* I wasn't built for casual sex?

There was no denying that my underwear was now damp from the best kiss a man had ever given me. I was wet from a make-out session. That had never happened!

While I tried to untangle my increasingly confusing crush on Baird, Ainsley had sidled up with some redheaded girl and started dancing beside me. Baird's sister gave me a knowing smirk that I ignored, but I was grateful to her for keeping me company while Baird buggered off to the bar.

Four songs passed, and he didn't return.

That wasn't exactly the plan for damage control.

My gaze swept the bar, dreading seeing him chatting to some other woman. When I found him, relief moved through me. He leaned his back against the countertop, nursing a beer, and watching me with uncharacteristic broodiness.

That was hot too.

I was just about to make my way over to him, telling myself it was because there were eyes on us and we couldn't look like we had fallen out, when the track changed. A recognizable tune blasted through the speakers, those first pop synth notes slamming into me so hard I stumbled to a stop.

"Kids" by MGMT.

When the lyrics hit, my chest tightened as memories slammed through my mind. My skin tingled and I was suddenly lightheaded.

I could see Mum dancing across from me in the kitchen as we shouted the lyrics to each other. My happiest memories of her—and my worst.

I hated that goddamn song.

It rarely ever played anywhere.

But when it did …

I needed air.

Stumbling toward the exit, I was vaguely aware of Ainsley calling my name, of people cursing at me as I shoved them aside.

I was almost at the front entrance when a strong hand curled around my biceps.

"Maia."

Staring up at Baird's face, the nausea pitched in my stomach. "Air."

He cursed under his breath and wound his arm around my waist, leading me out and down the side of the front steps away from the waiting queue. As soon as we were a few feet from the building, I turned, bent over, and threw up against the wall.

Baird caught my hair with catlike reflexes, holding it as his other hand made soothing circles on my back.

Finally, I stopped retching, but I was trembling so hard, I couldn't even feel embarrassed as I straightened. I was too busy trying to breathe normally. What the hell? *What the actual hell?!*

"Shit, My." Baird lowered his face to mine. "What is going on? Are you having a panic attack?"

Was I? I stared up at him wide-eyed and terrified as I found myself hyperventilating. Was I going to die? I felt like I might die.

"Look at me, My. Breathe with me. It's okay. You're okay. Breathe in." He took a deliberate slow inhale. "Breathe out." He exhaled. And then he repeated it. I focused on his mouth and attempted to follow suit. It seemed to take forever, but slowly, my breathing normalized.

Shocked by what had just occurred, I burst into tears.

Baird wrapped his arms around me, pulling me into his chest. I heard his murmured words of comfort, felt his soft kisses across my head and temple. And I felt safe. I felt safe to just cry.

———————

"I texted Ainsley," Baird said, holding tight to my hand as we walked back to my place. "Explained we'd left."

I nodded, still shaken from what I'd experienced and, honestly, feeling stupid. Like I'd totally overreacted.

It wasn't the first time.

Back at uni, when I lived in London, in second year, my roommates and I were friends with a group of lads in our dorm. We were hanging out at theirs, having a few beers, having a few laughs. Music was playing in the background. A playlist one of the lads made up.

"Kids" by MGMT came on.

I'd been mid-conversation with my roommate Shelly when I'd been lambasted with memories of Mum and that song. Before I knew it, Shelly had my head between my legs, coaxing me to breathe.

Not once did I acknowledge I'd had a panic attack in that moment.

How could it be a panic attack when it was only ever triggered by that song? Beth had recently told me she had an anxiety disorder, and she suffered from panic attacks. They weren't triggered by only one thing.

Right?

Why a bloody song?

"What happened in there, My?" Baird asked quietly, never letting go of my hand. "I saw your face. You looked like someone punched you in the stomach."

How did I explain without sounding nuts?

He squeezed my hand. "My, you can tell me anything."

My heel caught on a cobble, and I toppled sideways on my shaky legs. Baird was there in an instant, his arm around my waist, steadying me.

"I've got you," he murmured.

Aye, he did, didn't he?

I stared up at him, a million wishes rushing up inside of me with frustration. Yet it wasn't his fault I was catching feelings. I was not allowed to be frustrated by that.

Baird might not have been my real fiancé, but he was my real friend.

Possibly my best friend.

I righted myself and he released my waist but not my hand. "I must look a mess," I whispered, ducking my head as we continued to walk.

"You could never be a mess, Maia."

I scoffed, finally feeling the embarrassment of Baird holding my hair back. Groaning, I covered my face with my free hand. "You saw me upchuck."

He tugged on my wrist, his tone amused. "Babe, do you know how many times I've thrown up outside of a nightclub?"

My lips curled in a grateful smile. "Maybe you shouldn't tell me the number."

His expression was instantly serious. "What made you sick? Because I know it wasn't the three cocktails."

"It's stupid," I whispered. "I'm so embarrassed."

"Maia, I don't know how to make you believe that you never have to be embarrassed with me."

Fine. He was right. Baird had never given me cause to not trust him with my feelings.

"It was the song."

"The 'Kids' song?"

I nodded, watching my every step carefully and wishing

like hell I could take my stupid heels off and walk the rest of the way home barefoot. Not in this city, though.

"What about it?"

That immediate emotion I'd felt after I was sick threatened to burst forth again. I swallowed hard around the lump in my throat and choked out, "It was my mum's favorite song. When I was about twelve or so, she would play it constantly. We'd dance in the kitchen to it, shouting the lyrics at the top of our voices. And she would ... it was like she was—" My voice broke, and I blinked rapidly to stop the tears, but it only caused them to flow over.

Baird tugged me closer as I swiped at them.

"It ... It was like she was singing the lyrics at me. Like she was telling me what she wanted to say but couldn't. That's what it was like with her for so long. One minute she'd make me believe there was a mum in there who did love me but just didn't know how to show it. Then she'd rip it all away and I'd feel hopeless again. Worthless."

He stopped us, pulling me back into his arms as I cried quietly, soaking his shirt all over again.

"It's s-so s-st-stupid. I'm th-thirty y-years o-old. It ... it sh-shouldn't still hu-hurt like this."

"It's not stupid, My. You could be eighty and this would still hurt. A mum is supposed to protect their child. To put their kid first. If she was here in front of me, I might fucking kill her."

I gripped tighter to his shirt, turning my cheek so I could speak, trying to calm my tears. "That's the second time I've heard that s-song and re-reacted like that. S-so weird."

"It's triggering panic attacks."

Gently, I pushed away from him. "I-I don't think it's a panic attack."

"Babe." Baird reached down to swipe his thumb over my cheek and I saw black on it. Mascara. Damn it, I probably looked like a raccoon. "I know a panic attack when I see one."

I frowned. "But why just that song? I've never had a panic attack about anything else."

"Because ..." He bent his head toward mine, expression gentle. "The song represents all the complicated feelings you have about your mum. It's the thing that hurts most—that she could have loved you the way you needed her to, but she chose not to."

My mouth trembled as fresh tears sprang free. He was so wise. I nodded.

Baird tried to catch the tears with his thumbs, his expression almost agonized. Like my pain was his pain. "You deserve so much better, Maia."

"Bear ..."

He wiped my cheeks again and pressed a firm kiss to my forehead. "Let's get you home, beautiful. I'll make you a cup of tea and some toast. That'll help."

I snuggled into his side, confused by my tumultuous emotions but grateful to him. "Thank you for taking care of me."

His response was gravelly with emotion. "You never have to thank me for that. It's my privilege, Maia."

CHAPTER NINETEEN

BAIRD

The air felt sticky and heady, the humidity so high the lads and I had all discarded our training shirts within the first five minutes. Sweat lashed off us and we were constantly stopping to hydrate.

Usually there was a comfort in the familiar shouts between my team. The sound of the coaching assistants' whistles. The laughter and the filthy jokes. The smell of deodorant and sweat and fruity electrolyte sport drinks. When I was younger, it was the smell of grass that made me feel at home. But now the turf was a hybrid mix of natural grass and synthetic for better durability. It didn't smell like the pitches I grew up on.

The pitch wasn't the reason I didn't feel at home here lately.

It was strange being here without John.

A hard smack on my shoulder drew me out of my daze, and I turned to find Callan at my side, so drenched in sweat, he looked like he'd just showered. We all did.

"I miss him too."

Fuck.

He was a good pal, Callan. Nothing got by him.

"Aye." I rubbed the back of my neck. "Place doesn't feel the same."

"Agreed."

"He's doing all right, though. Braden called me this morning about an issue with planning rights. I sent John to go see what's up. I think he's surprised by how much he's getting into it."

Callan took a swig of his sports drink. Once he swallowed, he nodded. "Good. Maybe he'll stay."

"I hope so."

"Is that the only thing bothering you this morning?"

I avoided my mate's perceptive gaze. "Just gearing myself up for this afternoon. Got another video shoot for the Pennington's campaign."

"You don't sound excited."

"Oh, aye, it's my life's dream."

Callan snorted. "I don't think any of us expected this thing to take off like it did."

Certainly not me. I mean, I thought it might grow some legs, but it had grown arms and legs and extra heads. The kiss I'd shared with Maia in the club last week had gone viral after people posted it online. Pennington's were salivating over how invested people seemed to be in our romance already.

The kiss was fucking hot. I was more than a wee bit proud of it. And I might have been smug and elated about how into that kiss Maia was, if she was still talking to me.

Okay, it wasn't like she *wasn't* talking to me.

But ever since she'd had a panic attack at the club and I'd taken her home and looked after her until she fell asleep, Maia had been distant. She'd erected a wall between us.

I glanced at Callan, considering asking him for advice. Then I reconsidered on the basis I didn't want to come off as being a cling-on fiancé. Not that Callan would ... well, we took the piss out of each other all the time, but we knew when to be serious and there for each other too.

My mate side-eyed me. "You want to ask me something?"

Grimacing, I hesitated.

"Is it a relationship thing?"

I nodded.

Callan turned toward me, shrugging. "Hit me with it."

Ach, fine. "Has Beth ever ... like ... opened up to you and then totally shut you out afterward?" I scrubbed a hand over my beard, feeling weirdly vulnerable. I did not like to be confused when it came to the female sex. It was not normal for me. Growing up with a mum and sister, I thought I understood women better than most blokes. I was starting to realize, however, I'd gotten most of my information from Ainsley, and my big sister was quite possibly the most laid-back, commitment-phobic lassie I knew.

For instance, Ainsley had never called me out on the flirting shit because she was the same. If she found a person attractive, of any gender, she was all up in their space with the flirting.

My guidepost for women was me with tits.

Turned out that wasn't the best guidepost.

Maia ... she had me in fucking knots.

Callan shrugged. "Maybe. I mean, Beth was pretty closed off at first because she thought I was only interested in sex. Maia has your ring on her finger. Why would she do that? Unless ... she's embarrassed by whatever she opened up to you about? Some folk hate feeling vulnerable."

"Aye, that's what I was thinking. Doesnae mean it doesnae fuck me off she thinks she cannae be vulnerable with me," I replied, my accent thickening with my irritation.

I thought Maia and I were finally making some headway.

The kiss in the club was real.

She started to believe it when I told her how gorgeous she was, how much I wanted her.

And when she let me take care of her after her panic attack, I thought I was finally in.

But since then, she'd dodged seeing me, sent me one-word responses to my texts, and was avoiding my calls. I started to feel like a few of the lassies I'd slept with who'd gotten the wrong idea about what a one-night stand meant. I'd never been deliberately cruel to a lassie, but I'd ghosted a few. Now I felt bad about it.

A whistle suddenly blew sharp and piercing, accompanied by frantic shouts. Callan and I jolted, looking toward the direction of the sound and then Callan was running toward the opposite goal where the team's backup goalkeeper, Peter Klintberg, had been training with a few players.

I took off after Callan as our teammates surrounded two players lying on the pitch.

As I processed what was happening, I slowed to a stop, the blood rushing in my ears. The ground seemed to pulse up toward me in waves, and I squeezed my eyes closed, forcing myself to breathe slowly so I wouldn't pass out.

"He's not waking up."

"Fuck, fuck, I'm sorry."

"Freddie, Freddie, can you hear me?"

"He's out cold."

"What happened, Peter?"

"I didn't see."

"It was me and Kaito," Baumann spoke. "We were messing around."

"Freddie. Freddie!"

"Call an ambulance. Now!"

I opened my eyes, watching as our medic rushed across the field and Baumann roared at the coaches to call an ambulance.

"Move." The medic pushed Callan aside and opened Freddie's eyes, flashing a light in them. "Concussion." He pulled his fingers away from Freddie's temple and they were covered in blood.

Fuck.

Fuck!

This wasn't happening.

My chest tightened as I stood there unable to move, to help.

"What happened?" The gaffer stood in front of Kaito and Baumann as the medic checked Freddie's vitals.

He wasn't moving.

Fuck, he wasn't moving.

He was just a kid. He'd barely even started.

"I was showing Eric how to land with feet after kicking ball in air." Kaito's voice shook. "Freddie ... Why? He jump to header ball as I kick. And I kicked ... how to say ... much *force*. I hit Freddie."

Stupid, stupid.

"Why would he do that?"

"He didn't realize. He just jumped in to take the ball." Baumann shook his head. "Stupid fucking kid."

"Show some respect," Callan spat.

Baumann flinched and nodded.

Through all of this, I said nothing. Watched as the paramedics appeared on the field and placed the still-unconscious Freddie on a stretcher.

"Baird. Baird."

The ground swayed under me.

"Baird!" Callan suddenly filled my vision, green eyes hard with worry. "Mate, you all right?"

I blinked, coming out of my trance to realize Freddie had been loaded into the rig and the rest of the team were heading off the field.

Callan had his hands on my shoulders. "You all right?"

I stepped back, giving him a half-hearted cocky grin, even though it felt like my heart was about to explode out of my chest. "I'm fine. It's Freddie you need to worry about."

"He woke up on the stretcher. Hopefully, it's just a concussion."

"Aye, that's good."

"Do you ... do you need to talk?"

"Nah, mate. I need a shower. Then I need to get going." I clapped him on the shoulder, grinning broadly. "All good," I lied and then took off across the pitch, forcing myself to walk straight, feeling any second now like I might pass out.

There were a couple of private shower cubicles, and I snagged one.

Inside, I concentrated on breathing in and out like I'd shown Maia. I ran the water cold, and the shocking sting of it grounded me. I dressed and left before Callan could say anything more, but I was exhausted. At least I didn't feel like I was going to pass out anymore.

Despite the exhaustion, something beyond restlessness buzzed in my veins.

Something reckless and wild.

I needed to blow off steam.

I needed ... to feel in control in the most out-of-control way I could think of.

CHAPTER TWENTY

MAIA

I very rarely ever took time to people-watch or take in my surroundings, but knowing I was about to face Baird for the first time since my freak-out over a song, I needed a minute. Instead of eating lunch at my desk, I'd gone out onto Princes Street to a coffee shop just along from Pennington's. Now I stood outside that shop, my back to the window, sipping my to-go cup and watching the world pass by.

Trams and buses paused on the long stretch of wide road, temporarily blocking my view of the gardens and the rocky volcanic base of Edinburgh Castle, the medieval fortress perched over the city, a majestic, everyday reminder of the history here. It drew the tourists who passed me, making Edinburgh the second-biggest tourist city in the UK after London. It was even voted the fifth-most beautiful city in the *world*. It made me proud to live here, to work here, and I knew the tourism was one of the few reasons Pennington's had survived.

The sounds of chatter in multiple languages filled my ears, along with traffic, the beeping of crosswalks, and the distant wail of a bagpiper. It was hot and humid today, and the locals were showing lots of skin in full summer wear, whereas the tourists, expecting Scotland's typical mild climate, were caught unawares in their rain jackets and jeans. Especially as it had rained yesterday.

Deciding I wanted air-conditioning enough to face Baird, I sighed, chugged the last of my coffee, and dumped it into a recycling bin before heading back to Pennington's. My heeled sandals clicked on the pavement, and I dug in my purse for change to drop in the cup of the two homeless people who sat on their sleeping bags outside of an empty store.

"Thanks, gorgeous." The guy grinned a yellowed smile at me after I dropped the money in.

I nodded and continued on my way. When I first moved to Edinburgh to be with my dad, there had been homeless people just like there were in any big city. But it was definitely worse now. As were the graffiti tags, the litter, and many commercial buildings that sat empty. It was a miracle Pennington's had survived.

But I guess that's what the campaign was for. To ensure they stayed relevant. To ensure their survival.

I felt heavy with emotion and knew it was partly hormonal. I was on my period. However, I was also incredibly confused about Baird. He'd looked after me without judgment—only care—and I found my crush deepening to disastrous levels. I didn't know what it meant or if I was reading too much into the way Baird treated me ... but it felt like things between us were shifting. It felt like there might be something real developing between us.

I didn't know if I could handle that.

Somehow, I knew that if Baird ever hurt me the way Will had ... it would destroy me.

Therefore, I'd done what I was good at and pushed him away all week.

I wasn't proud of my behavior. I knew I had to woman up and face him. He deserved better.

This afternoon, the marketing team wanted to talk to us both after the production team shot footage of us walking around the relevant departments of Pennington's. They wanted footage of us picking out the items for our wedding registry.

This weekend, we were supposed to start our hunt for the wedding venue.

Butterflies fluttered in my belly as I walked into the store because it reminded me that in a few short months, I'd legally be married to Baird.

————

He texted to tell me he was on his way upstairs, so I waited for him at the lift. I'd already changed into a summer dress Christina and I had selected from the current season. With the air-conditioning on blast inside the offices, I was a little chilly in the strappy A-line.

My breath caught as Baird stepped out of the elevator. His forehead glistened with sweat, but it did nothing to detract from how hot he was in his short-sleeve shirt and navy chino shorts. If anything, the sweat made me think of sex.

Don't think of sex!

Baird's shorts revealed the tattooed dragon that wound around his left calf and ankle. The preppy look was incongruous to the tattooed muscular physique and unshaven face and shaggy hair.

Sexy as sin.

"Hey ..." My greeting sounded a little breathless even to me.

His gaze washed over me with a thoroughness that made my skin tingle. "Oi, oi," he said his trademark greeting, but this time with a husky quietness that caused a low flip deep in my belly.

We stared at each other. I felt like a fish on a hook as my body unconsciously pulled toward him.

"Good. You're here." The annoying voice jerked me out of my Baird daze.

Becky eyed my fake fiancé like he was the pair of Jimmy Choos she had on layaway. "Don't you look the part."

Baird stared at her with uncharacteristic stoniness. "Who are you again?"

I struggled to swallow a laugh because I knew he knew very well who she was.

Becky's flirtatious expression faltered. "Becky. From marketing. We met ... before."

He looked at me, cocking an eyebrow. "Did we?"

Biting back a laugh, I nodded.

Baird winked and I grinned, relieved he wasn't holding the past week against me.

My colleague cleared her throat in annoyance, and I had to unlock my eyes from Baird's dreamy dark ones. Becky's expression was all pinched and uptight. "This way. Both of you."

We fell into step behind her, and I reached out to slow Baird down. As soon as we were far enough behind her, I whispered, "I'm sorry I've been MIA. When it ... when it comes to my mum, I tend to get stuck in my head about it. But I've been a shit ... friend. Especially after you were so good to me."

Baird shrugged. "Hey, no worries, babe. I get it. You do

what you gotta do." He gestured with his head for us to continue after Becky.

I frowned because there was something off about his blasé response. Something almost dismissive—and Baird was never dismissive with me.

Then again, I supposed I deserved it. I'd been dismissive with him.

Feeling even more out of sorts, I forced myself to smile as we strode into the marketing meeting room to find Hilary and two other assistants.

"You both look great." Hilary straightened from tapping at her tablet screen. "We want you to know how delighted Pennington's is with how successful the campaign has been so far. We dropped the link for the preorder for the dress you were wearing at the nightclub, Maia, and we're sold out before it even hits the store."

I raised an eyebrow. "Wow."

"Exactly. Wow."

"It helps you made the dress look like a million dollars." The male marketing assistant, Kal, I think his name was, gave me a shy, boyish smile.

"True." Hilary studied us. "Now ... are you sure you won't engage with some of these chat show requests? Not even a podcast?"

I shook my head.

Baird gave an impatient jerk of his chin. "Where's the production team? I've got shit to do."

Surprised by his agitated tone, I searched his profile, trying to read him. Was he still mad at me?

"The team are filming footage of the outside and inside of the store. While they do that, we wanted to run over some things." Becky tapped on a tablet and then turned the screen to us. There was an image of a stunning ivy-covered castle. "This is Almondbrae Castle just outside of Kirkliston. It's where you two are getting married."

Confused, I tentatively took the tablet to scroll through the photos. The venue was absolutely stunning but way more over the top than I'd ever pictured for my wedding. "I thought we were supposed to film our hunt for a venue."

"You will." Becky shrugged. "But you don't *actually* get to choose. Almondbrae is the only luxury wedding venue that has an opening in August. They had a cancellation, so we got a discount. Your wedding date is August 27, by the way." There was a spiteful glint in her eyes, like she was enjoying the fact that I didn't have a say in my wedding date or venue.

Honestly, what the hell had I done to piss her off so much?

I looked down at the tablet, my throat tight, because suddenly this was all so very real. I was going to marry a man who didn't love me, all for the sake of my career because my colleague was quite possibly a sociopath and had chosen me as her target for destruction.

If someone else had told me this was happening to them, I wouldn't believe it.

"All good." Baird shrugged. "Now can we get on with it?"

"We also want to discuss adding a few more filming dates to the schedule." Hilary perched her elegant bum on the desk and crossed her arms over her chest. "Our team and the film production team feel like with the level of interest in you two, we should throw in some fun stuff to keep people engaged. Not just blatant promotion of our products."

"Like?" I asked warily.

"Like footage of you living your lives together. Perhaps we could film you on dates."

"But interesting ones," Becky threw in unnecessarily.

"Bungee jumping." Baird suddenly looked animated. "Why don't we film us going bungee jumping together? I've always wanted to do it, and you said you wanted to have a bit of adventure."

I gaped at him. What the hell? "Bungee jumping?"

"Or skydiving." He waggled his eyebrows at me a wee bit maniacally.

What the ... okay, something was going on with him.

"I'm not—"

"My type of guy." Becky's hot eyes raked over Baird. "I bungee jumped at the one in Perthshire. I'd suggest we do the shoot there"—her eyes flicked to me—"but Maia looks a little green around the gills at the thought."

"I'm not green around the gills." If she eye-fucked my fake fiancé one more time ...

"It's okay, Maia." Her smile was saccharine sweet. "We're not all adrenaline junkies. It's okay to be too scared for adventure. We'll figure out something else for the date."

"You don't know Maia." Baird shot Becky an annoyed glower before he turned to me, expression softening. Yet there was still that wild glint in his dark eyes I didn't understand, or like, because I'd seen it before—weeks ago, when he was chasing chaos.

Damn.

Were we back there again?

"I can bungee jump." The words were out of my mouth before I really processed what I'd agreed to.

Baird let out a whoop, twirling me in his arms in his excitement. I would have been happy to see the return of fun-loving Baird McMillan if I didn't feel so uneasy.

"Save it for the camera." Hilary chuckled as Baird placed me back on my feet. "Now let's go over a few more things before the team is ready for you."

———

Three hours later, hungry, tired, and growing increasingly pissed off, I was glad when Bruno finally called a wrap for the day. Between having to share shivery soft kisses with Baird all afternoon, feeling his hand pressed firmly on my lower back, or having him cuddle into me as we selected products from the home department for our registry, all the while feeling alarmed about his current mental state, I was a mess.

Not only that, but I also hadn't realized how difficult filming us picking our wedding gifts out would be. Though I would never have a wedding registry, I had imagined a moment in my life where I picked out plates and glasses and appliances and soft furnishings with my future partner.

To do it for the first time and have it all be fake ... I mean, Pennington's was donating all this stuff to us (and believe me, I had guilt about that too), and we'd have to live with it for at least a year. Together? We hadn't planned to live together, but now we were under all this scrutiny. Would that go away after the wedding, or would the media continue to follow us? Would we have to pretend to live together?

How could two intelligent people seriously have not thought this through?

Moreover, there was definitely something up with Baird.

He was giving me the front-cover version of his personality. On steroids.

Fake smiles, shallow conversation, constant jokes. The deeper, more serious side of him that I loved was buried beneath something frantic and frayed.

There was still work to be done at the office, so I walked Baird out of the staff entrance where he'd parked his motorbike.

"I'll see you soon." He bent his head to press a barely there kiss to my cheek, and I grabbed his arm, halting him.

"Bear ..." I searched his face for answers. "What is going on?"

He frowned, gently tugging his arm out of my hold. Then he flashed me a cocky smile that didn't reach his eyes. "Nothing. I need to get going. Got shit to do."

"Aye, you said that ... before you suggested we go bungee jumping on film."

"It'll be fun." He retreated, walking back toward the motorbike. "C'mon, My, live a little. You could do with a wee push off a cliff."

I flinched. "What does that mean?"

Baird grimaced. "Not the way you're taking it. Just, you could loosen up a bit. Even Becky's bungee jumped."

Hurt, I stepped back toward the building.

Baird's gaze dropped, watching me as I retreated. A muscle in his jaw ticked and he turned abruptly, picking up his helmet.

"Are you ... Did something happen?"

He threw a smirk over his shoulder. "Nothing happened, babe. Nothing's wrong. Isn't that what you've been telling *me* all week?"

Another stab of hurt flared across my chest, and I turned around and pushed inside the building before he could even get on his bike. Way to throw my apology in my face by passively aggressively telling me he did not accept said apology.

I leaned against the door as soon as it slammed shut, tears burning my eyes.

The hope that I'd stupidly let build alongside my moronic crush began to evaporate.

Baird's inability to accept my apology when he knew how much damage my mum had done, and then to lash out at me for being distant this past week, was proof that he wasn't mature enough for a relationship. Damn it, he wasn't even mature enough for our friendship. I thought I knew him ... but today ... I didn't know that guy.

Feeling crushed by the demise of my crush, I pushed off the door and marched back to work, throwing myself into it because it had to be worth it. My job had to be worth the seemingly inevitable destruction of me and Baird.

CHAPTER TWENTY-ONE

MAIA

An hour later, I was cursing my contacts and wishing I could rub at my bleary eyes from looking at my computer screen so intently. My optician had told me I needed to take a ten-minute screen break every twenty minutes, but it was difficult to put that into practice.

My phone, however, made an alert tone that was different from texts and social media notifications. When I first became friends with Baird, I'd set a search alert on my phone for Caledonia United. Anytime there was Caley FC news, I knew about it.

Miserable and unsettled by the encounter with Baird, I reached for my phone to check the alert and then I froze.

CALEY UNITED PLAYER INJURED IN TRAINING

I clicked on the news article, my heart racing as I read that Freddie Dalguise, the youngest player on the team, had suffered a head injury in training that morning. He'd been rushed to hospital with a concussion but had been discharged and was recovering.

Slumping in my chair, I saw Baird's face in my mind

again. That wild flare in his eyes this afternoon suddenly made so much sense.

"Shit," I muttered, feeling terrible that I hadn't pushed him more. I'd let my hurt feelings get the better of me when I should've known the last time Baird acted like this level of arsehole was only weeks after his own head injury.

I'd thought these past few weeks meant he was moving on. That he was dealing with what happened to him.

But I had just been a distraction from it.

Until Freddie reminded Baird.

Heart rate increasing with worry, I hit Baird's name on my contact list, but his phone went straight to voicemail. I tried again. Straight to voicemail.

Shit, shit, shit.

Tapping on my screen, I brought up his main socials and searched for his profile. Once I was on it, I saw he had a new story. I clicked on it, hoping it would reassure me about his whereabouts.

It did not.

There were a number of new stories added in the last twenty minutes.

Baird was at a racing circuit. With his motorbike.

"Of course he is," I huffed in concerned aggravation.

We were back here again. Would the drinking and partying follow suit? The women?

Chest aching, I tried calling him again. When there was nothing, I left a voicemail. "Bear, it's me. Please call me. It's important."

By the time I got home from work, Baird still hadn't called me back. I didn't want to phone again and look like a crazy stalker, but after checking his socials and finding no more stories, I started to get a pit in my stomach. I'd barely been able to eat dinner, I was so unsettled.

Later, as I took out my contacts and washed my face, readying for bed, I went from worried to seriously pissed off. Was this punishment for my behavior this week? Or did I not even factor in? Was I not even a thought in his mind right now?

My phone blared from the pocket of my joggers, and I startled. Quickly drying my hands first, I reached for it. It was Baird's sister.

Fear catapulted through me, and I fumbled to answer. "Ainsley?"

"Maia, thank goodness." She let out an irritated exhale. "Baird just called me. He asked me to pick him up from A&E because he came off his stupid bike at a racing circuit."

My stomach churned. "Is he okay?"

"Other than being a fucking moron, aye, he's fine. Hurt his ankle. Bike is wrecked. Twat. I'm so mad at him! I thought we were over this kamikaze phase."

"I thought so too."

"I've tried talking to him. Mum's tried."

"So have I."

"Well, I need you to try harder, Maia. You are the only one he will listen to."

"Ainsley—"

"I'm in Inverness right now for a design job. I can't pick him up, and his phone is running out of charge, so I told him I'd call John to pick him up. I'm not calling John. Those idiots enable one another. I know you don't have a car, My, but can you jump in a taxi to go get him? He'll listen to you."

I winced, feeling terrible and like an utter failure. "I've tried. Believe me, he doesn't listen to me."

"Then make him listen. Even if you have to be cruel to be kind. Because I am done waiting for another call that my wee bro is in hospital. I can't go through what Mum and I went through last year."

Tears burned my eyes because I'd never heard Ainsley sound so vulnerable, so upset. She was kind of a female version of Baird but edgier.

"I'll do what I can."

"That's all I ask. You ... you have more influence than you know with him, Maia." Ainsley hung up.

I stared into the mirror. I was in my sloppy, lounging-around-the-flat clothes, hair in a messy bun, makeup off with my glasses on. Yet there was no time to put on a face or contacts in.

This was me. For once I didn't have time to care about my usual "armor."

I was too worried, confused, and pissed off.

I decided this was the version of me Baird McMillan deserved to see right now.

————

"Will you say something?" Baird pleaded as I parked the borrowed car next to his in the private car park in Dean Village.

Dusk was turning to night. I'd picked up Baird half an hour ago from A&E. He'd been somewhat shocked to see me behind the wheel of my stepmum's car. Dad and Grace lived ten minutes from the hospital, so I'd gotten an Uber there and she'd let me borrow the car. I'd return it in the morning.

Dad had wanted to accompany me, but I'd told them we'd be okay.

However, I found myself unable to speak to Baird I was that freaking angry with him.

He'd limped his way into the vehicle and tried to ask me why I'd shown up, where was John, what was going on ...

I didn't speak.

I couldn't.

Because I might throttle him.

Pushing out of the car, I rounded it to help him, but Baird had already unfolded his large body and was closing the passenger door.

Shooting him a filthy look, I gestured for him to let us into his flat.

Baird happened to live in the coolest apartment I'd ever seen. Dean Village was medieval and among the most beautiful spots in the city. It was set down by the Water of Leith, an eclectic mix of Victorian and Tudor-style buildings. Baird's was an iconic nineteenth-century building perched on the banks of the water.

"Maia?" He gave me a pleading look as he let me into the flat, all signs of the arrogant, cocky avoider from earlier gone.

I still didn't say a word as I walked into his apartment and stood in the middle of the cavernous main living space. Once a social hall, the building had been split into flats, and Baird's was the largest and most unique. The main space was cathedral-like, with ceilings so high it barely felt residential. The period windows had been retained, as had the gigantic, tiled fireplace on the west end of the room. Rows of windows on either side gave away its historic use.

Baird had tried to make the space homey with the help of Ainsley's keen designer eye. Dramatically long curtains hung at every window, a twelve-seater dining table down one side near the fireplace, and a large corner sofa with chairs situated around a coffee table, all pointing at a large television screen beyond the dining table.

On the east end of the room was a stylish kitchen with a six-seater marble island. A mezzanine bedroom sat on a mounted base above the kitchen. A glass balustrade was the only thing between the bedroom and the hall.

No privacy, but epic design. A doorway on either side of the kitchen led up winding, narrow staircases to two more bedrooms. I knew because one time when we had movie night, I'd been too tired to travel home, so I'd stayed in one of his guest rooms.

Will was seriously pissed off I'd stayed over, so I never did that again.

"For fuck's sake, Maia, talk to me." Baird threw his keys on the coffee table. "The silent treatment is driving me crazy."

"You have more influence with him than you know, Maia."

Bolstered by Ainsley's confidence, I crossed my arms over my chest to singe him with my fiery gaze. "*I'm* driving *you* crazy? I'm not the one who needed picking up from A&E!"

He gestured to his bandage-wrapped right ankle. His leg was also covered in bruises and road rash because he'd been wearing those stupid chino shorts while arsing around on a motorbike at high speed. "It's just a sprain."

"Oh, yeah, well, explain that to your gaffer." I shook my head at him. "What's next, Baird? Partying, drugs, and women too? Are we back here again so soon?"

His dark eyes flashed, and he pointed a finger at me. "Don't. I told you I wouldn't do that shit and I meant it. It fucks me off you'd even think that."

"It fucks me off that you could have been killed tonight."

Baird's expression turned boyish and pleading. "My, it was just a wee accident."

"Aye? Or did you go out and do the most moronic thing you could think of doing because Freddie got injured in training today?"

I watched him freeze, his expression turning wary and distant.

I hated that look. It was so not Baird.

My shoulders slumped and I took a step toward him, my tone placating. "Bear ... you need to deal with this. You need to face the fact that you're not dealing with how much last year's injury impacted you."

That muscle in his jaw ticked, the sudden ice chips in his eyes warning me off. "My therapist cleared me."

"Was that before or after you started doing life-endangering bullshit just to prove you're not terrified?" I asked, my tone gentle.

He flinched and then scoffed. It was an ugly, grating sound. "Me?" He took a limping step toward me. "I'm not the one who's terrified, My. I'm not the one who pushes anyone away who gets close. Who actually got engaged to a guy *because* he wasn't interested in getting close to her."

His words were like a punch to the gut. "Baird."

"I live, babe. You just exist."

Angry that he was deflecting (and doing it with some harsh truths), I let my hurt and Ainsley's earlier suggestion guide me. "Maybe I have been too cautious. That's true. Maybe I've tried to control everything a wee bit too much because I know what it's like to live a life where you have no control," I reminded him, and he winced again, his remorse clear.

But I wasn't done. Ainsley was right. Sometimes you had to be cruel to be kind to shake someone out of their destructive spiral. "There is a difference between living life to the fullest and recklessly trying to prove to yourself that your mortality doesn't scare the shit out of you. I'm asking you to think of the people who care about you."

He'd grown paler, his features taut, as my words hit their target.

I'd expected my Baird to make an appearance. For him to soften.

But pointing out his fear only pissed him off.

As it turned out, easygoing Baird McMillan could skewer a woman with his words. "I gave up the partying, the drinking, and other women for you for the next three months. For this fucking campaign of yours. But you don't get to tell me how to live my life beyond that. You've made it pretty fucking clear this past week that what we have is fake, so you need to remember that. You don't want anyone to get close to you, fine. Goes both ways. So don't come at me with your bullshit amateur psychological analysis because I'm not the one who needs fucking therapy, Maia. I'm not the one who is going to end up alone and unloved!"

Stupid tears burned my eyes as I held back my physical gasp of pain at his words.

Everything these past few weeks ... I'd been living in a goddamn dream world.

I knew it.

I knew if I let myself feel that way about him that he'd hurt me.

A bitter laugh escaped me as I looked back at him. Baird's expression had slackened, but I wasn't paying attention. I couldn't see or hear anything beyond what he'd just said.

"You know what I can't believe ... that for a second I actually thought something real was happening between us." I scoffed, blinking back the tears. "But I was right the first time, wasn't I? You flirt and you're casually affectionate and you make someone believe that you ... you ... but now I know what you really think of me. And the funny thing is ... I did let you in more than I've ever let anyone in. So, thank you. Thank you for letting me know that you're just another person I can add to the list of people who believe I'm unlovable." I stepped toward the front door.

Baird moved toward me and limped, flinching. "Maia—"

I reached for the handle.

"Maia, please." The words were guttural. "I'm sorry, I ..."

"I'm clearly not the right person to do it, but please find someone to talk to. For your sake. For your mum and your sister's. They don't deserve to go through seeing you in the hospital like that again. Or worse." Fear of the future crashed down on me, but I forced the words out. "You're off the hook. I'll tell Christina and Hilary the truth. You're a free man. Don't call me ever again, Baird. I don't need another person like you in my life making me feel like shit about myself." I slipped out of the flat, slamming the door shut behind me.

The tears came as soon as he was out of my sight. I swiped at them angrily beneath my glasses and hurried to Grace's car. As I swung it around, Baird limped out of the flat, trying to wave me down.

I was too hurt to stop.

This hurt worse than leaving Will.

Therefore, I did what I'd been doing since I was a kid, my only defense to survive my mum. I hardened my heart against Baird, drawing on the numbness that had gotten me through the worst last years with her.

By the time I parked up on Hart Street Lane, Baird had charged his phone and was calling me. Remembering how he had a habit of turning up at my door, I restarted the car and drove to Beth and Callan's, only three minutes from my place.

Dad and Grace would just get angry at Baird if they saw me right now. Weirdly, there was a part of me that didn't want that.

Beth and Callan loved Baird.

They were Switzerland.

I needed Switzerland for the night.

Beth was surprised to hear my voice on the other side of the intercom and the concerned look on her face only grew more so at whatever she saw on mine when she opened the door to their penthouse flat.

Callan hovered at her back.

"Maia, what's wrong?"

"Can I stay here tonight?" I asked, my voice sounding strange even to my ears.

"Of course." My cousin ushered me inside, shooting her fiancé worried glances. "Maia, what happened?"

I shook my head. "Can I explain later?"

"Okay."

"I'm tired." I sounded like a robot.

"I'll show you to the guest room."

"Don't tell Baird where I am." I turned to Callan. He pinched his lips together but nodded. "Thanks." Numbly, I followed Beth down a hall to their guest room.

"Can I get you anything?" she asked quietly.

I shook my head, slowly lowering onto the bed. "I just want to sleep."

"Maia, you're freaking me out."

Guilt suffused me. I was crashing at their flat and acting like a weirdo. I tried to infuse some feeling into my words.

"I'm fine. I'm avoiding Baird. I'll explain in the morning." When the truth would finally come out.

I was going to lose my job tomorrow.

I'd lost Baird.

And I'd lost my job.

I clung to the numbness like I was hanging on to a cliff for dear life. Because if I let go, my cousin would witness an emotional breakdown the likes of which would embarrass me for the rest of my life.

"Tomorrow," Beth whispered and slipped out of the room, closing the door behind her.

It was deeply unsettling ... how quickly your life could change.

CHAPTER TWENTY-TWO
BAIRD

A bang woke me up from a fitful sleep.

Exhaustion pulled at my eyelids, my limbs; my back hurt, my arse was numb, and my sprained ankle throbbed like a motherfucker. Scrubbing my face, my beard prickling against my palms, I tried to wake up. Nausea rolled through my stomach, and not just from a lack of sleep, as I blinked against the light now spilling across the landing outside Maia's flat.

I scrambled for my phone to check the time.

Six thirty and she hadn't come home.

Worry gnawed at my gut.

Along with remorse and self-loathing.

Last night was a big fucking wake-up call.

Aye, okay. I could admit it. I was messed up about cracking my skull open last year.

I didn't want to face the fact that I was scared every time I walked onto the pitch now. I didn't want to face that it had fundamentally changed how I felt about a sport that was so much a part of me, I considered it a piece of my personality.

Football had been the one thing in my life I was class at. School had never come easy because I hated having to sit still for long periods. Reading and spelling had never been my thing, and I was better at digesting information through more interactive mediums.

I constantly felt like I was failing in the classroom. But the football pitch was where I excelled. It became the place where I could play out all my frustrations and worries, all the adolescent anger I'd felt toward the dad who had abandoned me. It was the place where I succeeded and made my family proud. It was the place I found blokes just like me who had become an extension of my family.

It was my safe place.

Until it wasn't.

And that broke something inside me.

But that was no excuse for what I said to Maia last night. Just because she'd seen right through my bullshit, I'd punished her for it in the worst way. I'd made her feel ... emotion clogged my throat as the look on her face kept flashing across my mind.

I'd hurt the one person who meant everything to me.

My chest burned with the ache of how painful that was.

"You know what I can't believe ... that for a second, I actually thought something real was happening between us."

Goddamn it.

"I did let you in more than I've ever let anyone in."

Fuck, fuck, fuck.

"Don't call me ever again, Baird. I don't need another person like you in my life making me feel like shit about myself."

That ... that was my wake-up call. Raising my phone to call Maia again, I winced as it rang for two seconds and cut out. It didn't even go to voicemail. Shit, I hoped she hadn't blocked me.

The bang that had woken me out of a dazed sleep rang through the building again, and I realized it was the front entrance. Footsteps sounded, ascending toward me. I tensed, phone dangling from my fingers as the footsteps kept coming.

Then there she was.

Relief and apprehension mingled as I straightened from my slump.

Maia abruptly stopped.

Her eyes looked tired behind her glasses and her hair was a mess. Her clothes were rumpled, like she'd slept in them.

She was the most gorgeous thing I'd ever seen.

Her lips parted, her nostrils flared. "What ... how long have you been there?"

I winced, pushing up to my feet and feeling every inch of having slept outside her flat. "All night."

"What?" She fingered her keys nervously. "Why would you do that?"

"Because I was waiting for you to come home." I rubbed a hand through my hair, heart rate increasing. "I was worried when you didn't."

She skirted past me, as if trying to avoid us touching.

Damn it.

"Where were you?"

Maia cut me a wary look, which hurt worse than if she'd glared daggers at me. "Beth and Callan's."

At least she'd been somewhere safe. "Maia, I need to apologize."

She stuck her keys in her door, shaking her head. "I have to get ready for work."

"You're right. I'm scared," I blurted out.

She paused but didn't look at me.

"Every time I walk on that pitch, I'm scared. And it … it fucking hurts, My. Because it's been my home for most of my life. It's been who I am. I don't know how to exist in a world where the pitch isn't a safe place anymore."

At the choked emotion in my voice, Maia looked up at me. Despite the nasty lies I spewed at her, those gorgeous violet eyes were filled with pain. For me. "Bear …"

I forced myself not to go to her. To maintain a distance for her sake. "You were right about everything. I've been trying to psych myself out of it by doing stupid shit that could hurt me, or worse. Trying to numb it with partying and drinking."

She waited for me to continue.

"I lashed out at you because you were trying to make me face the truth."

Tears flooded her eyes, and I could feel the burn in mine because I hated that I was responsible for them.

"I said what I said because I'm a dick. I'm a dick because I let my fear do that. But not just my fear." I leaned into her, feeling the truth brim over. "It was my frustration and impatience … because I've wanted you as more than a friend since the moment we met."

Her lips parted with surprise.

I shook my head. "That it could shock you that my feelings for you have never been platonic pisses me off because you should know how special you are, Maia. How fucking *lovable* you are," I said pointedly. "There is no way you will ever end up alone or unloved. Never. I feel sick to my stomach that I said that to you."

"Bear …" Her breathing hitched as she searched my face for the truth.

"I said yes to a fake marriage with you because I fully intended to make you see how real it could be for us."

There.

The truth was out.

Maia gasped. "What?"

"You heard me." I stepped in close now, my palms resting on her door above her head, caging her in. Our noses almost touched and there was that wee hitch in her breathing again. That wee hitch gave me hope. "I'm sorry, My. I'm sorry for hurting you. You are the last person I would ever want to hurt. And I want to be with you. Not just for the campaign. But for real."

Her breathing was harsh, short, and sharp, her cheeks flushed. "Even ... even knowing what you know about me?"

Jesus, I could kill her mother for the damage she'd wrought. "What I know is that there is no one like you and any man would be lucky to belong to you," I whispered.

Her eyes turned glassy again. "I have serious trust issues, Bear."

"I know. I'm not scared of your trust issues."

"We would be diving into the deep end. We're supposed to get *married* in two months."

"I know. It was my idea." I grinned, sensing her defenses crumbling.

"I ... I don't like when you flirt with other people, and you need to be able to be——"

Damn it. "Not flirting with other people because it means something to you isn't a hardship. I'm quite happy to direct all my sexual energy at you."

"You can be a one-woman guy?"

"I've been a one-woman guy since the moment we met."

Something flickered over her expression. "No, you haven't."

"Emotionally, I have. For months, I thought I'd have to

watch you marry another man, and you have no idea how much that killed, My. If you think for one second that now that I have a shot at making you mine I would jeopardize that by fucking around, then you don't know me at all."

"Bear—"

"I will convince you." I stepped back, even though it was the last thing I wanted to do. "I'm going to let you process everything because as much as I want you, I want you to want me back and not just physically."

She continued to gape at me as I retreated toward the staircase. "Bear ..."

"Take all the time you need," I forced out. "I'll be here when you've decided what you want." Then with all the willpower I had, I turned and began to descend the stairs, trying not to wince at my bad ankle.

"Text me when you get home so I know you're okay," she called out, her voice shaking.

"I will, beautiful."

"And we're going to talk about the football pitch no longer being a safe place. You can't just tell me that and expect me to forget about it or leave you alone in it."

I grinned, knowing whatever happened, I was forgiven. "I know. I promise we'll talk," I called back. "See you soon."

Hopefully sooner rather than later.

CHAPTER TWENTY-THREE

MAIA

At the beep of my phone, I stuffed my hand in my dress pocket, in such a hurry to see if it was Baird responding to my text that it flew from my fingers when I plucked it out.

It bounced off the back of the head of the man in front of me.

I gasped. "Oh my goodness, I'm so sorry!" My cheeks flamed hotly as he turned to glare at me.

Grace, who sat on my left, smothered her laughter as I awkwardly fumbled to collect my phone from the space between our feet. Once my phone was in hand, I pushed back my hair and straightened in my seat, offering the man another hurried apology.

His expression softened into a flirty smirk. "I'll forgive you if you put my number in your phone."

Okay, I had to hand it to him—that was smooth.

Before I could respond, my dad's palm shot out between me and the guy. "Not with my daughter, Ric."

Ric's gaze flew to Dad who had stretched past from his position on Grace's left to intervene. We were currently sitting in the stands of a local football ground near Grace and Dad's house, watching Lockie play against a team from Glasgow in the under 16s league.

"Your daughter?" Ric gaped, glancing between me and Dad. "Never, mate."

"Had her young. That still means you're too old for her, so keep your eye on your son and off my kid." Dad's tone held more than a hint of warning.

"She's engaged, anyway, so the point is moot," Grace reminded us with a sweet smile, trying to deflect the tension.

"Aye, okay." Ric seemed unbothered but then turned around while rubbing the back of his head.

I did feel guilty, but it didn't stop me from holding my phone screen up to my face.

It *was* Baird.

Before we arrived at the game, I'd texted him.

> I know you're giving me space, but I'm checking in. I'm here if you need to talk.

I was so worried now he'd finally admitted he was messed up about the game after his injury.

He'd finally texted back.

> All OK. Wth the lads at Blantyre 2day. U ok?

My fingers flew over the screen.

> Watching Lockie's match. As long as you're really OK??

I'd barely lowered the phone when it beeped again.

My heart flipped at Baird's response.

I'll be fine. Next time u txt or call it'll be cos
ur ready 2 talk about us.

Muttering under my breath at his stubbornness, I tucked the phone back into my pocket.

"Yes, Lockie!" Dad suddenly roared, standing up and clapping with a bunch of other parents.

Damn it, I'd missed my brother score a goal. "Bloody men distracting me," I huffed, watching my wee brother celebrate with his teammates.

Grace nudged me with her shoulder even as she clapped along with Dad. "You know the last time you acted like this over a boy was when you had a crush on Charlie!" she yelled over the cheering.

Charlie had been my high school boyfriend and my first big infatuation. I'd met him when I moved to Edinburgh to live with Dad, and we'd dated all through high school until I left for university in London. He went to Aberdeen, and I didn't want to do the long-distance thing. Looking back on it, it was because I didn't trust him not to fall for someone else. At the time I thought what we had was love, but if it was, it was puppy love. It wasn't all-encompassing, passionate, can't stop thinking about him, miss him when he wasn't there love.

Neither was what I'd felt for Will.

I was starting to worry I was incapable of letting go long enough to feel that way about someone. If Baird was as deep in it with me as he proclaimed ... well, he was the last person I wanted to hurt by not being able to fully commit.

Was that what was holding me back from going for it with him?

I leaned into Grace as the cheering died down and the game resumed. "After ... can we talk? Just you and me?"

Grace's brow furrowed with concern, but she nodded. "Of course, sweetheart."

————

The noise from the impromptu garden party could be heard throughout every single room in my parents' home. Lockie's team won because he'd scored twice, and he wanted to invite some of the lads back to our house. Dad had agreed, and now ten kids and their families had crammed into Grace and Dad's back garden while Dad grilled burgers and hot dogs on the rarely used barbecue.

I'd scored a cheeseburger before asking Grace to follow me upstairs.

We could hear Lockie giggling as we walked into Grace and Dad's bedroom. I followed the sound to the window and looked out to see Dad making my wee brother laugh as they worked the grill together.

Grace sighed contentedly at my side as we watched them for a few seconds. Lockie was a miniature version of Dad. They were like two peas in a pod in more ways than one. Strangely, I was more like Grace, even though we weren't blood related.

"I wish every day was like today," Grace murmured, a familiar tender love in her eyes. "But then we'd never recognize how precious these moments are if life was plain sailing."

It was that kind of perceptiveness and love that had brought me and Dad together and held us together through the turmoil of him finding out he had a surprise daughter. It was Grace's love that helped Dad through the trauma of his imprisonment. I still remembered his night-mares and how much they scared me. How Grace seemed to be the only one who could soothe him. That was still true.

"Do you think I'll ever love anyone the way you love Dad? The way he loves you?"

Her gaze flew to mine in surprise. "You already do. You love us that much."

"Of course I do. I meant ... romantically."

"Oh." Grace took my hand and led me over to the end of the bed to sit with her. "Is that what you wanted to talk about? Is it about Will? Or Baird?"

"I haven't heard from Will." It was true. After he showed up at my flat, I hadn't heard from him again. "It's a relief to have cut him out, and I don't know what that says about me."

"It says you didn't love him. More than that, I think it says he didn't make you feel good about yourself."

See? Perceptive. "Did you know that before I broke up with him?"

Grace nibbled on her lip a little nervously.

"Grace?"

She exhaled slowly. "You're a grown woman and so I leave you to make up your own mind about people. But did I have my doubts about Will? Yes."

"Did Dad?"

Grace wrinkled her nose. "Well ..."

"Grace!"

"Your father didn't like him. He was only nice to him for your sake. But he thought he was pretentious and cared too much about money."

"Why didn't you guys tell me that?"

"Because our opinions matter to you, and as lovely as

that is, we didn't want our opinion screwing anything up for you."

Impulsively, I pulled her into a tight hug. Grace snorted in surprise but embraced me in return. She kissed the top of my head and asked, "What's this for?"

"For being the best parents ever." I sighed and pulled back, revealing all my troubled thoughts in my expression.

She cupped my face tenderly. "Sweetheart, what is going on?"

I told her everything. About my friendship with Baird. My growing feelings. My worries about his mental state. Our argument when I tried to get him to talk to me. Running off to Beth. Beth who had been checking in with me every day to see how I was doing, even though I'd updated her on the ongoing saga between me and Baird. Then I revealed what Baird had told me about having real feelings for me from the start.

"Well, anyone could see that, sweetie." Grace gave me a disbelieving look. "How could you not?"

"Seriously?"

"Seriously. Even your dad said Will was in trouble the moment he saw you and Baird together."

"No way!"

She chuckled. "Yes, way. My goodness, Maia ... Baird might be a gregarious character and a flirty charmer, but he watches you like a hawk when you're in a room together. He follows you around like a puppy dog trying to entertain you and garner your affection."

My lips twitched at her description.

"Why do you think I was worried about the engagement? I was worried for *his* sake. I thought you were in denial about his true feelings for you."

"I wasn't in denial," I replied a wee bit breathlessly,

disbelieving I could have been so blind. "I just ... Baird is gorgeous and popular and a total player. Why would he give up his chance with as many women as he wants to be with me?" Tears brightened my eyes. "He said I'm all he wants and I'm all he's wanted since we met. But why is it so hard for me to believe that? I'm so afraid to believe it because he could hurt me. And I'm so afraid that even if I give into this thing between us, I'll always have a hand up, holding him back ... that I'll never let myself love him because of it."

My stepmum's eyes brightened with sympathetic tears as she reached to cup my face in her palms. Her thumbs wiped at my falling tears. "My darling Maia ... you and I are so similar in so many ways. My family, just like your mum, made me feel unworthy. And small. And somewhere along the line, I started to believe it. So ... when a very good-looking man moved into my building, one who was so much of a player he makes Baird's escapades look like child's play, I was immediately on the defense with him."

"Dad," I whispered. I still remembered the day I turned up at his flat to tell him who I was, and he was out on the landing arguing with Grace. There was such a spark between them even then that I thought they were a couple in the middle of an argument.

"I couldn't imagine why it would be me, of all women, that would make him want to settle down. Doesn't it sound familiar, Maia?"

My shoulders slumped. "I hate that you felt that way." Grace was the classiest, smartest, kindest woman I'd ever met. She challenged Dad. She always had. And he challenged her back. No one in their right mind would look at them together and think they were anything but a perfect match.

Her lovely eyes washed over my face. "I hate that your mum planted a seed that's grown so out of control in your mind that you can't see past its weeds and thorns to what everyone else sees. Maia, you're beautiful in all the ways that really matter. You're kind and thoughtful and you abhor bullies and try to make everyone feel seen. You have the capability and drive that people often mistake for confidence when it's just sheer determination to never return to the life you were born into. Then there's the beauty you have on the outside. I hate to say it, Maia, but I think it's just as much to blame for the way you see yourself as your mum's neglect was."

"What do you mean?"

"You have a physical beauty that terrifies your dad and always has because it makes you a target for unkind people. Yet the fact that you're so spectacularly unaware of how lovely you are is one of my favorite things about you. But not when it stands in the way of you seeing yourself clearly." She leaned closer so our noses almost touched. "There will always be shallow people who see your physical beauty as a threat. They'll make assumptions about your character. And they'll either try to tear you down so you don't see yourself clearly anymore or they'll *want* you because of the way you look, and they'll put so much stock into its value, they'll try to make you believe you're not that valuable, just so they don't lose you."

I sucked in a breath at her revelations because I knew she was talking about Will.

And possibly every other boyfriend I'd ever had, except for Charlie, who was too sweet to do that to anyone.

"I'm not that pretty," I huffed out.

Grace shook her head, laughing quietly, sadly. "Yes, you are, my darling."

"People are shallow arseholes, aren't they?" I muttered, tears burning my eyes as I thought about interactions and relationships I'd had over the years. Truthfully, I had been judged before people really knew me. I think my use of clothes and makeup to present myself to the world in a way that I wouldn't be shamed had only reinforced people's preconceived ideas about me.

"They can be. But Baird sees you for more than that, My. When he looks at you, he's really looking at *you*. And he very much likes what he sees."

Had Baird really been that obvious? Had I really been that blind? "Really?"

"Yes. You know I would never steer you wrong. So, when he tells you that he's wanted a real relationship with you from the moment you met, *I* believe him. I think if you dig deep enough, you do too."

———

BAIRD

The sea air ruffled my hair as we stood on the balcony off the second-floor ballroom, staring out toward the coast and the sea beyond. Blantyre Castle and Estate had captured my and Callan's attention because of its location. Close to the city but on the coast. Views from the bedrooms and public rooms. Large, manicured grounds.

Thankfully, the grounds had been maintained over the years, so it was just about upkeep. However, expensive things hadn't been updated. Like the roof and plumbing and electrical. Since walls and floors needed to be ripped up, that meant there was also a massive level of redecoration and restoration currently in progress. The construction of the spa building on the west of the property was also well underway. Once it was all completed and we came up with a solid marketing plan, we intended Blantyre to become the ultimate luxury destination.

"What do you think?" John asked at my side.

"It's on track, looking good."

"Lads."

We turned to find Braden Carmichael and Callan standing in the ballroom, dust sheets and scaffolding everywhere.

"Lunch is being served on the terrace." Braden gave a jerk of his chin and turned. Callan fell into step beside him, and John and I followed.

John chatted about the spa construction. Up ahead Callan said something that made Braden laugh. The older man squeezed the back of Callan's neck in a fatherly gesture.

I smiled to myself, happy for Callan. When Beth turned out to be his neighbor, I knew his antagonistic response to the gorgeous woman from his past meant something. I'd been a bit of a fucker and tried to push him toward her, with whatever means necessary. Including making him jealous by flirting my arse off with her.

Finally, they'd gotten their shit together, started a casual thing that anyone with a brain could see was going to blow up in their faces. I'd never seen my best mate so gone for a woman. It was a relief to all involved when Beth and Callan admitted they were in love and got engaged.

The bonus for Callan was Beth's parents. My mate had lost his mum and stepdad when he was a teenager. His dad was the shittiest dad that existed. He was so bad, it made me glad mine was in the fucking wind. Braden was an over-protective father and was slow to trust anyone with Beth. But he was a good guy. He recognized Callan was serious about her. And since he knew Callan's dad from back in the day, he also knew what Callan had to deal with. He'd set aside protective dad mode and set about making Callan feel like a son.

For that alone, Braden would have my loyalty and thanks. The fact that his experience in the business world and in real estate was making our investment in Blantyre worthwhile was second to what he'd done for Callan personally.

"Your mind is elsewhere," John observed, hands in his pockets as we walked through the castle and onto the grounds where a table had been laid out. Servers waited to serve us lunch. This was the life, eh?

"Just wondering if you're happy?" I responded, not untruthfully.

My friend sighed. "I'm not going to lie to you and say I'm not depressed about not playing ... but I'm into this." He gestured around us. "More than I thought I'd be. And it is the smarter avenue to invest my energy in. Football players retire early even when there are teams clambering to sign them."

That they did. Which was why Callan and I had started our property management business five years ago, making sure we invested our six-figure contract money into some-thing that would last beyond our football years.

I'd always assumed I would retire in my late thirties either because I'd aged out or because of injury.

Now I wasn't so sure about anything. Especially after finally admitting my fears out loud to Maia.

We took a seat at the table with Callan and Braden.

Callan's soon-to-be father-in-law was tall, broad of shoulder, thick of biceps. There was no middle-aged belly to be found on the bloke. The guy was kind of my hero. I saw women checking him out all the time, even though he didn't so much as glance at them. I wouldn't either with a sexy wife like his. Not that I'd say that to his face. I'd learned the hard way when I flirted with Joss Carmichael at one of their house parties. Braden Carmichael was possessive, even decades into their marriage. He'd given me a look that might have killed a lesser man. And when I'd responded, "Got it. No flirt-y without permission-y," Joss had gently shoved me away and whisper-shouted, "Run. Save yourself."

I think she was only partly joking.

Once the food was in front of us, Braden took a sip of coffee and eyed me with a glint in his steely blue gaze I wasn't sure I understood or liked. "So ... the social media campaign for Pennington's is going well."

John groaned as Callan grimaced.

Braden frowned. "What? Did I say something out of turn?"

John shook his head. "I just ... wouldn't bring it up."

I'd told the lads about my fight with Maia, mostly because Callan already knew. I'd told them the truth about everything (John had already guessed, anyway) and explained I'd confessed all to her and that Maia was taking her sweet time processing. I didn't tell them she was also texting me every day out of concern and how much that wasn't helping me not love her more than I already fucking did.

Braden narrowed his eyes on me. "What did you do?"

"Me?" I huffed indignantly. "Why do you assume it was me?"

"Maia is like a niece to me," he explained, his tone filled with warning. "Until proven otherwise, you're the guilty party. What happened?"

Shit. I forgot these people were like a fucking Scottish clan of old. They all saw one another as family, even though they weren't blood related. I usually thought it was class. But not now because it also meant they all thought they were entitled to know everything that was going on within their clan.

"Just tell him." Callan shrugged. "You've already told her, and she's probably told her mum and dad."

"I haven't told her everything. I don't want to frighten her off."

"What *have* you told her?" Braden asked with a casualness that belied his predatory countenance.

These fucking clansmen.

Ach, well, what did it matter, anyway? "The campaign was fake. Maia got roped into it at work and needed a fiancé fast after she and Will broke up. I stepped up to the plate and agreed to be her fake fiancé and marry her for the campaign."

"What?" Braden shook his head and turned to Callan. "See what you inspired?" He referred to the fact that Callan and Beth started out as a fake relationship because Beth was trying to deter a bloke who fancied her and could mess with her business if she turned him down. Not that most people knew that at the time. They'd confessed it all later.

Callan snorted before taking a sip of water.

Braden turned back to me. "Being straightforward usually works better."

"Does it?" I scrubbed a hand over my beard. "I only said yes because I have real feelings for Maia and thought this would finally wake her up to what she and I could have. But

I told her I really care about her, and I said she should take time to think about it ... and fuuuuuck, is she taking time."

The older man considered me. "Is Maia just a passing fancy or—"

"She's the one," I bit out, not liking any hint of suggestion that I just wanted to fuck her. "Though I haven't explicitly told her that. She's gun-shy. Don't want to scare her off. But maybe I already have."

Braden grinned, shaking his head. "You of the younger generation lack something quintessential when it comes to women."

"Aye?" I raised an eyebrow. "Enlighten us, Obi-Wan."

He cut me a dry look. "Patience. And then if patience doesn't work, I found that bulldozing your way through a woman's defenses does."

"Bulldozing?" I shook my head. "That's sounds red-flaggish. I'm a green fucking flag, mate."

"I'd agree if I knew what you were talking about. I don't regret what I did to get past Jocelyn's mile-high defenses. I ended up with the kind of marriage most people could only dream of having." He shrugged arrogantly.

Curiosity had me asking, "What did you do?"

His grin was wolfish. "Jocelyn didn't want to care about me beyond sex. I used sex to get past her defenses. Got her to talk to me, confide in me. When I knew what I was dealing with, I played dirty. Made her jealous so she'd see that one day I might not be around and that the thought of me with someone else was painful. Woke her up to admitting she was in love with me. It pissed her off, but making up afterward was fun."

"Did you cheat?" John asked curiously.

Callan tensed. "I don't think I should be hearing this."

Braden's expression hardened. "No, I didn't cheat. I

flirted. We weren't exclusive, so I might have lied about being with someone else just to get a reaction."

"That's brutal." Callan gaped at him.

"It was, but with Jocelyn it was necessary. And it worked. So while I felt like an arsehole at the time, I can't regret it now."

"Baird is good at flirting with other women," John stated the obvious.

I shook my head. "Trust me, flirting with other women will only push Maia away."

"Then don't. Know your audience. Maia ... I assume you're aware of her past?"

I nodded.

"Then you know why Maia has walls up. She has good reasons. Whatever you do, you don't give up with someone like Maia because that's what she expects. To not be worth the effort when we both know she is. Even if it hurts your pride, you keep at it until you win her trust. Otherwise, you don't deserve her or her trust."

"Pride?" John sought to defuse the sudden tension. "McMillan has no pride when it comes to Maia."

I shrugged. "He's not wrong."

Braden chuckled and relaxed in his seat. "Good. Anyway, I had a reason for bringing the subject up. Is the wedding venue booked for the campaign?"

"Pennington's booked Almondbrae. August 27. Also, you can't tell anyone what I told you, or me and Maia will both be in deep shit legally."

"Do I look like I gossip with the ladies over tea and crumpets?"

I felt it was safer to just shake my head.

"Right. Can Pennington's get out of that contract with Almondbrae?"

I raised a brow. "Why?"

"Because I think we can get the ballroom finished in time for the wedding. You could have the ceremony in there. The reception out here." Braden gestured around us. "All for free in exchange for being featured in the social media campaign. We'll have our system up and running to take bookings eighteen months in advance."

Eighteen months was when we expected to open.

"That's genius." Callan nodded. "What do you think, Baird?"

"I wish I'd thought of it," I agreed. "But it'll be up to Pennington's."

"Somehow I think you'll persuade them." Braden grinned the cocky grin of a man used to getting what he wanted. "Who can turn down free?"

I snorted and nodded. "Fair enough. I'll see what I can do."

Hopefully by the day of the wedding, when Maia said "I do," it would be as real for her as it will be for me.

CHAPTER TWENTY-FOUR
MAIA

For the umpteenth time that morning, I found my mind drifting to Baird, the dress in my hands blurring before me.

I missed him.

He was doing as promised and hadn't been in touch all week. We had a promo shoot tomorrow, so I knew it would be better if we had a chance to talk before then.

However, now my heart was causing my brain to do emotional, mental gymnastics. Like ... was the reason Baird hadn't texted because he'd decided with some space that he didn't want to be with me for real after all? Rationally, I knew I was most likely wrong since he'd explicitly said we wouldn't talk again until *I* was ready to talk about us. But I wasn't feeling very rational about Baird, which also scared me.

I was spiraling. See me spin in descent.

"Maia. Maia?"

I blinked rapidly, the vivid, color-blocked, calf-length tea dress coming back into focus. Looking up, I found Eli peering at me.

"Are you all right?" they asked, waving a long-nailed hand at me. "You completely spaced out there."

"Sorry." I winced. I needed to focus on my job. We were supposed to be curating a special summer collection for next year's Ascot to be sold in our London stores. Lifting the dress, I grimaced. "I think it's all wrong. Nay for me."

"Agreed." Eli pursed their lips. "It's giving me Lady Gaga rather than Lady FitzRoy."

Nodding, I placed the dress on the rack for the products we had discounted. Designers sent us samples from their upcoming collections, and we decided what we wanted to sell in store. However, we were pulling the Ascot feature together from clothing we'd already decided to sell in store next summer, which meant going through the entire wardrobe of samples we'd collated for the next year.

"Knock, knock."

I tensed at the sound of Becky's voice but turned to watch her walk into the room. She beamed at Eli, gesturing to their platform mules. "You bitch. You beat me to the Gucci!"

Eli grinned smugly. "I told you I would, Becks. Don't they look fabulous?" They twisted their ankle so "Becks" could get a better look.

"So fabulous. You wear them better than I ever could," she said with apparent genuineness.

It wasn't a shocking interaction. Becky was always friendly to Eli and Liza. As she focused on me, there was a barely perceptible chilly transformation.

"Sorry to disturb you, but Hilary has asked to see you. It's urgent."

Eli made an *O* shape with their lips.

A sense of dread took over as I instantly began to worry

if Becky had done something else to fuck me over. "Is anything the matter?"

She gave me a shrug, but I didn't like the spiteful gleam in her eyes. "She needs to talk in five." She threw Eli another smile. "Drinks. The Dome. Seven o'clock. Liza too."

"We'll be there, darling, Gucci and all."

"Not even a hint?" I asked Becky's back.

She glanced over her shoulder. "You'll see," she replied in a singsong voice before strutting off.

And I knew.

She was up to something.

Eli's brow furrowed. "What is that about?"

It shouldn't bother me that Becky was so friendly with my members of staff or that they couldn't see the passive-aggressive nastiness and fake sweetness she treated me to. But it was irritating and made me feel paranoid and isolated.

Yet, after my chat with Grace, I was beginning to wonder if that wasn't exactly what she intended. Maybe I hadn't done anything to upset Becky, and maybe it was time to stop questioning and start sticking up for myself.

I wasn't being paranoid.

"Did ... I don't suppose Becky said something to Liza about me?"

Eli pursed their lips and turned to snatch up a tailored pencil dress. "This is more Ascot, no?"

My pulse rushed in my ears. "Eli? Please, if you know something..."

They rolled their eyes with a sigh and put the dress back on the rack. "Okay, but Becks and I are friends, so I'd feel like I was talking out of school if I were to tell you."

"Eli?"

"Ugh, I'm only telling you this because I'd quite like to know your reasons myself. Becks let it slip to Liza that you were the reason Liza and I didn't get a Christmas bonus last year. She said you told management we hadn't done anything to deserve it and that assistants and assistant buyers shouldn't be considered for bonuses."

My heart pounded harder. "What?"

Eli raised an eyebrow. "You look genuinely shocked by that."

"That's because it's a lie!" I shook my head, lowering my voice. "Eli, why would you believe that? Does that seem like the kind of boss I am? Plus, Becky has no insider knowledge on those things. She works in marketing, not payroll."

"She said Hilary told her."

"I've worked for this company for almost a decade, and I can tell you right now that Hilary Erstwhile does not talk out of school. Becky lied. And just so we're clear, I will be speaking to Liza about this as your boss," I reminded them gently. "I will always be honest. You did not get a Christmas bonus last year because it wasn't in the budget. *I* didn't get a Christmas bonus, and Christina refused the one she was offered in solidarity. So, I hope you both feel really silly for believing that nonsense."

"It was a lie?"

My head whipped around to find Liza standing in the doorway, gaping at me.

It was then I realized I hadn't just let Becky walk all over me; I'd let my so-called subordinates. "Yes, it was a lie."

Liza stepped into the room, cheeks flushed red. "Why would Becky lie?"

"I can't answer that. What I can tell you from now on is that I won't be treated with disrespect in my own department. For too long I've allowed your bad attitude to continue, wondering what I'd done to upset you. It turns out, nothing." I glanced angrily between my two employees. "Liza, I expect you to treat me better from now on, or I will find another assistant buyer. I'm done being walked over by you and by Becky. Are we clear?" My hands were shaking so hard, I clenched them into fists at my sides.

Liza nodded, wide-eyed. "Of course. I'm sorry."

I looked at Eli.

They grinned. "Brava, boss. That was a long time coming and I'm very proud of you."

"Well, thank you. I think I'll go be sick now."

They chuckled as Liza stared at me in confusion and embarrassment.

"Not before you see Hilary."

"Oh hell." I almost forgot about that. "Keep working. Liza, help Eli. Hopefully, I won't be too long."

My legs were still trembling as I made my way to Hilary's office, but I didn't have a pit of dread in my stomach. In fact, Eli's response had bolstered me. I decided that if Liza was willing to believe Becky's nonsense, then I didn't really care about what she thought of me. As long as she started treating me with respect, then that's all that mattered.

Knocking on Hilary's door, I wondered if I should have insisted on Christina being here for whatever this was.

Becky opened it, gesturing for me to come in. I concealed my need to glare at the snake as I strode inside. What other wee lies had she been whispering into the ears of my colleagues?

My boss's boss abruptly ended the call she was on and stood, gesturing for me to take the seat across from her desk. Her countenance gave nothing away as to the reason she'd called me in here.

Becky, to my everlasting irritation, remained in the office, standing by the door.

As soon as I took a seat, Hilary rounded the desk to sit on its edge. "It's been brought to my attention that there is trouble in paradise."

My chin jerked in surprise. Not what I'd been expecting. "Excuse me?"

"Apparently, you and the groom-to-be aren't on speaking terms."

What the ... I looked at Becky ... and there! She let that malicious smile shine. Hilary cut her a look and Becky wiped her expression clean. Like a naughty schoolgirl hiding her evil intentions from the teacher.

Anger threatened to boil over, but I wouldn't give Becky the satisfaction. I held Hilary's questioning gaze instead. "I don't know what you've heard, but you've been misinformed. It seems there's a lot of that going around."

"Whatever do you mean?"

I didn't want to play into Becky's games by informing Hilary her marketing manager was a conniving cow. "Just that you've been misinformed."

"Really? Because Becky overheard an argument between you and Baird, and apparently, you haven't been seen together all week. You could see how this might negatively impact our campaign."

Stay calm. Stay calm.

I didn't know what Becky's intentions were with this new manipulation. Moreover, I didn't know how far she would take whatever this bullshit vendetta was against me, but was it possible she was following me?

No. She was a catty colleague. She wasn't unstable.

Right?

"I think Becky must have misheard something because I know she wouldn't intentionally misinform you," I replied with a polite tone that deserved an award for its ambivalence. "Baird and I are still together, still in love, and still very much dedicated to the campaign. It's been a busy week for him with his other business and his summer training, so we haven't been socializing in public. That doesn't mean we're not with each other at home." Becky couldn't prove it otherwise, unless she was willing to admit to some creepy stalking.

Hilary nodded and stood. "Good. That's great to hear. I'm sorry for interrupting your workday, but you understand we have a lot invested in this and I had to ask." She cut Becky an annoyed glower and gestured for her to move away from the door. "Let Maia return to work and you should too."

The door to Hilary's office had barely closed behind us when Becky stepped into my path, cutting off my escape.

"I know you're lying. I'm just politely warning you now that I will be the first person to come after you if you put this company's reputation in jeopardy."

I'd had enough.

I was sick of her treating me like crap and doing it under the guise of the company's welfare. "Accusing a colleague of lying is a serious accusation, Becky, and one I don't take lightly. For instance, I would never accuse you of telling Eli and Liza that I'm the reason they didn't get a Christmas bonus last year."

Her cheeks flushed red, giving her away. "I don't know what you're talking about."

Feeling brave from having stood my ground with Liza and Eli, I continued. "I don't know what your problem with me is.

But if I find out you're peddling lies, I will be forced to act because I do take slander seriously. If you accuse me of lying again or interfere with my career by, say, putting me forward for a campaign I didn't give you permission to include me in, I am no longer willing to sit back and do nothing. One more misstep and I'll report you to HR." I moved to walk around her.

She grabbed my arm, shocking the heck out of me.

"Release me, or you accosting me right now will be the first complaint I make."

Becky dropped my arm, cheeks beet red, eyes flashing with hatred. "Do it, and I'll tell Hilary you and Baird are faking this."

I tried not to flinch. "Excuse me?"

"That you're a known liar. I know you lied about Will for a month. You didn't split up with Will because of Baird. You split up with Will because he left you for my friend Birgitta. I even know the day he left you. It was the day I told you about the campaign."

Shock and understanding dawned. Was this why she hated me? Because she was poisoned against me by Birgitta?

Wait.

Did she just inadvertently admit she knew we were broken up when she put me forward for the campaign?

"If you knew the day I left Will, then you put me forward for this social media campaign knowing Will and I had broken up, and it would put me in a really difficult position with Pennington's if they chose us."

Her expression slammed closed as she took a step back.

"You did this deliberately. To damage my reputation here."

No answer. Just that stony glare.

"Why?" I wanted to know for sure. "What have I ever done to you, Becky? Please tell me. Is it because you're friends with Birgitta?"

She sniffed haughtily. "I don't have a problem with you, Maia. You should really talk to a professional about your paranoia." She smiled that saccharine fake smile and strutted past me.

Angry, frustrated tears threatened. I didn't have an answer for Becky's behavior, but I knew with certainty that this wasn't over. She was determined to make things so hard for me here ... to make me leave? To get me fired? And she was doing it in a way that made it hard to prove.

In that moment, there was only one person I wanted to see.

The person who did believe me.

As if Baird heard my thoughts, he texted me during my lunch break.

> We should talk b4 the venue promo shoot
> 2mrrow.

I started to spiral again, wondering if that meant he'd changed his mind. Had I left it too long to respond to his declaration?

My fingers trembled as I replied.

> Why don't we meet for a swim tomorrow
> before the shoot?

His response was instantaneous.

> Usual time. C U there.

No flirting. No banter. Straight to the point.

Oh goodness. My stomach flipped unpleasantly. What if he'd changed his mind?

Panic suffused me at the very thought.

Just like that, with such inconvenient timing, I knew exactly what I wanted to happen between us.

I had to hope I wasn't too late.

CHAPTER TWENTY-FIVE
MAIA

Between today's revelations about Becky, the anticipation of seeing Baird tomorrow, and not knowing how things between us would pan out, I was a jittery mess when I rang Joss and Braden Carmichael's doorbell that evening.

My pseudo-aunt and -uncle were hosting a college graduation party for their son Luke. Luke was the middle Carmichael child. Beth was the eldest and Elle the youngest at sixteen. Luke had graduated from Glasgow in prelaw and was attending Edinburgh's law school after the summer. He'd decided to come back home because his Portuguese boyfriend Afonso was attending the same law school at Edinburgh and Luke didn't want to be without him. They'd been together since freshman year at Glasgow and were madly in love.

Luke was big into his designer clothing, and I often used my Pennington's discount for him. If the party was for anyone else, I'd possibly make my excuses, but I loved Luke, and he deserved to be celebrated for his hard work.

Joss opened the door and pulled me into a hug. "Your

dad and Grace are running late. Apparently, Lockie wanted to sleep at a friend's house tonight so they're dropping him off first."

I rolled my eyes. "Sometimes I'd like to shake some sense into that kid. He doesn't know how lucky he is to have a family this big who want to spend time with him."

She gave me an understanding smile but said, "He's a teen boy. His family are pretty much furniture at this point. He'll come around."

Nodding in agreement, I followed Joss through the huge townhouse to the large kitchen/family room where everyone was already congregated, drinking, snacking, and listening to music as they chatted.

There was Luke and Afonso, Elle, Uncle Braden, and then Braden's sister Aunt Ellie and her husband, Uncle Adam. There was Aunt Shannon with her husband Uncle Cole, and Uncle Cole's sister Aunt Jo and her husband Uncle Cam. Uncle Cam's best friend Uncle Nate and his wife Aunt Olivia, Aunt Ellie's half sister Aunt Hannah, and Aunt Hannah's husband Uncle Marco.

Then all of us kids.

I was the oldest of the second generation. Beth was second eldest. There were also the younger kids who I could hear out in the garden—my cousins, Aunt Shannon and Uncle Cole's kids, Freya and Catriona, and Jo and Cam's youngest, Louis, who was a late baby. There were seven years between him and my cousin Belle, who I didn't see in the room.

I spotted Beth, though. She stood by the island laughing. With Callan *and* Baird.

As if he sensed me, Baird glanced over at the doorway and his dark eyes warmed.

I felt a wee bit breathless. I hadn't known he'd be here. Yet seeing him ... it felt like forever since I'd seen him.

"I'm going to let you process everything because as much as I want you, I want you to want me back and not just physically."

His words from that night replayed in my mind for the millionth time.

"Maia, you made it!" Luke pushed gently through his relatives to cross the room.

I beamed, always happy to see my handsome pseudo-cousin. "Happy graduation!" I held out the package I'd wrapped.

His gorgeous blue eyes lit up. "You didn't have to get me anything." He leaned in to kiss my cheek as he took the gift.

Afonso appeared at his side and eyed my outfit. "Maia, looking chic as always."

I glanced down at my leopard-print slip skirt, cropped black T, and brown leather brogues. This was my casual summer evening look. "Chic? Really?"

"You could wear a paper bag and make it chic," Afonso opined in his lilting Portuguese accent. "It's so unfair. I should hate you for it, but you're so lovely I cannot."

"Well, the gift is for both of you, if that makes you less inclined to hate me," I teased.

The couple's eyes lit up and Afonso gestured for Luke to open it.

During this entire interaction, I was doing my very best not to look over at Baird.

And failing.

January, Lily's younger sister, had appeared beside Baird like a gorgeous wee fairy. The memory of Lily telling me January was crushing on Baird hit me seconds before she pressed her palms to his chest and cocked her head flir-tatiously.

My fingernails bit into my palms, but I focused my attention back to Luke and Afonso.

Luke plucked not one but two bottles of the very expensive cologne I knew they both loved but couldn't afford. Pennington's stocked it, so I'd gotten a discount. "You didn't ..."

I shrugged, thoroughly enjoying the glee on their faces. "I did."

Just like that, I found myself embraced by two very handsome men who peppered my cheeks with kisses. Laughing, my gaze inadvertently met Baird's. His eyes were warm and tender on me.

Hope bloomed in my chest.

Then January cupped Baird's bearded cheek in her palm, somewhat aggressively pulling his attention back to her.

"What the fuck?" I muttered before I could stop myself.

"Oh, aye, that." Luke cocked his head in their direction. "She's been flirting with your fiancé since he walked in the door. You might want to have a wee word."

Before I could approach to do just that, January pressed her entire body against Baird and whatever she murmured to him had him throwing a panicked look in my direction.

That little ... "Excuse me, gentlemen." I marched across the room and Beth turned to greet me before I could snap January like a twig. She threw her arms around me and said between gritted teeth, "Please don't kill her."

My response was a toothless, annoyed smile and a bitten-out hello to Callan. My eyes locked with Baird's. A long, tension-filled silence stretched like there was a string attached to each of us, and it was pulling tauter and tauter ...

Everything—the chatter, the music—all faded around me as I stared into his warm brown eyes.

"Oh, I didn't think you were coming, Maia." January grinned at me like her hands weren't still on my fiancé's chest.

I gave her a pointed look.

Wicked humor lightened her expression as she dropped her hands to her sides. "I was just telling Baird that I suspect your engagement is fake."

Oh, holy hell. Tone even, I asked, "What makes you say that?"

"The evidence is substantial. You were barely broken up with Will. This campaign with Pennington's. Baird's escapades in the newspaper. The fact that the club has a new owner and maybe he didn't like Baird's escapades being in the newspaper. I'm thinking you needed a fiancé, Baird needed to clean up his act, and voilà!"

She really was too smart for her own good. If I wasn't the object of her sleuthing, I'd be so proud.

The only obvious thing to do was to squeeze past Beth, gently maneuver January to the side, and stand so close to my so-called fake fiancé my breasts brushed his chest. I heard his breath stutter as I whispered, "Hi," and then slid my palms over his hard pecs and up behind his neck. The scent of his familiar aftershave and the feel of our bodies touching sent tingles shooting down my nape and around my breasts. Pushing up onto my tiptoes, I feathered my lips over his mouth, once twice—

His arms banded tight around my waist so he could capture me in a deep, entirely inappropriate kiss that made my head spin and arousal tighten deep in my womb.

The wolf-whistling was the only reason Baird released me.

For a moment, we just panted against each other's mouths. My skin was on fire and a throbbing need made itself known between my thighs.

Oh boy.

Remembering we weren't alone, I lowered my heels and looked over my shoulder at January.

Her dark eyes brimmed with amusement. "So ... does that mean you're not up for stepping aside so I can have a crack at him?"

"Baird isn't an object you can have a crack at, Jan. I know men have objectified women for centuries, but reverse objectification is just bad feminism."

"I respectfully disagree."

"Respectfully? Okay, respectfully ... if you flirt with my fiancé again, it'll be me hiding dead fish all over *your* flat."

Jan saluted me. "Message received. I like this new aggressive you. And even though I'm not convinced this shit didn't start out fake, I almost combusted at that kiss, so I'm glad my meddling made you see sense. I'm happy for you, cuz. Will sounded like a bore. Baird is definitely an upgrade." She bounced off to cross the room to push between Lily and her boyfriend Sebastian. Whatever she said made Sebastian howl with laughter.

She'd deliberately flirted with Baird to push us together? "I think she might be the cutest, most devious person I've ever met," I muttered.

Baird squeezed my waist. "I wasn't flirting with her."

I gave him a reassuring smile. "I know."

He was so relieved, I felt his body relax. "You do?"

"I do." I stepped out of his personal space but couldn't help my wandering eyes. Like me, he wore a plain black T-shirt, paired with jeans and black trainers. His only adornment, other than his tattoos, was the carbon smart watch he wore all the time. "You look good."

"You always look good."

There was that strange pulling sensation between us again, like everyone else faded away.

Callan burst our bubble. "If you two are going to stand there eye-fucking each other, take it elsewhere. It's making me extremely uncomfortable."

Baird chuckled.

I shared an exasperated look with Beth. She jerked her chin upward. "The living room on the second floor is empty. It'll give you some privacy to talk."

Grateful, I thanked her and then held out my hand to Baird.

He took it without hesitation, his grip on me unyielding, almost like he was afraid I'd let go. Instead, I led him out of the party, unable to avoid my aunt Shannon's curious gaze. Although I'd chatted with her on the phone about my engagement to Baird, she and I hadn't had a chance to talk face-to-face. I knew by her expression that would change very soon.

The Carmichael townhome was the stuff of Edinburgh dreams. I'd babysat and slept over in this house, so I knew it well. On the ground floor, three doors split off to the huge kitchen Joss and Braden renovated a few years ago, a TV room, a guest bedroom, a bathroom, and Uncle Braden's office. On the next floor was the primary suite, a huge second living room, and Aunt Joss's office where she wrote her bestselling novels. The top floor had belonged to Beth, Luke, and Elle growing up. They each had a bedroom and shared a bathroom. Now I guessed it was just Elle up there. The Carmichaels had modernized the house without taking anything away from its Georgian architecture.

"This place is boss," Baird broke the sizzling silence as I led him upstairs.

"Mmm-hmm." I could barely speak. My heart raced. I was a little lightheaded. Because once he and I stepped into the living room, things between us would change forever.

The problem was we couldn't stay where we were.

We had to change.

I was so scared of losing his friendship.

However, as nervous as I was, I was more afraid of losing out on the possibility of an *us*.

Inside the moody, comfortable living space, I closed the door and released Baird to lean against it.

He stared at where I'd dropped his hand, his expression guarded as he wandered farther into the room. "You wanted to talk?"

"I miss you," I blurted out.

Baird jerked toward me, standing between the coffee table and the large U-shaped sofa. His thoughts were written all over his face, and it gave me courage.

I pushed off the door. "Bear ... if you tell me you're serious about me and that you will never intentionally hurt me, then ... I promise to believe you."

His eyes flared and he took a step toward me, his voice gravelly with emotion. "Maia, I'm serious about you and I will *never* intentionally hurt you."

The blood whooshed in my ears and my pulse raced frantically. My lips trembled around my next words. "Then I'm already yours."

Baird stared at me as if he wasn't quite sure he'd heard me correctly.

"Bear ... are you—"

The distance between us was gone in seconds and his

mouth cut me off as it crashed down over mine. I moaned in relief and hunger. Baird wrapped his strong arms around me, crushing me to his hard chest, and in an instant, my skin was aflame with need.

This was over a year of pent-up sexual attraction turned emotional connection igniting in seconds.

Baird groaned as I met him kiss for desperate kiss and suddenly, my feet were off the floor and his hands were gripping my thighs as we moved backward. He'd lifted me with a startling ease that was a total turn-on. My back hit the door, and my legs wrapped around Baird's hips as his hungry kisses intensified.

When his lips finally left mine, it was to trail kisses along my jaw to my ear, his beard bristling against my skin, my senses on overload. My head spun and somewhere in the back of my mind, I knew we shouldn't be doing this here, but I couldn't make my mouth form the words to stop. Baird's lips returned to mine for another scorching kiss, and all I could think about was him and how he made me feel more alive than I'd ever felt in my life.

He was hard and we were grinding on each other, groaning and moaning with avarice. My hands dipped beneath his tee to explore his sculpted body, and I desperately wanted him naked so I could map every contour with my lips.

Baird suddenly broke our kiss, and I panted for breath, my body trembling with unsatisfied desire. There wasn't just lust in those beautiful dark eyes. There was awe. Baird McMillan looked at me like I was ... *everything*.

The pulse between my legs became insistent. "Bear." I didn't know what I was asking for, but he seemed to know. His features hardened with determined want. I gasped as he lowered me to my feet only to grab the fabric of my skirt, coasting it up my thighs, as he held my gaze.

We shouldn't.

Not here.

We really, really shouldn't.

"We sh-shouldn't," I forced out breathlessly.

"I can't wait." I'd never heard his voice like that. It was this deep, masculine growl dripping with sex, and apparently, it had a direct connection to my erogenous zones. I practically moaned at his tone. "I have been fantasizing about licking your pussy for nearly two years, and I can't fucking wait any longer to taste you."

Oh. My. Holy. Fuuuuuuuuu—my knees literally buckled at his words.

Baird's triumphant expression was followed by his fingers curling into my underwear. I let out another huff of excitement as he roughly yanked my knickers down. "Bear!"

"Ssh, gorgeous." Baird held my eyes as he slowly and deliberately lowered himself to his knees before me.

I widened my thighs. Baird's head disappeared between my legs.

"Oh!" I cried out at the first touch of his tongue and then covered my mouth with my hand. He licked his way up to my clit, and I groaned as sensation spiked down all four limbs. Arousal tightened in exquisite need low in my belly as my hot blood pounded in my ears.

I reached for Baird's head, so unbelievably turned on by the sight of him between my legs I thought said limbs might give out.

His fingers dug into my thighs as he expertly licked and sucked at my clit, tormenting the bundle of nerves until I was struggling to contain my cries and moans of pleasure.

"Bear!" My fingers threaded through his thick hair and curled tight. He growled at the tug and thrust his fingers inside me, the sensation of fullness overwhelming. Weeks of tension shattered with an abruptness that took me aback. I couldn't stop my cry of release as I shuddered and shook against his mouth. Baird lapped up every drop of my orgasm, as if he couldn't get enough.

I sagged against the door, my body tremoring with aftershocks. Baird slowly rose to his feet and pulled me into his arms. His hands soothed down my back as mine caressed his and tears brightened my eyes and stung my nose.

Good tears.

Because even though that was the sexiest thing a man had ever done to me ... he'd also made it feel like more than sex. He'd made me feel ... loved.

"Bear."

"I'm never letting you go now," he whispered in my ear.

"We were supposed to talk," I whispered back. "I ... I want to make sure you've thought this through. Because we'll be launching our relationship straight into the deep end. Marriage in less than two months, in case you forgot that tiny detail."

Baird pulled back to cup my face in his palms, drinking in every aspect of my face. This was the intensity he rarely revealed to anyone. But he let me see this side of him. And I loved that. "I'm already in the deep end, My."

My heart lurched. A euphoric smile flirted with my lips. "Then I think you better take me home so I can return the delicious favor you bestowed upon me."

His grin was big and boyish, the Baird I knew and adored. "You can return that favor after. First ..." His voice roughened, "I need to take you home so I can come inside you."

My cheeks flushed at the imagery that flashed in my mind. I swallowed hard. "What are we waiting for, then?"

CHAPTER TWENTY-SIX

MAIA

We were in no state to talk to anyone, so our plan was to sneak out of the house. However, my aunt Shannon bumped into us as she came out of the downstairs powder room.

Aunt Shannon and I shared the same violet eyes as Dad, except instead of dark hair she had loads of stunning red hair. While I was average height, Aunt Shannon was tiny. She had the kind of youthful appearance that meant people often thought she was far younger than her actual age.

Usually, I loved seeing Aunt Shannon.

But right now, recognizing that knowing gleam in her eyes, I wanted the floor to swallow me whole.

"Leaving so soon?" She quirked an eyebrow, glancing between me and Baird.

"We have somewhere to be."

"Urgently." Baird gave me a gentle nudge toward the door.

Embarrassment scalded my cheeks.

Aunt Shannon shook her head, lips twitching. "I'll tell your dad and Grace something came *up*."

Baird snorted. I groaned in mortification. Aunt Shannon laughed as she strolled off. "Have fun and be safe."

"No, no, no," I huffed out as Baird tugged me toward the door. "That didn't just happen."

He laughed. "It did. Your aunt is funny."

"But she knows we're leaving to have sex," I whisper-shouted.

"I'm pretty sure she knows you're not a virgin, My," he teased, hurrying me down the front stoop and down Dublin Street.

"I just hope she doesn't tell my dad and Grace." I covered my face with my free palm.

Baird released my hand to slide his arm around my waist. "You're so adorable."

I pouted up at him. "No, I'm not adorable right now. I'm sexy. We're in a sexy mood. Adorable is for field mice and puppies."

Baird threw his head back in laughter, almost tripping on a paving stone and taking me with him. I gripped onto him, grinning as he righted himself. There was that look on his face again. Like I was everything. Wow, I could seriously get addicted to that look. "Maia MacLeod, sexy, adorable, wearing your glasses or wearing nothing, I want you all the time, anytime."

"Really?" I bit my lip, pleased.

"Oh, aye." He nodded and then waggled his eyebrows. "And at some point, I want you naked wearing only your glasses."

Laughing, even as my body pulsed with arousal, I replied, "You're so weird."

"But sexy, right?"

"Oh, completely. Now let's hurry up before I combust on Dublin Street."

"That was the longest walk in the history—" I was cut off, hauled into Baird's flat and against his body. His mouth slammed down on mine, and I whimpered, wrapping my arms around him. My fingers curled into his lush hair, and I had a fleeting memory of squashing many a fantasy about tugging Baird's hair out of his manbun. I'd been in denial for a very long time about how much I wanted him. Baird's kiss was thorough and just a wee bit dirty, and I loved it. I met him lick for lick, suck for suck, flicking my tongue against his, our kiss so deep we stumbled backward. Our momentum forced the flat door shut with a crash and we broke away, gasping.

My laughter was cut off by Baird's uncharacteristically severe expression. He looked ready to eat me alive. I shivered, my breasts feeling heavy, my skin burning hotter than it was even five minutes ago as we hurried through New Town to his flat in Dean Village.

I was wet and aching and had been ever since he'd made me come.

Anticipation had me shaking. "Do I have something on my face?" I teased on a whisper.

Baird slowly shook his head. "Nah, I'm just ... I can hardly believe you're here and we're ... here."

He really did want this. Want me. I wish I hadn't been so blinded by my own insecurities. "We're really here," I promised.

He yanked me to him, his hands coasting down my waist and around my back to slide over my bottom. He squeezed gently, and I moaned at the feel of his prodding erection. I rubbed against him, and Baird's hips undulated against me. "Bear, I don't want to wait any longer," I gasped out.

He bent his head and kissed me, and I knew I'd never want to kiss anyone but Baird McMillan ever again. I wanted only his taste, the feel of him. I loved the way his size was dominating and reassuring all at once. My fingers slid under his shirt, tracing the hard, smooth lines of his well-developed six-pack and I sucked on his tongue. Hard.

Baird shuddered and made that growling sound but this time in my mouth.

A mini orgasm fluttered low inside. "Oh!" I pulled back, eyes wide with surprise.

Because it had never been this intense with someone before. This needy. This passionate. Part of me had almost thought all the loved-up couples around me were lying about sex to make themselves feel better.

But they weren't.

It really could feel like every nerve ending in your body was alive and sizzling and sparking at the slightest touch and sound and scent.

I pushed on my tiptoes to press my lips to his again, moaning into his mouth as the kiss turned wild and dirty and breathlessly exciting. Baird's hands gripped my waist, and he lifted me with ease, still kissing me as he walked us in the direction of the back of the room. I lifted my knees so my feet wouldn't drag as I broke the kiss to pepper his bearded cheeks and down his throat.

"Fuck, fuck, fuck," he huffed out. "I don't know if I can make it to the bedroom."

"I don't care." I licked his throat. "I just need you inside me."

Quite abruptly, we slammed into the wall by the staircase, and I let out a laugh of surprise, one that disappeared into Baird's mouth as my feet hit the floor again. His warm, rough hands tugged at my skirt, yanking it down my legs until it pooled at my feet. We broke apart so I could step out of it and kick off my shoes at the same time. Then Baird's hands were shoving my knickers roughly down and a rush of wet between my thighs made me frantically shimmy them off.

Baird's hands tightened on my waist as he stared down at my naked lower half, chest heaving, cheeks slightly flushed. He squeezed his eyes closed as if he was in pain.

"Bear?"

He shook his head. "I just ... I'm, like, right at my edge. This has never happened before."

A glance at his crotch revealed his cock was pushing, probably painfully, against the zipper of his jeans. He still had his eyes closed.

"What do you mean?"

He huffed and the noise sounded almost a little ... embarrassed. "I mean ... I'm about to fucking come in my boxers." His eyes flashed open, his expression mortified. "Because it's you. I didn't know ... sex would feel so much more ... *more* ... when I felt about a woman the way I feel about you." He laughed, a short, harsh sound. "And now the one woman I want to impress, I'm about to fucking humiliate myself in front of."

This explosion of feeling bloomed across my chest.

Tenderness. Awe. Smugness.

I pretty much felt like the sexiest woman in the world right now.

So I told him that.

Baird's eyes flared. "Really?"

"Baird McMillan, heartbreaker and sex aficionado, just told me that he's so excited to be with me he can't control himself. Not embarrassing. I'm flattered beyond belief." I reached for the zipper on his jeans, and he covered my hands to stop me. "Trust me," I whispered. "We just need to take the edge off."

"Maia." His chest heaved again on a shuddering breath, but he let go of my hand so I could pull the zipper down on his jeans. For my sake, I tugged his T-shirt up and he raised his arms so we could whip it off. I bit my lip, taking in his beautiful torso and all the stunning ink tattooed up his arm and across his upper chest and throat.

"You looking at me like that is not helping," he gritted out.

Biting back a smile, I quickly shoved his jeans and boxers down until his cock bobbed out.

I gasped.

Baird was a big guy and I'd seen the shape of him through his swim shorts. Minutes ago, I'd felt his hardness against me. But I was still taken aback by the size of his cock and equal parts terrified and excited about the thought of it inside me. Will hadn't been huge, but he had girth, and that's what really mattered.

Baird had it all.

I was pretty sure dildo companies would want to make molds of what he was packing in his football shorts.

Right now, his cock was so hard it was an angry purple red with precum dripping from the tip. The veins popped along it, and it was visibly throbbing.

"Now I think I might come," I whispered without thinking.

"Fuck!" Baird huffed out as more precum released from his tip.

"You're … huge."

"Aye, not helping." He squeezed his eyes closed.

I wrapped my palm around him and his eyes flew open. "My!"

He pulsed against my skin, hot and smooth, stiff and hard. Wetness flooded between my thighs, thinking about him inside me. "You're going to come," I panted. "Like I said, take the edge off."

Baird stumbled forward, forcing me back against the wall as his hands braced on either side of my head, his lips inches from mine. "Expect me to come in two point four seconds."

I let out a little moan as I gave his cock a hard jerk.

"Oh fuck ..." He panted against my lips, eyes holding mine. "Say my name, My."

"Baird." My lips feathered over his. "Baird." I tugged again.

His cock throbbed and he let out a rough cry as he climaxed. His sticky cum flooded over my fingers as he shuddered against me, his forehead on my shoulder as he shook through his orgasm.

I think I might have had another mini one.

His cock only semi softened and I gently released him.

Baird slowly lifted his head from my shoulder to study my face. There was that awe again and maybe a little bit of wary confusion.

"Feel good?" I whispered.

He nodded as determination etched into his features. "Give me a minute to get hard again."

I grinned as he pushed away, and we both looked down to find cum splattered all over my T-shirt. "Well, that definitely needs washed now," I joked as I wiped my hand on a clean area.

"Lift your arms."

At his gruff command, I did just that. He pulled the

fabric away from me so it wouldn't touch my face as he lifted it over my head.

"Bra off." His eyes were hot as he threw the T-shirt next to his discarded clothes.

I unclipped it but didn't take it off, gaze roaming over him and his own cum-splattered jeans. "You next."

He kicked off his trainers and shoved his jeans and boxers down, revealing his thickly muscled thighs and carved calves. There was faded bruises up his right side from his motorcycle incident but they did nothing to mar how perfect I thought he was.

"You're really unfairly beautiful, you know that?"

"I've never been called beautiful, but I'll take it. Now. Bra. Off. I want to see you. I've dreamed about your tits for months."

I shook my head, laughing softly. "What kind of dreams?"

He cocked his head, grinning flirtatiously. "The kind where I lick, suck, and fuck every inch of them, every inch of you. They weren't really dreams since I was awake and in the shower with my hand around my cock."

"No wonder you came so quickly if I've been the star of your masturbatory fantasies for months."

He narrowed his eyes at my teasing. "Every. Single. One. And now that I finally have you here, I'm eager to get started on the *fucking every inch of you* part of the fantasy."

Since I was too, I dropped the bra.

My nipples peaked beneath his hooded stare.

It suddenly occurred to me that it was a monumental task to live up to his fantasies. How did reality measure up?

I shifted uneasily, my hands fluttering as if about to cover myself, but Baird bit out roughly, "Fuck, fantasy doesn't even come close to how beautiful you are, My.

You're so beautiful I feel it in every part of my body, every nerve ..." His hands flexed at his sides and his cock strained toward his stomach again.

The perks of being a testosterone-fueled, twenty-six-year-old athlete.

Yet, his words soothed me. "Can you just get inside me now, please?"

Baird's answer was to swing me into his arms bridal style, my breasts bouncing with the movement. "What—" But he was practically running upstairs, and my question ended in giggles of excitement that made him laugh too.

He placed me on his bed with a gentleness that belied our eagerness. Like I was precious to him. We kissed as he fell between my open thighs. Hungry but tender kisses that made me short of breath. He trailed said kisses down my neck, his beard tickling my skin as he explored my body with his mouth and tongue and hands. He squeezed my left breast as his lips covered my right nipple. He licked and sucked until I was writhing and flushed, my hips undulating against his cock.

This pleasurable torment continued until both my nipples were swollen and red from his attention. Following a path down my stomach, Baird kissed my body until his face was buried between my thighs again.

"This pussy," he whispered hoarsely, "is mine to worship."

I pushed up on my elbows, my thighs falling open for him. "Bear."

Our eyes met.

"Did *he* ever go down on you?"

I tensed, knowing he referred to Will. "No," I barely wheezed the word out. "He didn't like it."

Baird's eyes flashed with something like disgust but

quickly softened to tenderness. "Good. Then this is mine. I love your pussy. I love the taste, the smell, the feel of you coming on my tongue. And anytime you want it, you just say the word and I will get on my knees for you, Maia MacLeod."

I knew there was more than sexual intention in his declaration, and with my body in a heightened state of arousal, the emotions pushed hard at me.

As if Baird sensed it, his tenderness eased into a flirtatious grin. "Or I'll lie on my back and you can ride my face. I'd enjoy the fuck out of that too."

Arousal rippled through me, and I groaned, arching my chest, my head falling back at the imagery.

"Oh, aye, we're definitely doing that," he muttered before I felt the first lick of his tongue.

I cried out, my eyes flying open to watch him devour me.

It didn't take long. I flew over the precipice, shuddering against his mouth.

"Soaked." Baird pushed up, wiping a palm over his mouth and beard. "You're soaked, My. For me." His chest puffed up as he gripped his cock and gave it a stroke.

I was sprawled on my back, shaking and shivering and still needy.

I'd never experienced sex like this.

And I didn't want it to end.

Baird rolled off the bed to march to his bedside table where he pulled out a roll of condoms. I had a brief, flickering thought about how many girls he'd been with, and I obviously didn't wipe that thought from my expression quickly enough.

"I'm clean," he forced out as he returned to the bed.

"We get tested at work. I haven't been with anyone since my last test."

I nodded, grateful to him for telling me. "I'm ... I haven't been tested since Will. I'm on the pill. But I'll get tested so we don't have to use condoms."

He was mid tear of the condom package when he froze, staring down at me with this renewed intensity.

"What?"

"I've never ... I've never done it without a rubber."

Oh. Oh God. Maybe I'd overstepped. "We don't have to."

His hot gaze raked over my body with wicked intent before eyeing between my thighs. "Oh, I want to. I ... get tested soon, My. Because the thought of taking you bare ... fuck." He quickly donned protection and was suddenly over me, our chests brushing with delicious friction as he kissed me.

I gasped at the feel of him prodding me as he guided his cock to my entrance. He braced his hands over my head and broke the kiss as he pushed inside me. My hands found his waist, sliding around his strong back to hold on. His skin felt so hot to the touch. We were both burning up for each other.

A sharp, uncomfortable sensation took me by surprise, and I let out a little cry that had Baird freezing mid push.

"You okay?" he asked, his voice hoarse with need.

I nodded frantically. "Just ... big. But don't stop."

"Fuck." He gritted his teeth and carefully pressed in until I wasn't sure he could go any farther.

"Bear!"

"You okay?" he bit out again.

"I just ... I need a minute." My fingernails were digging into his back, I realized. "Sorry." I gentled my touch.

"Don't apologize." He shook his head, arms trembling as he kept himself still. "Everything about you feels fucking amazing." His eyes were glazed with need. "You feel amazing."

My inner muscles clenched around his cock in response to his words, and he grunted.

The fullness of him was feeling good now.

Really good.

"You can move," I told him softly, stroking his back.

"You sure?"

I loved that he wanted me to be totally sure, even though he was clearly using a lot of control to stop himself from thrusting.

"Yes."

Baird began to withdraw slowly, his teeth gritting as I gasped at the pleasurable drag of his cock against my inner muscles.

"Good?"

I made a mewing sound as my nails dug in again, my thighs tensing against his hips. "Don't stop."

He gave an experimental thrust and my back arched with the sensation. I planted my feet on the bed and lifted my hips against his.

"Jesus." Baird gripped my right hip to hold me down. "I'll blow if you start fucking me from the bottom."

"Then speed up," I pleaded. "Harder. Faster."

"Don't need to ask me twice, beautiful." He pushed up onto his knees, gripping my arse in his strong hold to lift it off the bed.

"What the—ahh!"

He drove into me, harder, faster, just as I'd asked.

And the way he held me I couldn't do anything but take it, to watch him taking me.

It was the sexiest moment of my goddamn life.

Baird's gaze swept over me like he didn't know where to look next. My face, my breasts as they trembled against his drives, between my thighs where his cock pushed in and out. No man had ever looked at me like this during sex. Like he wanted to eat me alive.

It made me feel powerful.

Beautiful.

And strangely safe.

Seeing his eyes flare every time I whimpered in pleasure, I let my cries out. Will had always asked me to keep it down during sex because of his neighbors.

But I naturally wanted to be loud.

Loud was hot.

Baird thought so too, his drives quicker and harder as my cries of pleasure grew in volume.

"Come, My!" he gasped out. "Come for me. Fuck, I've dreamed of you coming for me."

That was it.

The final trigger.

The tension inside of me shattered, and I was aware of how tight my pussy muscles throbbed around Baird's cock because the sensation prolonged my climax. But mostly I was trying to process the mind-blowing experience of the best orgasm of my life. Because of that, I almost missed Baird's reaction.

His eyes and nostrils flared as his grip on me loosened with a "Fuck! Me!" Then I felt the pulse of his cock as he released into the condom.

Baird's hips jerked and shuddered and then he collapsed over me, his face in my neck, his hands coasting absentmindedly over my breasts, squeezing roughly as his hips continued to shake against mine.

He groaned, long and deep into my neck, his thumbs scraping over my nipples making me shiver.

Then there was only the sound of our harsh, labored breathing.

My limbs felt like jelly, and I was pretty sure we'd fully merged with his mattress.

Eventually, we caught our breaths and Baird pushed off me to stare down at my face. His was now relaxed, satiated.

"That was …" I let out a little laugh of disbelief. "I didn't know … wow."

Baird's grin was slow but affectionate … and awed too. "I didn't know either. Guess sex really is better when …" His words trailed off and he lowered his eyes. "When it's you."

It seemed like he was about to say something else, but I was too doped up on endorphins to pursue it. Instead, I cupped his face in my hand and replied, "When it's you too."

Baird kissed me in answer, and I was shocked by how quickly my skin flushed again, how I pulsed around his cock. I wanted him. Usually after sex I was sleepy and ready for bed. But it was still early, and I felt energized. He broke the kiss, searching my face. "You got another round in you?"

"Apparently." I chuckled.

He grinned. "Let me deal with this condom and then we're doing that again."

CHAPTER TWENTY-SEVEN

BAIRD

Light prodded at my eyelids. In my semi-conscious state, I realized I'd forgotten to close the curtains in the living room. Which was a problem when your bedroom opened out to the rest of the flat.

Groaning, I turned to bury my head in my pillow and instead felt the silky soft strands of hair and inhaled the smoky, vanilla scent of familiar perfume. My eyes flew open and last night came back to me in a flood of scorching memories.

My chest suddenly felt tight with emotion as I lifted my head, blinking the sleep from my eyes. Maia was sleeping on her stomach, only her profile visible. The sheets were pulled down to her waist, so I had an excellent view of her slender back and all that gorgeous smooth olive skin.

Unsurprisingly, I had woken up hard.

We'd had sex twice last night. She'd ridden me after the first time. And then we'd just explored each other's bodies with our mouths until both of us were wrung dry.

Maia MacLeod in my bed.

I was starting to think I might be the world's luckiest bastard.

Got to do my dream job and then I got my dream girl.

I stiffened at the thought. Not the dream girl part because Maia was definitely that. But the job part. I *was* lucky. How many lads grew up dreaming of playing professional football? Especially lads like me who didn't have an academic bone in their body. And how many of those lads actually made it in the Professional League?

For eight years I'd played the beautiful game.

If it didn't last beyond that, then at least I'd had it.

That's how I had to look at it. Live in gratitude rather than resentment. Every day I would remind myself of that until the panicky dread I'd been experiencing for over a year finally went away.

Something settled over me. Something like peace.

And I had this gorgeous, sweet woman in my bed to thank for it.

Skin flushing hot, I glanced back at the bedside table to my alarm clock. We still had plenty of time before we needed to be at the video shoot. Next to the clock were the condoms. Reaching for one, I bit open the packet and then rolled it on, groaning at how fucking primed I was already.

Reaching for Maia beneath the sheet, I trailed the back of my fingers down her spine and over the lush rump of her arse. She wiggled in her sleep as I caressed her pussy. Her little moan made my balls draw up tight.

I'd enjoyed sex for far longer than I probably should have, but when you were already six feet at thirteen years old, girls tended to think you were older. I was also an early bloomer so to speak. And I loved sex. As apparent by my active sex life. I'd had really good sex over the years. I'd even had multiple group sex moments that were unforgettable. Well, except for the ones where I was wasted.

Yet never since my first few times as a teen had I been so turned on that I couldn't stop myself from coming. In fact, lately there had been times when I was worried about my sex drive because my cock was uninterested in other women and had needed some coaxing.

I'd been like an excited teenager with My last night. Like, I thought I might burst out of my skin I was so eager.

Callan had made comments about sex being better when you loved the woman you were with, but I'd cracked a shitty joke and he'd shut up.

But he was right.

It was a hundred million times better.

I'd never come so hard as I did last night.

I was addicted to it.

I was addicted to her.

Maia made another mewing sound, her fingers curling into the pillow as she grew wetter against my fingers. Finally, I pushed them inside her slowly and her eyes flew open. I watched her lashes flutter. Then she glanced over her shoulder, gaze still sleepy, but widening when she saw me.

Her lips parted on a gasp as I continued to finger-fuck her. "Bear." She licked her lips, moaning as she pressed her body toward me.

My chest heaved, my breathing quickening at just the thought of sliding inside her. "I want you again. Are you … are you too sore?"

She dipped her chin, biting her lower lip as she stared at me through sexy hooded eyes. "I'm a little sore."

I immediately stopped pumping my fingers. "Shit—"

"But it feels good." She moved to turn, but I stopped her when she was still on her side.

"Like this." I slid into position behind her so I was spooning her. I rested my right arm along the pillow above her while I caressed her breasts with my other. Her nipples were pebbled and tight. My cock throbbed. Sliding my hand down her satiny stomach, I instructed gruffly, "Bend your knees a wee bit."

Her breath stuttered. "O-okay."

I guided my cock to her pussy and pushed in.

Maia gasped, arching her back as I gripped her hip to thrust all the way in. Her tight, wet heat clamped around me, and I gritted my teeth against the urge to shove her onto her stomach and fuck her like a possessive beast. That was new. Who the fuck was that guy?

"You okay?" she gasped out.

I realized I'd frozen.

Nuzzling her neck, I nodded, rocked against her, gently easing out and then pushing back in.

Maia made a humming, groaning noise, her cheeks flushed, lashes fluttering wildly. "Uh!" She pressed her cheek into the pillow. "Bear!"

Excitement thrummed through me at her reaction. Every time I pressed back in, she cried louder.

Was I hitting her G-spot?

Fuck me.

I rocked a bit faster, clenching my jaw against my own need to come.

Maia first.

Her cries of pleasure grew higher and louder, her eyes slammed shut as her lower body undulated against my rocks with increasing friction.

Then she let out a hoarse half scream as her body tensed and shattered around me. Her inner muscles clamped down around my cock, throbbing and pulsing with a fierceness that took my breath away as she drenched me. My thrusts now made a wet sound as I moved against her.

"Fuck!" My mind turned hazy with pure, unadulterated lust, and Maia let out a gasp as I released her but only to manhandle her onto her hands and knees.

"Bear!" Her arms shook as she looked over her shoulder at me, eyes still glazed from her climax.

Then I was pushing into her, and she moaned, her head dropping forward.

I kicked her knees wider with mine and then thrust back in.

I powered in rough and hard, testing the waters.

Maia huffed out and then murmured, "Oh my god," as I felt her inner muscles pulse around me.

My grin was feral with wicked intent. I was going to make her come again.

It took more control than I knew I had to hold back my own orgasm because watching Maia shake and moan and cry out as I fucked her doggy-style was high up in my fantasy playbook.

There was nothing but her.

The sound of my grunts mingling with her groans, our bodies smacking together, and the scent of sex.

Sex with Maia.

Fuck it.

I reached between us and started rubbing her swollen clit.

"Oh! Oh my God! Bear!" she cried, squeezing around me again as her arms gave out.

But I kept her arse in the air, fucking her through her second orgasm until I couldn't hold back anymore.

"Maia!" I bellowed my release as heat shivered down my spine and pleasure erupted through my limbs. Shuddering and shaking, I kept a tight hold to her, wanting her to feel every inch of how hard I was coming, wanting to stay connected to her for as long as possible.

Finally, I relaxed my grip on her hips, belatedly realizing how tightly I'd been holding her, hoping I hadn't left bruises.

I bent my head to kiss her lower back and then gently eased from her.

"Fuck," I muttered, because we'd almost lost the condom I'd come that hard. "Let me just deal with this."

After I returned from the bathroom, I smiled at Maia, now lying on her back, her bare breasts a sight to behold. She giggled as I clambered over her like an excited pup, pressing kisses to her gorgeous tits and licking at her nipples.

Her fingers threaded through my hair, making me shiver.

"You're insatiable."

I raised my head. "You have no idea."

Her cheeks flushed. "I think I saw stars this morning."

"G-spot," I opined. "That was fucking hot, beautiful."

Her eyes widened. "I thought the G-spot was a myth."

I braced myself over her, stroking my thumbs over her cheeks. "Did it feel like a myth?"

Maia chuckled. "I guess not."

"We should shower," I murmured, tracing her face with my fingertips like I could memorize every inch of it. "We have the video shoot in two hours."

"Oh my God." She pressed her palms to my chest. "I forgot about that! We need to move."

"We will." I bent my head to nuzzle her throat, pressing wet kisses as I caressed her body.

She moaned. "Bear ... we need to move. And we can't have sex again. I'm definitely sore now."

A weird mix of remorse and triumph thrummed through me. She'd feel me between her legs all day and I couldn't say I didn't like that. Raising my head, I nodded. "Okay, let's shower." I frowned. "When you say we can't have sex again—"

Maia slapped my chest, laughing. "I meant today. Just let my vagina get used to your monster cock, okay?"

I threw back my head in laughter and rolled off her.

She shoved at me. "Don't let that inflate your ego."

"You just called it my monster cock. How do I not let that inflate my ego?" I waggled my brows. "Or the way you came for me *multiple* times."

Her eyes narrowed as she sat up to slide off the bed. "I wasn't the only one who came multiple times or came hard, Baird McMillan."

"I know, beautiful. I've never come harder in my life. Trust me."

Maia's expression softened with the shyness that was incongruous to the confident woman she presented to the world. It had me jumping out of bed and grabbing her up in my arms to carry her to the shower. Her giggles made my chest tighten and expand as I gently eased her onto her feet.

That feeling, this overwhelming feeling that wanted to explode from me ... it was happiness, I realized.

It was fucking bliss.

Those three little words bubbled on my lips, and I kissed her to stop them. She wasn't there yet. But I had hope now more than ever that she'd get there, eventually.

CHAPTER TWENTY-EIGHT
MAIA

I had to borrow one of Baird's tees after we showered. It was massive on me, hanging off one shoulder and bagging over the top of my skirt. My wet hair was knotted on top of my head to be dealt with once we arrived at my place. As I waited for Baird to dress for the day, I sipped a coffee and tried hard not to rub at my eyes.

While the most phenomenal sex of my life was worth the blurred vision and gritty pain of wearing my contacts overnight, they were really starting to bother me. I was itching to rip them out of my eyeballs. In fact, the irritation was almost, but not quite enough, to ruin my afterglow.

Every time I thought about last night or this morning, my skin would flush from the tip of my toes to the top of my head. I wasn't kidding when I told Baird I was a wee bit sore. The last time I'd been sore after sex was the first with Charlie. It wasn't just Baird's "monster cock." It was Baird. Sex with him ... I'd never felt so free in bed before. It was invigorating and vigorous!

I realized up until last night, I'd been an overthinker during sex. Not that I'd slept with a ton of people, but I'd had three boyfriends between Charlie and Will. With every one of them I'd thought: *Is he enjoying it? If I move my hips a little, would it help make me come? Would that make me seem greedy? Do I look good from this angle? Did the fact that he didn't look at me mean he's bored?*

Toward the end of my relationship with Will, I'd gone from overthinking it to feeling apathetic about his or my own enjoyment. Sometimes it was good. Sometimes it was meh. I still used my vibrator a fair bit whenever I was by myself in my flat. With Baird, I doubt I'd have time to even think about my vibrator unless he was using it on me.

With Baird, it was like everything condensed down to *feeling. Experiencing.* I lost myself in the bliss of being with him. There was no overthinking. Because I believed he was lost in it with me. When he looked at me ... goodness, I could come from that awed expression on his face alone.

I smiled dreamily even as I rubbed at my eyes.

"Where did you go?"

I looked up from my perch at Baird's island to the blurry vision of him standing opposite it. "Huh?"

"You didn't hear me walk in because you were daydreaming. Where did you go?"

"Where do you think?" I hopped off the island and squinted at him.

"My ..." Baird grew a little less blurry as he approached, his face clearing slightly when he pulled me against him. There was a frown puckering his brow. "What's going on? Your eyes are red."

"I left my contacts in overnight, and these are only daily disposables, so they hurt like a bitch. We need to get to mine so I can take them out."

"Take them out now."

"I don't think you understand how bad my vision is, Bear."

"Is it any worse than it clearly is now? We're leaving here, getting in my car, and going to your flat. I think I can get you there safely. Take them out."

He was right.

"Can you walk me to the powder room because everything looks like blobby shapes to me right now."

Baird clasped my elbow. "Were you just going to pretend you could see? Why didn't you tell me?"

"I didn't want to be a nuisance."

"You're never a nuisance." He swung me up into his arms and I lost my breath for a second.

"You have to stop doing that!"

Baird chuckled and strode to the powder room. He lowered me to my feet in front of the mirror and stayed behind me, bracing his hands on the sink so I was caged in.

"Are you going to watch? Because it's not pretty."

"I'm going to make sure you make it safely out of my house and to my car. Next time, you bring extra contact solution and an extra pair of glasses that you can leave here."

I paused, pulling my eyelid down.

"You should probably bring some other stuff too. Extra toiletries and clothes. And I'll do the same for yours until we move in together after the wedding."

I gaped at his blurry reflection.

"What?" he asked quietly, uncertainly.

"Nothing," I whispered, my heart in my throat. "It's just … feels nice to not play games with you. For you to just … for you to really want me in your life and not be afraid to say it."

Baird pressed his chest to my back, his lips lingering at

my ear. "The only way I'll ever not be in your life is if you ask me to go. And even then ... I'll fight for you."

Tears threatened to spill, exacerbating my current problem. I elbowed him. "Don't make me cry right now!"

His body shook against mine with amusement. Then he gently slapped my butt. "Hurry. We're going to be late."

I muttered under my breath about arseholes saying perfect things when you had your finger in your eyeball, which only made him snort-laugh. As quickly as possible, I removed the contacts and dumped them in the trash with Baird's guidance.

Everything was blurry, so it was hard to gauge the distance between objects. Once Baird had everything he needed, he took my hand again and guided me outside. He locked up one-handed, not letting me go, and then helped me over the cobblestones toward the building's car park.

His grip was gentle but firm, and I bit back a giddy smile.

Will wasn't the hand-holding type.

Charlie was. I'd loved holding hands with him when we were kids.

"What are you thinking?" Baird asked as we stopped by his car.

Realizing I could pretty much say anything to him, I smiled at his blurry face. "I love holding hands with you."

He squeezed said hand. "Then my hand is yours to hold whenever you want it."

There went those damn tears again. My nose stung trying to hold them back. "Seriously, you have got to stop saying the nicest things."

His face drew closer, his lips brushing mine. He whispered against them, "Never. Not until it sinks in."

"What sinks in?"

Baird didn't answer. Instead, he opened the passenger door and helped me into my seat.

"What sinks in?" I repeated.

He closed the door and rounded the bonnet, sliding into the driver's seat.

"What sinks in, Bear?"

"No time. We need to get moving. I hope you like a little El Camino in the morning." Music blared to life, and I recognized the opening riffs of a song by The Black Keys. Baird, like me, had an eclectic taste in music. One minute he was listening to rap, the next techno, the next rock—whatever struck his mood.

I guessed we were done with the questioning portion of the morning.

I didn't ask again, but I pondered his words all the way to my flat.

————

Not only was I tired from lack of sleep, but my body ached all over. And not just from Baird rolling me around in his bed last night but from walking around venues all day. Thankfully, the acting in love and happy part of the venue shoot was easy because Baird and I were still high from finally getting together.

On the way to the first venue, Baird told me about Braden's proposal to use Blantyre as the location for the wedding ceremony and reception. I was fully on board, so as soon as we met up with the director and crew, they called the project managers to relay the proposal to them. They said if we could get permission to film there tomorrow so we at least had the footage, they'd talk with the higher-ups about switching venues.

The thought of another day of traipsing around luxury wedding locations might have made me want to curl into a ball if Baird's presence didn't inject me with adrenaline.

He could barely keep his hands off me.

At one point, during the second venue shoot, he'd waited until the crew was distracted and then he'd hurried me into the empty ballroom to press me up against the wall and kiss me breathless.

He'd been perfect all day.

My eyes were too sore for contacts, so I'd chosen to wear my glasses after Baird convinced me I looked hot. Bruno was being an arse about them.

"They reflect light! We can't see her eyes, and they're her best feature."

Baird lost his good-boy charm in an instant. "Wrong. Her heart is her best feature, which is why she's too nice to tell you to fuck off. I'm not. My fiancée's eyes are sensitive today so she's wearing her glasses, and if you say one more word about it, I'll take Maia back to my car and we'll drive out of here, leaving you to explain why your pissant behavior lost Pennington's precious pennies today."

The crew all went silent, though I saw an assistant or two trying to cover their smiles.

I didn't bother covering mine. I beamed, like the proud fiancée I was.

Bruno swallowed hard, his face blanching as if realizing he'd just upset the fiancée of a six-foot-five Scottish goalkeeper. "Right. Of course. We'll manage fine as we are."

Will had never stood up for me like that. Neither had Mum. Grace had. Dad had. But no one since them.

Until Baird.

In the empty ballroom, when he finally let me up for air, I'd squinted up at him because he'd pushed my glasses up into my hair so he could kiss me. I whispered hoarsely, "Thanks for having my back today."

Baird stroked my cheek tenderly, before popping my glasses back onto my nose. His gorgeous features sharpened into focus as he eased away from me. "You're my family now, My. In my family, we always have each other's backs."

I grinned a little too giddily. "Same."

If my smile gave away too much of my feelings, Baird seemed delighted, not frightened. He hugged me into his side, pressing a slow kiss to my temple before we reluctantly rejoined the crew.

By the time we got into the car to drive home, I switched my phone back on to a ton of texts from friends and family. Grace was annoyed we'd left the party before they'd arrived and insisted that we make it up to her, Dad, and Lockie. Even though I was exhausted, I promised her we'd have dinner with them in the coming week. Baird agreed amiably. It was refreshingly unlike Will who always hemmed and hawed and insisted he needed to check his calendar a thousand times before committing to spending time with my family.

I had a missed call and text from Beth. A text from Lily, one from January, and even one from Luke. I really needed to apologize to Luke for bailing on his graduation party. However, the fact that all their texts were filled with cheeky innuendo about why we'd left early meant my responses could wait. *Nosy buggers,* I thought with a small smile on my face.

That was seconds before I dozed off.

I woke up to Baird trying to lift me gently out of the car. I assured him I was awake when I was really only semiconscious, and I sleep-drunkenly got into my flat with his help.

We had this to do all over again tomorrow, and I just wanted to snuggle into Baird's chest and sleep for a hundred hours first.

Instead, Baird insisted I stay awake long enough to eat the takeout he'd apparently picked up on the way home. I'd slept through him stopping to go into a Chinese restaurant to collect food!

"You were totally out." He stroked my cheek after I watched him place lettuce wraps on a plate. It was the exact right thing to order for me.

He saw me gaping at the wraps and stated, "Lettuce wraps when you're not that hungry. Kung pao chicken when you are. And I got vegetable spring rolls."

It was weird. Even after all the lovely, amazing things he'd said to me when he confessed that he'd wanted me romantically since the beginning ... it was at this moment when it finally hit. Our entire friendship, Baird had been so into me, he'd soaked up every minute detail. Including the fact that when my stomach was feeling a bit sensitive or I wasn't hungry, I always ordered lettuce wraps.

"What else do you know about me?" I whispered.

Whatever he heard in my tone, Baird's expression turned serious. "I know you swim three times a week, not just for the fitness but because it's the one place your mind focuses and all your stress melts away for a while."

Facts.

I held my breath, waiting.

"I know you love fashion and that you take your time presenting yourself to the world, not because you're hung up on your looks but because it's your armor. Because your mum's situation made people look at you like you were less than, and you never want to feel that way again. I know you listen to Taylor Swift when you're in a good mood,

Paramore when you're pissed off, and Lord Huron when you're chilled out." His lips twitched. "This is just a guess, but I think Hozier might be when you're horny."

My lips parted on a "Uh!" squeak as I whacked his arm. "How did you know that?"

Baird threw his head back in laughter.

I was half shocked at everything he said.

When his laughter trailed off, his eyes still danced with humor. "I pay attention, My. And believe me, there were days I came over and you were listening to Hozier, and I wondered what the fuck Will *wasn't* doing for you, and it was really hard not to make an arsehole move."

My cheeks flushed. I was now fully awake again. "Oh my god."

His gaze smoldered even as he reached for the cutlery. "I know your favorite dishes are cacio e pepe if it's Italian, kung pao chicken if it's Chinese, pad Thai noodles if it's Thai, a haggis supper if it's from the chippy, and butter chicken—Indian. You love fish but can't stomach most shellfish. A mojito is your favorite cocktail. Champagne is your favorite overall, but you're not a big drinker and you'd prefer to nurse a glass of bubbly because you think most alcohol tastes like, and I quote, 'Swill.' Whatever that means. I know you love traveling for fashion month, but I can tell you're uncomfortable around industry people because when you talk about it, there's always this wee telltale wrinkle between your nose and that light in your eyes when you talk about the actual clothes winks out. I know—"

I reached up to cover his mouth with my palm, my pulse pounding in my ears. His eyebrows rose in question.

"If you say much more, I'm going to melt into a puddle

at your feet." I felt his smile against my palm. "And then die of guilt."

Baird frowned, pulling my hand from his mouth. "Why?"

"Because ... because while you are the one person who has ever given a shit enough to notice all those things about me ... I didn't even notice you felt that way." Tears brightened my eyes. "I was such a blind idiot. Literally and metaphorically."

Baird grinned, bending his head to press a soft kiss to my mouth. He pulled back to search my eyes. "No guilt, My. We were in different places. Now we're in the same place, and that's all I care about." He leaned back and lifted the plate to me. "Now, eat something before you fall asleep. Go sit. I'll make tea and grab some water."

He was taking care of me.

In fact, Baird McMillan had been taking care of me for far longer than I realized.

I promised myself as I settled on the couch that I was going to start taking care of him right back.

So as tired as I was, I said, "Uh-uh" when Baird reached for the TV remote. "We're going to talk. About what you said the night you told me you had feelings for me. About football. How you feel about it now."

He swallowed his bite of stir-fried noodles. "Sneak attack, eh?"

"Well?"

"We can talk about that later. It's been a long day, My."

"We'll talk about it later if that's really what you want, but I'd like to talk about it now. I want to make sure that my fiancé isn't dreading going to training every day."

His expression softened. "I had a bit of a ... what do you

call it? Epiphany? Aye, an epiphany today." He then went on to explain how I'd helped him feel grateful for what he had in life. How so few young men who dreamed of playing professional football ever made it into the league. How he was grateful for the eight years he'd played. "That's how I'm going to keep looking at it. And if I start to think that my fears really are winning and I'm not enjoying the game anymore, I'll walk away and be grateful for how long it lasted. I just ... I still need time to figure out if I'm ready to walk away or if I want to fight for it. There's no magic answer. Just ... time."

Pride flooded my chest, so I told him I was proud of him.

He gave me a boyish grin. "Aye?"

"Aye." I smiled, lowering my eyes so he couldn't see my *overwhelming* emotions. "You know, behind that gregarious 'life of the party' demeanor, you're more mature than men ten years older than you. Maybe even more mature than me." I shrugged self-deprecatingly.

"Och, I wouldn't go that far, beautiful."

I looked up to meet his tender but wicked smile.

"After all, it's a bit of a kink for me that I've bagged myself an older woman."

I promptly plucked a mushroom out of my lettuce wrap and threw it at him. "Don't ever call me an older woman again."

He shook the piece of mushroom out of his hair, shoulders shaking with laughter. His voice trembled with it as he taunted, "You do realize when you're forty, I'll only be thirty-six."

"I hate you."

Baird laughed harder. "It's a four-year age gap, gorgeous. Not ten. No big deal."

A sudden thought flashed in my mind, making my smile slide right off my face.

"What? What just happened?"

"Nothing," I squeaked out. It was way too soon to bring it up.

"It's definitely something." Baird put his plate down on my coffee table and turned his body into mine. "Talk to me. Because I can't have you getting in your head—not when I finally know how fucking good it is between us."

His concern incited my remorse. I didn't want him constantly battling against my overthinking but ... "If I told you what just crossed my mind, you'd run so far and so fast I'd see a Baird-shaped hole in my front door."

He grinned that sexy grin of his. "I doubt it. Tell me." At my hesitation, he prompted, "Did you know I'm like a dog with a bone when I want something?"

The fact that he'd stuck around for over a year waiting for me to open my eyes and see he was the better choice, I think I did. Oh well. Here went nothing.

"I'm thirty. By thirty-five ... pregnancy is considered high risk."

One thick handsome eyebrow quirked up toward his forehead.

"Rethinking the Baird-shaped hole?"

"Keep going."

"I ... thought I'd most likely have a child by the time I was thirty-five."

"And that won't happen now why? My swimmers are all in working order, as far as I'm aware."

I gaped at him. "But ... but ... you're only twenty-six."

"And?" He shuffled closer to me. "Obviously, I want you to myself for a bit longer. But I also want to be a young dad. I want to have energy to raise my kids."

He just … he just kept surprising me. Over and over again. "I … you want kids? You've thought about it?"

"Of course. I was never not open to finding the right person and starting a family just because I played the field."

After several long seconds of me staring at him, Baird bent his head to mine. "Are you ever going to speak again?"

I shook my head.

His lips twitched. "That would be a shame because I enjoy the sound of your voice." He waggled his brows. "Especially when you're screaming my name."

I shoved him playfully, almost losing my dinner plate.

He rescued it for me and asked quietly, "So … are we good, My?"

"We're more than good, Bear. I'm … you make me happy."

His chest moved upward in one heave of *feeling*. When he exhaled, he let out hoarsely, "You make me happy too."

As we cuddled into each other, picking at our food, I squeezed my eyes closed, soaking in this unbelievable contentment. Joy. Thrill. Hope. For a beautiful future together.

I did my very best to shove back that insidious wee voice in my head that whispered I couldn't be this lucky. That something or someone would find a way to take Baird McMillan away from me.

BAIRD

The past week had been a blur. I was an optimist, so the good far outweighed the bad, and thankfully, Maia seemed to feel the same way. I kept glancing at her as I drove through Falkirk, watching her curious expression as she took in the town where I grew up. She'd told me she'd never been here before, so I promised her we'd drive down to see the Kelpies, our most visited tourist landmark, once we'd had dinner with my family.

Ainsley had a work thing so she couldn't make it this time, which was probably a good thing since she was the reason Maia and I had to jam a second family dinner into an already packed week when all we wanted to do was fuck. That was the straight-up truth. The woman made me horny all the time.

I put a leash on it, though, knowing we were heading to my childhood home.

Instead, I wondered what Maia was thinking and hoped it was all about the present and not about some of the shitty things that had happened this week.

Last Sunday we'd done the second video shoot for the

venue part of the campaign, including filming at Blantyre. Good news was Pennington's went for our idea, and we were now going to get free marketing for our hotel. Bad news was when the video went live, we discovered the film crew had included private footage.

Neither of us really wanted to look at the campaign posts. Maia, however, gave into her curiosity and had scrolled through the comments during her lunch break.

There were comments like:

Ugh, this is obviously so fake. I want to see REAL people getting married.

Eh ... like Maia and I weren't real people. What the actual fuck?

He's so hot. He could do way better than her.

Why did women do that to each other? Especially when it was straight-up bullshit.

There are people dying in the world. Maybe talk about that!

So, because it's just occurred to you that people die, you don't want anyone to talk about anything else ever? Make that make sense.

And then there were nice comments like:

They look so in love. I want this!

And then confusing comments like this:

I think my ovaries just exploded.

I'm afraid to admit how many times I've rewatched that kiss.

Find a guy who kisses you like this!

That kiss was a bit NSFW, no??

It was that last comment that prompted Maia to watch the video because our kisses for the camera were polite. She'd then called to tell me to watch the video. One of the fucking cameramen had followed me and Maia at the venue where I dragged her into the ballroom to kiss the life out of her. Now, don't get me wrong, the kiss was hot. But it was a private moment that should not have been part of the footage. It was the kind of kiss some sickos might get their rocks off to, and I didn't want anyone seeing my fiancée like that.

Maia requested a meeting with her boss Hilary, I joined in via video call, and we pretty much demanded nothing like that ever happen again. Hilary was apologetic and assured us she'd talk to marketing, the director, and the crew, and also to legal.

Marketing responded by being total dicks, insisting that the kiss made the video go viral. Thankfully, legal assured them they were opening themselves up to a lawsuit if they pulled anything like that a-fucking-gain since it clearly stated in the contract that Maia and I only agreed to use of permissible footage. Since he'd filmed us behind our backs like a fucking creep, it was not permissible. I went a step further and asked for a new cameraman and I also insisted we see the final posts before they were published.

I'd never cared before about anything I did making it into public consumption. But I cared about people witnessing intimate moments between me and Maia. Moments that were supposed to be ours. I cared that because some bitchy twit called Becky had a problem with My that we were in this situation in the first place, swinging Maia's arse out there for anyone to make shitty comments about her or use content of her for their own perverse desires.

I couldn't protect her from that, and it fucked with my head more than I expected.

It was one of the reasons I hadn't told her that the tabloid media had started planting themselves outside the club every morning before training, hounding me about the campaign and about my "sordid" past.

I'd looked up that word and I did not think my past was *sordid*. Since when did having sex and partying here and there become a bad thing in the twenty-first century? Fucking tabloid journos twisted everything.

Another crap thing that happened was that Pennington's informed us they'd booked our date for the bungee jump. Now that I was in my right mind again, there was no bloody way I was putting Maia at risk by throwing us off a platform suspended forty meters above a river. Maia, however, decided she wanted to do it. We got into an argument, which I hated. She insisted Will had made her feel boring and unadventurous, and she'd like to prove to herself that she wasn't. Who could argue with that? I put my overprotectiveness to one side and realized that my inability to say no to this woman did not bode well for me in the future. Though ultimately it wasn't up to me whether she did the bungee jump. She was a grown woman, and it was her decision.

Whether I liked it or not.

The fact that when we went to dinner at her parents' house and her dad found out and wasn't happy about it almost made me want to throw my support behind him ... until I saw the sheen of tears in Maia's eyes as she argued her point. She wasn't getting upset to get her way. Maia often got teary when she was frustrated, which just frustrated her even more. I thought it was adorable, though I knew better than to tell her that.

Other than the bungee jump discussion, dinner with her parents and Lockie went well. Lockie was a bit in awe of me, so I tried to make him comfortable and answered his million questions about football and the Professional

League. Maia's dad treated me with an assessing politeness, but he warmed up toward the end of the dinner and joined me and Lockie in our discussions.

Maia's stepmum Grace was a sweetheart, as always. She was one of the classiest women I'd ever met and had one of those posh English accents that made everything she said sound smart as fuck. She and Maia had a bond that transcended blood, and I decided Grace MacLeod had my loyalty for life.

Ainsley, of course, had then let it slip to my mum that we'd had the long overdue family dinner, and Mum's response was worse than if she'd just been annoyed. No. She sounded butt hurt instead and I couldn't handle that, so I asked Maia if we could do dinner at my mum's Friday night. Maia's answer was an instant "Of course."

So here we were.

We slowed to a stop outside my grandparents' house. "This is it."

Maia looked up at the end-of-terrace home with its large front bay window.

At her silence, I asked, "What are you thinking?"

She turned to me. "That this seems like a nice house, a nice street, to grow up on."

Emotion clogged my throat. To most folk, this was a modest house on a modest street. Totally ordinary. Nothing special.

Maia saw a family home. A street where kids could play safely together.

She saw that because she'd grown up in a dangerous, poverty-stricken area of Glasgow, never feeling safe inside or outside her home.

And I hated it.

I wish I could erase every second of the first fifteen years of her life.

Yet I also knew Maia wouldn't be Maia without them. Life's twisted sense of humor. Because she was a kinder person for having experienced those years.

"It was," I answered roughly.

It was getting harder and harder to hold back those three little words.

"Let's go in."

Maia had met my mum at the hospital when I was injured, but she hadn't met my grandparents. In her usual dry tone that confused most folk, Gran couldn't stop commenting on how beautiful Maia was. I could see not only was Maia embarrassed, but she wasn't sure if she was being complimented. I made a crack about it giving me a complex, like she was too gorgeous for me or something, and Gran laughed. She also didn't say it again, though she kept glancing at Maia in this searching way that I knew Maia probably thought was assessing. But she looked at Ainsley the same way. My gran liked what she saw in Maia. Which made me want to puff up my chest in pride because as much as their opinion wouldn't change my feelings for Maia, I did care what my family thought. Granddad kept sharing conspiratorial looks with me as if to say *Well done, my boy*. I grinned, chuffed to fucking bits.

I knew Maia was nervous because she told me she was, but I also witnessed it in her slightly strained smiles. Over time, because my family was friendly, she relaxed more and let her personality shine. She cracked jokes, and when Gran teased her with her dry sense of humor, Maia teased right back, which Gran loved. They asked her about her job and about the campaign and about us.

It was good.

It made the last amazing week with her feel more real.

Sometimes I still couldn't bloody believe it. I'd wanted her for so long.

After dinner Maia offered to help Mum with the dishes. I got up to help too, but Mum pressed a hand to my shoulder. "You keep your grandparents company."

It occurred to me a bit belatedly that Mum might be mumming in the kitchen. And by that, I meant switching on momma bear mode. Fuck.

"I need another drink. Want anything?"

My granddad shook his head while Gran muttered, "Took him long enough."

I took that to mean she knew Mum was up to something.

Fuck.

Trying not to hurry, I stepped out of the living room and into the hall and froze at what I heard from the kitchen.

"What I'm trying to say, Maia, is that you seem like a nice girl, but I need to know you're in this for real before Baird gets hurt."

Fuck!

I moved to step into the room, but Maia's response stopped me on the threshold. Their backs were to me as they stood at the sink.

"I would never hurt Bear," she replied vehemently, sounding offended. "He's my favorite person in the whole world."

My chest tightened. In a good way.

"Bear?" Mum asked.

"I call him Bear. Because he gives good bear hugs."

Mum laughed softly. "He does. He always has."

"His hugs make me feel safe," Maia continued quietly. "Your son is one of the best humans I've ever met. He makes me feel good about myself, he makes me feel safe to just be me, but he also makes me feel like I can be more than who I am right now. Like there's more in me and I don't have to be afraid to explore that with him. It's exciting. It's ..." She trailed off.

My heart was in my fucking throat.

Blood whooshed in my ears.

Hope grew so big inside me I could barely breathe around it.

"You should tell him that," Mum said, her profile soft. "He deserves to hear it."

I cleared my throat. "I just did."

Maia whirled on a gasp while Mum beamed from ear to ear. She looked between us, at Maia's pink cheeks, and then at me. Whatever she saw on my face made her bridge the distance between us. Mum stroked the back of her knuckles over my cheek. "I'm so pleased for you, sweetheart."

I nodded because I didn't think I could get the words out.

Then she looked back at Maia. "Did you know your wedding invitations ask the guests to RSVP in just one week?"

The abrupt change in conversation made Maia blink rapidly. "No. What? One week?" Her shoulders slumped. "Unfortunately, none of the decisions regarding the wedding are ours to make. Part of the agreement."

"Not even your dress?" Mum was aghast.

"Thankfully, since I'm the bridal buyer for Pennington's, there are very few gowns I don't like in our collection."

Mum *hmm'd* and then patted my shoulder as she passed.

I knew that noise. Just as I saw the sadness and frustration on My's face. It hadn't bothered me when we made the deal with Pennington's. I hadn't thought beyond using the campaign as a way to show Maia what was really between us.

But hearing her say those phenomenal things about how I made her feel ... knowing that this was *real* between us ... it was shit that Maia didn't get to choose how our wedding would go down. Mum clearly thought so too.

And this was it.

Me and Maia ... it would take an apocalyptic event to end us, and maybe not even then. Which meant our wedding was going to happen and we would be legally married. And it wouldn't even feel like us.

I could practically hear my mum telling me to fix it.

I just didn't know how.

Yet.

CHAPTER THIRTY

MAIA

I was at war with myself.

The river rushed below us, wild after last night's rainstorm.

The control freak in me, the person who planned her life to the exact letter to limit the number of bad things that could happen, wanted to run back off the platform, through the trail in the woods, and straight back to Baird's car.

But that other person, the girl who bravely hunted down her real father and swung her arse out there to be hurt in the hopes of changing her life, she still existed in me. For better or worse, the chaos of this campaign being forced upon me had brought her to life again. Falling for someone like Baird who was a red flag on paper but a row of green flags with smiley face emojis in real life ... it had proved to that girl that she deserved more of a say.

That girl wanted to throw herself off a platform to experience the thrill of free fall.

"Maia."

I looked at Baird as the instructor did his final safety

checks on the harness strapped around my waist, under my bottom, and around my thighs.

"You don't have to do this. Or I could go first."

I'd won (or lost, depending on your perspective) the coin toss to go first on our bungee jumping date.

Did I mention I had a camera strapped to my helmet? There were camera people on either side of the river and one right behind us on the platform, filming everything for the campaign.

Who was it going to be?

I stared up into Baird's soulful dark eyes, feeling humbled and honored that I knew him better than most people ever could hope to.

Was the Maia who needed to be in control of everything going to take the reins and bail? Or did the girl who used to crave adventure get another chance to prove that the most terrifying things in life often provided the most rewards?

I leaned up on my tiptoes to press a quick kiss to Baird's lips. When I pulled back, I whispered, "I really wish Tom Petty's 'Free Fallin'' was playing right now."

He grinned. "A girl who knows Tom Petty is a girl after my own heart."

Laughing, I pulled back and nodded at the instructor.

We'd spent the morning here for Pennington's, and the instructors had gone over all the safety talks with us. The air was crisp, and my senses were filled with the battling scents of the woodlands. Flora and fauna attempted to overpower the petrichor—that heightened, earthy smell after the rain. It was enervating.

It was time.

To just ... let go.

My belly was alive with a million butterflies, but at the instructor's go-ahead, I dove! I dove like I was diving into a pool. I was vaguely aware over the sound of the wind in my ears of Baird's whooping shouts of support from above.

It felt like everything inside me was forced toward my throat with gravity. I didn't scream, though. Upon the rapid descent, the wind whipped against my face and the river with its foamy rapids tunneled toward me.

Suddenly, I was halted and hauled upward, my stomach swooping, my heart lurching, with the abrupt jerk on the harness. I accelerated downward again and then back up several times until the motion caused this weird surge of laughter I couldn't explain.

Finally, I was hanging above the river, all the blood rushing to my head in this pressure that wasn't entirely comfortable. Yet as I looked around at the woodlands as I swayed back and forth over the river, I couldn't help but let out a whoop of joy.

I did it!

I heard Baird's shouts and applause from above and laughed until tears of relief burned my eyes.

It had been a free fall in bigger ways than physical.

———

Baird was like an impatient puppy as they winched me back up to the platform. He was practically popping up and down on his heels, desperate to get to me, grinning so hard it was a wonder his face didn't break.

Utter joy filled me as I grinned back at him, unbuckling my helmet with the camera and handing it off to Gail, my crew assistant. As soon as I was free from the harness, I squealed with excitement and threw myself at Baird like a monkey. He laughed, catching me as I wound my arms and legs around him. I cut off his amusement with a kiss that was probably a wee bit too risqué for Pennington's, but at that point, I'd totally forgotten about the cameras.

Baird stroked my back as he kissed me.

I finally let him up for air. "I did it!"

"I saw that, beautiful."

"It was amazing!"

"Aye? Now I can't wait." He stared into my eyes, his so full of tenderness and affection that I could feel the words, those three words, bubbling toward my tongue.

"We're ready for you now, Baird." The instructor spoke before I could.

Reality returned, and I realized what a giant mistake it would be admitting my feelings to Baird in such a public way. My truth wasn't for anyone else. Only him.

I dropped my legs from around his waist and lowered to my feet.

"You've got a lot of energy after that." Baird eyed me suggestively.

"Not going to lie, the pressure on the head is a little ..." I shook my hand at him, grimacing. "But otherwise, aye, I have lots of energy. To expel. Lots and lots and lots."

He bent his head to whisper in my ear, "I'll collect later on that surplus."

Chuckling, I nodded and then watched with anticipation as they buckled him into a harness and Gail handed him his camera helmet. My legs were still shaking with fear and adrenaline and joy, and I had to hold on to the platform railing.

"Ready." The instructor patted Baird on the back.

He winked cockily at me and dove off with no hesitation, yelling, "Oi! Oi!"

Of course he did.

I collapsed into giggles as his trademark greeting was

cut off by the wind and I watched his large body jerk back upward.

Though it was hard to hear over the river, I was pretty certain he didn't yell or whoop, which was surprising because Baird was an extrovert who let his experiences all hang out. When they pulled him back up, his face was flushed, and he shook his head. "Naw. No thanks. Never again."

"No?" I gaped, taken aback. Baird usually enjoyed his thrill-seeking exploits.

"It was the tug back upward and down like a yo-yo. Didnae like that." His accent thickened. "Didnae like it at all. Skydiving. There's none of that in skydiving. We shoulda done that."

His fingers trembled as he unbuckled the helmet to hand it off to Gail and my heart melted. I wanted to wrap him in my arms and hold him until he stopped shaking. He was such a big guy that it was disconcerting to see him like that. Just like it was when I visited him after his injury. I'd hated every second of seeing him felled, even if it was temporary. Hell, I was so in denial even then about my feelings for him.

"We can go skydiving," I offered, trying to distract him.

"Aye?"

"I mean, not today. But definitely, yes."

Freed from the harness, Baird stumbled a bit, and I hurried to him, worry chilling my happiness as his face turned chalk white. "Baird?"

His eyes looked a bit glazed and he swayed, his breathing sounding tight.

I whipped my head toward the camera. "Off. Camera off. Now."

Thankfully, the cameraman lowered the equipment as I turned back to Baird. "What's going on? Are you okay?"

He shook his head, his grip on me tightening.

I led him quickly off the platform, frightened by how much he seemed to need to lean on me. Fury ripped through me as a camerawoman stepped into our path. "Switch that off! You do not have permission to film this." I caught sight of Bruno. "No filming!"

Bruno glanced between us. "What happened? Does he need help?"

"No, My, no." He shook against me. "Just need ... privacy." He gritted out.

"We need to be alone." I shooed them away, glad Pennington's had paid to close the bungee jumping attraction for the morning so there was no one else around but staff.

Finally, Baird seemed to relax as we reached the end of the trail that led to the car park. He slumped to his arse so suddenly, I thought he was passing out.

"Baird." I dropped to my knees.

He waved a weary hand at me in reassurance.

"What happened?" I smoothed a hand over his bent knee.

"I ... I had the thought a few seconds after I jumped. When you mentioned the pressure on your head, it hit me that maybe this was a bad idea for me."

Oh God. Oh heck. Why didn't I think about that? His injury. I squeezed his knee.

"It's probably fine." His voice was rough. "But once I felt the pressure, I started to panic down there and every time I yo-yoed, the pressure felt worse. By the time I got back up ..."

"The lightheadedness is anxiety," I realized.

Baird looked embarrassed but nodded. "Aye."

"You know that's totally normal, right?" I pushed against him, gently turning his face to meet my eyes. "Baird, you suffered a traumatic head injury. You nearly died. The fracture might have healed, but the mental fractures from a near-death experience ... those take much longer to heal. There's no shame in that."

The muscle in his jaw clenched. "I hate that I can't control when I'm going to feel this way about something. It just fucking happens. This time on film."

"I will personally ruin any arsehole here if they ever publish that footage, Bear."

His lips twitched. "Aye? Are you my protector now?"

There were those words again, desperate but terrified to squeak out of me. "Aren't you mine?"

Baird's expression turned tender. "Always."

"I'm always yours too." I leaned in and brushed my lips over his.

When I pulled back, his countenance had turned somewhat intense. "Maia, I—"

"Everything all right?"

Annoyance sliced through me, but I gritted my teeth against it and turned to see the instructor standing a few feet from us, a worried look in his eyes.

"Do you have water? And maybe a piece of chocolate or something?"

"I'm all right," Baird insisted.

"You will be," I promised.

Bruno joined us as the instructor darted off to retrieve the water and chocolate.

"I've had the camera crew delete the last few minutes of footage," he assured us as he approached. "Is everything okay?"

"Baird didn't eat before we left for the shoot," I lied, covering for him. "His blood sugar dropped with the adrenaline." I had no idea what I was talking about, but I hoped it sounded plausible.

Bruno seemed to think so and slumped with relief. "Oh, I'm glad to hear it's nothing serious. We have what we need if you two want to go home."

"Thanks, Bruno, I appreciate it." The director had been much nicer to us ever since he got a scolding from Hilary Erstwhile about the footage permissions.

As Bruno departed, I helped Baird to his feet.

Without a word, he hauled me into his arms for a spectacular bear hug. He held me, his face buried in my hair, breathing me in.

My return embrace was tight, almost pulling, like if I could, I would have soaked up every bit of PTSD his injury had left him with.

No words were needed.

We just held each other.

Yet I fell faster and deeper in that moment than I had throwing myself over that river.

CHAPTER THIRTY-ONE
MAIA

The music in the club was a wee bit too loud, but my friends were enjoying themselves, shouting over it to be heard, nursing their beers and cocktails. Callan had pulled some strings and gotten the entire VIP mezzanine for us. He said it was so we could dance in privacy if we wanted to since our escapades last time had gone viral on social media. I was looking forward to this campaign being over so Baird and I could explore our relationship in a normal environment.

My fiancé had his arm around the back of the booth behind me, his side pressed to mine as he talked and joked with Callan, John, and Sebastian. Ainsley had come with us and had brought a date, a gorgeous blond dude called Alex. The two of them had disappeared down onto the dance floor thirty minutes ago. I was being grilled by Beth and Lily about the wedding plans since the two of them, along with January, Belle, and Elle were my bridesmaids. I was grateful they'd said yes, considering how quickly everything had come together.

Two weeks had passed since the bungee jump. Bruno

kept to his word, and we approved the final edit of the video. The public loved it, so Pennington's asked permission to follow us around on a "typical date night." Baird had taken me out for dinner and drinks while the public stared at us, wondering why there were two camerapeople and a director following us around town.

It had been a whirlwind few weeks. Pennington's really ramped up the schedule for the campaign, and we'd filmed everything but the wedding and honeymoon. Thankfully, the company had decided it was more cost effective to book a studio with a pool and use green screen and just pretend they were filming us on our honeymoon than send an entire crew with us for the duration. They had some footage from the resort they'd booked for us in Bali (I couldn't say I wasn't excited for that!), and Baird and I would take hand-held footage that Pennington's would edit together with theirs. Our "honeymoon" shoot wasn't for another week.

We had a break from filming for the campaign for a while, and I was glad because I wanted to focus on us.

After the bungee incident, Baird had agreed to reach out to the therapist the club had hired after his injury. He'd had two sessions with her so far, and we were both optimistic it would help. Baird assured me that just confiding in me had lifted a huge weight off his shoulders, and I felt incredible and humbled that I could do that for him.

Despite how busy we were, we'd managed to grab alone time. And while my period momentarily interfered with our sex life, as soon as it finished, we were all over each other. I swear I had a little more definition in my abs from how athletic the sex was.

And yet, my favorite standout moment of the last few weeks was just a few nights ago. Christina informed me Becky would be accompanying me to Paris Fashion Week for some cooked-up reason she'd whispered in her boss's ear, and I was stressed and pissed off. Baird had given me a key to his place, and I was supposed to be meeting him there. He'd called to tell me a property management work meeting was running late. I'd decided to fill my time by running a bubble bath in Baird's oversized, egg-shaped tub to decompress from the terrible news. I hadn't had a bubble bath in forever.

I was luxuriating in said tub, Hozier playing from my phone, when Baird came running into the bathroom, giving me the fright of my life.

His cheeks were flushed, and he was already tugging at his tie.

"What on earth?"

He grinned even as he devoured me with his gaze. "I heard Hozier."

It took me a second and then I burst into laughter. Laughter that only got more hysterical as I watched him tear off his clothes like an excited schoolboy. He knocked over a plant pot, stumbled into the sink trying to get his trousers off, skidded on the bath towel I'd laid down and nearly landed on his arse ... it was chaotic and hilarious. There were tears in my eyes by the time he lunged into the tub, sending water cascading over the sides.

I'd squealed as he reached for me, totally uncaring of the mess he was making. Even as he kissed me, I burst out laughing again. "I'm sorry," I wheezed, "I just keep picturing it."

He grinned at my teasing, completely unabashed by his less than suave seduction attempts. "You're ruining Hozier."

I snorted. "I think you ruined Hozier."

"Aye?" He dipped his hand in the water between us and

I sucked in a breath at the feel of his thumb on my clit. "You sure about that?"

"Hmm ... maybe ... maybe I can be convinced otherwise." I gasped as he pushed his fingers inside me.

From there, Baird made languid, decadent love to me in his bathtub and we didn't get out until we were both wrinkled and pruned. He made me scarily happy. For the fifty millionth time in two weeks, I held back the words *I love you.*

I didn't know why I was holding myself back.

Correction: I did know why. I just didn't like thinking about it.

I was terrified of rejection, abandonment.

Therefore, I was waiting for Baird to take that first step.

Beth brought me back from the memory to the nightclub with a teasing comment. "Can you at least tell us if the dresses will be 1990s 'I hate my bridesmaids' or twenty-first century 'I want my girlies to look hot'?"

"You two would look hot in a bin bag and you know it."

Lily shrugged. "You know I don't care either way."

Beth side-eyed her. "Make me look bad for caring, why don't you?"

Lily grinned unapologetically, her dimples creasing her cheeks.

"You know I can't stay even pretend mad at you when you pull out the dimples. No fair." Beth flicked a cocktail stick at her.

"They're lethal, aren't they?" Sebastian dipped his head into our conversation. "I can never say no to her. It's terrible. Dimple terrorism, I tell you."

Lily chucked the cocktail stick at him in answer, and he chuckled and turned back to the guys' conversation.

"I thought you were both coming to the store on

Thursday to pick dresses?" That's what the so-called wedding planner had told me. I'd had all the bridal party options already shipped to my department.

"We are." Beth nodded. "That doesn't mean I'm not curious."

"All the options are good. Trust me."

"I trust you." Lily shrugged. "You're the chicest person I know."

"You're determined to make me look like the annoying bridesmaid, aren't you, wee cuz?" Beth narrowed her eyes teasingly.

"It's not my fault you're so nosy." She stuck her tongue out at Beth.

I'd just let out a laugh that froze in my throat when the familiar opening synth pop beat of "Kids" by MGMT flooded the mezzanine.

No.

Bloody hell.

Not again.

Why was this DJ so obsessed with this song?

The blood rushed in my ears, my cheeks flushing, and I was vaguely aware of an insistent nudge against my upper arm. Turning blindly, I barely processed Baird's concerned face and him gently trying to get me out of the booth.

Like I was on autopilot, I slid out, my legs shaky as the memories flooded in like clockwork.

Mum standing in the kitchen, looking much healthier than the last memory I had of her, grinning as she spun me around, shouting the lyrics at the top of her voice. Her cupping my face in her palms to whisper them, bright tears in her eyes, like I meant something to her.

Like she did love me.

"My." Baird tugged me toward the middle of the mezzanine where there was a little more room to maneuver.

I tried to pull my hand away. "I need to leave."

He hauled me into his arms, a tight band around my waist as I tilted my head back to look at him in anger. What was he doing?

"She doesn't get to do this to you," he said, just loud enough to be heard over the music. "This song ... it's ours now. Okay?"

"Baird ..."

"Whenever you hear it, you'll think of this. Us." He abruptly let me go and started jumping on the balls of his feet. "Control yourself ..." He shouted at the top of his voice, grinning encouragingly at me.

My heart thumped in my chest.

Baird kept singing and bopping more than dancing, totally loose and uninhibited. He ignored the guys shouting good-natured abuse at him, his gaze fixed firmly on me.

"Control yourself ...," I whispered, forcing my legs to move.

He reached for me, twining his fingers through mine as his movements vibrated down my arm, making me move too.

My voice grew louder, my hips looser as I focused on Baird. And instead of the memories of Mum, I let the memories of the past few months flood over me. Baird's confession about wanting to be with me, the way he knew me, *really* knew me, his protectiveness, his encouragement, his belief in me. The way his body felt wrapped around mine, his sweet kisses, his hard kisses ... his utter devotion.

I laughed as Baird tossed his head like an idiot, his hair that he's growing out flying around as he winked at me, trying to keep me with him in this moment.

It was then that I realized how unfair it was to wait for him to say the words *I love you* when he'd been making all the first moves from the very beginning.

Knowing the song by heart, I knew when the last refrains of it were dying, and I stopped dancing.

Baird did too, concern puckering his brow as he waited to see if he'd done the right thing.

Be brave, Maia. Be brave for him.

My heart thumped so hard I felt sick, but I took a breath and then I let it out on three words, "I love you."

Baird's expression slackened.

Oh shit.

"I—"

He abruptly stepped into my personal space, his grip on my hips almost bruising. "Say that again," he demanded harshly.

I refused to look away as I licked my very dry lips. "I love you, Baird McMillan. I'm in love with you."

There. I'd said—

Baird kissed me hard, rough, desperate, and I clung to his shoulders as I tried to match his ferocity. Suddenly he pulled away, physically turning us and nudging me back toward the booth. What the heck ...

He snatched up my purse, barely looking at our companions. "Maia and I need to leave. Catch you later."

"What—" I shot my friends a look of apology as they catcalled after us, seeming to understand the situation better than I did.

"Baird!"

"Keep going." He gently pressed on my back as I descended the mezzanine stairs.

"What is happening?"

Baird did not answer. Instead, he grabbed my hand as

soon as we reached the bottom and bulldozed his way through the crowd of dancers, leading me out of the club.

"Hey, that's McMillan and his bird!" some bloke shouted.

"Oh my God, it's Maia and Baird!"

A phone appeared in my face. "Can I get a selfie?"

"No!" Baird barked, tugging me after him.

It was a chaotic departure, and my heart was pounding. "Baird, will you talk to me, please?" I demanded.

"As soon as we are alone," he replied breathlessly.

"Baird!" I jerked on his hand, almost stumbling on a cobble.

He glanced back at me and bit out a curse at the uncertainty in my expression. "No, Maia." He cuddled me close, cupping my cheek. I was surprised to feel his erection prodding my stomach as he confessed gruffly, "I've been in love with you since we met."

"Really?"

"Aye, really. And you telling me you love me is the greatest thing I've ever heard in my life. Problem is, my cock thinks so too, so I need to get you alone. Now."

Joy bubbled out of me in a flood of giggles. "Oh."

Baird chuckled. "Aye. Oh. Can we hurry this along, please?"

From there we were a bundle of giddiness as we ran to my apartment. I nearly went over on my ankles a few times on the bloody cobbles, but Baird kept me upright.

He also practically dragged me up my flat stairs, but when we got inside, my laughter fled at the utter adoration in his eyes. He locked the door and held out his hand. And I wanted to burst into tears—the good kind. I held it together as I threaded my fingers through his and let him lead us at a far less hurried pace to my bedroom.

Baird released his hold on me to unbutton his shirt, throwing the expensive piece of fabric on my bedroom floor. He was so beautiful. I reached out to press my palms to his pecs and trailed my fingers over the artwork tattooed on his skin. One day, as we'd lain in bed, I'd asked him about each piece. Most of them were art he saw, loved, and wanted on his body. The Celtic tribal mandala mishmash design that faded as it scribed its way up around his neck. The dragon breathing fire on his leg. The Caley United logo caught between the thorns of a few roses as they spread down his arm and across the top of his hand. When he was drunk, Ainsley dared him to get the word *Love* tattooed across the top of his knuckles, so he did, and he didn't regret it.

"It's what life is about at the end of the day. What we love, who we love ... that's what gets us up in the morning," he'd whispered in my ear, and I'd held my breath waiting for him to tell me he loved me.

But now I knew that he was waiting for me to make that move, not because he was playing games but because he didn't want to scare me off.

"I want you on here somewhere," Baird suddenly whispered.

My gaze flew from tracing his ink to searching his dark eyes. I swear I nearly melted to the floor at his meaning. "Really?"

He swallowed hard and nodded. "I already know what I want." He pointed to his left pec that was free of any ink. "Violets, for the color of your eyes, with the letter M entwined in them. Right over my heart."

Emotion choked me. "Are you sure?"

He cupped my face in his big hands, bringing his nose to mine. "You are forever for me, Maia. Permanently tattooed on my fucking heart, whether I get it done in ink or not."

"I love you so much," I gasped on a slight sob.

Baird squeezed his eyes closed as if in pain. Then he pressed his forehead to mine, his reply rough with feeling, "You have no idea how long I've waited to hear that."

"I'm sorry I made you wait."

"Och, don't you worry, gorgeous. It was worth every agonizing second."

"You always say the most perfect things to me."

"You make it easy." He brushed his mouth over mine, and I sighed into the tender kiss.

Then his fingers tickled my stomach as he pulled gently on the cropped camisole I'd worn tonight. We broke apart so I could lift my arms as he pulled it over my head. His nimble fingers plucked off my strapless bra next. As soon as it was gone, Baird wrapped his arms around me, crushing my bare breasts to his chest as he kissed me with a deep but slow, tender passion.

Baird kissed me like I was cherished and precious, and I wanted him to feel that in return. I reached up onto tiptoes, pushing into him as I wound my arms around his neck and curled my fingers into the soft, thick hair at his nape. Our tongues met in sweet, languid exploration.

He guided us back toward the bed but didn't break the kiss even as we laid down on it. Finally, we broke apart, panting, and my belly swooped with arousal as he lifted me with ease into the middle of the bed.

Holding my gaze, Baird moved to kick off his shoes and unzip his jeans. I shivered at the fierce, possessive look on his face. My hungry eyes traveled over his six-pack, to that miraculous V-cut of his obliques that I loved to explore with my tongue. His cock sprang free from his jeans and boxer briefs. I licked my lips possessively. Because every inch of Baird McMillan belonged to me too.

"I want you bare tonight ..." There was a question in his gruff words.

I'd gotten my health check, but we hadn't yet had sex without a condom. I didn't know if it was because Baird was being extra cautious or if he was waiting for me to suggest it. Now I realized he'd been waiting for me.

"I want that too."

I tingled with anticipation as he kicked off his jeans and underwear and then bent over to slip off my high heels. He reached up to unzip my wide leg trousers. My nipples peaked into tight buds, my stomach muscles fluttering as he yanked down my pants, along with the barely there lacy knickers.

I didn't know why I bothered with nice underwear because Baird took very little time to appreciate it before he whipped it off me.

He braced his hands on either side of my hips, his greedy eyes lingering between my thighs before climbing my body. The muscle in his jaw clenched as he drank in my breasts and then when his gaze reached my face, my breath stuttered.

There was such longing there mingling with the lust. Longing, lust ... and love.

I realized then he'd been looking at me like that for weeks. Maybe even months.

Baird *loved* me.

A tear escaped down my cheek before I could stop it, and I reached up to flick it away.

"Good tears?" Baird whispered.

I nodded, my lips trembling.

In answer, he pressed a reverent, sweet kiss to my stomach, and I threaded my fingers through his hair as he trailed his knuckles across my belly and up toward my breasts. His touch was gentle and claiming at the same time as he stroked my breasts, his thumbs brushing over my nipples. I arched my back as he trailed kisses down my stomach toward where I wanted him most.

I groaned in need as Baird moved back upward instead. I could feel his cheeky smile against my skin as his beard and lips sent my senses into overload. Wanting my mouth again, he kissed me until I was breathless, then his lips moved down my chin in a path of affection along my throat and breasts.

He rolled us suddenly, again with such ease, until he was flat on his back, and I was braced over him. He caught my breast in his mouth, and I cried out at the sensation, straddling his waist and holding on to the headboard as he sucked and licked and laved at my nipple before moving onto the next.

By this point my skin was flushed and damp with sweat and I needed him inside of me. I needed to be connected to him in every way possible.

I pulled away, but only to straddle him properly, rubbing against his erection while I trailed my fingers over his pecs and abs. Baird let out a little groan, his stomach muscles flexing at my touch, and there was an answering throb in my clit.

Just as suddenly, my desire to thrust down over him was overwhelmed by my desire to claim every inch of him. I kissed him again, hungrier, greedier, and his grip on my hips turned bruising as I rolled them over his cock. Baird groaned into my mouth, and I rolled a little harder, making him break away to pant the word *fuck* against my lips.

A smile of pleasure curled my lips and his dark gaze

heated at the sight. I bent my head again, but this time to kiss his throat. He liked having his throat kissed. It was one of his many erogenous zones. Honestly, though, Baird was just one big walking erogenous zone. The thought made me smile as I trailed kisses down his chest. His rough palms felt wonderful as he caressed my back, my breasts, my stomach, my arse. My breath hitched as his thumb slipped between the crease of my cheeks.

I licked his left nipple and then sucked it between my teeth. He squeezed my arse, pulling me hard against him. His body was tense with anticipation, but I wanted to devour all of him. I kissed down his stomach, licking the sweat off his abs as I traced his sculpted contours with my tongue.

As I slid farther down his body, his hips jerked upward. "Fuck. Maia ... fuck."

There was no need to tease him. I didn't want to. Instead, I took as much of him as I could into my mouth and fisted the base of his cock, stroking the length that was way too much.

"Fuck!" Baird's thigh muscles contracted, tightening up as I took a pulling suck at the same time jerking him tightly in my hand. We'd done this enough times for me to know exactly what he liked.

The wet between my thighs intensified, as did the swooping lust deep in my belly. Glancing up at Baird's flushed face, I grew more and more aroused by how undone he was.

"Fuck!" he gritted out. "My, My, My ... stop, stop, *stop*."

I abruptly did, my heart pounding in my ears.

Baird tugged on my arm, pulling me upward. "I need inside you, My. I want to come inside you, not your mouth. Not this time."

Understanding, I moved over him, straddling him, bracing my hands on his strong shoulders as he reached between us. I sucked in a breath as he pushed his fingers inside me.

His nostrils flared. "Oh, aye, you're ready."

So ready.

I wrapped my hands around his cock, pushing up on my knees to guide him. Baird clasped my hips, his hands huge and masculine. Because of his size, every time he entered me, it was overwhelmingly full. It always took me a second to adjust.

I let out a humming noise I couldn't hold back as all the nerves in my body electrified.

Baird grunted my name, his features harsh with pleasure as his fingers bit into my skin. "You good?" he bit out.

"Just ... just a sec ..." I pressed my palms to his pecs, adjusting my position a little.

"Fuck," he panted, his eyes flashing as they roamed over my body. "Do you even know how good you feel? Your pussy is my favorite place in the world."

My answering laugh abruptly turned into a moan as my lower body jerked with the motion. I lifted slowly and then pushed back down on a groan of pleasure.

We held each other's eyes as I unhurriedly rode him. "I love you."

"I love you too. Fuck, do I love you." He guided me back down, rolling his hips under mine in a way that made my *eyes* roll in the back of my head.

"Oh God!" My hands moved over his fevered skin as his grip tightened until he was riding me from below.

The tension coiled tighter and tighter inside me, but I forced myself not to go too fast. I wanted to draw out every inch of this moment.

Baird had other things in mind.

Suddenly, he flipped me onto my back. "Bear!"

He swallowed my gasp in a passionate kiss that left my head spinning. I curled my fingers in his hair, holding on for dear life. My lower body jerked at the touch of his fingers, of his thumb circling my clit, and my thighs widened, opening for him to explore.

As he pressed down on the bundle of nerves at my apex, my legs trembled, my stomach tightened, and my feet pressed into the mattress as the tension became too much.

Baird circled my clit harder and just like that, I shattered in his arms, breaking his kiss to gasp and moan as I shuddered beneath him.

"I love you, Maia," Baird groaned against my throat before kissing down my body again, muttering over and over like he couldn't stop saying it. He tormented my nipples with his mouth until they were red and throbbing and I was pleading for him to make me come.

In answer, he pushed my thighs open and took my swollen clit into his mouth.

"Uh!" I cried out, my back bowing at the pleasure-pain that burned through my nerves as he suckled me.

I tried to reach for him as he held my gaze and devoured me, licking and kissing my pussy. Thrusting his tongue into me until I was a writhing puddle of need, begging him to come back inside me.

His lips and tongue tormented my clit, pushing me over the edge again. This time I was glad for no neighbors on this side of the wall as my cry of release echoed off it. I was still shivering from the intensity of my climax when Baird climbed my body to brace himself over me. I felt the hot nudge of him and then he thrust inside.

My thighs fell open, my hands smoothing over his hot, damp back as he pumped into me in slow, hard drives.

"I love you," he grunted out, his eyes dark with hot possessiveness. "I love you so much. You're everything, My. Everything."

"You too!" I gasped, planting my feet to move my hips against his drives.

Baird's features hardened, his teeth gritted with need as he sat back on his knees. He gripped my thighs so my bottom and feet were lifted off the bed and pounded back into me.

"Oh my god!" I curled my fingers into the sheets, unable to do anything but take what he needed to give.

"You love me, Maia?" he demanded on a powerful pump of his hips that pushed my back up the bed.

"Yes!"

"You're mine?"

"Yes!"

"Fuck aye!" His hips undulated quickly as he thrust in and out, so deep and hard and bruising and needy. "I'm yours, My. Every fuckin' inch of me, baby. I'm yours!"

My scream was hoarse with emotion as everything in me seemed to release into him. The clench of my inner muscles was so intense, I felt them throb around Baird like a tight fist. He made a guttural sound of pleasure before his hips froze and he erupted inside me. I felt something else I'd never felt before. I felt him empty into me.

His awed, breathless expletives filled the bedroom as he jerked and trembled. His chest heaved as he continued to twitch inside me, pulses of his prolonged climax.

We looked at each other, flushed and sweaty, our minds blown by the ferocity of our orgasms. Baird's gaze lowered between us as he gently pulled out. I felt the wet rush of his cum and Baird growled, "Fuck me, why is that so hot?"

I let out a satisfied giggle, branded by the heated look in his eyes and the feel of him dripping from me.

"Mine," I whispered without even thinking.

Baird's expression softened to tenderness, his words gruff as he replied, "Aye, you better fuckin' believe it. Yours for life, Maia MacLeod soon-to-be McMillan."

CHAPTER THIRTY-TWO
BAIRD

If Maia consumed most of my thoughts before she admitted she loved me, the woman was now my full-blown obsession. We were only three weeks out from the wedding, and I was the happiest I'd ever been in my life.

She loved me back.

I'd convinced myself I'd be happy with Maia's love, even if she never quite loved me as much as I loved her, but I would have been wrong. Because knowing Maia was as crazy about me as I was about her was the most euphoric fucking feeling in the world, and I couldn't have settled for less in the end. If I'd done anything right in this life, it was being loved by Maia. What bloke wouldn't feel like a champion if Maia MacLeod fell in love with him?

We had more photoshoots to do for Pennington's and then it would be the wedding. I was itching to marry Maia. To be able to call her my wife. Fuck, it made me hard just thinking about it. Since I thought about it regularly, we seemed to spend most of our free time having sex. Since my fiancée felt safe with me, she also felt safe to experiment, and I was having a lot of fun trying out different positions with her.

It was Sunday morning. Maia had no work, I had no training, and there was no Pennington's video shoot to do. We'd gone out with our friends last night, but our evening abruptly ended when the paps showed up to follow us from dinner to the nightclub. I was looking forward to that bull-shit being over with. We'd gotten in a taxi and asked it to drive around to shake them off before we returned to my flat where our friends were waiting for us. It was a chill night, and Maia ended up falling asleep before Callan and Beth had even left.

That morning, I'd woken her so she could help me with my Sunday morning glory. An hour later we were still at it, both of us dripping with sweat, skin flushed, while I had Maia positioned on her back, legs straight up and then crossed at the ankles, resting on my shoulders. As I sunk my cock into her tight, wet heat, the angle meant I hit her G-spot every time. Maia's face was screwed up in pleasure, her lips parting on cries that grew louder and louder as her fingers clenched the pillow behind her head.

"That's it, gorgeous," I encouraged roughly, holding tight to my own orgasm because I wanted her to come first. I grunted loudly because Maia liked it loud.

She cried out hoarsely as I pushed her toward climax.

"That better be Maia, wee bro, or I am going to kill you!" my sister's voice screeched like a banshee. It was worse than a cold fucking shower.

Maia's eyes flew wide, and she promptly slapped her hands over her face in mortification.

It took me a second to process what the bloody hell was happening.

"Ains?" I barked.

"Aye! Maia texted me yesterday and told me she was going to be at her dad's this morning!" I could hear my sister's voice trembling with anger. "So, who is up there with you?"

The fucking mezzanine. I glared over my shoulder where my bedroom balustrade was. Thankfully, Ainsley couldn't see us. But she'd heard us!

"Are you serious?" I yelled. "You barge into my flat and then accuse me of cheating on My!"

"Well, excuse me for letting myself in with the key you gave me! I thought we could go for breakfast!" There was real emotion in her voice, and despite my frustration I turned back to Maia who was peeking at me between her fingers.

"Will you tell her it's you, please?"

Maia groaned in embarrassment but removed her hands from her face. Squeezing her eyes closed, she yelled out, "It's me, Ainsley! Sorry for the confusion!"

"I've lost my fucking hard-on," I muttered grumpily, pulling out of Maia.

Maia giggled. At least she was amused.

Ainsley called back up, "Thank God!"

Right. That was it.

"Where are you going?" Maia sat up, her breasts trembling with the movement.

I stared at her forlornly, cursing my sister to hell for interrupting what was about to be a spectacular orgasm for us both. I'd already pulled on my joggers and was reaching for a tee.

"To kill my sister."

"Bear!" Maia tried to reach for me, but I was gone, taking the spiral staircase down to the main floor.

Ainsley stood at the kitchen island and gave me a sheepish grimace. "Sorry."

"I don't know what I'm more pissed off about—that you interrupted a private moment between me and my fiancée or that you thought I'd cheat on My. In fact, I do know. I can't believe you thought I'd cheat on Maia!"

My sister winced. "I'm sorry. It's just she told me she was going to be at her dad's this morning, so I thought I'd hang out with you. And then I heard sex noises …" Her gaze turned uncharacteristically pleading. "I'm sorry. It was shitty to think that. I know you never would."

"Bugger." We heard Maia say from above us. Fuck, you really could hear everything up there.

"What's up, gorgeous?" I called out.

"I forgot I am supposed to be at Dad's. I'm jumping in the shower."

I slumped, disappointed she was leaving.

Ainsley snorted. "You've got it bad. Can't be without her for a day, huh?"

"No." I stuck my tongue out at her like I was five. "Jealous?"

"Uh, no. I do not want to be so obsessed with someone I can't function without them."

"I can function." I moved into the kitchen. "Coffee?"

"Sure. I brought bagels." Ainsley pushed a carrier bag along my island. "Sorry for interrupting."

It occurred to me that since I'd started seeing Maia, I really hadn't seen as much of my big sister. Guilt made my cheeks hot. "Sorry for being … MIA."

"Don't you mean MIM?" she teased.

"Eh?"

"Missing in Maia." She snorted at her joke.

I laughed but shrugged because who gave a fuck if it was true.

We were halfway through our coffees and bagels when Maia rushed downstairs, wet hair in a messy bun, glasses on, cheeks flushed, wearing a pair of sports leggings and a cropped T-shirt. She was at my place so much, she'd started leaving clean clothes so she had something to change into.

"Coffee?" I asked.

She hurried over, shaking her head. "I have to go. I'm already late for brunch." She kissed me quick and hard and then squeezed Ainsley's shoulder as she passed. "Enjoy your bagels!"

"Okay." I jumped off the stool, following quickly as she moved toward the front door. I reached for her, drawing her back against me.

"I'm late." Maia laughed as I hauled her close for a cuddle.

"We need to get a place with a bit more privacy," I murmured as I nuzzled her neck.

She tensed.

I pulled back, eyebrows drawn together. "What?"

Maia's violet eyes searched mine from behind her glasses. "We ... we're getting a place together?"

I grinned. "Aye. We are getting married, My."

"Right." She tried to hold back a cheesy smile but failed. She was so fucking adorable.

I cupped the nape of her neck, holding her to me for a proper goodbye kiss. When I had her panting and flushed and looking at me regretfully, like she hated she had to leave for brunch, I finally released her. "We'll start looking for a place."

"Okay." She bounced on her feet to give me another quick kiss and then flashed me a happy smile. "Love you."

"Love you," I replied gruffly, my heart in my throat as I watched her walk out.

I missed her already.

This was crazy.

I turned with a big sigh to find my sister grinning in absolute delight.

Not because she was happy for me (though I knew she was that too), but because I was giving her enough material to rip the piss out of me for years to come.

"Did you hear that?" She cocked her head, eyes wide.

I narrowed mine. "Hear what?"

"I think … I think … it sounded like a whip lashing."

"Fuck off."

"Or was it your independence dying?"

"Fuck the fuck off."

"It could have been Maia tugging on your leash."

"You know, just because we're blood related doesn't mean we have to be friends."

"Maybe it was your balls being crushed by the vise of impending marriage."

"I officially hate you."

Ainsley cackled. "Ach, you know I'm secretly happy for you, wee bro." She crossed her arms on the countertop and leaned into me. "She loves you back."

I waggled my eyebrows. "I know."

Ainsley pursed her lips.

"What? Just say it."

"Okay, so when you started this thing with Maia, I was more worried about her hurting you than you hurting her. But now—"

"Ains—"

"I know I came in this morning and accused you of something you would never do, and I'm sorry. But that doesn't mean that down the line you might not hurt her. Unintentionally."

I was irritated by the turn in conversation but tried to be patient with my sister. "People in even the best relationships are going to unintentionally hurt each other. That's life."

"The thing is ... I don't know if you've noticed, but Maia's like a totally different person around you. I, honestly, used to wonder what you saw in her. Like, I know she's gorgeous, but I always thought she was kind of aloof. But now I get it. You open her up. She's warm and sweet and she can be silly with you. You make her feel safe to be herself. And that's amazing. But she hasn't completely changed. She's still the same person who was willing to fake a marriage for her career. And she's thirty. Doesn't she want kids soon? Like ... be sure you both are on the same page here."

"Ains, I really appreciate where you're coming from, but I'm not fifteen anymore. Maia and I have talked about all this, and it's between us. Just me and her. Okay?"

"So ... I don't get to have a say at all? I tell you everything about my relationships."

"Aye, too much. There are some things a brother doesn't want to hear. Or have be heard by his sister," I said pointedly, glancing up at my bedroom.

"Oh, please, I've walked in on you doing worse."

"Not the point. I love you, Ains. But my relationship with Maia is between me and Maia. No one else."

My sister searched my face and then weirdly, she smiled. Not the reaction I was expecting.

"What?"

"I've just realized that lately ... you're different too. But in a good way. You're more ... mature. More settled in yourself."

I nodded because she was right. I was.

It was all Maia. She made me want to be a better man. The kind of man she could count on. And part of that meant growing the fuck up.

"You're both handling the campaign madness well," Ainsley offered.

"Aye. We're ignoring it. Seems like the best way to handle it."

"Well, people are obsessed with you as a couple."

"Of course they are. We're the shit."

"Cocky arsehole."

I shrugged, grinning unabashedly.

"For your sakes, I hope it dies down after the campaign," Ainsley said. "It would be a nightmare trying to navigate a marriage with people constantly filming you when you're out in public. And you being in the Professional League isn't going to help the publicity go away. It might affect your marriage eventually, if that's the case."

"Gee, Ains, did you come over to be a big ray of fucking sunshine or what?" My tone was teasing but worry flickered through me at my sister's words. However, I couldn't let those worries sink in too deeply.

I had to believe that the public would grow bored with us and move on to something else because there was no way I wanted either of us to have to deal with that level of scrutiny for too long. I had a feeling Ainsley was right and that eventually, it could impact my and Maia's relationship.

The thought filled me with so much trepidation, I immediately chucked it away.

If only I'd prepared myself better ... because I had no

idea the campaign was about to throw us a devastating curveball.

CHAPTER THIRTY-THREE

MAIA

"**D**on't you swim three times a week?" Gail, the production crew assistant, gave me a narrow-eyed look. She wore a slight air of impatient annoyance.

I did swim three times a week, but there was hardly anyone in the pool and I wasn't strutting out there in a bikini that left very little to the imagination.

Unpleasant butterflies roiled in my stomach as I opened the robe again to look at myself in the mirror. I'd provided Pennington's with a bunch of swimwear options for both me and Bear for the fake honeymoon shoot, and the campaign management had chosen a fuchsia pink bikini set for me. It wasn't that I didn't like it or that I wouldn't wear it under normal circumstances. It was the knowing that millions of people would see me in it that bothered me.

The bikini had a pink print inspired by Spanish tiles. The top was a halter neck with a deep V and padded cups that pushed my boobs up and together. The bottoms had a high cut with a peekaboo strip on the hips and showed a good deal of my arse cheeks.

"It's just a lot of skin to bear to a lot of people," I murmured.

Her expression softened. "You really are nervous, aren't you?"

"I don't particularly enjoy the idea that these images will be on the internet forever for anyone to look at any time they want."

"Ugh, yeah, didn't think about that." She cocked her head. "If it makes you feel any better, any dirty bugger could take a photo of you on the beach and look at it anytime he wants."

Oh my God. I whirled around, lips parted in horror.

Gail tried not to laugh at my expression and failed. "Sorry."

"That is going to be embedded in my brain forever now." I shuddered. "People are creepy."

"Some really are, but we can't stop living because of it."

I blinked at her words because she was right. We couldn't stop ourselves from doing things because of the actions of a few. Nodding in agreement, I shrugged out of the robe and strode across the dressing room. "Let's do this."

"You look gorgeous," she assured me.

"Thank you."

I tried not to meet anyone's eyes as Gail walked me down the hallway and into the studio. There were cameras and crew and a green screen behind the pool. Outdoor furniture available to buy from Pennington's had been set up around the pool—lounge chairs, bistro set, and inflatable armchairs, as well as smaller pieces of summer décor.

Baird stood in navy swim shorts that had a fuchsia stripe down the side to match my bikini. He was chatting with Bruno, and I immediately felt safer at the sight of him.

"Is it okay for me to tell you that your fiancé is smoking hot?" Gail murmured.

"You only speak the truth."

As if he sensed me, Baird's head whipped in my direction, and I tingled all over at the way his eyes moved down my body and back up again.

"Oh my God. How do you not combust at the way he looks at you?" Gail asked like a giddy schoolgirl.

"Maybe I do." I was glad for the padded cups of my bikini because I was pretty sure my nipples were hard from that look alone.

Baird broke away from Bruno, striding toward me with that confident swagger. It was sexy that he knew he was good-looking but that he wasn't a complete prick about it. His hair had grown out a bit, and he could tuck it behind his ears now. The manbun would be back before long.

He gave Gail a brief nod of acknowledgement before pulling me close. "You good?"

I'd told him I was nervous about this one, and he'd told me if I really wanted to, we could find a way out of it. However, I hadn't wanted to cause a fuss. The truth was I wanted this campaign to be over so everyone would leave us in peace. "I'm good," I promised.

"You look incredible." His hands coasted down my back, one smoothing over my arse with a casual possessiveness. "Too good." He waggled his brows at me suggestively.

I rolled my eyes. "You can keep it together for a couple of hours."

"I can," he agreed. "But I can't promise that my monster cock can."

My laugh was part groan as I rested my head on his chest, feeling it shake with his amusement. As promised, Baird hadn't let me live that comment down.

A throat cleared and I realized Gail had overheard him. I playfully shoved him away. "Behave."

———

Even though the pool was heated, I was pretty done with the shoot by hour two. I was weary of being directed to do things that felt unnatural, like posing midair in a jump into the pool and lying on a lounger like some kind of glamour model.

Now Baird and I were on a set of inflatable armchairs, fake splashing each other and grinning into each other's eyes, even though I could tell Baird was over it too.

We pulled the chairs out of the water to film in front of the green screen, pretend-drinking mojitos and enjoying the sun. It was then I became aware that the plastic under my skin felt looser.

I finally processed the whistling sound.

My head whipped toward Baird who was looking down at himself and that's when I realized his chair was deflating.

And so was mine!

Our eyes locked, and with hilarious abruptness, the whistling grew louder as we lowered toward the floor. Either they'd burst or unplugged somehow. Baird reached for me as I reached for him, trying to pull each other out before they completely deflated. We couldn't have stopped our hysterical laughter if we tried.

By the time the chairs flattened, I was collapsed over Baird, and we were laughing so hard I was crying. We could hear the crew trying to get us to pull it together, but we were too far gone.

The pressure and weirdness of the campaign had finally gotten to us and the laughter was a release.

Finally, Bruno stood over us, holding out a phone. "Pull it together, Maia! Hilary is on the line!"

I sucked in a breath, trying to calm down as I wiped at my face, and Baird helped me sit up. Why was my boss calling? Had Bruno tattled on us for ruining the shoot?

I exchanged a confused look with my fiancé and then reached for the phone. Pressing it to my ear, I asked tentatively, "Hilary?" Her name came out a little croaky because of my laughing fit.

"Maia."

Her tone sent a chill through me and any amusement abruptly fled. "What is it?"

"A news article broke in a national tabloid an hour ago. I know you're locked in the studio and most likely haven't seen it. We need you to come into the office."

"What's the news article about?"

"It's your mother, Maia. She sold a story to the papers."

Blood rushed in my ears. Lips suddenly numb, I only vaguely processed the words. "What kind of story?"

"About where you grew up. That she's a recovering addict. And you ran away when you were fifteen, leaving her to fend for herself."

Leaving her to fend for herself?

"You need to come in. We have to talk response strategy. Bruno knows. The shoot is over. Get dressed and get here." She hung up.

Baird pressed a hand to my back. "Maia, what's wrong?"

I stared at the phone as that fifteen-year-old girl I used to know screamed from the back of my mind in absolute fury and heartbreak.

"Maia?"

Suddenly his face was in mine, his hands clasping my cheeks. "Maia, talk to me."

CHAPTER THIRTY-FOUR
BAIRD

My stomach was sick with worry as I drove a silent Maia back to her place. After Hilary's phone call, we'd googled the article in question and sure enough, there it was, front-page headline in the same national tabloid that published the photo of me partying a few months ago. Same fucking journo too. Craig Bennet. There was a picture of Maia from the campaign plastered on the front and then a picture of Maryanne Lewis, Maia's mother, looking surprisingly well and not at all the haggard heroin addict Maia had described from her childhood.

The headline stated:

SOCIAL MEDIA SWEETHEART ABANDONED ME IN MY TIME OF NEED

The subhead: *Maia MacLeod's mum speaks out about her addiction and how her estranged daughter left her behind to fend for herself while she pursued fame and money.*

The double spread article had more photos of Maia when she was a kid, more of Maryanne Lewis, and was just a bunch of bullshit that any moron could see through. How does a kid abandon their heroin-addict parent? She stated that Maia had left their home when she was fifteen to go live with her dad and that Maryanne had felt abandoned by her. That she was clean now and working to help other people get sober. She said she was shocked to see Maia online and it had brought back a lot of painful memories.

I fucking despised the woman, and I'd never met her.

"Not only did she sell a lie, but she got sober," Maia whispered. "She got sober and ... she never reached out. Instead, she sold a twisted version of events to the public."

"Baby ..." I reached over to squeeze her hand, but it was limp in mine.

Fear crawled through me at how distant she was.

"Even if she's clean now ... she ... she hasn't changed. She still cares more about herself than she ever cared about me. I can't blame the addiction anymore. It's her. She's just a terrible fucking person."

I didn't know what to say because I knew deep down there wasn't anything I could say to make it better, and I hated that.

I felt powerless in the worst way.

I'd driven Maia to Pennington's, and her bosses Hilary and Christina were kind enough about the situation. I'd wanted to wipe the smug smirk off that rat Becky's face. The marketing team had decided the best response was no response. It seemed from the commentary online that most people weren't buying the sob story, anyway. A lot of people were on Maia's side. But there were also a loud few calling Maia fake. There were also a lot of arseholes using filthy language they'd never dare use in front of me as they suggested I dump Maia.

Becky took a wee bit too much satisfaction in relaying those comments.

"Enough," I'd snapped at her. "We don't need to know what people are saying."

Her lips had pinched together in that sour way of hers. "Well, actually, we do need to know what the public response to this is and how damaging it is to our campaign and to the company."

Maia had sat in shocked silence throughout the whole conversation, only murmuring agreements when asked to. "Maia isn't her mum. Maia has nothing to do with her mum. Maia is a hardworking member of staff who has, quite frankly, given a lot to this company."

"No one is saying she hasn't," Hilary assured me. "And we're grateful for the boost in sales Pennington's has seen nationally because of the campaign. We just needed to talk strategy and make sure we're all on the same page. Ultimately, we think we shouldn't fan the flames by giving either Maia's mother or the tabloids the satisfaction of a reaction."

Even though I knew that was smart, it didn't mean I didn't want to kill Craig Bennet for writing that article. Or Maia's mum for hurting her. Again.

Maia's phone had blown up with friends and family trying to contact her. Her dad and Grace were the only people she spoke to. It had been a quick call, and she'd promised to call them again when I got her home.

That could wait, though.

I parked on Hart Street and rounded the car to grab Maia's hand as she got out.

"I'm okay," she murmured, finally giving me a wee squeeze.

"Let's get you inside, eh." I locked up the car and held tight to her hand as we strode down the lane to her apartment building.

Once inside, I settled her on the couch, kneeling to help her out of her trainers.

"I'm fine." She attempted to shove me off, but I insisted on helping.

Her tan cheeks were a concerning chalky color.

"I'll make you some tea and toast."

"I'm not hungry."

"Just try to eat a wee something." I marched into the kitchen and quickly made her a snack.

Maia looked at it like it was a pile of shite.

"Please." I nudged the plate toward her.

On a heavy sigh, she took it and placed it beside her on the couch. She wrapped her palms around the hot mug and relaxed against the sofa, closing her eyes.

"I want to wake up from this nightmare," she whispered.

"We'll get through this, My. I promise."

Before she could respond, my phone rang in my back pocket. It had been blowing up too. Callan and John had called to check in. So had Mum and Ains. I had a bunch of texts from friends and family and even from the gaffer, but I hadn't looked at any of them.

My plan was to send the call to voicemail, but it was Brian. A text and a call? Bugger.

I groaned. "It's the gaffer. I need to take it."

Maia nodded. "Of course."

I answered as I strolled out of the living room. "Everything all right?"

His gruff voice rumbled down the line. "I'm sorry to call bearing this news on such a shit day, McMillan, but we have a big fucking problem."

I paused in Maia's hallway. "What kind of problem?"

"Fred saw the article today about your fiancée. He also saw the response online, and he's furious."

Fuck! Fred Burbank had been the bane of my existence this year. I didn't want Maia to overhear this conversation, so I stepped out of the flat. "Why is he furious about the article?"

"Because of how it looks to the club that his goalkeeper's fiancée's mother is a recovering junkie who sells private stories to tabloid newspapers."

"This had nothing to do with Maia."

"It's her mother, Baird."

"Only in the biological sense. Maia has no contact with her."

The gaffer sighed. "I know it's not her fault. But I warned you that you were on your last life with Fred. This is it. He's done. He wants you to end your engagement to Maia, end this campaign immediately, or ... fuck ... we'll have to reconsider your place at this club."

Boiling rage flooded through me so fast and furious, I hung up before I said something I might regret.

"Fuck!" I gripped my hair in my hands, lowering to my haunches, taking in deep breaths to try to calm the hell down before I jumped in my car to annihilate someone. I just wasnae sure who I'd kill first—Maryanne, Craig Bennet, or Fred Fucking Burbank.

The hitch of a breath had me launching to my feet and whirling around.

Maia stood in the doorway, violet eyes shimmering with tears. A sob caught in her throat, and she forced out hoarsely, "I heard. And I won't let you lose everything because of this."

My heart lurched. "My—"

"Call him back. Tell him it's over between us. This campaign has done enough damage. I'm sorry. I'm so sorry, Bear." Her voice broke on the last word as she swung the door shut in my face, the lock sliding aggressively into place.

It happened so fast, I didn't have time to react.

No.

Fucking no way!

"Maia!" I jiggled the door handle, but it didn't budge. "Maia, don't! I'm not losing you over this!"

I heard her sob on the other side of the door and tears thickened in my throat. "Maia, open the door. Let me in. We can fix this."

"I—I a-am fixing i-it. You-you d-deserve better t-than this. Than me." She sobbed harder, and the sharp ache in my chest made me breathless.

Tears burned my eyes as I banged on the door. "Maia." Her name caught on a sob, and I didn't care if she could hear me crying. "Maia, I love you. Don't do this. Don't fuck this up and twist it in your head, baby. Don't let her win."

In answer, her crying grew quieter as she moved away from the door.

Panic suffused me. "Maia! Maia!" I pounded on the door, begging her to open up. I didn't know how long I slammed on her front door before a voice cut through mine.

"Right, that's enough!"

I whirled to find an older woman I'd never seen before standing in the doorway of the flat opposite.

Her hard expression softened at the sight of me with tears on my fucking cheeks. "Och, I see. Well, I'm sorry, lad, but if the lass doesn't want you at her door, then you need to leave. Or I will call the police." She pointedly had her mobile ready to go in her hand.

Wrath at her, at the whole fucking world, threatened to

consume me. I wiped at my cheeks and forced myself to walk away.

Temporarily.

This wasn't it.

There was no way a bunch of arseholes would interfere in our relationship.

But it wasn't really them I was afraid of.

It was Maia's demons.

That seed her mum planted in her mind all those years ago, the one she'd worked so hard to get over ... only for this to happen and prove that bullshit was rooted deep.

Deep enough to stop what was growing between me and her.

My chest felt tight at the thought, even as I tried to convince myself that in twenty-four hours, once she'd calmed down, Maia would come back to me.

She had to.

I'd never get over it if I lost her.

CHAPTER THIRTY-FIVE
BAIRD

While I'd been lucky so far in life to not have lost someone I loved, I knew from my injury how the course of your existence could change in an instant.

The dark place I'd fallen into after my career-disrupting accident was nothing compared to the black fucking hole that yawned before me at the thought of losing Maia forever.

I think I was still in shock because it had happened so quickly. She hadn't given me a chance to tell her that there was nothing in this world that would ever make me walk away from her.

Maia had shut me out completely, and according to Callan, she wasn't answering Beth's calls either. It had been a full day since I'd seen her, and a quick call into Pennington's told me she hadn't turned up for work.

"She called in sick," Eli informed me. "She didn't tell you?"

"No." I'd forced the word out. "I'll go check on her."

Eli's voice lowered. "Tell her we're here too. I know what it's like to have a crap parent."

"Thanks." I'd hung up and tried Maia again, but her phone went straight to voicemail.

That morning, I missed training because I was afraid I'd spew my rage all over the gaffer and he didn't deserve it. Ultimately, Fred was the money, the owner, and he made the final decision, even if the gaffer didn't agree with him. That left me at home, pacing and stewing. When the notifications sounded on my phone and I picked it up to see people on socials were sharing a new article, I lost my shit.

The journalist had followed up the story with an article on Maia's dad and the fact that he'd spent time in prison for assaulting his sister's ex-boyfriend.

The thought of Maia seeing that, of the hurt and guilt she'd feel for bringing her dad and aunt into this, was the straw that broke the camel's back. My mind wiped blank of everything but rage. There was nothing but a need to mete out justice for this bullshit. I googled the address I wanted and then I thundered out of my flat. I'd just reached my car when the sound of car doors slamming and my name being shouted registered.

Callan and John were hurrying toward me from Callan's Defender, their expressions tight with worry. "Where are you going?" Callan pressed a hand to my driver's side door to stop me from getting in.

I knocked it away, throwing it open. "To fucking kill that wee prick!"

He winced as John paled. "What prick?"

"Did you see? Did you see he wrote another fucking story about Maia—except this time it's about her dad?"

"We saw." John gripped my shoulder. "You can't go

after a journo, Baird. Your career, and possibly your life, will be over."

"My career is already fucking over," I spat. "Fred says I need to break it off with My or I'm out."

Callan's eyes flared with anger. "No fucking way."

"Aye. Way." I jumped into my car and my best pal held the door open. "Keen, let go o' the fuckin' door. Now!"

At my bark, he let go and I slammed it shut.

The lads were already hurrying back to the Defender, but I didn't care. I was out of there. The hour and a half drive it took to get from Edinburgh to Glasgow was cut down by at least twenty minutes with the speed of my wrath.

I parked illegally and tore out of my car and into the office building that housed the tabloid newspaper. I thought I heard someone shout my name as I got on the lift, but I stabbed the button for the newspaper's floor and the doors closed on the yells. Blood rushed in my ears and my fists clenched at my sides, ready to mash the journo's face into a wall.

Stepping onto the floor, I eyed the security guard who stood outside the glass double doors that had the newspaper's name etched on it in gold. I forced myself to be a bit smart about this. As smart as I could be in the moment. I approached the receptionist. "Aye, could you point me in the direction of Craig Bennet? I have an appointment with him."

The woman's eyes narrowed as she searched my face, and I knew she recognized me but couldn't quite place me. "Let me just call his desk."

Shit.

Fuck.

I threw a shifty glance at the security guard who was

scrolling on his phone. Christ, I could probably walk right by that idiot.

I was contemplating it when the receptionist sighed. "His line is busy. One second and I'll go see if he's available. What was your name?"

"John Keen," I lied because I was intending to follow her, anyway.

Sure enough, the security guard just gave her a barely there glance as she pushed open the double doors, so I snuck in behind her, letting him think I was supposed to be following her. Then I slowed, waiting for her to make her way through the busy open-plan office. There were messy desks everywhere and while there were privacy screens between desks, everyone was loud and social as they went about the business of publicly gossiping about people's fucking lives.

I sneered at them as I followed the receptionist through the room. When she stopped at a desk, I picked up my pace. I'd almost reached it, seeing the top of a bloke's bald head when my arm was yanked.

"Baird!"

Callan was somehow there and had a hold of my arm, expression hard and determined.

John stood behind him, glancing over his shoulder at the security guard who stood nervously at the top of the room watching us as he spoke into a walkie-talkie.

"He's not worth it, mate." Callan's grip tightened.

"Maia is." I yanked my arm and turned back to see Craig standing, looking nervous but with a defiant tilt to his chin.

"Baird McMillan." Craig Bennet had a reedy voice that irritated me as much as his crap journalism did. "I think you should listen to your teammates and leave before we call the police."

I was going to knock his teeth out and then break his fingers. See how he'd get on writing his shitty articles then.

"Baird." Callan leaned in, tone harsh. "You do this, and you really lose Maia forever. You'll lose everything."

I breathed hard, shaking against the urge to take it all out on this bloke. Because someone needed to pay for the pain Maia was in right now, all the pain I couldn't fucking fix! "You said in your latest piece-of-shit article there was a source. Who?"

"I can't tell you that. They emailed me the information and asked to remain anonymous. I have to respect that."

"Respect that? I'm going to—"

Callan tightened his grip. "He's not worth a prison sentence. And Maia needs you."

"She broke up with me," I gritted out. "She thinks ... she thinks I deserve better."

"Jesus." Callan squeezed my shoulder. "She's just hurting, mate. She doesn't mean it. You'll fix it."

"I can't!" I turned on him. "That bitch fucked her up so badly and *he*"—I stabbed a finger in Bennet's direction—"fucking let her do it again!"

Callan gripped the front of my shirt and shook me. Hard. "I know where Maia is right now," he hissed under his breath. "I've been right there in her shoes. And trust me ... she'll come around. But she can't come around if you are in prison for beating the shit out of a sad wee prick who doesn't deserve a single second of your time."

"He's right, man," John urged softly. "Let's go. Walk away."

Callan's wisdom started to penetrate, and the fog of fury that had driven me here dissipated as his words gave me a bit of hope. While my dad had walked out of my life when I was a bairn, I'd had my granddad to fill that void.

Callan had his stepdad and mum, but when they were killed in an accident, he was left with nothing but a waste-of-space dad. His dad had screwed over Braden Carmichael when they were younger and that history had messed with Callan. He'd almost lost Beth because of his own bullshit about it ... but she'd pulled him back.

Which meant I could still fix things with Maia.

Shit.

I sagged as the worst of the anger drained away and Callan sighed heavily in relief as he released his hold on me.

It was then I realized it had grown quiet in this part of the room as people waited to see what would happen next. I eyed the receptionist who had stepped to the side, nervously, afraid of me.

Fuck.

That cooled my fury fever too.

Bennet still stood, but he swallowed hard as he forced himself to hold my gaze.

"You're not worth it," I told him quietly. "You're bottom-feeding scum. And I feel sorry for you that your life's work is basically fucking gossiping and not giving one shit what damage your stories do to people's lives. I wish you a lifetime of misery and loneliness, you pathetic. *Little*. Turd."

Bennet looked away, the muscle in his jaw clenching, and I scoffed, turning and nodding toward the exit. "Let's go, boys."

John and Callan couldn't hide their relief as they fell into step and accompanied me out of the building. The security guard eyed us warily as he moved aside to let us pass.

We didn't talk until we were outside and I saw Callan's

Defender parked behind my car. They must have flown down that motorway to keep up with me.

"I think I just shit myself." John tried to ease the tension with a joke. "Seriously, Keen nearly killed us chasing you down that motorway. I ... Man, I've never seen you lose it like that."

I scrubbed my hand over my face. "I dinnae ken what came over me."

"Maia did." Callan shrugged. "Mate, I get it. I'd want to kill anyone who tried to hurt Beth. But My doesn't need you doing something stupid. She just needs to know you're there."

"I've called her a stalker level number eh' times since last night." I leaned back against my car, squeezing the bridge of my nose. My accent thickened as it always did when I was tired or emotional. "I dinnae ken how tae get through tae her right noo."

"Aye, you do." Callan's expression hardened.

I read that look in his eyes and nodded, determination thrumming through me. "I need tae get tae the club."

"I've got your back."

"Me too." John patted my shoulder. "Civilian life isn't so bad, you know."

Aye, well, I was about to find that out for myself.

CHAPTER THIRTY-SIX
MAIA

My phone was currently turned off and hidden in a shoebox in my dressing room. Honestly, I was just too in shock, too busy spiraling, to think about it. Which was why my parents had shown up at my door last night. All I could do was cry. I couldn't speak. Until Dad asked where Baird was and I somehow managed to choke out that I'd broken it off with him. They had questions, but the pain in my chest was so bad I thought I was going to be sick.

They hadn't wanted to leave me, but they had to get home for Lockie, and truthfully, I needed space. Dad was so furious at Mum that his anger hurt me as much as it soothed me.

When they left, I cried so hard I did throw up, and it was at that point I knew I needed to find a way to calm down. I tried some mindfulness techniques Beth had taught me, but every time my head grew quiet, a sentence from the article would pop up, breaking my heart all over again. Or I'd hear Baird's gaffer loudly telling him he needed to dump me or he'd lose his place at the club.

Terror had filled me in that moment.

Of ruining Baird the way my mum seemed to ruin everyone in her orbit.

I wouldn't be the reason he lost the thing that made him feel safe. The club was his home.

I didn't feel worthy enough to sacrifice that for.

In fact, I felt ... small and unclean, just like I used to when I was young and everyone whispered behind my back about how I was the kid of a junkie. About how my mum would have sex with anyone who could get her a hit. There were even rumors that she sold me out for sex, so boys at school used to proposition me, say disgusting things I didn't even understand until I was older. I hadn't yet told Baird that part.

Everything I'd worked so hard to forget, to leave behind, had been wiped away in the space of a few minutes.

But this time it wasn't because I was the child of an addict. It was because I was the child of a woman who put me through that, made me feel guilty for not being able to deal with an addiction that was beyond her control, and then when she got clean ... she still sold me out. She sold lies and sob stories about her own flesh and blood, and for what? A payday?

All these years I'd blamed heroin for taking my mum from me.

But she'd been clean for years and not only had she not sought me out, she had betrayed me. She *used* me.

And Baird. Now he was tarnished by association.

That's what Fred Burbank thought. Maybe even his teammates. The public definitely thought that.

That night, I barely slept, tossing and turning between crying jags. Wishing she still didn't have the power to hurt me this much. Crying for Bear. Missing him. Missing his big arms around me, making me feel safe and loved … and worthy.

It took everything I had to call in sick to work, grateful it was Eli I spoke to and not my boss. They tried to talk to me, reassure me, but I cut them off, hanging up rudely. Hopefully they understood.

My heart leapt into my throat at the loud pounding on my door at 9:00 a.m. Part of me hoped it was Baird and the other part knew I'd crumble to pieces if it was.

It wasn't him.

Beth, Lily, and January stood on the other side of my door.

"What are you doing here?"

"You weren't answering your phone." Beth pushed in, throwing her arms around me in a tight hug.

That was all it took for me to burst into tears.

A wee while later, we sat in my living room. I'd finally stopped crying, and Lily had made me a hot cup of tea. Beth sat by my side, her arm still around me, while the girls waited patiently for me to talk.

Even January was uncharacteristically serious. Not so uncharacteristically, she was beyond pissed off with my mum.

Feeling terrible that I'd worried them so much that they'd ditched their work and school to come check on me, I turned my phone back on.

"Just don't look at social media," Lily advised. "At the end of the day, strangers' opinions about you are not your business."

I knew her words were wise, and I really tried to let them sink in. Yet, Baird's boss wasn't a stranger and, unfortunately, his opinion was my business. My boss was not a stranger, and it mattered to me what Pennington's thought about all of this. I was terrified to find out.

Thankfully, I'd turned off my social media notifications weeks ago because of the campaign. I did have texts and missed calls. So many from Baird, I started to cry silently. Then my heart lurched in my throat at a text from an unknown number.

> Three years we were together, and you didn't tell me about your mum. No wonder. Not so superior now, My? Guess I made the right choice.

I sucked in a breath at the callous text, and Beth peered at my screen.

"Is that from Will?" Her tone was low with fury.

Nodding, I blocked his number.

"What is it?"

Beth relayed what the text had said, and the room went chilly with their anger.

Jan seethed. "I'm definitely breaking into his flat and leaving a dead fish in his closet."

"I still have a spare key."

Her eyes sparkled. "Nice."

"I can't believe I was going to marry that prick."

"You never would have." Beth rubbed my shoulder. "My, you didn't tell him about your mum because deep down you must have known that would be his arsehole response."

"Did ... did you tell Baird?" Lily asked tentatively.

My lips trembled and the sob escaped as I nodded.

"And I bet he was lovely about it," Beth guessed.

All I could do was nod again, my chest aching so badly, it felt like it might actually be in the midst of cracking.

"Oh, My." She pressed her forehead to my temple. "Did something happen with Baird?"

Through fits and starts and sobs and whispers, I told them what happened with the call from his gaffer and me immediately shutting him out.

"Look." I handed Beth my phone, tapping the screen so she could see how many missed calls and texts there were from him.

"You should talk to him." She pushed the phone back to me. "Call him."

"Why? So he can give up everything he loves just so I don't feel like shit? He would, you know. But then one day, he might wake up and realize he gave up everything for someone who didn't deserve that kind of sacrifice."

"Of course you do!" Jan huffed. "Nah, you can't talk about yourself like that, My."

Lily placed a hand on her knee to quiet her. Then she turned to me. "This is about your mum and how she made you feel?"

I shrugged, feeling the oily shame of my mum's behavior all over again.

"Maia, you know that the people who really matter don't believe you are your mum. And I know you'll have very complicated feelings about her addiction and how she got sober and didn't get in touch only to do this to you, but good people won't judge you for that. I know I don't. Her actions aren't a reflection on you. They're a reflection on her. You know that, right?"

I stared at my sweet, sweet cousin, a lump of pain constricting my throat. "That's how you see it, Lily. But that's not how I've been treated. Growing up, I was treated like scum because of my mum. I hated her and I hated myself for hating her when I know this addiction was beyond her control. But it turns out she got clean. She got clean after I was gone. What does that say about our relationship? Was I the reason for her addiction in the first place?

"And maybe I could understand her not reaching out because it might have been too much for her ... but I will never understand or forgive her for vilifying me publicly. For money. We haven't spoken in fifteen years, and she betrayed me for what? A thousand quid at most? I hate her for that. And it hurts. It really hurts. And I hate her for how people will look at me because of her. Like ... I'm trash. Either because of her addiction ... or because I left her behind because of her addiction. I'm trash either way."

Beth sucked in a breath. "Please don't call yourself that. You are not that, and who cares about people who don't matter?"

Lily eyed me thoughtfully. "I don't think the problem is what other people think. I think the problem is that her inability to fight her addiction to be the mother you needed has made you feel like you are less than. That you are unworthy. And then she goes and chooses money, and not very much at that, to sell you out, reinforcing those old feelings."

My chest heaved as her words hit their target, and I buried my face in my hands to cover my shame, because I despised that she was right.

"Oh, My." Beth pulled me into her arms, stroking my hair. "That's not true. You have to know that's not true."

"Baird adores you." Jan's voice hitched, and I glanced over through my tears to see she was wiping her own from her cheeks. "He looks at you like you're his whole world. Let him be here for you through this."

"I can't." I shook my head, wiping at my snotty nose

and cheeks as I pulled from Beth's embrace. "I love him too much to watch him throw everything away for me." Sucking in a huge gulp of air, I tried to take calming breaths. "I love you girls. Really. And I know you mean well, but I have to end this before he gets hurt any more than he already has been." Determination cut through my pain. "I need to go to Pennington's and tell them the campaign is over. I need to fix this for him."

Jan's face turned red with apparent frustration *"You're* making a mistake."

"When you fall in love, Jan ... you'll understand. You'll do just about anything to protect that person. Even if it means walking away."

Jan pushed to her feet, shoving her shoes back on. "Sorry, My. I love you, but I can't stick around to listen to this martyr BS. And I say this with all the tough love in the world, but, girl, you should talk to someone. A therapist. Or your childhood trauma is going to fuck up the rest of your life." She leaned over and pressed a quick kiss to the top of my head, I think to soften the blow of her words, before she strode out of my apartment.

Stunned, I gaped at Lily who sighed heavily. Is that what she thought too? Her opinion meant a lot to me, not just because she was one of the most levelheaded, kindest people I knew but because Lily was in postgrad to become a psychotherapist. "My sister can be blunt. Sorry."

But was she right?

"I hate to sound like a therapist-to-be." Lily cocked her head in thought. "But ... I have to ask if you truly believe Baird thinks you're unworthy."

"Of course not." I shook my head. "He makes me feel special every day."

"But you think you know better? That you're a bad person?"

I frowned. "Well ... no."

"That you would not be a supportive wife?"

"Of course I'd be a supportive wife."

"So, you wouldn't cheat on him?"

"Never!" I was affronted by the suggestion.

"You wouldn't shut him out when you were having a bad day?"

"No, he always gets it out of me."

"So, you wouldn't judge him if he ended up in a career where he wasn't making as much money as he is now?"

"Lily, you know me better than that. I'd take Baird no matter what he does for a living. Though, stripping might bother me." I made a face at Beth, who chuckled.

"What if his swimmers don't work and he can't give you kids?"

I frowned and shrugged. "We'd adopt."

She raised an eyebrow. "A tabloid printed a story in the paper saying he'd cheated on you?"

My heart lurched at the thought, but I couldn't imagine a world in which Baird would do that. He was big on loyalty. I knew now how tabloids could twist lies into fake truths. "I'd give him the benefit of the doubt," I answered with true honesty.

"His mum got ill and needed to stay with you?"

"Then she'd stay with us. I'd hope he'd feel the same way if it was my dad or Grace."

Lily smiled. "I think you sound like the kind of fiancée every guy would feel lucky to have. Listen back to everything you just said, Maia ... and can you honestly tell me you don't deserve Baird? That you wouldn't be the right choice for him if he had to choose?"

I gaped at her as Beth laughed quietly at my side. "You are very sneaky, Lily Sawyer."

"She's going to make a hell of a therapist." Beth beamed at her proudly.

Lily's olive cheeks flushed but she shrugged. "Sometimes we get something so stuck in our minds and hearts, we can't see the woods for the trees."

Slowly, I nodded, letting her wisdom sink in. "I ... I still think I need to end the campaign. Baird deserves the chance to have more time to decide without the pressure of something that seems so shallow now."

"Your career was on the line," Beth reminded me. "That's not shallow."

"Now his is. And maybe ... maybe ending the campaign will be enough for the club owner. Once everything dies down ..." Hope blossomed in my chest. "We'll be able to be together again."

CHAPTER THIRTY-SEVEN
MAIA

The last few years, I'd allowed my career, Will, and my own confusion over my future distance me from the family I'd been adopted into at fifteen years old. I'd made friends at uni in London, and we still texted and called each other now and then. Leigh, my old high school friend, and I still kept in touch, but it wasn't a deep friendship anymore. I'd started to feel like there was something missing from my life. I'd watched how close Grace had become with Aunt Shannon, Joss, Liv, Ellie, Hannah, and Jo, and I'd always hoped that one day I'd have friends like that. Not the casual acquaintances of work colleagues or uni friends or even Leigh.

As Beth and Lily abandoned their own schedules that morning to wait with me as I showered and dressed to visit Pennington's, I felt bolstered by their love and support. Even January with her blunt tough love made me feel cared for. I realized that I already had what I'd been looking for in these girls. We might not be in one another's lives every minute of every day, but they showed up when it mattered, and I vowed from this day on to show up for them.

They even walked me to Pennington's, offering to wait for me. I told them I'd be fine, and they should get back to their own schedules. We hugged one another tight, and I thanked them for being two of the best people I knew.

Once they left, my knees shook as I took the staff entrance into the department store. Colleagues nodded at me with curious, questioning stares, and I knew they'd all seen the story. I tried not to let it make me feel sick with humiliation. Because Beth was right. It was time to stop allowing public opinion to affect me so much. The only opinions that mattered were the ones that directly impacted me.

My stomach roiled as I took the lift to the office floor. I'd dressed in armor—a pale blue, long-line blazer with matching wide-leg trousers, a cropped pale pink cami, and stilettos. Beth had helped me with my hair and makeup so that on the outside, I'd never looked more put together. It might seem shallow to some, but it helped glue all my shattered pieces together.

I'd already called ahead to ask to meet with Christina and Hilary, so I went straight to Hilary's office. Her assistant let me in, and I gritted my teeth at the sight of Becky. I didn't look at her. I couldn't. Instead, I greeted my bosses and took the seat they gestured to.

Informing them that I wanted to end the campaign was probably going to end my career.

"So, we should start with this morning's latest article and how it impacts the company," Becky announced in a no-nonsense tone.

I stiffened. Not looking at her, I turned to Christina. "What article?"

"You don't know?"

Oh God. What now? I shook my head, sweat prickling under my arms.

"It seems that someone found out about your father's time in prison," Hilary offered quietly.

The room tunneled around me.

No.

No!

My immediate thought was about Dad and Grace and Lockie. And fuck, Aunt Shannon! Their private business plastered all over the national news. I was instantly sick to my stomach.

"I ... I n-need to call my dad." I moved to stand, but Christina squeezed my arm.

"You will. Please sit. I was going to call a meeting myself, and I wanted Becky to be here."

It was a struggle to process my boss's words because I had to get to my family. To apologize. *Oh my God*. Had they called this morning? I had so many missed calls I ... fuck!

"Maia, are you okay?" Hilary asked.

"I think the better question is, is Pennington's okay now that the sweetheart of our campaign has a history that's quite frankly scandalized the country?" Becky sucked in a breath. "I'm so sorry to be blunt, Maia, but we have to treat this situation factually for the sake of the business."

"We do, Becky," Christina agreed. "Which is why it is of great concern to Pennington's that one of our own marketing managers would sabotage our campaign by sabotaging her colleague."

Wait.

What?

The worry for my family was momentarily put to one side as I gaped at Christina. What was she talking about?

Hilary looked deeply uncomfortable as she straightened

from her desk. "Usually this wouldn't be done in front of an audience, but your actions directly impact Maia, so we felt it was only right she was here in the room so you might explain yourself."

I looked at Becky.

She was chalk white as she stared wide-eyed at our bosses. "What are you talking about?"

Christina narrowed her eyes. "A colleague anonymously confessed that you were the one who reached out to Craig Bennet, the tabloid journalist, about where to find Maryanne Lewis. So, the tech department logged into your emails, and we discovered for ourselves that it was true. If you're going to sabotage the company you work for, Becky, you probably should have used your personal computer to email Bennet."

Oh my fucking ...

Becky shook her head frantically. "No ... no ... I ..."

Hilary waved an abrupt hand. "There's no denying it. The evidence is there. We have all the emails you exchanged with Bennet, including the encouragement to look into Maia's father's past. Why would you do that? You seemed to value your position here, so it beggars belief."

My heart pounded as I searched Becky's face for answers. I knew she disliked me. I didn't know why. However, I couldn't imagine what I'd possibly done to her that she'd jeopardize her own career to hurt me like this.

The panic in her eyes hardened and she stood to her feet. "I'm pretty sure this, in front of other members of staff, is against regulations. I don't have to answer your questions, especially if I'm already fired."

Hilary heaved a disappointed sigh. "Unfortunately, we can't employ someone who would do such public damage to the company."

Her lips pinched together, tears brightening her eyes. But Becky lifted her chin defiantly and moved to march past me. I stood, blocking her path, and she glared at me with such hatred, it made me flinch.

"What did I do?" I asked softly. "Just tell me."

Becky sneered. "You're pathetic, you know that."

Then she was gone, leaving me as confused as ever.

It was Christina who broke the silence. "When I started out in my career, I had a colleague whom, for reasons I never discovered, took an immediate dislike to me. She bullied me. It was passive aggressive, where other colleagues couldn't see. But slowly she started manipulating people, telling them things about me behind my back, until my colleagues isolated me. It got to the point I was so sick with the stress that I was physically ill, and I decided to leave that job." Christina's expression remained neutral, stoic. "I wish I'd fought harder, but sometimes these situations become untenable. It took a lot for me to gain my confidence back and decide to never let that happen again. The problem is bullying is insidious and sometimes very hard to prove. Unless you have a boss who recognizes the signs."

Emotion choked me, but I didn't want to cry in front of these two women I admired so much. I wanted to be strong, even though this person I barely knew had just blown up my entire life.

"I won't have my senior buyer, who is damn good at her job and has sacrificed her personal life for this company, be run out of here by a bully who can be easily replaced with a team player."

Admiration for my boss filled me because she'd put her neck out for me too.

Hilary peered at me. "I won't lie. Normally, I hate drama

of any kind. I don't stand for it. Grown adults should be able to figure these things out between themselves without tattling to the boss."

I stiffened at that, and Christina's expression turned carefully blank.

"However, I would hate to think, as would my brother, that Pennington's is a place that fosters workplace bullying. I trusted Christina's gut instincts and we have proof Becky wasn't a team player. So that's done. We're over it." She leaned back against her desk, crossing her arms. "Now we have to discuss damage control."

And all I wanted to do was go to my parents.

But I had to be honest with my bosses and tell them it was all over.

It seemed an ugly way to pay Christina back for her kindness toward me.

I let out a shaky exhale. "I—"

The door to Hilary's office flew open, and we all startled.

Standing in the doorway, a little sweaty and out of breath, was Baird. Longing flooded my system. His dark gaze zeroed in on me as he stumbled into the room.

"I apologize, Ms. Erstwhile." Hilary's assistant popped her head around Baird's arm. "He just burst in."

"I'm sorry." Baird ran a shaky hand through his hair. "But what I have to say can't wait."

CHAPTER THIRTY-EIGHT
BAIRD

Seeing Maia, recognizing the heartbreak in her big violet eyes, I knew I had made the right decision. I'd do just about anything to make her eyes light up with happiness again.

Beth had called Callan while I was leaving the club and told him that Maia was going into Pennington's to end the campaign.

I couldn't let that happen.

Not just because I didn't want her to lose everything she'd worked so hard for but because I had my heart set on marrying her in two weeks.

Leaving the club had been bittersweet. I'd been with Caley since I was sixteen and played for them professionally for the last eight years. For the longest time, the grounds of Caledonia United was my home. But truthfully, it had stopped being that place for me since my injury. I was never able to look at it or feel about it the same way.

I left there at peace with my decision.

"Can I talk to Maia alone?" I asked the two classy older women.

Hilary Erstwhile raised an eyebrow. "You do realize this is my office?"

"We'll talk in My's office, then." I nodded at my stunned fiancée. "All right, My?"

"Oh, it's fine." Hilary waved Christina to go ahead of her. "You have five minutes and then we really need to discuss the campaign."

I nodded, stepping aside to let them pass. As soon as the door closed, I knelt at Maia's feet and took her hands in mine. "Baby, are you okay?"

She searched my face, sounding a bit breathless. "What are you doing here?"

"Stopping you from stopping this. Did you tell them yet?"

"How did you—" Realization dawned, and she grimaced. "Beth?"

"My, you cannot quit this campaign. There's no point. You and I *are* getting married in two weeks, and it would be nice if we didn't have to pay for it."

Pain etched in her gorgeous face as she tugged unsuccessfully on her hands. "I can't let you do that."

Frustration roiled in my gut, but I tamped it down. "It's done. I've been to the club, and I told the gaffer I quit."

Maia shot to her feet, wrenching us apart. "No!"

"Aye." I stood slowly, reaching for her waist to pull her to me.

She shoved gently at me, but for once I refused to let her go. I pulled her close, bending my forehead to hers. Maia whimpered at the connection and stopped struggling.

"I can't let you throw away your career. Not for me. We'll end the campaign and then when things blow over, maybe Burbank won't care anymore."

I jerked back, disbelieving. Maia wouldn't meet my gaze. I cupped her face. "My."

Waiting, my heart in her fucking hands, I stayed silent until she finally lifted her eyes to mine.

They shimmered with unshed tears. "Bear ... it's your safe place. Your home. I can't take that from you."

"Aye? You can't take my safe place, my home? Okay, well, the fucking club is not that. You are. You are my safe place now. Maia ... I love you so fucking much." Emotion got the best of me, my voice catching. "If I thought the injury threw my life off course ... bloody hell, My, losing you would destroy me in ways I won't ever come back from. I have never loved anything as much as I love our relationship. *Anything.* It was a pretty fucking easy decision to tell Burbank where to stick his fucking club. I didnae mean tae swear so much during this convo, so sorry about that, but the only thing that terrifies me is losing you. Awright?"

Her tears brimmed over as she squeezed her eyes closed, her fingers sliding around my wrists as she melted against me.

Relief eased the cloying panic in my chest. "Football was never going to last. I mean, I'll have to move out of my apartment because I won't be making as much until Blantyre takes off, but—"

"You know I don't care about that stuff." Maia jerked away. "I would live in a shoebox with you."

My lips twitched. "Aye, it'll no' come to that."

Her eyes dimmed. "Did you see the article today? I haven't seen it. But apparently, he wrote about Dad being in prison."

As tears spilled down Maia's cheeks, part of me wished I'd beat the shit out of Craig Bennet after all. Yet I knew if I had, I wouldn't be here to wipe those tears away. "I saw, baby."

A wee sob escaped her lips, breaking my fucking heart. "I haven't spoken to Dad or Grace yet. Or Aunt Shannon. I feel so selfish. When we started this ... I was so set on doing it that I didn't allow myself to really think about how this could impact them."

"My, you couldn't have known Bennet would write about your family. I know for a fact they'll be more worried about you than you are about them."

"I want to go to them. I need to."

"Then I'm coming with you."

She searched my face and despite the love she couldn't hide, I still waited nervously for her response. "I'm sorry for pushing you away. It's only because I love you so much."

"I know, My. But please, don't do it again. It ... hurts."

New tears spilled free. "I'm sorry."

I kissed the tears away. "No more sorries," I whispered. "It's done. We're good."

A throat cleared behind us, and I cuddled Maia protectively to my chest as I glanced over my shoulder. Hilary and Christina stood in the doorway.

Hilary appeared uncomfortable. "I hate to break this up, but we really do need to discuss the campaign."

"We do that, then Maia gets the rest of the day off so she can go see her family," I negotiated.

Christina smirked, I think in approval, behind Hilary's back.

Hilary sighed. "Fine."

"Fine." I wrapped both arms around Maia, not letting her go as her bosses entered the room. "The wedding's still on. I spoke to my publicist, and she suggested we don't fan the flames. Especially as the campaign is almost at an end. No response. Continue on as we have."

Maia gently extricated herself from my arms, wiping at her cheeks. I let her go because she was in a professional situation and I knew she wanted to respect that. However, I felt her fingers twine with mine at our sides, her grip tight as she met her bosses head on. "I agree with Baird."

Crossing her arms, leaning her arse on her desk, Hilary sighed. "Well, there's been some negative backlash about Pennington's not checking their employee history carefully enough. As irrational as that sounds, we do have to listen to public opinion. Our publicist suggested you make a statement distancing yourself from your family. Including your father."

Maia sucked in a harsh breath. "I'm sorry, but that's never going to happen."

Pride swelled in my chest even as I felt like hunting down their publicist and telling them to buy a fucking soul.

"I thought that's what you'd say." Hilary gestured to Christina. "Christina insists you're invaluable to the company. I can't argue that you're very good at your job, Maia, but I do have to protect my company's reputation. Iain and I will not be the people who ruin Pennington's. I'm afraid I will need you to make that statement."

"No." Maia jutted her chin. "Go ahead and fire me. End the campaign. For all your talk of loyalty, Ms. Erstwhile, please do be a hypocrite and give into the minority of irrational voices who just happen to be louder than the masses. Punish the person who has given a decade of her life and sacrificed her personal privacy for this company just to appease a couple of morons on the internet."

I squeezed her hand, wishing I could fucking whoop with joy at the sight of Maia letting go of her people-pleasing ways to stand up for herself. Christina bowed her head to look at her shoes, but I witnessed the smile she was trying to hide.

Hilary raised one eyebrow and pushed off the desk. Her cheeks flushed red, and she opened and shut her mouth. I could practically hear Maia's heart pounding, and I rubbed a thumb over the pulse at her wrist, reminding her I was right there.

Finally, her boss crossed her arms over her chest. "While I don't appreciate your tone, I can't deny there's truth in what you said."

"Hilary," Christina spoke up. "This will all blow over. As soon as they see the video of Maia walking down the aisle in her wedding dress and saying her vows to her ridiculously good-looking footballer fiancé, they'll forget everything else. And our bridal sales will go up."

She considered this while I kept my mouth shut about the fact that I was no longer a professional footballer. That was something we'd deal with later.

Hilary glanced among us all, her expression unreadable.

"Fine." She nodded. "No response it is, then. But I am suggesting to marketing that we end the campaign after the wedding if the conversation keeps turning back to Maia's family."

Maia slumped against me, and I wrapped my arm around her. "So, we're good?" I asked.

"We're good. But I expect you back in the office tomorrow, Maia."

She nodded. "I'll be here."

"Right, well, I have a business to run ..." Hilary waved in a shooing gesture.

Maia thanked her and I walked her out with Christina at our backs.

"I hope your family is okay, Maia," her boss said as we walked toward the lifts.

"Thank you, Christina. For everything."

She raised a dismissive hand. "I told you my reasons. And to be clear, I don't hold anyone's family against them."

"My dad is a good man," Maia said instantly, tone brittle.

Christina nodded. "I have a younger sister. I don't know what I'd do if someone hurt her, so I understand."

"Thanks," Maia whispered. "I just ... I hate that everyone knows their private business. I hope my aunt Shannon can forgive me."

"Go to your family. I'll see you in the office tomorrow."

Guiding Maia into the lifts, I was about to tell her how proud I was of her when an arm appeared to block the doors from closing.

An out-of-breath young woman with blond hair that ombré'd into pastel pink stood there, eyes wide. "Maia."

"Liza?" Maia pulled away from me. "Are you okay?"

Liza stepped onto the lift with us and the doors closed. I knew she was Maia's assistant buyer and that there had been some weirdness between her and My because of Becky.

"I wanted you to know that it was me." She pressed a button so the lift couldn't descend.

Confused, I watched Maia note the move and ask cautiously, "What was you?"

"I was the one who told Christina about Becky emailing that journalist."

Wait, what had I missed?

My fiancée gaped at Liza, but the girl continued quickly, "I knew she'd found out about your mum and got the journalist to contact her. And I felt horrible about it, Maia. I felt sick. Becky kept telling me you were this terrible person, but you're like the best boss I've ever had."

What the fuck?

It was Becky!

"Liza, it's okay," Maia insisted.

"No, it's not. When I ... last night she told me about your dad and about the article that would appear in the paper today." Liza's gaze moved to me, but she couldn't quite meet my eyes before she returned her attention to Maia. "Let's just say, I know what your aunt must have gone through, and I had someone in my life who did what your dad did, but he got away with it. It would have killed me if he'd gone to prison for protecting me."

Fuck me.

Suddenly, I realized what her look had been. She was uncomfortable divulging this info in front of me, and honestly, I felt like shit for not being able to escape and give her and Maia privacy.

"Oh, Liza." Maia reached out to squeeze her arm.

"It finally cemented the truth—that Becky was the horrible person in this scenario, so I told Christina."

Clearly, I'd missed a big revelation today.

"Thank you, Liza. Thank you for being brave enough to do that."

"It wasn't brave. Brave would have been standing up to Becky months ago." She shrugged, cheeks flushed.

"I'm still grateful." Maia nibbled her lush lower lip and then asked, "Do ... do you know why she hates me? I know it shouldn't bother me, but it would be nice to know her motivations."

Liza shook her head. "She never said. She did mention she was friends with your ex-fiancé's new or old girlfriend or whatever and that he said you were a bitch. But that's it.

But ... *I* think she was jealous of you, Maia. Like a not-normal kind of jealousy."

"Jealous?" Maia huffed. "Why?"

"Because you're gorgeous and smart and all the higher-ups love you here. She used to say stuff that was, like, factually incorrect, as if she was trying to convince herself. Like 'Oh, Maia's not even that pretty if you take away her hair and makeup.'"

I grunted at that fucking bullshit and Liza smiled.

Maia absentmindedly reached out to squeeze my arm.

"And she'd say like 'Oh, you could do Maia's job better, Liza, but she's got Christina wrapped around her finger' and ...' She grimaced. "Some not nice things about why your fiancé was probably with you. It all reeks of—"

"Crazy jealousy," I agreed. "Told you, My."

Maia shook her head, dazed. "That's nuts to me. Nuts! That can't be the reason why she tried to destroy my career."

Liza shrugged and hit the button to open the doors again. "It's the only thing I can think of. Anyway, just wanted you to know. So ... we're all good, boss?"

In answer, Maia drew Liza into a hug and the young woman blushed and laughed.

"I'll take that as a yes."

"It's a yes." Maia released her and stepped back into me. I placed my hand on her hip as she waved at Liza. "Keep things going for me today. See you tomorrow."

As the doors closed and the lift descended, Maia rested her head on my arm. "As you might have guessed from that conversation, Becky was the one who found my mum and urged Craig Bennet to reach out to her and encouraged him to publish the story about my dad. She did it from her work computer, so when Liza told Christina, Christina and Hilary had the tech department log into Becky's emails. Becky just got fired for sabotaging the campaign. And now I'm emotionally exhausted."

Bloody hell. Silver lining was that Maia didn't have to put up with that rat anymore. "I know, babe. I'm right here, though."

"I know." She turned to press a kiss to my bare arm before looking up at me, gaze bright with worry. "And I'm going to need you when I face my family."

The truth was I couldn't imagine her dad or aunt being mad at Maia about this, but I was ready to protect her from anything, even them. "I'm not going anywhere, Maia soon-to-be McMillan. Not ever again."

CHAPTER THIRTY-NINE
MAIA

Even knowing Baird was right beside me on the couch, his hand tight in mine, I felt ready to crumble. I loved my dad so much, and his opinion could make or break me right now.

He sat across from me with a pale-faced Grace and I had done my best not to turn into a sobbing mess as I apologized for putting them in this position, that they'd woken up to my dad's private history plastered across a national tabloid.

Grace had hugged me at the door, but she was upset because Lockie's school had called to tell her Lockie had been in a fight with someone about the article. Already.

I didn't want them to feel like they had to comfort me when they were the ones whose lives were blasted all over that paper, so I was trying to hold together the painful sobs that filled my chest.

The very idea of hurting the people I loved most broke me because I never wanted to hurt them the way my mother had hurt me.

Dad rested his elbows on his knees, his hands clasped

together as he studied me with the violet eyes I was grateful he gave to me. His were always a little harder because of what life had carved out of him, which meant when they softened with love, it was the greatest feeling in the world.

"Did ... were you worried about this happening when I told you about the campaign?" My voice shook. "Because I feel so selfish for not considering it more."

Dad shifted a little in his seat and Grace reached over to squeeze his knee in support. "Maia, I won't lie and say it didn't cross my mind. But I will never ask my family to make decisions about their lives because of the choices *I* made in mine. *I* went to prison. No one else. It's not on you that this is something from my past that people can dig up to hurt you. That's on me."

My heart lurched. "Dad, no."

"Aye, Maia. It is. You're sitting here, looking like I'm going to stop loving you, and that kills me." His voice was rough. "Because me and your mum did that to you."

I sobbed. "No, you didn't. You never did." It wasn't Dad's fault that Mum never told him I existed. As soon as he found out about me, he'd been there for me every day for the past fifteen years.

Baird hugged me into his side.

"I am so sorry that you've carried the burden of responsibility on your shoulders for your mum. For me. The choice for Maryanne to get clean had nothing to do with you. It should have. You should have been the reason, but it wasn't your job to make it happen. I won't be another parent in your life who puts their choices on your shoulders. I protect you. Not the other way around. Lockie was always going to find out the truth, and he left this house this morning proud of his old man for protecting an aunt he adores. That's what the fight was about at school, and I would be a hypocrite for punishing him for protecting his family when I've done the same."

Gratitude toward my dad made it hard to speak, but I choked out, "It was still selfish of me not to consider it more."

Dad abruptly pushed to his feet, coming around the coffee table to sit on my other side. He cupped my face, drawing my head down to kiss my forehead. I squeezed my eyes closed, more bloody tears spilling free. I felt like I'd cried a decade's worth of tears in the last few months. As though something blocked inside of me had been released.

"There isn't a selfish bone in your body, lass," Dad insisted. "I'm so proud of who you are. I'm so fucking proud that the world gets to see that you are a prime example of the fact that we are not defined by where or who we come from. We are who we choose to be and you, sweetheart, have always been extraordinary. One day, I hope you finally see that too."

Movement at my other side drew both our gazes to Baird who was wiping his thumb across his eyes. He was completely unabashed by this show of emotion as I shared a watery smile with my fiancé.

I loved him so much.

"I've decided I like him," Dad said quietly.

Baird sniffled and replied gruffly, "Thank fuck for that because you're stuck with me."

At that I half giggled, half sobbed, falling against him even as I held my dad's hand.

My gaze met Grace's tender one from across the room, and despite the stress, despite the conversations that still needed to be had, I'd never felt so completely loved in my entire life.

CHAPTER FORTY
MAIA

Our next stop was Aunt Shannon's studio.

My aunt and her husband Cole were two of the most artistic people I knew, and that was saying something since a lot of folks in our extended family had very creative jobs. Uncle Cole was co-owner of one of the most renowned tattoo studios in Scotland, INKarnate, and people came from all over to have their tattoos designed by him. Aunt Shannon was a painter, and after she had the youngest of their three children, she'd transitioned to wallpaper design and was doing amazingly well.

She rented a studio and store near Dean Village, and we found her there. Baird wanted to give us privacy, so he stayed in the store with Aunt Shannon's sales assistant, Meg, and I followed Shannon into the privacy of her studio.

As soon as we were alone, I blurted out a loud, broken apology.

Aunt Shannon bridged the distance between us, folding her arms around me. The height difference meant I had to bend down to hug her, but I did so, almost afraid to let go.

"We're okay, we're okay." Aunt Shannon rubbed my back. "It's okay, sweetie."

When she released me, I bit my lip to stop tears. I was so tired of crying, but more than that, I didn't want her comforting me when I was the one who should be comforting her.

"There aren't enough apologies in the world. I can't believe that I put you in this position."

Aunt Shannon tucked a long wavy lock of red hair behind her ear. "You didn't put me in this position. Some arsehole at a tabloid newspaper did."

"You know what I mean."

"No." She shook her head vehemently. "Maia, you know things are strained between me and my parents and your aunt Amanda." She referred to her and Dad's older sister. I wasn't super close with her, just like I wasn't super close to my paternal grandparents, but they'd always been kind to me. I knew they hadn't been kind to Shannon, though. "Even before everything that happened, I felt like the odd one out. Logan was always the favorite. With all of us. My parents and Amanda told me I made bad choices, including with men ..." She lowered her gaze. "So, when the abuse from my ex got to the point it did, when he attacked me and I ran to your dad without thinking about the consequences, they were so angry at me."

I knew this. And to be honest, it had tainted my view of them.

"They blamed me for Logan going to prison. They blamed it on my choices. There was never any support or empathy or kindness toward me for a situation that I realize now was not my fault. And it broke me in ways that can never be fixed." She reached out to take my hand. "Therefore, I will never blame you for a situation that is not your fault. You will never have anything but my love and support."

"Aunt Shannon," I whispered, beyond grateful for her.

"The kids are too young to know what's being said in the papers. My only social media is my business accounts, and I have someone running those, monitoring them, so I'm not even aware of any discussions that might be had about me. I have no shame or guilt about my past now and neither does your dad, which is what matters to me. So, I don't want you to be burdened by that, okay? I'm more worried about you than I am about your dad and me, and I know he feels the same way."

I exhaled shakily, holding back fresh tears. Then I told her everything. The real story. About Becky, Will, the campaign, Baird. All of it. "I'm feeling a million things. Guilt. I can't help that. Guilt for lying, even though everything turned out true in the end. Guilt for dragging you into this. Hurt that someone I didn't even know tried to sabotage my life. Resentment at Maryanne for not caring enough, for never having cared enough."

"Sweetheart."

"But gratitude," I hurried to say. "To you and Dad and all my family and friends because you've all just been amazing throughout this. And ... I'm so deeply, deeply in love with that man out there." I gestured back to her shop. "It terrifies me to think that one day I might not have him anymore."

Shannon wrapped me in another big hug, swaying me from side to side. She pulled back, reaching up to cup my face, a beautiful smile wreathing hers. "I know that kind of love, Maia, and I am so excited for you. Just know that it is terrifying at first. It takes a while for that to settle. But you'll get there, and when you do, there's only the love."

"Thank you for being my aunt."

"That, sweetheart, is a privilege. No thanks required."

————

Baird held my hand tightly in his as we drove the five minutes to his place. He seemed to know I was in processing mode and so he talked quietly to me, but his next words had me on alert. "Mum, Ains, and the grandparents called. They're asking for you."

"What was their reaction to the articles?"

"What do you think? They're angry at your mum and feel bad for your family. No judgment. Granddad said your dad sounds like his kind of bloke."

"Did you ... did you tell them about the club?"

"Aye. They're proud of me." He gave me a pointed look. "They didn't raise a man who would choose anything over family. And you're my family, My."

"You're my family too. How are you, really? You've spent the whole morning by my side, dealing with my stuff, and you went through something huge too."

"Maia, I meant it. I am totally at peace with my decision. I wouldn't lie about that just to appease you."

"I'm here if you do find yourself needing to talk about it."

"I know, gorgeous. I promise. I'm good."

"Have you told Callan and John?"

"They were with me when I did it. Callan wanted the gaffer to know that as captain, he felt it was a catastrophic decision for the team." He grinned. "That was the word he used."

"He's right. You're an amazing goalkeeper."

"Aye, well, Fred Burbank thinks he knows best, and I don't want to waste my energy on an arsehole like that."

"I'm proud of you."

"Proud of you too."

"God, we're sickeningly cute."

Baird chuckled and nodded in agreement.

After we parked outside his place, he rounded the vehicle to take my hand again. "You must be exhausted."

I was definitely emotionally drained. Yet I needed something more than I needed rest.

Baird turned to me after closing the apartment door and I wound my arms around his neck, pressing the length of my body to his. "Make love to me," I whispered.

He squeezed my hips. "Are you sure that's what you need right now?"

"Yes. I just want to feel you. Only you."

It had quickly become apparent over the months that Baird genuinely found it difficult to say no to me. That wasn't something I'd ever take advantage of, so I didn't push. I waited.

His answer was to kiss me with a tender sweetness that was always a prelude to lovemaking. Baird had tells for whatever sexy kind of mood he was in. If he wanted athletic, energetic sex, his kisses were hungry and needy. If he wanted to take his time, his kisses were softer in their passion.

We climbed upstairs to his not-private bedroom and undressed one another. He kissed me all over, paying extra attention to my clit to bring me to orgasm. Afterward, he moved up my body, and I wrapped him up in me, arms around his shoulders, legs around his waist, holding him close. Tears of relief pricked my eyes as he pushed inside me with slow, deep undulations.

Those salty tears fell at his murmured love words and my soft cries of pleasure filled his ears as he kissed the tears from my cheeks.

Looking into his eyes, seeing his love for me, feeling the beauty of his body on mine, finally allowing it to sink in that Baird McMillan loved me and would support me and protect me and always *choose* me ... it was the most beautiful moment. For the first time ever, we climaxed together, as if cementing physically the agreement that we were one now.

We spooned afterward, talking quietly about all that had happened, and all that was still to come. At some point I felt him harden against me and sighed in pleasure as he kissed my upper back as his thumb rolled between my legs over my swollen clit.

"I-I'm thinking about getting a tattoo there," I murmured and then hissed in reaction to his touch.

Baird lifted his head. "Where?"

"On my upper back."

"Here?" He removed his hand from between my thighs to touch the exact spot I was thinking of.

"Aye." I glanced over my shoulder to find that he liked that idea. A lot. "Don't get excited. I'm thinking I'll get it once we're finished having kids."

He raised a questioning eyebrow.

I smiled coyly. "I was thinking your name and then our kids' names. Three, just so you know. And the names will make the shape of a heart."

"Three kids?" Baird's grin was big and beaming and my heart melted.

"What do you think?"

He smoothed a hand over my hip as he guided himself

to my entrance. His voice was rough as he replied, "I'm thinking why stop at three?"

My answering laughter cut off on a gasp as Baird pushed inside me. His lovemaking this time was harder, a little rougher, as he filled my ears with vows of love that drove me toward the peak.

As I shattered around him and felt him release inside me, his heavy weight pushing against my back as he gave me everything, I knew, without a shadow of a doubt, that my future included a heart tattoo and a love beyond measure.

A love that grew from friendship into something deep, abiding, and filled with respect and kindness. That it just so happened to come with this kind of passion made me feel like the luckiest woman in the world.

All my life I'd been looking for a place where I could be fully *me*, and I could curse myself for not realizing sooner that my place was Baird McMillan's heart.

I knew now, though.

And I was never, ever going to forget it or take it for granted or let a day go by when he didn't know my heart was that place for him too.

CHAPTER FORTY-ONE

MAIA

As much as I hated the fact that I didn't have a real sense of closure about the situation between me and Becky—why she targeted me, for instance—I walked into the office feeling lighter than I had in nearly two years. In fact, I hadn't quite realized how stressed I was about my working relationship with Becky until I didn't have to deal with her anymore. I looked forward to work again in a way I hadn't in a long time.

Colleagues, especially those who had worked closely with Becky in marketing, had come forward to whisper in my ear about Becky's escalating behavior over the last couple of years. Apparently, she'd taken credit for the work of assistants, had been passive aggressive toward more than just me, had bullied assistants into doing work for her, threatening their jobs if they didn't, had forced one of the marketing assistants to work the day after her gran passed away, laughed at an intern who was crying over the death of her dog, and a million other little things that had all added up to an uncomfortable workplace situation.

Becky fished for compliments when she wasn't already

complimenting herself. They told me she was self-important and how she was preoccupied with looks and the way she was perceived but also seemed to have an unhealthy obsession with me. If I was brought up in conversation, she'd randomly talk about how gorgeous I obviously thought I was, how I thought I was better than her, how she worked harder than me but no one recognized that. To the point they were all talking about it in the marketing department. I wished they'd mentioned it to me at the time.

Between these facts and her behavior toward me, escalating from mild comments to outright lying and eventually sabotaging me, I spoke to Lily. Lily was cautious as ever about an amateur diagnosis, especially of someone she herself hadn't met or counselled, but did say Becky showed signs of narcissistic personality disorder. I took that to mean that I would never get the closure I desired. Ultimately, I had to ask myself if answers were even worth pursuing.

They were not.

The atmosphere at work was how I remembered it. Hectic and stressful but fun and creative, and there was a sense of lightness and togetherness in the team again. Therefore, I was happy to leave Becky in the past.

We were a week out from the wedding, and I was nervous. Not about marrying Baird—I knew it was normal to go into your wedding with doubts and fears, and I always thought I'd be that person. However, I could honestly say, hand on heart, that I desperately wanted to be Baird's wife and to know that he was my person for the rest of forever. The nerves were more about the public spectacle. The gossip and negativity had died down a little, but I knew the wedding would stir things up again. And yes, there was a big part of me that was sad that our wedding had been orchestrated by other people and that we'd been limited to the choices they'd set before us.

But I could deal with that knowing I got Baird out of it. He was worth it because he was compromising on the vision he saw for us to help me keep the job I loved.

He proved how lucky I was time and again. During a fortnight that should have been dedicated to just us and our impending nuptials, he stood by my side while I paid a ton of attention to my family. I was feeling extra clingy with my parents and Lockie and with my aunt Shannon. We spent time with them for my own reassurance that the articles hadn't disrupted or impacted their lives in a big way, and that we were all good. Baird understood that.

We gave equal time and attention to his family and Ainsley, because it was becoming real for them too that what had seemed like a whirlwind relationship was going to end in something legal and permanent.

In among all that was the pain of discovering my mum had been in recovery for over a decade and that she'd betrayed me. Baird had suggested perhaps I should talk to someone because he'd found counseling helpful, and I said I would consider it. The trauma from the hurt my mother had caused had impacted our relationship in the past, and I didn't want that to keep happening.

Baird, my family, my work, the upcoming wedding, did a lot to distract me from Maryanne Lewis.

Therefore, it was a shock when one week out from the wedding, I was in the middle of booking flights for myself, Eli, and Liza to attend Paris Fashion Week when Eli popped their head around my door.

Their expression was difficult to read as they cleared

their throat and very slowly relayed, "There is a call for you … from someone claiming to be Maryanne Lewis."

It was amazing how her name could set off a fight-or-flight response. I instantly felt my breathing grow rapid, sweat on my palms, my entire body tense and trembling. I experienced a rush of lightheadedness.

"Do you want me to put the call through? Maia?" Eli stepped into the room, frowning. "Maia, do you want me to put the call through?"

I closed my eyes, my mind whirring as the blood pounded in my ears. "Um … okay."

"You sure?"

I nodded, looking at the phone on my desk.

I was aware of Eli leaving. As I waited, I contemplated the idea that the person calling wasn't really my mum. That it was a scam. That someone was trying to mess with me. But if it was my mother, why was she calling? What did she have to say? Did I want to hear what she had to say?

I was going to throw up.

The phone rang on the desk and I literally jumped in my seat. Sucking in a shaky breath, I exhaled and reached to pick up the handset. If it was really her, I wanted to be calm and cool and collected. Detached, almost.

"Hello?"

"Maia?"

A rush of nostalgia was quickly followed by resentment, heartbreak, anger, all the ugly feelings I wished I could let go of.

It was really her.

"Maryanne?"

"Aye … it's me."

I waited, my ears throbbing from how hard and fast my

heart beat the blood around my body. "Why are you calling me?"

"I ..." The line crackled as she let out a shaky sounding exhale. "I wondered if you would ... I mean, we can talk here on the phone, but I wondered if you would meet me."

"Why?"

"I have some things I'd like to explain."

I squeezed my eyes closed because she sounded like how she used to before her addiction got so bad she could barely string sentences together. Her speech was so greatly abused by the heroin. But here she was on the other end of the line, sounding sober and clear.

"That newspaper thing ... it wasn't ... that bastard edited out so much of what I said and ... and he made it look like I was blaming you, and that was not my intention."

I gritted my teeth. "Why talk to him at all?"

"I want to explain in person." At my lengthy silence, she continued, "I'm not ... I'm not expecting a relationship with you, Maia. I'm not after anything. But if I were you, I'd be feeling a certain way right now, and I ... a long time ago, my sponsor told me that I should make amends with you first and foremost, and I couldn't do it. I don't even know if you care or if anything I do affects you or affected you ... but I owe you amends. Now more than ever."

It was hard for me to reconcile the voice on the other end of the phone with the woman who had put me in danger, who had left me to grow up and take care of myself, and whose negligible and abusive actions had pushed me to the point of running away.

I could hold on to that resentment and let it eat me alive with all the unanswered questions between us ... or I could face her and try to find as much closure as was possible.

"Where do you want to meet?"

I heard her wee harsh intake of breath. Her voice shook as she replied, "I could come to you, or you could come to me. I live in West Lothian now."

My God, she was physically closer than ever, and she'd never bloody reached out! That heartbroken fury rose its ugly head, and I knew I didn't want her in my home. I wanted to be able to leave if I needed to. "I'll come to you."

———

I stared at the small bungalow, a wreck of emotions. Mostly I wondered what my childhood might have been like if I'd instead grown up in this house on this quiet street where people looked after their gardens and neighborhood watch signs hung from the lampposts.

"Are you sure you want me to stay in the car?" Baird asked from the driver's side.

It was the day after the call with Maryanne, a sunny Saturday morning, and Baird had driven me to the well-looked-after development on the outskirts of Blackburn, a town in West Lothian, less than fifty minutes from the city center.

I didn't know how Maryanne had gone from the worst area, worst tenement in Glasgow, to this nice wee house, but part of me needed to know.

Baird's frown was deep between his brows, and I knew he was worried about me facing my mother. We'd talked about it at length last night because for Baird, he genuinely didn't desire or need closure from his birth father. He was at peace with the idea of never knowing him because he felt so strongly about his abandonment. I think he found it hard to understand why I needed to talk with my mother because he didn't think she was worth it, but I wanted the door on this painful chapter in my life to close for good. I didn't know how it would close, what that looked like, but I needed to walk away from this discussion having gained clarity about who she was.

"I'll be okay," I promised him, reaching out to squeeze his hand. "Knowing you're outside waiting for me makes it easier to walk in there."

He reached over to brush his mouth over mine in answer.

My answering smile was shaky with nerves, so I shoved open the passenger door and got out before I caved into my fears.

Walking up her front path was surreal. Part of me still didn't believe she lived here.

But the door opened a few seconds after I pressed the doorbell and ... it was her.

Not the skinny, decaying mess of a human being who used to slap me around when she was agitated and in need of a hit.

This was an older version of the Maryanne from my early childhood.

She was a healthy weight now that she wasn't injecting heroin into her body. When her lips parted in a strained smile, I was surprised to see white veneers. The last time I saw her, her teeth were wrecked. Somewhere along the line, she'd gotten the money to fix them. Her dark hair, while still quite thin, was shiny and styled poker straight around her face. The T-shirt and jeans she wore were clean and quality. The only giveaway to her past was her skin, which had a weathered look beyond her age.

Her dark eyes roamed over me and to my surprise, they brightened with tears. She stepped back. "Come in, Maia."

My legs shook as I stepped into the hallway of the small

but modern home. It was well-decorated and nicely furnished. And it didn't smell like human waste, which was how I remembered our flat in the end.

She gestured for me to follow her into the living room, and I could tell by the way she kept crossing and uncrossing her arms that she was nervous too. "Can I get you anything? Tea, coffee, water?"

I shook my head and stared around the space, taking in the good furniture and the large TV. There was framed artwork ... and photographs of her ... with a man and two kids. The more I looked, the more I realized that there were photographs of those kids everywhere.

Agony sliced across my chest as I realized she didn't live here alone.

"Please sit."

I turned back to stare at her, trying to reconcile this person with the woman I knew.

Slowly, I sat on the edge of the velvet corner sofa.

Maryanne nodded and sat down on the armchair next to it. "You must have a lot of questions."

I snorted bitterly. "You think?"

She rubbed her hands together nervously, and it reminded me of when she used to do that when she was itching for a hit. "If you'll indulge me, I'd like to tell you my story and not that shite you read in the paper."

"So, you didn't say I abandoned you?"

She winced. "That arsehole of a journo took it out of context. I felt abandoned, My, but I said more than that. I had no idea he was going to come at it as an attack against you."

"Why talk to him in the first place?"

"Because I was naive and ... I've faced everything else in my life but you. You represent all of my behavior I'm most ashamed of, and I've found you the hardest to face." She looked away even now, unable to look me in the eye. "I took the coward's way out by never reaching out to you when I got clean, and I ... when that dickhead approached me, I stupidly thought it was a way to reach out without forcing it on you."

My emotions were rocked because this wasn't what I'd expected. At all. And I honestly didn't know what to believe. She'd played with my emotions so much as a child.

Maryanne finally met my gaze. "When I was fucked up, it was difficult for my brain to process anything but wanting the escape that I got from smack. Smack was all I could think about. But when your dad came to me and I knew you'd found him, there was this wee part of me ..." She struggled to speak, her jaw moving in and out as she tried to stop the tears from escaping and failed. Maryanne brushed impatiently at them. "There was this part of me leftover that was still your mum and as callous as it seemed at the time, I knew you needed to be away from me."

"That's not quite how you put it." I glared, refusing to give in to the tears that stung in my own nose.

She shook her head. "I can imagine. I can't remember everything I did, but I remember some stuff, and I know it was bad, My. I know that I put you in situations that no fucking bairn should ever be put in. I know that. And believe you me, I work every day to fight my self-loathing over it."

I stared at my shoes.

It was all I'd wanted to know.

If she felt remorse.

Or if my own mother was a villain.

To know that she'd felt remorse was a relief.

But it didn't miraculously wipe away all my heartbreak and resentments.

"It's … it was about six months after you went to live with your dad and … well, the universe has a funny way of fixing what's broken. I was in a car accident with Kells. I don't know if you remember him."

My eyes flew to her in surprise regarding the car accident. I did know Kells. He was her dealer. I nodded.

"Kells died. I was in a coma for a couple of weeks. I had no choice but to go through withdrawal in hospital. I'd have never gotten clean otherwise, Maia. There was a nurse there who really cared about me getting clean and staying sober, and so she went above and beyond. Her name was Karisha, and she was one of the most amazing women I've ever met. She took me in and drove me to AA meetings and she got me involved in her local church. She got me a job working for a charity, and I lived with her for four years until she passed away."

I gaped at her in shock. I'd wondered how she'd gotten sober, but the idea of her going to church and working for a charity seemed unreal.

"I was very lucky." Maryanne nodded, sensing my disbelief. "During all that, I went back to school part time to study psychology, and I worked toward becoming a counselor, specializing in addiction."

"Oh my God," I whispered.

She shrugged, seeming embarrassed. "I've spent the last decade helping other people make amends to their loved ones, and I couldn't even reach out to my own daughter to tell her how sorry I was."

Rage flushed through me like someone had lit a kerosene fire at my feet, but I sucked back the urge to roar at her. Cheeks hot, fists clenched, I took deep breaths because I didn't want this to descend into a fight. But how could she? How could she be so selfish in her cowardice?

"Did you even want to know me?" I asked.

"Of course. I ... googled you. Found your socials. Saw you seemed to be doing well, and I was relieved. I was relieved that I hadn't royally fucked you up." She half laugh, half sobbed.

"But you did." I stared at her like she was nuts. "You fucked me up, Maryanne. I ... for years, I've carried the weight of not just your inability to love me like a mum should have, but the years of abuse and torment from other people because of your actions. I loved you. I was your parent, not the other way around. You slapped me when I told you one of your boyfriend's tried to assault me."

She covered her mouth, squeezing her eyes closed, but I wasn't done.

"I left you because I was scared what might happen to me, to you. Every day I lived in fear of coming home from school to either find you dead or find you so strung out that you couldn't stop it if one of your loser boyfriends raped me."

Maryanne made a sound like a wounded animal, but I continued.

"Reading that you felt abandoned by me was like having the worst thing you believe about yourself be proved true. To the whole fucking world. Because I did feel ashamed of leaving you behind. Even though it felt just as much like you were throwing me away. Did I leave you behind, or did you throw me away? My heart couldn't tell the difference. All I know is that I loved you and cared for you for years and then I went to stay with my dad, so I'm just as bad as you are."

"No. You were a kid. *I* was supposed to parent *you*, so

you need to get that out of your head now, Maia. That isn't true. That's not your guilt to bear."

I calmed a little at her words, hoping they'd sink in and free me over time. "I don't want to hurt you," I offered. "But I have other things I need to say."

She straightened as if bracing herself. "Then say them."

"I ... I bore years of having people look at me like I'm less than, like I'm scum. People who sexually harassed a fucking child because they thought I was less than human because of you. And I know that's not directly your fault, but it's something I've carried for years. I cared way too much what people thought of me because I was ashamed and embarrassed, like I was unworthy. If my own mum could throw me away, could defend a trash human being who tried to assault me rather than protect me from him, then there had to be something wrong with me. I have a beautiful man out there"—I gestured toward the window, to the car parked outside—"who I could have lost because I couldn't accept ..." I sobbed before I could stop it. "I- I couldn't accept that s-someone could love me like he does. Th-that I'm worthy of that love."

Maryanne wiped her tears from her face as she stood, as if to come to me.

"Don't." I sniffled, wiping in frustration at my own tears. "I can't."

She sat back down, her shoulders shaking from trying to keep her sobs at bay.

We sat in silence for what seemed like forever and then finally I spoke. "So, you moved here?"

"Aye. I ...got a counseling job in Livingston. I met my husband, Peter, at an AA meeting there. He's a recovering alcoholic."

I raised an eyebrow but let her continue.

"He's been sober for two decades, but he's never stopped attending the meetings. Anyway, he'd gone through a rough divorce and the meetings meant more to him than ever."

"Did you tell him about me?"

"I did." She nodded emphatically. "I told him about everything. He ... Peter has two kids, Gemma and Ben. They split their time between us and their mum. We've been married for three years, and we moved here about a year ago."

I wouldn't lie and say that didn't break my goddamn heart.

To know she'd pulled her life together and could be a stepmum to kids who weren't even hers when she was barely a *human* to her daughter.

"When I saw you in that campaign for Pennington's, I couldn't believe it." She smiled, her eyes shining. "I couldn't believe that beautiful girl was my daughter and that I had absolutely nothing to do with making her into that beautiful woman."

"Does it hurt?" I asked.

"Aye, it hurts, Maia. It will always hurt."

I nodded, wiping away my silently falling tears.

"I didn't take any money for that article."

I tensed.

She leaned toward me. "You can call the paper and they'll corroborate it, but I didn't do it for money. I really, stupidly, naively thought that I could say everything I'd always wanted to say to you, and you could hear it in a way that felt safe for both of us." She huffed bitterly. "Fucking ... Peter warned me. He told me not to trust that guy. I should have listened."

"You did say *I* abandoned *you*, though."

"No, actually, he asked me if I'd felt abandoned by you and I said that in a way I did, but that I abandoned you first. He twisted everything, Maia."

"Do you feel like I abandoned you?"

"I did, but I've had years to look back on things, and I remember a small child making sure the flat was clean, that I'd eaten, tucking me into bed." Her chin trembled. "As awful as it is for me to have to admit, I know I abandoned you a long time before you went to your dad. It wasn't up to you to get me clean, Maia. It was up to me to get clean for you, to hold up my hands and say I wasn't strong enough. If I hadn't been forced to, I wouldn't be sitting here. I'd be dead." Maryanne sighed heavily. "Aw, Maia, all I wanted was to tell you in that article that I was here, I was good, and that I was so, so sorry for everything I put you through, kid."

I stood up slowly, smoothing my skirt with shaking hands. "See, I get that, Maryanne. I do. I can see that you're doing well, and I am happy you're sober. I'm sorry for leaving you. I know you think I don't owe you that, but I need you to know that leaving you was one of the hardest choices I've ever had to make ... But the fact that you thought speaking about our relationship, or lack thereof, in a public manner was a good idea leaves me with many questions about your judgment and about your trustworthiness."

She stood to face me, swallowing several times as she nodded and rubbed her hands together. "I understand."

"So, why? Why not just reach out to me directly?"

"I told you—"

"No. I know you said you were too afraid to ... but I question that because you weren't afraid to air to the entire country that you were a heroin addict. How could you be okay with that and not facing me?"

"Because it's easier to tell a bunch of strangers about your mistakes than to face the person who bore the brunt of those mistakes." Maryanne gave me a sad half smile. "I don't expect anything from this, Maia. I don't expect your trust or forgiveness. That's not what I wanted today. I just wanted the chance to tell you that I never intended to hurt you again with that article. And I wanted to tell you face-to-face that I am sorrier than you will ever know, kid. I know I'm not allowed to feel any way about you, but I am so proud of the woman you've become. I know I've left my wounds on you ... I know that, and I know that because I had shitty parents, My, and they were among the reasons I turned to drugs. So, I know what a crap upbringing can do to you ... and I am beyond proud that my daughter is so much stronger than I ever was. That you broke the generational trauma. That's huge, Maia. That speaks so much to your strength of character. If we never see each other again, I needed you to know that. That you"—her tears spilled over—"you are the best part of me, and I'm sorry I couldn't show you that growing up."

Her words were like a sword and a bandage all in one. I choked on my emotion, gave her an abrupt nod, and strode out of there.

Seeing Baird in the car, I hurried toward the vehicle. I slid in, slammed the door shut, and turned to look at him.

Everything I'd been holding in burst out of me. Baird cursed and tucked me against his chest, and I shook and sobbed uncontrollably in his arms.

"Do I need to kill her?" he asked gruffly, his own voice thick with emotion.

"No," I whispered and then sat back in the seat. My

nose was snotty, and I knew my mascara must be all over my face. Baird reached into the glove compartment and pulled out tissues for me.

He waited patiently as I blew my nose and wiped my cheeks and eyes.

Finally, I turned to him. "Let's go home."

He studied me, and whatever he saw had him nodding and turning on the engine.

We were about ten minutes down the motorway when I finally spoke again. "I don't know if I'll ever be able to reconcile all my feelings toward her ... but I'm glad I met her today."

"Aye?" Baird glanced at me uncertainly. "Because that was some breakdown, baby."

"It was ... it was a good breakdown. Cathartic." I reached over to smooth a hand over his knee. "I don't know if I will ever want her back in my life ... but I wanted to know that she wasn't this villain. That she was more complicated than that. That she ... that there was a part of her that was sorry and loved me."

"Did you get that from her?"

"I did. She ... I don't think I could ever trust her judgment. But ... seeing her healed something in me, I think. I'm ready to ... I'm ready to let go."

"Wow," he murmured. "Babe, that's huge."

A sense of peace settled over me as I relaxed against the seat. "Aye, it really is." My smile was slow and still a bit trembling ... but it was hopeful. "You changed my life."

Baird grinned at me and then at the road ahead. "Aye?"

"Do you even know how special you are, Baird McMillan?"

He shook his head, the grin softening to a smile. "I didn't. Until you told me you loved me. If someone as special as you can love me ... then I guess I'm a bit of all right."

I laughed, squeezing his knee. "You are definitely more than a bit of all right." My tone turned serious. "My whole life, I've taken care of myself because that's how it started out. I either took care of myself or no one did. Grace and Dad took care of me, but when I moved out, I reverted to independence mode. Looking back, I never let men take care of me. Will didn't even want to try, really. But you take care of me in all the little ways and in all the big ways, and it's like this weight off my shoulders I didn't even realize I was carrying. So, thank you. Thank you for taking care of me. Because even though I can take care of myself, it's lovely knowing I don't always have to. You're everything. You're my everything."

Baird let out a shaky exhale. "I will always take care of you, Maia. We'll take care of each other."

"I love you."

He beamed, his chest puffing up in that way that made me chuckle. "I love you too, Maia MacLeod soon-to-be-McMillan. I love you so fucking much."

EPILOGUE
BAIRD

One year later

It was the second time I'd watched Maia walk down the aisle toward me. Last time, there were cameras everywhere, Blantyre ballroom was decorated with over-the-top glamour, and there were people in attendance from Pennington's who we didn't even know. As special as it was to make her my wife that day, it wasn't what we would have planned.

The truth was, I wanted Maia to have the wedding of her dreams and, unfortunately, the so-called scandal surrounding ours did cast a pall over it that neither of us could quite shake.

For the past year, we'd let it go. Life as husband and wife made it easy to let the shit that didn't matter go.

But that didn't mean that I didn't want Maia to have her dream wedding, so six months into our marriage, I surprise proposed again and asked her to renew her vows with me. Under normal circumstances, of course, that would be nuts. However, our friends and family understood.

The last twelve months had been a whirlwind.

Fred Burbank faced pressure from many corners of the football world, including the public, after Callan exposed the truth of why my contract would end early. There was a fucking uproar and Burbank offered me a two-year contract to stay on with Caley United. As at peace as I'd felt walking away for Maia, there was still a part of me that wanted to see if the game still mattered enough to continue. I decided on a one-year contract because deep down, I knew it would be my last year.

We made it my best fucking last year because for the first time in decades, a non-Glasgow team took the title. Caley United won their first Professional League championship in twenty-five years.

It was a good way to retire.

Maia continued to do well at Pennington's, despite the craziness of the campaign. Sometimes she worked long hours, which was tough because I missed her, but it was worth it to see how much she got out of her job. When she had to leave the country for fashion weeks, it was difficult because I couldn't get the time away from the club to join her, but I hoped now that I'd retired, I could work my schedule so I could travel with her.

We both wanted to be able to see a bit more of the world. I'd traveled with the team but rarely got to see much of the cities we played in.

I'd given up my flat, and Maia had given up hers. It was harder saying goodbye to her place on Hart Street Lane because that was where so many big moments happened between us. It was the place she realized she loved me back.

But we needed our own place. When one of the leases on my favorite rental that Callan and I bought years ago finished, we bought Callan out and took the flat for ourselves. It was a large two-bedroom just above Dean Village, a very nice starter home for us. Once we decided we were ready for a family, we both agreed we'd like a house, which meant probably moving out of the city center. Neither of us was quite ready for that, though Maia didn't want to wait too much longer to have kids because of her age.

I was genuinely happy with whatever Maia wanted to do.

To be honest, I still couldn't quite believe that she was mine. I was a lucky, lucky bloke, and I'd never take for granted that my literal dream woman loved me back.

That was why, even though this was the second time she'd walked toward me in a wedding dress, I got choked up all over again.

Maia's last wedding dress had been this sexy number that fitted to her curves like a lacy glove with a dramatic train. She looked like a fairy-tale princess. The dress suited the over-the-top venue and décor.

This time, as she walked barefoot on the grass between two rows of storm candle holders that denoted the aisle between the guest seats, her dress fitted this smaller, private ceremony. We'd gotten permission to get married in the privacy of Queen Street Gardens. The gardens were across the road from Joss and Braden's townhouse, and they'd generously offered to hold the reception at their place.

Our friends and family were seated in the gardens, our wedding mostly hidden from public view by the trees that surrounded us.

I was in my kilt, but I didn't wear it with the full regalia —kilt jacket, waistcoat, shirt, and fly plaid—like last time. This time I wore a navy shirt with my kilt. My hair had grown out and was tied up in a knot.

Callan stood at my side; Beth and Lily in their summery bridesmaids' dresses stood opposite us after having walked down the aisle first. Maia's dad accompanied her, her arm through his as he brought her forward and held out her hand to me.

I murmured my thanks and then looked deep in those spectacular eyes of hers and told her she looked beautiful. Because she did. She always did.

As stunning as her last dress had been, this one felt more like My. It was softer with some lace on the bodice and arms and scattered over the skirt, but it had a fuller skirt and no train. Less drama.

She still looked like a princess, though.

My princess. My wife.

Maia beamed at me, eyes filled with nothing but trust and love and even after a year, it made my heart turn over in my chest. Without thinking, I cupped her face in my hands and kissed her a wee bit too passionately.

She laughed as she pulled away, and I heard our friends and family titter. "Too soon for that," Maia teased, gently pressing me back.

I didn't let her go fully, though. I held her hands in mine as we turned to the humanist celebrant, Anthea, we'd hired to marry us.

"Maia and Baird McMillan, your friends and family have gathered before you to witness the renewal of your vows in marriage—"

"I do," I cut her off.

Laughter erupted around us and Maia squeezed my

hands. I grinned unrepentantly as Anthea chuckled but gave me a mock look of warning.

"Someone's eager," she tsked.

I waggled my brows at My. "Always."

She rolled her eyes, grinning, used to my nonsense.

"Let's try again."

This time I let the officiant get through her speech and then it was our turn to say our vows. We'd opted for traditional vows at our first wedding because of how public it was.

"Maia and Baird have chosen to write their own vows." Anthea looked to Maia. "Maia."

My wife tightened her grip on my hands, her wide, nervous gaze searching mine and finding the comfort and reassurance she needed. "Baird Gareth McMillan, you are my everything. You are the safest place I've ever known." Her eyes brightened with tears so, of course, I choked up. "You love me for exactly who I am, and you make me feel like I am the best thing to ever happen to you, and that's saying a lot since you just won the championship." I grinned as John and a few others whooped from the peanut gallery. Maia's smile was so big it was fucking blinding. "I vow to spend the rest of my life making you feel the way you make me feel. To support you, to laugh with you, to cry with you, and to never stop being your best friend. I love you more today than I loved you yesterday, and I know I'll love you more tomorrow. I vow to never stop falling more and more in love with you, Bear."

I squeezed her hands, blinking back the tears as I cleared my throat. "How am I supposed to follow that?"

Everyone's laughter relaxed Maia's tense hold as she leaned into me.

My gaze washed over her face. "Sometimes it feels

surreal to look into your eyes and see how much you love me because I wanted that for so long. When you think the person you love will end up with someone else, you try to make peace with it, but it burns like nothing else could."

"Bear," she whispered like she hadn't meant to say my name.

"But I'm glad in a way that, for a while, I thought you would never be mine because now that you are, I know what I'm facing if I lose you. So, it's my mission in life, My, to make you so happy, you'll never want to be anywhere but by my side. Every morning, I wake up and see your face, and I can't believe that this kind of peace and joy exists. I vow that even on the mornings where life is hard, I will find a way to make you feel that same peace and joy. That I will be the person who reminds you all the bad is worth getting through when you have what we have found together. You're the kind of beautiful deep down in your soul, Maia, that it can't help but shine out. I feel lucky that it shines on me every day. I vow to protect that in you. To protect your heart and your goodness with my mind, body, and soul. I love you with everything I am. Forever and always."

I heard sniffling coming from the guests and was pretty sure at least one of the snifflers was my mum. Maia and I smiled, lost in each other's eyes. Just fucking lost in each other.

"Well, that was beautiful," Anthea said quietly, and then her voice rose. "Do you, Maia MacLeod McMillan, promise to uphold your vows to Baird Gareth McMillan, your lawfully wedded husband?"

Maia's smile could have lit up a Christmas tree. "I do."

"Baird Gareth McMillan, do you promise to uphold your vows to Maia MacLeod McMillan, your lawfully wedded wife?"

"I do." I'd barely gotten the last word out when I pulled Maia into my arms and kissed her like I hadn't seen her in ten years. Our family and friends clapped and whooped around us as my wife clung to me, swept up in the kiss. I didn't release her until she was flushed and breathless.

Then I murmured one last vow against her lips, "I'm never letting go. Even after our time here in this life is over, I will find you in the next."

Maia smiled and her tears spilled over. "You always say the most perfect things, Husband."

I rested my forehead against hers. "Only ever to you, Wife."

ACKNOWLEDGMENTS

Thank you to everyone who messaged me after they'd read *On Loverose Lane* and told me how much they'd fallen in love with Baird. I knew while I was writing book one in this series that Baird McMillan was giving off major main character energy, but your response just confirmed what I felt in my gut. He deserved his own story! Thank you for reaching out and loving on him because he's truly been the most fun character to write. I also felt a lot of pressure writing his story because I wanted to live up to that guy so many readers fell for in book one. I hope you love him even more now because Baird truly has been one of my favorite characters to write.

The writing journey, however, is always made easier by the support of those around me.

To my friends and family, thank you for always understanding how much this writing business means to me and for always having my back no matter what. I love you lots.

To my amazing editor Jennifer Sommersby Young who always fills me with confidence and encouragement just when I need it. You can never stop being my editor, Jenn. You're stuck with me!

Thank you to Julie Deaton for proofreading *Hart Street Lane,* catching all the things, and for the most beautiful commentary on Baird and Maia's story. Your love for them bolstered me more than I can say. I'm so sad this was our last book together but I wish you the most amazing next chapter!

And thank you to my phenomenal assistants, Ashleen and Jess, for helping to lighten the load and making my life so much easier. I'm so grateful for you both.

The life of a writer doesn't stop with the book. Our job expands beyond the written word to marketing, advertising, graphic design, social media management, and more. Help from those in the know goes a long way and I have my very own "social queens"! A huge thank-you to Nina Grinstead, Josette, Christine, Kim, Kelley, Sarah, Meagan and all the team at Valentine PR for your encouragement, support, insight, and advice.

A huge thank you to JR for doing all your techy ad magic to deliver my stories into the hands of new readers. You're a wizard!

Thank you to every single influencer and book lover who has helped spread the word about my books. You all are appreciated so much. On that note, a massive thank-you to the fantastic readers in my new content team. Seeing the content you create from the worlds inside my head is so very special. I'm grateful for your time, effort, and the way you selflessly donate your energy to helping spread the word about my books and the books of so many of my peers. It means the absolute world.

A massive thank-you to Hang Le for creating another stunning cover in the world of ODS. Your talent knows no bounds, my friend.

As always, thank you to my agent Lauren Abramo for making it possible for readers all over the world to find my words. Thank you, thank you, a million thank yous.

Finally, to you, my reader. Thank you for reading. I couldn't do this without you.

www.ingramcontent.com/pod-product-compliance
Lightning Source LLC
Chambersburg PA
CBHW010019200726

48283CB00015B/2985